W9-ABJ-674

Date: 1/6/15

LP FIC HALL
Hall, James W.
The big finish

THE BIG FINISH

Center Point
Large Print

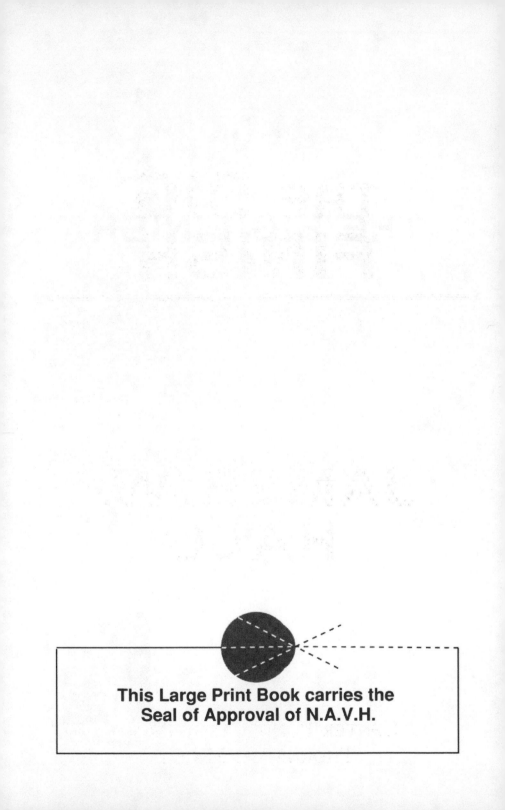

**This Large Print Book carries the
Seal of Approval of N.A.V.H.**

THE BIG FINISH

JAMES W. HALL

CENTER POINT LARGE PRINT
THORNDIKE, MAINE

Library of Congress Cataloging-in-Publication Data

Hall, James W. (James Wilson), 1947–
The big finish / James W. Hall. — Center Point Large Print edition.
pages ; cm
Summary: "Thorn sets off on a mission to a tiny North Carolina town
after receiving a postcard call for help from his son who has been
involved with an eco-underground group for the past year"—Provided
by publisher.
ISBN 978-1-62899-410-0 (library binding : alk. paper)
1. Thorn (Fictitious character)—Fiction. 2. Ecoterrorism—Fiction. 3.
Revenge—Fiction. 4. Large type books. I. Title.
PS3558.A369B525 2014
813'.54—dc23
2014037683

For Dutch

The greatness of a nation and its moral progress can be judged by the way its animals are treated.

—Mahatma Gandhi

Never wrestle with a pig. You get dirty, and besides, the pig likes it.

—George Bernard Shaw

PART ONE

One

It was a brisk, moon-dazzled November night when Flynn Moss and several of his closest friends were gunned down.

For a week, they'd been camping in a forest of evergreens on the bank of the Neuse River in eastern North Carolina. Might sound picturesque, but it wasn't. Nothing like the majestic Blue Ridge Mountains a day's drive west, or the gorgeous sweep of dunes and squeaky white sands two hours east along the Outer Banks. These woods weren't the least bit scenic, and neither was the flat, barren terrain surrounding them. And good lord, Pine Haven, the nearby town, if you could even call it a town, was as hellish a shithole as anywhere they'd staged an operation in the last year. Even the desolate coal mining settlement of Marsh Fork, Kentucky, was idyllic in comparison.

As for Flynn, he was once again nursing an acute case of homesickness, the familiar gnawing ache in his chest, the hard magnetic pull of the seaside city he'd cherished since he'd drawn his first breath. At the moment their campsite in the Carolina forest was just shy of eight hundred miles from Miami. Eleven hours by car, a long damn way. But somehow it felt even farther. Like suspended animation would be required to travel the light-years back home to the blue waters and soothing sunshine and those exquisite breezes flavored with nutmeg and cloves and ripening mangoes.

Around the dwindling campfire the other three were silent, everyone on edge, waiting for Caitlin to return. Late in the afternoon she'd received an SOS text from one of the two Mexican farm-workers she'd recruited as spies. Their attempt at espionage had apparently gone bad.

With a grim face, Caitlin had set off alone to discover just how bad.

Hours later, the group had settled into a fidgety hush. All the others had finished their dinners, while Billy Jack was still polishing off his third helping of baked beans. A brawny guy with black hair and a neck thicker than Flynn's thigh, Billy Jack had played football for Auburn. But after shattering an opponent's jaw in an on-field brawl, Billy Jack was tossed from the team and would've spent a stretch in jail except his girlfriend's dad bribed the injured man to drop the charges.

Caitlin was that girlfriend. A fragile, high-strung belle, Caitlin started out as a true believer, a nature-loving free spirit who'd impulsively enlisted in the Earth Liberation Front minutes after hearing one of Cassandra's rousing recruitment speeches near the Auburn campus.

Caitlin dragged Billy Jack along on the righteous adventure. Caitlin full of idealistic rebellion, Billy Jack simply along for the ride. But in the last few months their romance cooled, and while Billy Jack's thrill for combat kept him engaged in the group's efforts, Caitlin lost her fervor for the cause. Recently she'd confided to Flynn that she'd been sneaking phone calls to her daddy, and the old guy was begging her to cut loose and head home. A new BMW was waiting for her, no ques-tions asked.

In the twelve months Flynn had been a member of ELF, he'd seen recruits come and go, so her departure wouldn't be surprising. But Cassandra would be pissed because Caitlin had proved to be remarkably adept at using her powers of enchantment to the group's advantage. Gaining access to people and opening doors that would have stayed shut without her southern charms.

On the log beside Billy Jack, Jellyroll was hunched over his laptop, his fingers flying. Twenty years old, he looked thirteen. A black kid from Philly. His mother dead, father serving life in some supermax joint in Virginia, Jellyroll was the group's computer geek. Back in July he'd first appeared at a fracking protest rally in Allentown, Pennsylvania, sidled over to their group, and to establish his hacking credentials he presented

Cassandra with her entire FBI dossier on the same laptop he was using tonight.

"Half of this is total bullshit," she said when she finished reading.

"No worries," Jellyroll said. "I'm a wizard with the delete key."

By midnight, the dinner plates were cleaned and stowed, the fire was down to a red glow, and the moody silence had grown deeper.

Flynn said, "I'm going to look for her."

"No, you're not," Cassandra said. "We stay together."

"She's in trouble," said Flynn. "She should've been back hours ago."

"Wouldn't be surprised," said Billy Jack, "if that girl hasn't run off. Been months since her last manicure, those raggedy nails are driving her batshit."

"Probably her right now." Jellyroll motioned at the dark tangle of woods, the wobble of a flashlight heading up the trail.

Everyone rose and stood flat-footed, waiting.

Moments later Caitlin came thrashing out of the woods, halted abruptly, and washed the beam of her flashlight over their faces.

"It's over, we're finished," she said, panting from her run. She stooped forward, hands on her knees. "They caught Javier, they've got his camera. We need to get the hell out of here. And I mean right now."

Cassandra squatted by the embers, waved for Caitlin to quiet down.

"Whoa, girl. They've got Javier's camera? You're sure?"

"Jesús told me one of the security guys spotted the wristwatch, made Javier take it off, figured out what it was, and dragged Javier away. Jesús is scared he'll be next."

The tiny spy camera embedded in the wristwatch had remarkable clarity for something so small. They'd bought the two watches from an online dealer. USB interface, four gigs of flash memory, audio recorder. A battery that could last for two hours of continuous recording. A hundred and fifty bucks for each.

"Took him away?" Jellyroll was using one finger to slice and dice the touch pad on his laptop. "Is that a euphemism? Like they killed him?"

Caitlin said she wasn't sure, but it was likely, very likely because these people were fucking scary, far more dangerous than anyone they'd encountered before. She circled the dying campfire, behind everyone's backs, repeating over and over: *We're finished. We need to go. We need to go now.*

"Take a breath, Caitlin." Cassandra came to her feet. "Slow breaths, deep. Count them; one, two, three, four."

Technically the group had no leader, but Cassandra was the oldest by a decade and had by far the most experience in the movement, plus she had an intimidating-as-hell glare framed by wild and abundant red hair, so the others deferred to her, even Billy Jack.

"Okay, I've finished the edit," Jellyroll said. "Fifty-six seconds long. It's rough, but there's good shit here. This could kick some serious ass."

Flynn moved behind Jellyroll and the others crowded in to see.

"Did you hear me? We need to go," Caitlin said from across the fire. "If you don't want to, fine. But I'm done. I didn't sign on for violence."

"So go," Billy Jack said. "You see anybody trying to stop you?"

"Javier knows where we're camping," Caitlin said. "If they torture him, he'll confess. They could be on their way here right now."

"Play it," Cassandra said to Jellyroll. "Let's see what we got."

A few days earlier Caitlin, who spoke basic Spanish, had recruited Javier and Jesús and gave each a watch and a hundred dollars to wear them on the job. Both were senior workers, eight years at the Dobbins Farm with free access throughout the facilities. But Javier was either too nervous or too hurried to follow the training Caitlin gave him, various ways to keep the camera steady.

Despite the jumpy, off-angle images, the video was decent. It started with an establishing shot, the Dobbins Farm sign in green and gold. Then the bouncy drive up the entrance road. Javier with his arm out the truck's window, capturing the manure ponds, the giant Rain Bird sprinklers shooting arcs of hog shit over a pasture. Not a pretty sight, but nothing criminal.

Then a jump cut took them inside a containment barn. Noisy hogs full-grown, restless in their tight cages, jostling, snorting, biting each other, scarfing down food, shitting in their pens. Then another cut. A quick shot of Burkhart dragging a sick hog by its hind legs out of a pen and into the concrete passageway, then using a hand sledge to kill the animal. Two hard whacks to its skull. The animal on its side bleating and squirming. Two more whacks.

Some of the other hogs were bumping the bars of their pens in protest. Ten seconds of ugliness, fairly mild compared to the undercover videos Flynn had seen online, hogs being hung by their necks on steel cables, hogs covered in bleeding sores, their legs giving way under their unnatural weight, left lying helpless, some truly horrendous shit, all of it perfectly legal. Excluded from state cruelty laws, farm animals were regularly subjected to sickening abuse. That was part of the group's mission, to share the revolting realities of industrial food production and put pressure on state governments to change those lax cruelty laws. Make it hard for the public to ignore what was going on.

The video moved to a new location. Javier was entering a greenhouse, a gold Dobbins logo over the doorway. He walked slowly down the rows of tall flowering trees, their ghostly trumpet blooms facing downward. After three or four seconds scanning the blooms, the camera turned to the ground, showing the gravel path where Javier was walking, and a quick image of another Mexican worker passing by. The worker was wearing a surgical mask.

"Great shot," Cassandra said. "Rising tension."

Javier entered a door at the far end of the greenhouse, passed by the drying racks that were hung with blooms, and took a seat at a long table where a row of other men were working. All of them in similar surgical masks. Then a few seconds that showed the entire pill room.

The camera was badly tilted, but Flynn could still make out what was taking place. The man sitting beside Javier at the table poured a test tube of fine powder through a paper funnel and filled a small hole drilled into a block of wood. Then the worker inserted a brass tamping rod into the hole, tapped it twice with a rubber-tipped mallet, tapped it again, then turned the block of wood over and shook the block until a bright red tablet fell onto the table in front of him. Then the worker scraped the pill into a jar with dozens of other similar tablets and began the process again. A primitive production line.

"Bingo," said Billy Jack. "We got us some major felonies."

The video flickered and ended.

Everyone was silent for a moment. Caitlin moaned to herself and stepped away from the others.

"I thought we were here for the hogs," Flynn said.

"We were," Cassandra said. "But this trumps the hogs."

"Sure," Flynn said. "Maybe this could shut Dobbins down, send him to jail, but even if it did, it's a one-off. It doesn't do anything for the big picture. That shot of Burkhart killing the sick pig, that's the stuff we're after, animal cruelty, not some pissant drug operation. That just muddies our message."

"Dobbins is a big deal. Take him down, it's a blow to his corporate bosses, a blow to the industry."

"They'll say Dobbins was an outlier. Throw him under the bus. Their hands stay clean."

"How do we know that?" Cassandra said. "Maybe Pastureland is fully aware of what's happening at one of their farms and they condone this. Maybe they're even getting a cut."

"They make billions on pork. Why risk a sideline in dope?"

Jellyroll raised his hand like a kid in class. Cassandra nodded his way.

"If I'm going to post the video to YouTube, we need to drive over to Goldsboro to hijack a wireless signal."

"Use your damn smartphone," Billy Jack said. "Post it tonight."

"File's too large. Need a wireless connection. That motel we stayed at last week, we could get a room, take showers, upload the video, then blow this taco stand."

Billy Jack was all in for that. Scrub off the putrid hog stink.

"You deleted the video from the watch, right, Jelly? Before Caitlin gave it back to Javier?"

"I did."

"So even if they have the watch, they don't know what we've got."

"Big deal," Caitlin said. "They know we've been spying. They're bound to think the worst. They'll come for us. I know they will. We're finished."

"Once it's on YouTube," Jellyroll said, "we send a link to the authorities. Maybe use Flynn's FBI contact. Someone like that."

"Your buddy Agent Sheffield will handle it, right? If you ask him nice." Cassandra was smiling, giving Flynn some shit.

"He's not my goddamn buddy."

"Okay, your father's buddy." Cassandra and Thorn had crossed paths last year. Sparks flew, but not the romantic kind.

Flynn Moss was the product of a one-night stand between Thorn and April Moss, Flynn's mom, a fact both father and son discovered by accident a year ago. Flynn had grown up without a father and had no interest in having one now, especially this guy. A hard-core loner, Thorn lived in a primitive cracker house along the coast in Key Largo and tied custom bonefish flies for a living. The guy came across as mellow, living the laid-back life, but puncture the veneer, piss him off, endanger his friends, and molten lava spewed. The guy could flare so hot it was scary. Flynn had to admit he admired that. The lava part. A year after their first meeting, Flynn still didn't want or need a dad, but damn it, he wished he'd inherited more of Thorn's latent ferocity.

Jellyroll said, "I'm going to post on the message board. Not a mayday or anything, just let our associates know where we are, the broad outline, you know, in case some bad shit happens and we go dark."

"All right, that's it, goddamn it, I'm leaving," Caitlin said. "I'm packing my gear and taking my canoe."

"Happy paddling." Billy Jack shot her a grin. "Watch out for white-eyed rednecks strumming banjos."

Cassandra walked over to Caitlin, took hold of her shoulder, swept back her hair, and leaned in close. Cheek to cheek, Cassandra spoke for half a minute while the others watched. Caitlin's panicked expression slowly dissolved, she nodded, then her head sagged and she looked up at Cassandra.

"Okay, okay," she said. "One more night."

"We're tired, we're spooked," Cassandra said, facing the group. "A lot's been going on. But I don't think we have anything to fear from these yahoos. We've heard their kind of bluster before. Let's just absorb this news, get some rest; tomorrow we'll consider our options, figure out the best way to help Javier. He's been loyal. We can't just leave him and Jesús hanging."

"Fuck 'em," Billy Jack said. "They got paid. They knew the risks."

Flynn had first watch. He sat cross-legged with his back against a pine. He'd chosen a spot fifty yards from their campsite on the north bank of the Neuse River.

That Monday before Thanksgiving, the night was crisp and a bright full moon dusted the branches with a silvery powder, enough radiance for him to keep watch on the narrow trail that led to their campsite. Only that one way in. These woods were too snarled with thickets and vines for anyone to sneak up on the camp from another direction.

Cassandra and Caitlin were in their sleeping bags, stretched out side by side on beds of pine straw, Billy Jack and Jellyroll in the hammocks they'd rigged inside the group's Ford van.

Flynn was armed only with a whistle. If he heard anyone approaching, he'd blow it twice, a signal for the group to abandon their sleeping bags, grab their escape kits, and sprint the half mile along the bank of the Neuse to the sandy shoreline where they'd hidden their canoes. Flynn would take a different route to the same location. On previous operations they'd drilled for this contingency, joking at what seemed like a senseless precaution. But when they reviewed it a while ago, there was no laughter.

Running from danger was their only option. Weeks ago they'd voted to outlaw weapons, and they'd tossed the group's single handgun in a river in Marsh Fork, Kentucky. Cassandra wasn't happy about parting with her .38, but the group had spoken. Four to one against her. Having guns led to laziness and lack of ingenuity. If they couldn't resolve their conflicts peacefully, what good was their entire mission? Guns were antithetical to all they espoused.

Above him a breeze stirred the limbs. Flynn lifted his head and listened to them rustle, tried to make out any human sounds the wind might be concealing. Around him the strawberry scent of evergreen was banished and overwhelmed by the harsh reek of hog manure. The stench of it had given Jellyroll and Caitlin headaches all week.

Their eyes reddened and Caitlin's throat was raw. But their suffering was nothing compared to those in the communities living downwind of the farm. It's why they'd come. To give voice to the voiceless, stand against the powerful.

Most of all they were here to mobilize the locals and bring attention to the outrageous crimes committed against them. Only they hadn't counted on unearthing something like this. Their discovery had been unintentional but they saw immediately how volatile their information was.

It was well after midnight. Flynn was in the middle of a reverie about Thorn's oceanside house in Key Largo, surrounded by dazzling blue waters that teemed with manatees, brightly colored reef fish, and rolling tarpon, and the sky above it thick with pelicans and ospreys and roseate spoonbills, a gorgeous, Technicolor, heart-soaring vision.

When the intruders came, the rustle of the dried leaves jerked him alert and Flynn barely stifled a panicky yelp.

After he steadied himself, he leaned out for a glimpse.

Twenty feet away, out on the dirt track, the point man was carrying an automatic weapon and crouching low. The man flanking him held a shotgun. The man in the lead wore night-vision goggles, training them forward as he moved toward the campsite.

Silently, Flynn came to his feet, pressing his back to the pine. He raised the whistle to his lips. If he blew it now with the men so near, there'd be no escape for him. If he waited till they passed, the others wouldn't have time to get away.

Shit. He'd set up the watch post too close to camp. He saw that now. Stupid mistake. Should have realized it long ago and moved farther up the trail.

Halting, the point man seemed to sense a presence nearby. In the moonlight Flynn saw the snowy bristles of his flat-top. A guy in his sixties, Burkhart was his name, the duly elected sheriff of Winston County and head of security at Dobbins hog farm. A cold-eyed guy with a military bearing, he'd confronted Cassandra in town a few days ago. Reached out a big hand and trickled his fingers across her cheek. Drawling with mock courtesy, a threat masked in avuncular concern. It might be better if she and her friends stopped stirring up trouble and got their sweet asses out of town and didn't return. This, he told her, will be your one and only warning. You're a grown lady, so you'll have to decide, but he'd hate to see any harm come to such a sweetheart.

When Cassandra knocked his hand away, the man laughed, calling her a spitfire, and grinned into her eyes as though they'd forged an intimate bond.

Flynn moved behind the tree, squatted down

and patted a hand across the ground. He risked another peek around the trunk. Both men had halted. They'd begun to scan the area, panning their weapons in a slow circle.

On the ground a few feet away Flynn found a rock—something from his storehouse of Hollywood clichés. Toss it into the nearby brush, misdirect the bad guys, and while their heads were turned, make a run. Most of the clichés Flynn had absorbed from his thousands of hours of film study were bogus, never worked off-screen, but he hoped, by God, this one might.

He stepped back from the pine, keeping the trunk in the attackers' sight line, and he hurled the rock over their heads back into the woods behind them. It clattered into leaves and fallen brush. The man behind Burkhart swung around, tracking the noise, taking a step or two away from Flynn's hiding place, but Burkhart wasn't fooled. One-handed he adjusted his goggles and began a slow sweep of his weapon in Flynn's direction.

Flynn ducked back behind the tree. His chest so constricted, he couldn't draw a breath. The man hissed to his partner and Flynn heard the dry crackle of their steps fanning out around him.

Flynn brought the whistle to his lips and blew two sharp blasts. He blew twice more as he was sprinting away, the automatic fire shredding the trees around him, strafing the branches, spurting the dirt at his feet. The deafening bursts of gunfire made any more warnings unnecessary, but Flynn blew the whistle twice more as he raced through the darkness, leading the men deeper into the pine forest that smelled so lovely.

If his friends had followed their evacuation plan and fled into the darkness on foot, heading down the bank to the canoes, everything might have worked out differently. But they panicked, or Cassandra overruled them and herded them into the van, unwilling to abandon their vehicle and gear. He heard the van's engine cough and fail to catch, then turn over again. The damn starter motor had been cranky for weeks, but they were short on cash and hadn't replaced it. He heard one attacker change direction, rushing toward the campsite, and he heard the engine sputter to life, then the bark of gunfire, howls of rage, and even louder howls of agony.

Flynn veered toward the camp, sprinting low. He didn't know what he could do to help the others, but he had to try.

All around him the pine forest was thick with scent. It was that rich odor he was thinking of, the sappy sweetness of evergreen, when he felt the hard electric tug on his shoulder, then another in his leg, and a second later a stinging spray of buckshot, then a creamy warmth spreading down his back.

After a breathless moment, he felt a surge of unexpected joy, a release from the tension of these last few days, these last months, an exhilarating letting go, and for the next hundred yards as the mindless bullets ripped apart the air around him, Flynn Moss seemed to float above the rough terrain, fearless and strong, his feet barely grazing the earth as he saw the moonlit water up ahead, the silver current that streamed through this fertile countryside, flowing and flowing, as all rivers did, their waters inevitably returning to the welcoming sea.

Two

A week after Thanksgiving, an early afternoon in December, Thorn sat at a computer console in the Key Largo library, once again searching for news of his son, Flynn Moss.

He'd propped Flynn's latest postcard against the base of the monitor and was scanning the rows of photographs Google search had selected for him when he typed in the words "Marsh Fork, Kentucky." None of the images on the computer matched the green hills and lazy blue sky of the postcard.

On his screen there were maps of the area, placing Marsh Fork in the eastern end of the state near the West Virginia line, and there were images of miners with coal-smudged faces and hard hats standing shoulder to shoulder and staring into the camera with a resigned weariness. And photos of Marsh Fork Elementary School, a one-story, tired-out brick building surrounded by a tall chain-link fence. But most of the photos featured protest rallies inside gymnasiums or in green rolling fields or in front of Marsh Fork Elementary.

The protestors held up hand-lettered signs demanding the governor save their kids, save their elementary school, save their community, save their mountains. A few rows down from all the protest pictures were some images taken from a mile or so in the air that showed a lush green mountain range pockmarked with the gray flattened scars of mountaintop removal, a mining technique that wiped out the forests and blasted away the rivers and streams and obliterated the mountains one by one as giant cranes scooped out the black shiny coal.

There were aerial shots that included both the elementary school and a huge pond carved into the mountains just a half mile above the school. A caption described the pond as filled with three billion gallons of coal slurry. Thorn had to look that one up and found that coal slurry was the by-product of mountaintop-removal mining. A highly toxic blend of dissolved minerals. The Web page that listed the toxins in a typical slurry pond was full of multisyllable chemicals from benzidine to dimethyl phthalate. Thorn didn't need to look up any of those. The images of the foul brown liquid made it obvious.

Nobody sane would want their kids attending school in that brick building a half mile down-hill from a few billion gallons of toxic sludge held in place by earthen walls.

A few weeks ago when Flynn sent this post-card, this was where he'd been, Flynn and his cohorts in the Earth Liberation Front, the group of eco-avengers he'd gotten mixed up with late last year. The postcards had been arriving regularly at Sugarman's office. Sugar, Thorn's closest friend, ran a one-man private investi-gation agency and because of that, Thorn usually deferred to him in matters of logic, but since these postcards started arriving, he and Sugar had been at odds over what they signified.

"He's sending you a message," Sugar said.

"A few words would be a message. These are blank. This feels more like taunting, showing off, trying to prove he did the right thing by joining up with these people."

"He wants you to know where he is, that he's safe. He's trying to reassure you, keep the lines of communication open."

"Then he should include his goddamn address."

"You know he can't do that. He's got to stay at arm's length."

"He wants me to know what he's up to, but he doesn't trust me."

"The stuff he's doing, he's got to be cagey."

"Why send them to your office? Not directly to me?"

"Somebody could be snooping on your mail."

"Come on. Who would do that?"

"Whatever federal task force is hunting ecoterrorists."

"Flynn's no terrorist."

Sugar didn't reply. He was tired of arguing that particular semantic issue.

"Okay, sure, he's misguided, getting involved with these people. But he's well-meaning. This is civil disobedience, nothing worse."

"So he's not a terrorist. Fine. Use whatever word makes you happy. Point is, if he's caught, the kid's going to do some serious time. He's known to the feds and so are you. Since you're his father, I wouldn't be surprised if your mail is being monitored."

"They would do that?"

"That and more. If you had a phone, Internet access, they'd be all over that too."

Thorn spent a while longer scrolling through the images of Marsh Fork, Kentucky. Groups of forlorn women locked arm in arm marching somewhere, cops in riot gear blocking their way. More country folks, men, women, and children having a sit-in at the Kentucky governor's office. Save Marsh Fork Elementary.

He moved the computer mouse to the heading of the Google page and touched the arrow to "News." He hesitated, glanced around the library. The place was so quiet, so polite, the world of books and reading and thoughtful people. No one protesting. No one risking their lives for a higher principle.

The young librarian with purple hair and five nose rings was watching Thorn from behind the circulation desk, sending him "I'm available" smiles. Her name was Julia, and on several previous occasions she'd helped Thorn with the computer when the damn machine confounded him. A couple of times she'd asked about the postcards, but Thorn told her nothing. Julia had a pretty face and dark, striking eyes. Years ago he'd dated her aunt, a highway patrol officer who lived down in Lower Matecumbe.

When Julia winked at him and cocked her head coyly to the side, Thorn gave the young lady a cool disinterested smile. Julia read the look correctly, sighed, made a wistful nod, and got back to work. Game over.

Good. Thorn wasn't about to trifle with the daughters of women his own age. In Key Largo such men were not uncommon, but Thorn was determined not to become one. He'd gotten dangerously close a few times over the years, but lately some fuse had blown in his libido and his attraction to younger women had faded.

Still, Thorn continued to consider himself as relatively young, hovering somewhere between late twenties and early thirties, still in his twitchy prime. Though what he saw in the mirror was brutally at odds with that sensation. He was getting close to being twice the age he felt himself to be.

He clicked the mouse and went to "News." Though he'd heard nothing about it at the time, Marsh Fork, Kentucky, had been the subject of dozens of newspaper headlines and sensational TV stories in the last few weeks. That earthen dam had given way. A couple of billion gallons of waste slurry had sluiced down the hillside and swept away the one-story brick school in a toxic tsunami. Another school would now be built in a safer location. Exactly what the parents and the assorted protestors had been campaigning for all along.

The catastrophe had occurred around two in the morning on a weekend. That night the single security guard must've been alerted to what was coming and had called in sick.

No one was killed. No one injured. Dynamite had been set at four locations along the downhill portion of the dam. No group had taken credit for the sabotage, but the Earth Liberation Front was targeted in the investigation because they'd been the most outspoken critics of the dam and organized the local protests and the sit-in at the governor's office. And after the dam burst and the destruction of the school, no ELF members could be found anywhere in Marsh Fork.

It fit their pattern. An attack on the despoilers of the environment that was carefully calibrated to cause strategic harm to property without loss of life. Then they vanished.

Thorn scanned a few of the articles, searching as he always did for Flynn's name or any mention of Cassandra, the red-haired woman who led the band Flynn had gotten mixed up with last summer. Thorn met her and one of her badass lieutenants when the ELF gang commandeered his isolated house in Key Largo to use as a staging area and escape route after their attack on Turkey Point nuclear plant.

He'd done what he could to thwart that attack and pry Flynn loose from the band of environmental crazies, and he partly succeeded, but after the mission ended that violent night, Flynn walked over to Thorn, embraced him, said he loved him but he'd had a change of heart about this ELF cell. He'd decided to go all in, dedicate himself to their goals, become a full-fledged member. Then he climbed into a green panel van with his new comrades and drove away into the summer night.

Since that moment there'd been seven picture

postcards. With a little research on each location Thorn found the same pattern repeating each time. An environmental outrage committed against a community, followed by some kind of violent attack in response, each one an attempt to solve the issue or at least bring it to the public's attention. While they didn't all work as neatly as the Marsh Fork venture, Thorn continued to be sympathetic to their cause. Though he had to admit, it was hard to tell if Flynn's group was accomplishing anything of long-term value.

In any case, Flynn was now an outlaw, and though his name was not mentioned in any of the news stories Thorn found on the library computer, Thorn's friend Frank Sheffield, the agent in charge of the FBI Miami field office, had assured him that Flynn Moss was indeed on the extended Most Wanted list. Not hanging on the post office walls yet. But damn close.

Ordinarily Thorn wouldn't go near a computer. He lived in a clapboard-sided house built by his adoptive father. Surviving just fine in primitive simplicity with electricity generated by an ancient windmill and water heated by pipes exposed to the ceaseless sunshine of the Keys. His basic needs were few, his food and beer bought with the meager funds he made tying custom bonefish flies. His clientele was a faithful group of old-time Conchs and a set of young fishing guides who found in his handiwork a certain practical magic. His flies caught fish—more fish than their own handcrafted lures. Maybe not a lot more, but enough to tip the balance in their favor and bring those guides to Thorn's door.

Following the travels of Flynn Moss had become for Thorn a ritual of self-inflicted emotional pain, a masochistic habit he couldn't break. His heart pitched and twisted when he sat down before the public computers and began to read the details of Flynn's latest exploits. He wanted his son to return home safely, give Thorn a chance to make amends for all he had and had not done. But with each new stunt, the likelihood of that diminished. Off and on for the last two weeks he'd been tormented by the Marsh Fork postcard before he finally summoned the will to come to the library and confront his son's recent escapades.

Until a year earlier, Thorn hadn't known he had a son. Flynn was the product of a weekend fling decades back and only through a series of flukes had Flynn's mother revealed the truth and allowed father and son to meet.

An actor by profession, Flynn was a handsome, high-spirited young man. Initially, after discovering Thorn was his dad, Flynn's reaction was icy and distant. But months later, unknown to Thorn, he began to move in another direction. Inspired by a single visit to Thorn's primitive home in Key Largo, impulsively Flynn Moss bought a boat of his own and began to explore the waters of South Florida, some dormant outdoorsman gene awakening in his bloodstream. He began attending Sierra Club meetings, got involved in local environmental causes, and quickly grew more radical than the other members. In a matter of months, Flynn was recruited by ELF. And so it happened that within only a year of his visit to Thorn's spartan home, Flynn had quit his TV acting job, engaged in an assault on a nuclear power plant, then disappeared into the eco-underground, a fugitive on the run.

It weighed on Thorn, shadowed him through his daily chores, his hours of solitude beside the bright waters of Key Largo. For months he'd been plagued with guilt and a helpless simmering anger. Blaming himself for Flynn's dark turn and trying to imagine a way to undo the harm he'd done to his son.

Thorn sat for a while staring at the brittle light coming through the high windows and watching the clouds drift by. Those windows, those walls, that library had been built three decades earlier, part of a package deal the developer of the shopping center was forced to accept to mitigate the loss of the many acres of hardwood hammock that were bulldozed. After all that time only a few old-timers around Key Largo remembered those trees where Thorn and Sugarman and some of their buddies had tramped around as kids and built a secret fort where they held council meetings, making up adolescent fantasies about girls their age, tales of derring-do and mystery that always concluded in saving the skin of the girl in question and, of course, winning her undying love.

A lost hardwood forest, a gained library. In the grand scheme, a fairly even trade, but as much as Thorn loved books and libraries, he missed those lignum vitae and mahoganies, and the secret dens of raccoons and possums and the nests of osprey and ibis and egrets, making their homes and raising their young in the very spot where Thorn was now sitting.

As Thorn was shutting down the computer, Sugarman settled into the adjacent chair, reached into his shirt pocket, and slid a postcard across the table.

"Came today."

Thorn looked at the glossy image of a river twisting through the lush woods of some foothill wilderness.

The caption read: *The Neuse River, Pine Haven, North Carolina.*

Thorn turned to the computer keyboard.

"Don't bother," Sugar said. "I looked it up already."

"So tell me."

"The Neuse runs southeast of Raleigh, all the way to the coast."

"What's the issue this time?"

"That's the thing."

Sugarman took a cautious look around the library as if checking for eavesdroppers.

Sugar was Thorn's age, but was enduring the years far more gracefully. He seemed to be growing more handsome, more dignified, more calm. His caramel skin was still silky smooth, his dark eyes full of the quiet fire of youth. A man whose Jamaican father and Scandinavian mother had bestowed on him a lucky genetic legacy. An elegantly structured face, coffee dark eyes, and a thick mat of densely coiled hair that Sugarman had always worn short.

"What's wrong, Sugar?"

"What's wrong is this time there is no issue."

Thorn looked again at the card.

"I checked online news sites, blogs, Twitter, everything I could find. No protest, no mention of any outside agitators or an environmental issue."

Thorn sat back in his chair, glancing around at the quiet carpeted space. The clean December light was filtering through the tall windows. No one listening, no one looking in their direction.

"So whatever they're planning hasn't happened yet."

"A reasonable inference," Sugar said.

"Which makes this different. A different kind of message."

"Appears that way," said Sugarman.

"An invitation?"

Sugar's face was blank.

"Tell me what're you thinking."

He just shook his head, waiting for Thorn.

"Seems pretty obvious," Thorn said. "He's ready to come home."

Sugar closed his eyes. He massaged his forehead as if trying to drive away an ugly thought.

At the age of two, after his parents abandoned him, Sugar was adopted by an African American church lady who'd raised him in Key Largo's one black district. Under her influence, Sugar acquired a finely tuned moral sensibility. He resolutely followed the codes of decency and honor. Controlled and methodical and steady. In that way he was Thorn's opposite and because they'd been close friends since childhood, fighting side by side in more battles than Thorn cared to recall, Sugar had saved his ass dozens of times, snatching him back from the brink of one disaster after another. The good cop to his bad. The wise counsel to Thorn's impulse.

Sugar's gaze drifted to the windows across the room, his eyes faraway as though he was revisiting a time long past when their shared world was uncomplicated and their struggles manageable. Back when it was possible to be full of hope and confidence, before the losses and heartaches and ambiguities began to complicate every decision—a time when the future was as sharp and bright as the winter sky beyond the library windows.

Thorn had been at this precise point so many times before, feeling the first click of gears meshing, the revving heart, the flutter in his blood. Another long stretch of tranquility interrupted. He no longer deluded himself about his ability to resist. This was who he had become. A hermit on call.

"Let's say you're right," Sugar said. "Then what?"

"I'll go get him."

"And how would you do that?"

"Fly up to Atlanta or Charlotte, rent a car."

"Yeah? And how the hell do you accomplish that, fly commercial without ID? You going to go get a driver's license this afternoon? A Social Security number, a credit card. After all these years you're going to register your sorry ass with the U.S. government. Check in with Uncle Sam, say, hi, I've been living in the shadows for the last half-century, but I decided I want to take a plane ride, so I'm signing in."

"Then I'll drive."

"Goddamn it, Thorn." He stood up. "The shape it's in, your car wouldn't make it to Miami."

"I'll borrow your car."

"No you won't."

Sugar was shaking his head. Couldn't believe

where this was headed. Thorn searched Sugarman's eyes.

Sugarman looked away and said, "The last time you tried to get Flynn away from these people, flying solo, a lot of folks went down and you were almost killed."

"You offering to help me?"

"I'd have to be crazy to do that."

"Forget it. You've got a job, responsibilities."

Sugar snorted. He'd been complaining lately that in these rough economic times when people wanted to investigate somebody or track down a runaway spouse, more and more they handled it on their own. For a small fee to some online service, they had access to all the public records on their target. The Internet was taking a toll on Sugar's profession. All summer and into the fall his business had been dead. He'd been talking about putting the house he'd lived in for thirty years up for sale, forced to use the equity just to get by.

"Look at the card again, the back side."

Thorn picked up the postcard and turned it over. As usual the card was addressed to Sugarman at his office address, hand-printed in all caps. The message side of the card had always been blank. This time it wasn't.

Help Me was printed in the same blocky letters.

Thorn straightened in his chair.

"Now check the postmark."

The card was stamped, but there was no postmark, not even the faintest sign.

"That happens sometimes. Something slips through."

"Sometimes?" Sugarman said. "I'd say almost never."

"So Flynn came to your office and dropped this in your mailbox? Is that what you think?"

Sugar paused, looking off at Julia, the purple-haired librarian.

"Okay," Sugar said. "I'll drive you up there. I'll go along."

"You'd do that?"

"But I have to be back by next Friday."

"Friday?"

"A job interview."

"With who?"

"Sheriff's department, Monroe County," Sugar said.

"Your old job?" Thorn was staring at the postcard.

"Something new," he said. "Community affairs, media relations."

Thorn looked up, smiling in disbelief.

"Writing press releases? Crime-stopper meetings?"

Sugar nodded, halfhearted.

"You wouldn't be on the street, no real police work. You'd hate that."

"The interview is Friday at ten," Sugar said. "I

43

have to be back no later than Thursday night. This takes any longer, I don't know, Thorn. I got bills stacked so high I can't see out my kitchen window."

"No sweat, back by Thursday. What's today, Monday?"

"It must be nice," Sugar said. "Living in a timeless zone. Don't know the day of the week, what month it is."

"It's December," Thorn said.

"Today's Friday," said Sugar.

"No problem. It's probably a small town. Leave today, drive straight through. We find Flynn, grab him, back by Sunday, Monday at the latest."

Sugar fluttered his lips and shook his head. Whether it was Thorn's tainted karma or just his general recklessness, nothing ever turned out simply when Thorn was involved.

"A drive that distance," Sugar said, "I need to change my oil, check my tires. Throw a few things in a suitcase. I need to call Tina, tell her I'm leaving."

"Yeah, okay."

"So here's what you do. Get yourself ready, then take your skiff down to the docks at the Lorelei. Victor will let you dock it there for a few days. I'll meet you at the bar in a couple of hours."

"Why not just swing by my house, pick me up? It's on the way."

"Look, Thorn. If someone's monitoring your mail, they might be watching your comings and goings. Take the boat."

"What're you saying? This is a trick? The government playing games?"

"I don't know what it is."

"I'll tell you what it is. Flynn's in trouble. Serious trouble. Something he can't handle."

Sugar patted him on the back and got to his feet.

"*Tranquilo*. We'll find him, bring him home. It's going to be fine."

Thorn held up the postcard. The Neuse River. He'd never heard of it. But it was pretty, with a gentle flow, clear, sparkling water. Looked like a perfect spot for a family reunion.

Three

The last road trip Thorn had taken was decades earlier, a drive from Key Largo to Baltimore with his adoptive parents, Kate and Dr. Bill Truman. They'd driven straight through to drop Thorn off for his freshman year at Dr. Bill's alma mater, Johns Hopkins. Thorn had lasted exactly two months in college, flunking all his courses, bored by the aimless debates over current events, and tormented by the drab autumn weather which felt bitterly cold to Thorn, but which Baltimore locals described as the mildest fall on record. He dropped out and was back home in Key Largo by Thanksgiving and was never drawn north of Palm Beach after that. Until now.

In an old gym bag he packed underwear, long-sleeved shirts and jeans, along with his only sweater, a heavy black crewneck that years ago some girlfriend had presented him for his mid-summer birthday. A gift so weirdly inappropriate it seemed to signal both the great divide between them and the end of their affair. The sweater smelled as musty as a rat's burrow, but Thorn stuffed it into the bag anyway, along with the few toiletries he used.

There was no one to notify of his departure, no one to ask to keep an eye on his old Cracker house. His ancient thirty-two-foot Chris Craft would have to fend for itself. If someone wanted to steal it, all they had to do was untie the lines and find a way to crank that balky eight cylinder.

He left the front door unlocked so thieves wouldn't need to break a window to steal his loot. Happy hunting. If they gathered every valuable Thorn owned and pawned them all, they'd be lucky to clear enough for a fish sandwich at Craig's Diner.

On the boat ride down to Islamorada the ocean

was glassy and pulsed with pale blue wintery light. Earlier in the week a mass of Canadian air had swept in, and now as he headed out to deeper water the sharp sulfurous tang of the exposed flats gave way to the bracing arctic air that had flooded into the Keys, bringing the cypress and fir scent of old-growth forests and the undertone of melting glaciers, that blue ice that seemed to be releasing into the atmosphere precious molecules of oxygen so ancient they'd never been sullied by the lungs of humans.

He docked, found an empty barstool, ordered a bottle of Red Stripe. After he'd had a taste, a young man next to him tapped on his shoulder and asked if he could take Thorn's photograph. He was wearing a bright pink flowered shirt the same throbbing tone as his sunburn.

"Why would you do that?"

"For a project," he said. "College art class."

Thorn asked him what kind of project.

"A collection of Keys characters. And you, damn, you're perfect. You got that local-color Jimmy Buffett thing going on. The sandy hair, the jaw, that weathered skin. Like some crusty *Old Man and the Sea* desperado hanging out in Margaritaville. My professor will love it."

"You don't have people like me where you're from?"

"You kidding? In South Bend?"

Thorn declined as politely as he could manage.

Waited a decent interval, then got up, moved to a table alongside the dock. The thought of being in someone's local-color slide show made him feel even older and sadder.

When Sugarman finally arrived he had Tina Gathercole in tow. Sugar had been dating Tina for the last few weeks, though Thorn couldn't see the attraction. Tina was wired and fidgety and a breathless talker. She was barely five feet tall, wore her blond hair cropped in a scruffy pixie apparently meant to project a just-rolled-out-of-the-sack look.

She ran Island Treasures, a gift shop in Tavernier, a tiny space crammed with goofy sea-shell geegaws and row upon row of customized bongs. She created them at a hobby table at the rear of the store. Each was covered in peace symbols and flashy plastic beadwork. Patchouli or sandalwood incense burned in every corner of the space. If you weren't stoned when you entered Tina's store, you were at least a little dizzy when you left.

"I'm going with you guys," she said to Thorn. "Sugar called to tell me he was driving north and I asked could I come along, and my sweetie said yes."

"As far as Jacksonville," Sugar said, shooting Thorn a conciliatory look. "Tina's got an aunt in the hospital up there. So I volunteered to give her a lift."

Thorn said sure. No problem.

"What's the big mystery?" she whispered to Thorn as he was settling his gym bag in the trunk of Sugar's Honda. There was a full-size army duffel taking up most of the cargo space. "Come on, Sugar won't tell me a thing."

"It's a secret," Thorn said.

"I hate secrets. They aggravate my hormones, make me sweat like a camel."

"We'll stop and get you a bag of frozen peas. I hear that helps."

She brayed with laughter.

"And some of the girls say what a grumpy stick-in-the-mud you are. But no, you're funny, Thorn. You're a regular riot."

"Maybe three bags of frozen peas. One for each of us."

She rode shotgun, casting looks at Thorn in the mirror in her sun visor. Smiling at him, mugging, trying to get him to loosen up. It didn't work.

As they hit the nightmare of Miami traffic, Tina cleared her throat and sat up straight, ready for an announcement.

"I know what the mystery is. It's your son, Thorn. Flynn Moss."

Sugarman's foot came off the gas for a moment, and Tina said, "Bingo."

"What makes you think that?" Thorn said.

"It adds up," she said. "Everyone knows what happened with the power plant and Flynn.

49

Then he disappeared. Now you two are off on a mysterious road trip. It's just two plus two. Anybody could figure it out. And the postcards."

"Postcards?" Thorn said. "What postcards?"

"Julia Jackson—you know, Thorn. Works in the library, cute, with lavender hair. She works in my shop on weekends. We were talking and she said you're always at her computers, a picture postcard on the desk in front of you and you're Googling this and that. Looking at maps and photographs and newspaper stories. So we figured it was about your boy. He's sending you messages and you're checking up on him."

Thorn looked out at the traffic. Sugarman said nothing. Driving with full concentration.

"Now don't start thinking I'm a gossip," Tina said. "It's just the coconut telegraph. You hear things, you can't help it."

Thorn tightened his seat belt, settled back into the seat.

"Oh, okay. I guessed your secret, so now I get the silent treatment. I'm not welcome. You want to dump me on the side of the road."

"We're taking you to Jacksonville," Sugar said.

"You sure you don't want to talk about Flynn? I could give you a woman's point of view, help you out with whatever the problem is."

"Kind of you to ask," Thorn said. "But no thanks."

50

They drove in silence while Tina fiddled with the radio until she found a talk show and turned up the volume. Some blowhard was ranting about the president, ridiculing him for his lies and failures and corruption. They listened to the rant for several minutes, Thorn trying and failing to tune the guy out.

"Maybe some music," Sugarman said.

"Hey, I need my fix of straight talk," Tina said. "You're just biased against political discourse."

"Is that what that is? It sounds like hate speech."

Tina turned around to face Thorn.

"Me and Sugar have these arguments. He's so accepting. So naive about how the world works. I'm trying to convert him to a rabble rouser."

"Good luck," Thorn said. "First you need to get his pulse over thirty."

She brayed again. Sugarman reached over and punched a button on the radio and got a station playing seventies rock. Tina gave him a good-natured punch in the arm and turned back to Thorn.

"You know, all these years, I never had a chance to actually sit down with you, Thorn. But now I'm starting to see why you and Sugar are buds."

"Normally he's not this chatty," Sugarman said. "Thorn's said more to you in the last fifty miles than he's said to me in a month."

51

"I have that effect on men, honey. You know that. I open them up like cans of tuna fish."

"How many more hours to Jacksonville?" Thorn said.

"You know what helps make the miles go by faster?" She drew a fat joint from her shirt pocket and held it up. "Anyone use a toke?"

Sugar declined and Thorn said no, he was content in his present state.

"Suit yourself," Tina said, lighting up.

It did smell good. He could feel it riding heavy in his shirt pocket, the postcard from Neuse River. With a fingertip he touched the card through the fabric and sat back and watched the flat, empty miles. The winter migration of birds was filling fields and power lines with Cooper's hawks and ospreys and plovers and kingfishers, willets and terns. They seemed unperturbed by the outlet malls and the housing developments crammed along the highway. Somehow those traveling birds were still finding patches of green and standing water in drainage ditches. Getting by, making do, adjusting as all pilgrims must.

The first few bars of some big band music sounded, and Tina plucked her phone from her pocket, pressed it to her ear, and listened for a few seconds, then clicked off.

"Cool ringtone, huh?"

"She's proud of her ringtone," Sugarman said.

"It's the opening of 'La Marseillaise,' " she said

over her shoulder as she was putting her phone away. "In case you were wondering."

"You're French?" Thorn said.

"No, no. It's from that movie *Casablanca*, the scene at Rick's bar when the German soldiers stand up and start singing their national anthem with those deep masculine voices, and the French all get on their feet and sing theirs, the women joining in, competing, you know, and the French song is much prettier, and it becomes much louder, and eventually it drowns out the Germans, mainly because Rick gives the high sign to his band, and they chime in. 'To arms, to arms, ye brave. March on.' It's a great scene. So I use it on my phone. I always get chills when a call comes in."

Another twenty minutes up the road, outside of Vero Beach, Tina prodded Sugarman's arm, said she had to use the toilet. An emergency.

Sugar took the next exit.

"That one," Tina said. "The Shell station."

"Okay, sure. The Shell station."

"They're cleaner, that's all. Shell stations, their bathrooms are always cleaner."

While Tina headed for the john, Thorn joined Sugar at the pumps.

In a quiet voice Sugar said, "Don't look, but there's a white pickup two pumps over. It's been behind us since we left Key Largo."

"You sure?"

"Thirty years in law enforcement, I can spot a damn tail."

Thorn said, "I'll go get in the guy's face. See what's up."

"Stay put. First, it's not a guy. And second, she's heading over here."

Halfway between her truck and where they stood, the tall, dark-haired woman reached inside her jean jacket and withdrew a leather folder and flipped it open, closing in on them with her badge displayed.

"Oh, terrific," Sugar said.

"Afternoon, gentlemen."

Thorn leaned in to read the ID. Her name was Madeline Cruz, an agent with the FBI.

She wore faded jeans and a denim jacket over a black and white checked shirt. She was wide shouldered and slender and olive skinned. Her smoky eyes were a deep glossy brown. There was a bump in the bridge of her nose that looked like a fist might have cracked it a few years back. She was in her early forties, quietly exotic in that way that Hispanic women with a shot of Aztec blood can be. Not conventionally beautiful, but well north of pretty.

Sugar asked what they could do for her. Stiffly courteous.

"I'd like you to open the trunk of your vehicle, sir."

"What's this about, Cruz?"

54

"You need to open your trunk, sir."

"That badge only takes you so far. You need some probable cause."

"Well, for one thing, I smell marijuana coming from your vehicle."

"The FBI is in the drug business now?"

"There's another matter, a bit more serious."

Sugarman bent forward and took a closer look at her badge.

"I have reason to believe you're transporting illegal materials."

Tina was coming back across the parking lot drinking a Big Gulp. She halted when she saw the woman showing her badge to Sugar. Tina scanned the gas station, spotted a green sedan, its door open, engine running; its owner, a skinny girl in a baseball cap, was dumping some litter in a trash can.

Tina dropped her drink and sprinted to the sedan, slammed the door; the skinny kid crossed her arms across her chest and yelled at Tina as she peeled out of the station, swerving to avoid a Winnebago and screeching toward the entrance ramp for I-95.

Cruz flipped open her cell, speed-dialed, and said, "She's running. Green Nissan with dark windows. Yeah, call me when it's done."

"What the hell?" Thorn stepped close to the woman.

"All right, gentlemen. Back in your vehicle,

park over there beside the station. We'll talk. And don't curse at me again, is that clear?"

Sugarman drove them to the shade of a tamarind tree. She leaned over and pulled out the ignition keys and told them to stay put, then got out and went behind the car and popped the trunk.

"Jesus, Sugar. Is Tina dealing dope?"

"She smokes a ton of weed, and she's got some sketchy friends, but dealing, no. Anyway the FBI doesn't waste their time with drugs."

Cruz came back to Sugar's window and motioned for them to get out.

They followed her around to the rear of the car, the open trunk. She bent down and spread the duffel all the way open, exposing the stocky barrels and handgrips of a couple of oversize shotguns hidden beneath bundled bricks of cash. Old bills, twenties and fifties.

Cruz zipped up the duffel and slammed the trunk. Her phone rang and she plucked it from her jacket pocket, flipped it open.

"Okay, good," she said. "Take her back to HQ. I'll be in touch."

Sugar gave Thorn a gloomy eye roll. *Here we go.* They were only a few hours down the road and already their simple plan had spun out of control.

Cruz ended the call and directed a satisfied smile toward the ramp where Tina had fled. She snapped the phone shut and ordered them back in the vehicle.

"I didn't know about the weapons or the money," Sugar said when they were seated. "I put the duffel in the trunk, I never looked inside."

"Save it," Cruz said through Sugar's window. "I know you're innocent. Both of you."

"Where's Tina? Where'd they take her?"

"For questioning," Cruz said. "Palm Beach office."

"She needs an attorney," Sugar said. "Give me the details, her location."

"For the moment," Cruz said, "all legal protections are suspended for your friend, just as they are for all enemy combatants. It's Homeland Security's call. I'm sure their people will be contacting you in due course."

"Are you nuts? Tina's no terrorist."

"It appears you don't know Ms. Gathercole as well as you thought."

"If you know we're innocent," Thorn said, "then give us the keys and we'll be on our way."

"You'll stay put."

She left them sitting in the car and went to her pickup, drove over to the side of the station, and parked alongside them. She unloaded a computer bag and a backpack, put them in Sugarman's trunk, and got back in the front seat.

She handed Sugarman his car keys.

"Drive," she said.

"Where?"

"North on I-95. Same direction you were headed."

"You're not going to take us in, interrogate us?"

"You can't tell me anything I don't already know."

"So where am I driving?"

"North."

"Where?"

"I'll tell you when to exit," she said. "Don't worry, I'm not taking you out of your way."

"This isn't even close to police procedure."

"No," she said. "It's not."

"How far are we going?"

She drew a Glock from her jacket, lay it on the dashboard.

"Far enough for us to get acquainted."

Four

But no acquainting took place for the next half hour. Sugar peppered her with questions but Cruz stared straight ahead and seemed not to hear and finally he shook his head and went quiet. With each mile the silence inside the Honda grew more dense until the stillness solidified around them and the interior of the car felt so airless that human speech no longer seemed possible. The only sound was the rough hum of tires, the rumble of passing trucks, and their buffeting tailwinds.

Thorn slipped the postcard from his pocket and looked again at the Neuse River, the pines and dogwoods and sweet gums growing near its banks, the grassy field dotted with wildflowers.

He turned the card over and examined Sugarman's office address, printed in block letters. Those two words, *Help Me*. Looking some more. Spotting something odd.

He was no handwriting expert, and he'd need to have the rest of Flynn's postcards at hand to do a side-by-side comparison to be sure, but there seemed to be something different about the penmanship from the addresses on the previous cards. A subtle backward tilt to the letters. And the first letter of each word was capitalized.

Thorn tried to picture the others. Shuffling through the storehouse of images in his head. Visualizing the most recent one, from Marsh Fork, the one he'd had at the library just a few hours ago. He was almost certain those letters were printed in all caps.

Very close but not identical. Just the slightest hint of another personality. A backward-tilting, capitalizing human being pretending to be Thorn's son.

"Something's not right."

Cruz half turned and met Thorn's eyes.

"What is it?"

"Forget it. It doesn't concern you."

"Everything concerns me." She rested her arm on the seat back and swiveled around a few more degrees until she was facing him.

"Okay, this is total bullshit." Sugar slowed the car, checked the rearview mirror, then swung into the emergency lane and braked to a hard stop.

Cruz swiveled forward again, looked out her window, and from Thorn's vantage point her face seemed utterly serene, as if she'd been expecting this moment for a while and was fully prepared for anything that might develop.

"Look," Sugar said. "Read us our rights, arrest us, or let us go. What you're doing amounts to carjacking. You can't hold us against our will. That's beyond your authority or anybody else's, I don't care what federal agency you work for."

"No one's being arrested," Cruz said. "No need for legal formalities."

"She's singing from a different hymnal," Thorn said. "What do you think, Sugar? Toss her out right here, get back to our business?"

She didn't bother turning around again. Just kept staring out the side window at an empty field as the traffic blew past them.

"Thorn, Thorn, Thorn. Agent Sheffield warned me that you're the designated problem child on this team. Which makes him a better judge of character than I've been giving him credit for."

"You work with Sheffield?"

"I think his exact words were: 'a recluse with poorly developed social skills.' "

"Why were you talking to Sheffield about Thorn?" Sugar had switched to cop mode. Tough, no nonsense, Cruz's professional equal.

"Let's drop the adversarial tone. It won't be productive in the coming days. We need to foster a more cordial and trusting relationship."

"What coming days?" Sugar said.

Thorn said, "And what the hell're we doing with that artillery still in the trunk? Why didn't your people seize the duffel back at the gas station? Where's Tina?"

"All right," Cruz said, shifting in her seat, glancing back at Thorn, then settling her gaze on Sugarman. "These are decent questions. Good, let's get started. The first thing you need to know is that the weapons in the trunk aren't your ordinary street sweepers. What you're carrying back there are AA-12s. Either of you familiar with that model?"

Sugar said he wasn't, and Thorn said, "Go on, you have our attention."

"They are Atchisson Assault Shotguns. Fully automatic and drum-fed. They fire five twelve-gauge shells per second with great reliability and so little recoil that a strong man can shoot it one-handed. The AA-12 was developed together with the FRAG-12, an extremely lethal variety of cartridge. Each round is essentially a small high-explosive or fragmentation grenade accurate up to a hundred and seventy-five meters. In short, these weapons are not legal for civilian use."

"What's Tina Gathercole doing with a couple of elephant guns?" Thorn said. "Running them to Jacksonville?"

"Tina wasn't going to Jacksonville. That was only her cover story."

"I don't get it," Sugar said.

"She was along for the whole trip. She hadn't sprung that on you yet, but I'm sure she had a good story ready. She was going to sweet talk you like she's been doing the last few weeks. She was headed to Carolina, all the way."

"That's ridiculous. Tina didn't know I was going on a trip till a few hours ago."

"Wrong. She's known for at least a week."

"I'm not following you, Cruz."

"All right," she said. "Here's how it is. Last week someone contacted your friend Tina with a proposition. I know this because my team has been monitoring the communications of the person who made that contact. That person convinced Tina to take advantage of her relationship with Sugarman to hitch a ride all the way to Pine Haven, North Carolina, where some very dangerous people are hiding out near the Neuse River. Same place you're headed. You're now part of a larger federal operation that's being run under my command."

Sugar was silent for a moment, then said in a chastened voice, "Which explains how Tina knew Flynn was involved. That wasn't a guess."

"Why'd she need us? She could drive the guns there herself."

"She wasn't delivering weapons. Her job was to deliver you, Thorn."

"Do that again."

"Let's get something straight." Cruz turned and faced Thorn, then cut a harsh look at Sugar. "The woman back at the gas station, your so-called friend, she was conning you. Unwittingly perhaps, she had gotten mixed up with some bad folks, and she was leading you into a trap."

Sugar looked over at her, shook his head as if he hadn't heard correctly, then glanced at Thorn. A familiar expression. *You bastard, this is your fault.*

"The postcard from Carolina. That was Tina's doing?"

Cruz nodded.

"So Flynn, he's not part of this? Gun smuggling? That cash."

"Flynn Moss is at the heart of it."

"Goddamn it, Cruz," Thorn said. "Cut the double-talk. You want our help, you're going to lay out the whole story."

She was silent for a moment, then reached into her jacket and came out with a clear plastic case, the kind his clients carried in their fishing vests.

She opened it and held it out for Thorn to see.

63

A half dozen bonefish flies, an assortment of his own creations.

"You do nice work. Can't say I've actually tried them out myself, but from what I see, your flies have a certain aesthetic charm. This is my favorite." She plucked a red and blue feathered lure from its slot. "What do you call it?"

He hesitated a moment, then sighed and said, "Bone Crusher."

She eyed him carefully.

"Interesting choice."

"Get to the point," Thorn said.

"You're all about violence, aren't you? Trying to project yourself as this laid-back guy, but there's all this molten energy seething just below the skin. And every once in a while you show a glimpse of it."

"Bonefish flies all have names like that," Sugar said. "It's part of fishing culture. You're reading Thorn wrong."

"Yeah," she said. "You two defend each other. Have each other's back. You're a team."

"What do the flies have to do with anything?" Thorn said.

"I've been studying you to understand what makes you tick. Lately it's been my full-time focus. I wanted to be sure you could be trusted for the role you'll play. Agent Sheffield thought you'd be willing. Willing is fine, but I needed to be sure you'd be effective."

"What role would that be?"

She held the box of flies up so both Sugar and Thorn could see.

"This role," she said. "To dangle you in front of some very bad men, see if we can get them to bite."

And that was all she would give them for the next hundred miles.

Five

"Is that your name or your license number?"

The girl behind the motel counter was looking at the registration card he'd just signed.

"It's not my license."

"You're joking. Your name is X-88?"

He looked out at the falling twilight beyond the office windows. A Comfort Inn an hour shy of Jacksonville. A mile west of Twelve Mile Swamp, which looked to him like an excellent spot to dump a body.

Even that far away, he could smell the swamp, its notes of sulfur blended with rotting mushrooms and yeast and a sour undertone that reminded him of the used-up air of a big-city bus station.

"If that's your name, then damn, your parents did a number on you."

Standing beside him, Pixie said, "She's trying to be funny. 'A number on you,' X-88, it's like a pun."

"You got a problem with my name?"

"No, no. It's cool as shit." The motel clerk was a year or two older than X. No makeup, with clean straight chestnut hair with bangs that covered her eyebrows. The kind of girl you'd pass on the street, not give a second look unless you noticed that scorching body hiding under her baggy white dress.

The motel clerk looked at Pixie and said, "You got a number too?"

"I'm Pixie, like it's any of your business."

"Pixie's another good one," the clerk said. "Suits you."

Pixie edged closer to X, touching his arm.

She was a bony girl, flat-chested and narrow hipped, like a sexless twelve-year-old, which X found to be a turn-on. She was pale with naturally white-blond hair she streaked with rainbow colors, and her lips were always lit up with bright pinks and purples. Shaved eyebrows, wide-spaced gray eyes, a pointy nose. A little freaky, yeah, but she'd kept X satisfied these last few months, so shit, he overlooked her physical quirks.

As for X, he was as thick as Pixie was thin. Shaved head, olive skin tone from the Turkish blood on his old man's side, that motherfucker.

X had heavy lips and dark brown eyes. His arms and chest were smooth and beefy, which now and then some idiot mistook for blubber. And he had a wide back, strong enough to hoist a fifty-gallon drum full of body parts, lift it over his head, and toss it in a ditch. An accomplishment he'd recently added to his résumé.

"So are we checked in or what?" X-88 said.

"Just need a credit card," she said.

"I don't do plastic. I'm cash only."

An older gentleman with a rolling suitcase entered the lobby. White hair, hunched shoulders, closing in on seventy. Rumpled seersucker suit.

"We'll be just a second more, sir," the clerk told the old man. "So, X? Can I call you that?"

"It's my name."

The clerk swiped the electronic keys through the magnetic machine while X counted out the bills for one night at the Comfort Inn.

"You mind my asking how you came by it?"

"He picked it up at Raiford," Pixie said. "You know, the state prison."

"Oh, you were a bad boy. Did some time."

"What do you care?"

Pixie said, "Growing up, he had a normal name, but he hated it, hated the family that gave it to him. X-88 came to him while he was locked up."

"You guys in a gang?" the clerk said. "Crips, Bloods, like that."

"Fuck the Crips," X said. "Bunch of degenerates."

"So what are you?"

Pixie said, "We're straight-edgers, hardline vegans."

"Really? Like what? You beat up meat eaters?"

"Sometimes."

"Man, you've made my day. Pixie and X-88, hardline vegans."

"Yeah?" X said. "And what's your name?"

The old man standing behind them huffed. He came around to the counter and planted a hand on it.

"You mind having this personal chat after you've checked me in?"

"Be just a minute more, sir. I'm not quite finished with these guests."

"You were telling us your name," Pixie said. Challenging her, claws out, the way she got when a woman circled too close.

"My name," the clerk said, "is Varla."

"Varla," Pixie said, doing a dry spit like she had a hair on her tongue.

"Named after a Harlem chanteuse," she said. "A notorious pansexual."

"What the hell is that?" X said. "She was into kitchenware?"

The clerk smiled at X.

"My namesake was into anything and anybody that struck her fancy."

The motel clerk reached up to brush her bangs away from her eyes. Molecules of her morning shampoo broke loose. Nutmeg and honeysuckle.

"Hey, come on," the old man said. "I just drove six hundred miles. I'm a priority member with a reservation and I want to get in my goddamn room."

X-88 turned to the man.

"Mister," X said. "You ever been subjected to great bodily harm?"

The man took a few seconds to absorb the nut-crushing presence of X-88, then he sighed, shrank back, picked up a brochure of local amusements from the counter, and started paging through it.

Varla handed X the keys in a paper folder, counted out his change.

"In case you're interested," Varla said, "I get off at nine."

"You talking to me or Pixie?" X said.

Varla smiled, her voice going husky and slow.

"I believe I'm talking to both of you."

He and Pixie got in the car and moved it to the parking spot outside their room. Number 112, first floor, on the far end away from the inter-state. Pixie was quiet, fuming. Chin tucked, eyes mooning like a child who'd been slighted by a playmate.

"You didn't need to tell her anything about us," X-88 said.

"She made me mad."

"We can't be leaving a trail, people remembering us."

"I know, I know. But the way you were looking at her."

"What am I supposed to do, wear a blindfold around pretty girls?"

"You thought she was pretty?"

"And you told her all that about my name, the vegan stuff."

"She pissed me off, I couldn't help it. She was making fun of us."

"I'm used to it," he said. "Doesn't bother me. I'm proud of my name."

He parked, took the suitcases and overnight stuff out of the backseat. Carried them inside. Pixie tagging along.

X-88. Yeah, it was true. He'd acquired it during his five-year sleepover at Florida State Prison. And Pixie was just repeating what he'd told her. He hated his family, hated the name they chose for him. So shortly after he arrived at Raiford and started hanging with the straight-edge crowd, that new name came to him one night lying awake.

The letter X was the edger insignia, they tattooed Xs on their chests or arms or anywhere they could reach. Started in the punk-music scene, where Xs were marked on the backs of the hands of underage drinkers so the bartender wouldn't serve them. X becoming a badge of honor for abstainers.

88, that was his personal choice. He picked it because it was rugged, an upper-quartile number but nothing fancy. A big, strong, muscled-up, B-plus, a better-than-average blue-collar digit.

Before Raiford he'd never heard of edgers, but he connected right off. All white guys, most with some high school, and some, like X-88, had a year or two of community college. They were hardass punks who'd sworn off booze, drugs, meat, and meat by-products, and the other debased practices of the modern world.

On X's cell block, the king badass of the edgers was Manny Obrero. Older guy, doing a thirty-year stretch for moving tons of coke, the guy had wallowed in drugs for years, anything a man could snort, swallow, shoot in your veins, or fuck, he'd done it, and he claimed prison was the best thing that ever happened to him. Showed him the light. He got converted to the straight-edge abstainer way of life. Living pure. No poisons, no promiscuity, no caffeine, no cigarettes, no animal or dairy. Push-ups, weights, get strong. And Manny took on X's education, became his mentor, showing him how it was done. How to stay solid and uncontaminated. He learned to despise the indulgent drunks and junkies and the carnivores, "the meat people," Obrero called them. Worst of them all. Carnivores put guiltless animals in cages, cramming them, ten, twenty, thirty to a coop like they did to men at Raiford. Making them shit where they ate. Humans were meant to be free-range creatures like chickens and cows and pigs. It was the carnivores fucking up the metabolism of the earth. All those assholes hooked on bloody red meat and meat by-products and cheese and eggs.

X-88 fell right in. Read the pamphlets, got converted. Truth was, he'd been looking for something like them for years though he hadn't known it. He thought he was a diehard loner, a nonbeliever. But no, he liked Obrero, liked his no-bullshit approach. Old enough to be X-88's dad, Obrero treated X as an equal, appointed him second in command of his wing of straight-edgers. It fell to X to execute discipline, bust heads, break fingers, and in special cases take their rivals and enemies into the showers and mop closets and empty cells and step them across to the other side.

Seven guys he'd wasted in Raiford. Never got caught. Got good at it. Even started to see it as an art form, the unique method Obrero taught him.

When X-88's stretch was up, Obrero sat him down. Told him he knew a woman who could use his help, and she could help X-88 readjust to the straight life. Woman used to be Obrero's wife, now she was out there hunting down a killer. Would X look her up, would X, only if he felt like it, help her out, maybe also look after Obrero's little girl. And one more thing, look after the bankroll Obrero left with his wife, over two million in cash. Watch over all of that till Obrero got back, mother, daughter, and money, and when Obrero was free, then he and X would partner up for real. Kick some serious ass.

X-88 was honored. He promised Manny all that, swore a blood oath, and here he was a year later in St. Augustine, Florida, not more than an hour east from Raiford, putting everything Manny taught him into action.

He slid the credit card key into the door lock and pushed it open, then stood there a minute and sniffed the putrid air. Turned around and looked.

Goddamn if there wasn't a hamburger joint across the parking lot, cars lined up at the drive-through. Its stink carrying on the breeze. Fried grease, dead meat sizzling. There it sat, a beef and pork and chicken dispensary, right next to their motel, like an evil enticement calling out X-88's name.

They went inside, set down their stuff. X went into the bathroom, splashed some water on his face while Pixie fiddled with the crappy TV.

"Time I did the deed," X said from the bathroom doorway, drying his face with a towel. "I'll drive around till it gets dark, look for a place."

"Can I come?"

"I'll handle it. Catch up on your TV shows."

"That girl," Pixie said. "You really think she was pretty?"

"I'm not going to lie to you."

73

"You want her?"

"Hell, yes. I want every woman, even the ugly ones. I'm a fucking man. You got any doubt about that?"

Pixie watched the TV, the six o'clock news coming out of Orlando.

"She's off at nine," Pixie said. "I'll get her if that's what you want. I've slept with plenty of girls. Girls are fine. Softer, sweeter."

"Is that what you want, a three-way?"

"I got everything I want right now."

"Nobody's got everything. We all want shit. Till the day we die."

"Not me," Pixie said. "I'm content how I am, with you, doing what we're doing, going where we're going, our goals, our togetherness. That's enough for me."

X-88 didn't feel like getting bogged down in one of Pixie's weepy loyalty tests. He'd told her from the start she was welcome to be his girl, but nothing was permanent. He'd protect her, take her places, buy her shit. But when it was over, which it would be one day soon, it was over. Take it or leave it. Those were the terms.

"I want you to love me," Pixie said. "Before one of us dies, if it's only for a few minutes. That's what I want. A taste of true love."

They'd been over this ground so many times, X had nothing left to say.

"This shouldn't take more than an hour."

"You're not going to kiss me good-bye?"

"An hour I'll be back. You need a kiss to get you through an hour?"

"I do. I need a kiss."

He gave her one, quick and dry, but afterward her chin was still tucked, eyes mooning, not looking at him.

"Maybe you should call the front desk," X said. "Ask that Varla to come sleep with you. See how she is, maybe if you hit it off, you two could live happily ever after. St. Augustine isn't such a bad place, it's got an ocean, a beach, an old fort."

"Aw, come on. Don't do this. You feeling bad, X? Your head hurting again? Is that why you're saying this? The migraine thing. You need some tofu, baby, some good vegetable protein."

"I'm fine, Pixie. But baby, I'm not going to lie. That midnight train's rolling into the station. Pretty soon you've got to pick some place to get off, today, tomorrow, the next day, the way it's going inside me now, the way my head is, this ride isn't going to last much longer."

Six

First X drove over to the burger joint and got in the drive-through lane. At the speaker he ordered three regular hamburgers, plain, no sauce, no cheese, no lettuce, none of that shit, nothing but burger and bun, paid at the window, and drove forward to pick them up. The black kid in the window said, "Wow, nobody orders plain regular burgers."

"I just did," X said.

The kid shrugged and handed him the bag, smiling.

"I say something funny?" said X.

The boy shrugged again, the smile on his lips melting away.

"What you're doing here, kid, purveying slaughtered animals by the millions, that's some seriously sick shit. You know that, don't you?"

"Yes, sir."

"Yet here you are, still purveying, and giving your customers scornful, smartass grins."

"I didn't mean nothing, sir."

"You know where those cows and pigs and chickens come from you're cooking in your deep fat fryers and your griddles? You know the grim life they lead? Do those creatures ever see the sun, boy, feel its heat on their hide? They ever smell the natural grasses they were meant to eat? They live their lives in pens and cages, they can't turn around, their legs collapse under their weight. They chew off each other's tails out of boredom. You know that?"

An older woman moved behind the boy, put a hand on his shoulder.

"There some kind of problem here, Anthony?"

He shook his head at his boss.

"Is there a problem, sir?" she said to X-88, bending forward to see him.

"Your business is an abomination. Do you consider that a problem?"

X-88 didn't wait for an answer. He rolled out of the drive-through and eased across the parking lot.

Turning onto the highway, he stripped the burgers from their buns, rolled down his window, tossed the bread and paper sack out the window, and stacked the three warm patties on the passenger seat. Sickening smell.

A mile down the road he saw right away that Twelve Mile Swamp wasn't going to work. He'd been picturing a wild, deserted marsh where human flesh decomposed fast. Instead it was a state park, high fenced, with all its entrance roads blocked with gates and guardhouses.

So X-88 circled back and cruised past the

cluster of motels and fast food joints and kept heading west onto the narrowing two-lane, leaving behind the 7-Elevens and gas stations and stoplights, the glow of civilization, driving out into the piney woods that covered most of Florida when you got fifteen miles inland from the coast.

A few sandy roads sprouted off the main highway. Hardly any traffic. A house or two, then not even that. Just dark woods and empty sky. No moon, no scattering of stars.

Brights on, X-88 drove another mile into the wilderness, chose a side road, pulled off, bumped over potholes and rocks and lumps that scraped the undercarriage, went about a half mile as the road tapered, branches brushing both sides of the car. No mailboxes or house lights through the trees. He'd have to back all the way out, but overall it felt right.

He shut off the ignition, cut the lights, lowered the windows. Listened to the crickets celebrating the darkness, the whir of insects, a distant car passing on the lonesome highway. He sat for a while staring out the windshield into the night until he heard a muffled thud that woke him from his daze.

He left the parking lights on, picked up the three patties, and got out, went to the trunk. He stuffed the meat into his trouser pocket, then opened the trunk and stepped back. You couldn't be too careful with a woman like this. But the gag had held and the flex cuffs were still locked around her wrists and ankles.

"I'm going to let you out. Don't fight me. I'll get rough if you do. That's not what I want. Do you understand?"

She stared at him. Unbelieving. X-88 patted her arm, what he meant as a reassuring gesture, but she cringed.

"Do you understand what I just said?"

She stayed frozen.

"I regret you had to spend so much time in the trunk. There was no way to avoid that. You're probably dehydrated, dizzy, confused."

She grumbled something rude through the gag. Still not trusting him.

"Okay, here we go. I'm going to stand you up."

He cradled her body, lifted her over the lip of the trunk and set her on her feet on the sandy roadway. Holding her steady until the wobble had gone from her legs. Little woman, mussy blond hair cut short. He couldn't see her face that well in the light from the trunk. But he'd gotten a good look at it before when he hauled her out of the stolen car. She was in her fifties, showing some road wear. A pugnacious attitude. Smart mouth.

"Now let me get this off."

He unknotted the gag, squatted down, flicked out his knife blade, and freed her ankles. She was breathing hard, still swaying.

"I'll cut loose your wrists, but first we come to an understanding."

"Like what?" Her voice hoarse and breathless.

Something rustled in the woods, an animal moving through the brush. X looked toward the sound, made out a clumsy shadow and caught its scent. Woodsmoke and musk clinging to its fur, the pungent tang of spoiled garbage. When he was a kid he'd smelled the same scent at a roadside zoo. Black bear.

A needle-sharp ping stabbed him in the frontal lobe. He breathed his way past the pain and shifted back to the woman, put his knife in his pocket.

"Why're you doing this?" the woman said. "What did I do wrong?"

"Not a thing."

"You work with Cruz, I met you in Key Largo."

"Now see, that right there is the entire issue. You met me, you saw me, and you recognized me. That, Tina, is the reason we're out here right now."

She couldn't speak for a moment, swallowing. Looked X-88 in the face, then stumbled backward, bumped the car fender, nowhere to run.

Again he got a whiff of the bear. Crushed grass in its coat, its teeth moldy and rotten. An old fellow, not long left either.

"Tell me what you want. Money?"

X was looking off at the woods. Enduring this

out of respect for the victim. If she wanted to prolong her last moment, try to bargain her way out of this, who was he to deprive her of a little extra time?

"I'm not motivated by money."

Her wild eyes roved his face.

"Christ almighty. She double-crossed me."

X-88 sighed.

"What's your name? Tell me your name."

"Not relevant."

This was a woman used to talking her way out of things.

"Look, I did what she asked me to. Everything, exactly the way she said. I dropped that postcard in Sugarman's mailbox, it got them going like she wanted, and there at the gas station she pulls out her badge, and I make a run, steal that car, that green car, and she said that would be the end of it. I drive to Key Largo, leave the car in a lot somewhere, walk home. She never mentioned you forcing me off the road, grabbing me, holding me hostage."

"Plans change."

"I did what I was supposed to. Now I'm supposed to go home and wait. This isn't how it goes. She and I worked it out. The step-by-step process. I cooperated. I was a hundred percent certain Sugar would go along with Thorn, and before he left the island he'd call me and tell me he was leaving, and I had my story ready. It was all planned out. It went off without a hitch. Until now."

"You talk a lot."

"Did you hear what I said? Cruz is a federal agent. She's tracking terrorists. She's after Thorn's son. I was just helping out her investigation."

"Sure you were."

"I was being a good citizen."

X-88 said nothing.

"You're not going to let me go. You're going to murder me."

"Don't take it personally."

"Does Cruz know you're doing this? Does she?"

"This is you and me, Tina. Is Cruz here? Do you see her? We're off the reservation, you and me. This is my play."

A tear broke loose from one of Tina's eyes. Then a second tear.

"Did you hear what I said? This isn't the plan. I did what Cruz asked, every single thing. She's your boss, right?"

"Nobody's my boss."

"You got to let me go. I won't tell anybody about all this."

"Let me ask you something," X said. "I were to let you go right now, what would you do? Give it to me, the play-by-play. What would you do?"

"Find some way to get home, ride a bus,

whatever. And I'd never say a word to anybody. Never a word."

"This guy, your boyfriend, Sugarman. He cuddles up to you later on, it's late at night, you've made some sweet love, and he whispers in your ear, asks you real nice, what's the deal, Tina? You're not going to tell him anything?"

"Nothing," she said. "I'd never say a word."

"Yeah, yeah, you say that. But, Tina, you're a talker. I'm around you two minutes I can see that. You like to gab. Am I wrong?"

She licked her lips.

"No," Tina said. "I'd never speak to a soul about any of this."

"But see, I can't trust your word. And I'm in an awkward position. This woman, Cruz, she's got one thing on her mind and one thing only, like Ahab and his great white shark. And she's in such a goddamn hurry to accomplish that one thing, she forgets about loose ends. She never thinks what might come back to bite her. And that's fine for her, maybe nothing will ever bite her. But I'm not that way. I don't like loose ends, see. Because sooner or later one of them is going to come back, and before you know it that loose end has wrapped itself around your throat and you're hanging from it."

"It was a whale, not a great white shark. Ahab and his whale."

"Really?"

"Really. It's a book about whales."

"I been saying it wrong all this time?"

"You're thinking about *Jaws*, that's the one with the shark."

"Ahab and his whale," X said. "Well, thank you."

"Look." Tina put her hand on her heart. "I swear on my mother's grave I won't say a word, never, ever."

"I'm sorry, sweetheart, but that part's over, we're finished with it, okay?" X looked up at the dark sky, easing into this. "So listen, Tina, you familiar with 'gavage,' the word?"

Since she seemed confused he spelled it for her.

She drew back, eyes tightened as if peering at him from a great distance.

"Before Raiford, I didn't know it either. What it means is force-feeding. You know, how they handle a prisoner on hunger strike, jam a tube down his throat. And how they do ducks and geese to fatten them up for foie gras. Gorge, that's the literal meaning."

"Look, I know what," she said. "You got a cell phone. Let me call Cruz, talk to her. At least let me do that. Maybe you misunderstood some-thing, she can straighten it out."

"Tina, Tina. Don't you hear me? Cruz isn't here. This is you and me. We've moved on. We're done haggling. Look around you, look at the sky overhead, the stars, take it in. It's time to say good-bye to all this."

"No, no, you're a good man, you're good. Please."

They always said please. Every one of them. *Please, please.* Like if you got polite, made nice, the abracadabra word they'd learned when they were kids, that would set them free. *Please, pretty please.* Never once had X-88 said the word, not in his entire life. Never heard it in his house growing up. Lots of other words, but not "please."

"Oh, mother of Christ." Tina looked away into the dark woods, swallowing again, buying a few seconds, then in a defeated voice said, "Look, do this for me, at least do this. Will you? Tell Sugarman something, will you?"

X was quiet, waiting for her.

"Tell him I meant no harm. Cruz came, I told her what I knew, the postcards Thorn gets. She offered money if I'd help. I needed it. My shop, I'm bankrupt, can't pay my lease. Tell Sugar, okay? Will you? I didn't mean for anyone to get hurt. Tell him I love him. That's the truth. Tell him that for me, I love him, I really do. Will you do that for me?"

"If I meet up with him, sure, I'll repeat every word of that speech. Now, you ready for this, or you going to talk some more?"

"Oh, holy Christ."

With his left hand he clutched Tina's hair and

rocked her head back. She fought him, twisting side to side, but X outmuscled her, got her still.

"Think of this as drowning," he said to her. "Everybody says drowning isn't such a bad way to go. So this is drowning, only not in water."

Using his free hand, he dug out the three hamburger patties.

He balled up the meat one-handed and crammed it into Tina's mouth. When most of it was inside, he clamped his hand over her lips.

Tina gagged, snorted, tried to bite the palm of his hand. But X held his hand firm against her flailing, plugging up her airway to a count of ten, to a count of twenty.

When he felt her weakening, he released her hair, pinched her nose shut, cradled her in the crook of his arm like a waltz partner until Tina's struggling slowed and she grew still. Her weight slumping against him.

That's the technique Manny Obrero taught him at Raiford finishing school, the hands-on, natural way to keep the target from howling for help. Brutal and simple. Steal something solid from the cafeteria, ball it up, back the target in a corner, no tools, no blade. A mouth packed with food, keep the lips shut. A reverse Heimlich. Manny liked to say killing this way sent a message to the intemperate indulgers, the gulpers. Put the fear of god into them. A method so quick and outrageous, some didn't even put up a fight.

X-88 hadn't thought to bring a shovel.

He dragged her body fifty yards through lashing branches and spiderwebs, so far into the forest he could barely make out the parking lights.

He laid her out flat. Looked at her body for a moment. He spoke her name, *Tina Gathercole*, like a last rite, then he turned and left her remains behind.

Fresh meat. An offering to that sick old bear waiting in the shadows.

Seven

Just after eight, Cruz told Sugar to take the next exit, look for a motel, Holiday Inn, Hampton, one of those.

"We're driving straight through," Thorn said. "Sugar's on a schedule."

She turned, flashed a hard smile, and said, "Pine Haven is not a town you want to arrive in the dark."

Sugar said, "I'll stop, but you level with us or we're ditching you here."

"It's very simple. To locate Thorn's son, you're going to need my help. You barge into this without knowing the cast of characters, chances are very good Flynn's a dead man."

Thorn and Sugar shared a quick look. Neither trusted her, but damn it, this wasn't a risk they could take.

Along motel row, Cruz pointed them to a Best Western. A Waffle House on one side, burger joint on the other.

They carried their bags inside, Cruz handling the duffel. She set it in her room, unlocked the door on her side. Sugar did the same and swung it open.

Thorn stood in the center of the motel room, eyeing the anonymous furniture with a nagging sense of dread. A hard pressure was growing in his chest, and the atmosphere seemed to have thickened as it does just before a thunderstorm, a density and weight to the air that registered against the skin as lightly but as surely as the first brush of a bull shark.

He sat on the foot of the bed, absently ran a hand across the bedspread, its surface tacky from the fluids of the strangers streaming through the room. There was an undertone of mildew.

"Listen, guys, I'm starving," she said. "Would you mind, Sugar?" Cruz motioned through the open drapes at the burger joint glowing in the night across the parking lot. "I'll lay out the details over dinner."

"You keep stalling."

"Over dinner," she said.

Sugar shrugged, took their orders, and on his

way out the door he shot Thorn a warning look. *Don't try some harebrained stunt while I'm gone.*

When the door shut, Cruz went to her room and returned with a laptop computer, set it on the desk by the front door, and switched it on. She got on the Internet, typed in an address, and stepped back.

Thorn rose from the bed. He didn't believe in premonitions, but the burn prickling across his shoulders was impossible to ignore.

Through the window he watched Sugar trudge across the parking lot, head down, shoulders slumped, reduced to an errand boy.

Cruz turned the laptop around. Motioned for Thorn to sit. He moved over, lowered himself into the chair. The chills still jingling across his back.

"This is a Web site," she said, "the press office section for ELF. I believe you're familiar with the ELF."

"I am."

"Use the down arrow to scroll."

At the top of the page there was an image of a man in a black ski mask cradling a young goat against his chest. Below him was a series of mug shots with a paragraph posted next to each face.

"What's this have to do with anything?"

She nudged the laptop closer to him.

The page's headline: "Snitches and Informers."

"The people in these photos were activists busted by the FBI or another branch of law enforcement. Once in custody they saw the light and flipped, took a plea deal, cooperated, wore a wire, testified in court, things of that nature, and for their cooperation they either got a reduced sentence or immunity. And their faces wound up on this Web site."

"Why're you showing me this?"

"Scroll down."

Thorn pressed the arrow key and the pages rolled by. Most mug shots were of white kids in their twenties, mainly guys, a few females, a single Asian, and a black woman. He read about a couple. The crimes they were busted for, their plea deals, the names of those incarcerated because of them. Their eye and hair color, distinguishing features, tattoos, scars. Last known location.

"And that?"

He nodded at a photo of a pudgy young man with long curly hair and thick glasses. There was a bright red X marked across the photo image.

"It's not obvious?"

"They caught him."

"And dealt with him."

"Say what you mean."

"That particular case, I don't know the specifics, but if the kid was lucky, a bullet to the back of the head."

He paused, staring at the screen, tried to focus, concentrate on the young man's face, block out the dizzy spin of the room.

"What does this have to do with Flynn?"

"Keep scrolling."

He tapped the down arrow, continued to scroll through the page until he came to a dark-haired girl whose eyes stopped him. Intense, but with an impish squint. A vague familiarity. Another red X across her face. Printed in bold letters, her name was CARMEN SANDIA CRUZ.

He looked up at Madeline and she closed her eyes and nodded.

"In that photo she was nineteen," she said. "Since the time she was old enough to walk she adored animals. The kid who brought home snakes, iguanas, stray dogs, birds wrapped in fishing line. We built cages in the backyard for the possums.

"She went off to vet school in Georgia, befriended a woman in the ELF. This person is taking courses in the daytime, spending her nights breaking into chimp labs or SUV dealerships, tearing up the places. Her new friend talked Carmen into going along on a raid. Carmen thought it was a harmless political protest for a cause she believed in, but it turned out to be more than that, a lot more, and afterward she felt so guilty about the vandalism they'd committed she confided in me and I passed along a few names to my superior at the FBI and some of the culprits went to prison. Though not her friend, not the leader."

"And her friend figured out where the leak came from."

"Yes," Cruz said. "She did."

She stared out the window at the shadowy parking lot.

"When did it happen?"

"Sixteen months ago. Carmen was thrown from the rooftop of a four-story apartment building in Atlanta. Supposed to look like suicide."

"And you've been tracking this woman."

"Since it happened, every hour, every day. I've gotten close, lots of near misses. But now I think I have her. Where you and I are headed, Pine Haven, North Carolina, the woman who did this to Carmen, she's holed up there, she may be injured. She and your son, Flynn, are members of the same group. In fact, I believe you may have crossed paths with her before. She calls herself Cassandra."

Thorn repeated the name quietly.

Cruz said, "Red hair, thick and curly, a tall woman. Athletic. Imposing."

Thorn nodded. That was her. That was Cassandra.

"And Flynn?"

"Cassandra and Flynn and a few others were in Carolina, planning some kind of action against a hog farm."

"Hog farm?"

"Concentrated animal feeding operation, known as a CAFO. A high-density process, large number of animals crammed into tight quarters. A heavy environmental impact on the surrounding community. Just their sort of target."

"I don't understand," Thorn said. "What about Tina, the guns, all that?"

She tapped him on the shoulder, motioned for him to get up.

She took his place in front of the computer and brought up a Web page with a black background and faint yellow print. Lots of boxes filled with brief messages.

She scrolled through several pages until she found the one she was after, then stood up and signaled for Thorn to sit.

"What you're looking at is a message board where the radical ecocommunity congregates. A public forum, so they mostly speak in code, it's not easy to follow. But this particular message is straightforward. Posted ten days ago, just before Thanksgiving. Jellyroll, the one who signed it, he's a member of Cassandra's cell."

Dobbins Hog Farm, NC. U dont hear from us tmrow, come lookin for bodies.

He turned to look at her.

She pursed her lips and expelled a breath as if blowing out candles.

"That was a week and a half ago," she said. "Nothing's been posted since."

He absorbed her words and the message on the screen for a long while then came slowly to his feet. He drew in a deep breath but it did nothing to relieve the swelling inside his chest. He moved toward Cruz.

She stared into his eyes and held her ground. He came close, raised his hand to her chest, pressing her against the wall.

"This is a lie. Flynn's not dead. I'd know if he was. I'd feel it."

"Every parent thinks that. But would you? I know I didn't."

He cocked his arm, pressed his forearm against her throat. Trying to hold himself back, to quiet the teakettle's scream in his ears.

"Step back."

"This is a lie, it's a fucking lie."

"Step away from me, Thorn. Do it now."

He got a breath down and said, "It can't be."

"No one's said your son is dead."

Thorn lowered his arm and turned away. His heart floundering.

"The group was attacked and some of his associates were killed. We believe Flynn was shot, injured. He and Cassandra have gone into hiding. They're still in the area. That's why I need you, Thorn. You can entice him."

"What does that mean?"

"He learns you're in town, he'll seek you out. That's the outcome I'm looking for. You get your son back, I get Cassandra."

"How do you know this? How do you know he's injured?"

"I went to Pine Haven immediately after I saw the post on the message board. I met Webb Dobbins, the owner of the hog farm, met the sheriff, got the lowdown."

"How badly is he hurt, how'd it happen? I want details."

"We don't have time for this right now. You'll have to trust me. I've got a plan. You'll get Flynn, I'll get justice."

"Trust you? Why should I? A couple of hours ago you were talking about dangerous people hanging out by the Neuse River, a larger federal operation under your command, Tina's job was to deliver me, she was leading me into a trap. Now it's something else. It's about Flynn and Cassandra."

"What I said earlier was for Sugarman's benefit, not yours. What I'm telling you now is the truth."

"Then you lied pretty goddamn easily."

"Okay," she said. "So don't believe me. Go ahead, you go to Pine Haven, you and Sugarman. Go on your own, fumble around in this mine-field, see how that works out."

"How do you know Flynn was hurt? That he's still alive?"

"Listen. We have to sort out Sugarman before he gets back."

Thorn couldn't name the feelings rocketing through his chest. His face was hot. His ears rang. Body clenched.

Cruz said, "Sugarman can't be involved. It's got to be you and me, Thorn. Just the two of us."

He gripped the back of the chair, looked around at the unsteady room.

"He *is* involved."

"Not after tonight."

"I don't understand. I don't understand any of this."

Thorn was struggling to fill his lungs. He settled into the chair.

"I want a name. The fucker who shot my son."

"I can't do that."

"But you know who it is, the shooter."

"Right now there's only one thing you need to know. You and I have a common objective. You want to rescue Flynn, I want Cassandra. I know the lay of the land where they're hiding out, and you have the ability to draw them into the open. What that means is we have no choice but to work together."

Eight

"After we get to Pine Haven I'll give you everything I have about the man who attacked your son. Not before. If I revealed it now, you'd jump ship, try to settle this on your own. You have that history, Thorn, a reputation. So not until we're there, until we've finalized our plan, gone over everything."

"Sugar," Thorn said. "He's coming."

She looked out the window, saw him crossing the lot carrying the bags of food, seconds away.

"I know he's a good person," Cruz said. "I have no doubt. Sheffield speaks highly of him, and we could use the manpower, but he can't come."

"Why?"

"Because he believes in the rule book. We can't have that."

Thorn pulled himself from the screen, stood up again. He blinked his eyes clear and stared at Madeline Cruz.

"Why?" he said. "Because we aren't going to be playing by the rules?"

"No," Cruz said. "Because where we're going, there *are* no rules."

He looked back at Sugarman out in the darkness.

"Your friend, is he willing to step over the legal line? Way across that line? Do whatever it takes to accomplish our goal, despite how many laws we have to break?"

"No."

"Then you have to cut him loose. This is going to be messy."

"You're not FBI, are you?"

"I was for many years."

"But not anymore."

"That's correct. Not since I lost Carmen."

Sugar came into the room, set the sacks of food on the desk.

When he registered the look on Thorn's face, he halted.

Madeline stepped over to the laptop and shut the lid.

"We need to talk," Thorn said.

"Aw, great." Sugar rolled his eyes to the ceiling, then looked back at Thorn. "God help us every one."

"We're not going to need you anymore," Thorn said. "Cruz and I are going to take it from here."

Sugar's gaze drifted from Thorn to Cruz, then to the window and the open blinds.

At that second the even-tempered, all-enduring look on Sugarman's face sent Thorn back to an afternoon from twenty years earlier, Sugar still in his deputy's uniform, he and Thorn drinking a beer at the Caribbean Club in Key Largo, where tourists stopped in to see the local badasses misbehave and where the local badasses came to put on a show for the tourists.

Thorn couldn't recall why they'd wound up there, but he remembered Sugar was talking to a college girl from a little town in Mississippi Thorn had never heard of. Sugar was married at the time, a devoted husband, not the least bit flirty, simply doing his best to shield the girl from the roughnecks in that bar. He and the girl were having a good time, Sugar being funny in the wry, understated way he had, not trying to make her laugh, not trying to charm her, simply describing his afternoon shift, a domestic spat he'd broken up between two eighty-year-old men who'd been roommates for the last half-century but now were trying to claw each other's eyes out over whose turn it was to do the dishes. And one of the badasses across the bar took exception to the fact that the Mississippi girl with the languid eyes and the molasses in her laughter was enjoying the company of a black man in a cop uniform, and he came strutting around the bar, long-haired guy with a drunk's sloppy smile, wearing only a leather vest over his sunken chest, and he wedged in between Sugarman and the Mississippi girl, planted his elbow on the bar, and proceeded to call her a nigger-loving little cunt who should get her ass back in her rental car and

99

keep on driving down to Key West, where the faggots would be more accepting of her nigger-loving ways.

Thorn took hold of the badass's ponytail and gave it a jerk, which was Thorn's hands-on approach to introducing the asshole to civilized behavior.

And the badass swung around, spoiling for what came next, but Sugar already had the guy's left wrist cuffed to a piece of angle iron that supported the bar. The guy swung and lurched but the cuffs had him caught. Sugar and Thorn and the college girl moved around the bar and continued their conversation on stools with a view of the red sun dissolving into Blackwater Sound while the badass swung his free arm and cursed until he was all used up. On the way out of the bar Sugarman unlocked his cuffs, never saying a word to the bigoted asshole, and he and Thorn walked the college girl to her car, and with his blue lights flashing, Sugar saw her safely back to the motel where she was staying a mile down the road and then he drove home to his wife.

That was Sugar, the rules he played by. The man Thorn was dismissing.

Sugarman turned on Cruz.

"Where's Tina being held?"

"Tina's fine," Cruz said. "Don't worry about her."

Sugar rubbed the back of his hand across his

mouth as if to smooth away the hurt that was showing there.

"Where is she?" Sugar's voice was tightly controlled, eyes hot.

"Tina was questioned by my associates, she's agreed to cooperate with their investigation, now she's headed back home to Key Largo."

"Driven there by Homeland Security agents," Sugar said.

"That's right."

"I tried calling her, but there's no answer."

"Try again, she's probably home by now."

Sugar dug his phone out of his front pocket. He went to the corner of the room, made the call, must've gotten her voicemail. He left a message that he would talk to her tomorrow, speaking in a soft voice, consoling, but with an edge of urgency.

When he was done, Sugar said, "How you getting to Carolina without a car? Hitchhike?"

"We'll manage," Cruz said.

Sugar faced Thorn, peering into his eyes, trying to determine if this was legit or being done under duress. One last chance.

"Come outside," Thorn said.

"Wait a minute," Cruz said. "What're you doing?"

"I'm having a private conversation with my friend."

She gave him a warning look. Thorn put his arm

around Sugar's shoulder and steered him to the door and led him out into the dark parking lot.

"All right, old buddy. What the hell is going on?"

"Do you trust that woman?" Thorn said.

"Does a bear shit in the Vatican?"

"Yeah, well, neither do I."

"Okay, so let's get our luggage and go."

"I can't do that. I need to stick with her. For Flynn's sake."

"And me?"

"And you need to go find Tina."

"Tina wouldn't mess with guns or any of this bullshit. I know her better than that."

"So go track her down, make sure she's okay. I'm staying with Cruz. I'll call your cell tomorrow. It's going to be all right."

"Is it?"

Sugar searched Thorn's eyes, saw his resolve, and responded with a grim smile. They'd danced these steps before. The push/pull of a prickly loner and his bighearted buddy. How many rebuffs had there been? How many more could their friendship endure?

"You might as well get started," Thorn said.

Sugar blew out a breath and took a half step back.

"That's what you want? You don't want to sleep on it?"

"Good luck with your job interview."

"Yeah," Sugar said. "I'll knock 'em dead."

They went back into the motel room. Sugar got his bag, didn't look at Cruz, didn't bother with Thorn either. He carried his bag out to the car, pitched it in the backseat. Through the open drapes Thorn watched him back out of the slot and drive off into the darkness. Standing there Thorn felt as hollowed out and useless as a sloughed-off cicada skin clinging to a branch.

"Good work," Cruz said.

"That was all bullshit, the Homeland Security stuff, Tina agreeing to cooperate. What's really going on?"

"When we get to Pine Haven, it'll all be clear."

"And those shotguns?"

"There's a high likelihood we'll be needing them."

Thorn moved past her and walked into her room. He went to the bed, where the duffel was lying beside her suitcase. He unzipped it and hauled out one of the AA-12 shotguns and turned to her, holding its serious weight in both hands.

"Okay," he said. "Show me how to work the goddamn thing."

Nine

Thorn lay on the motel bed in the dark, staring at the ceiling. He played back every second he could recall of his brief time around Flynn Moss. From the first moment he saw him on the set of a television show Flynn was starring in, to the night when Flynn embraced Thorn, told him good-bye, and drove off with his radical friends. Then he played it back again. This might be all he'd have of the kid, these aching memories, so he worked to retrieve each second, stash them in some long-term storage file. He worked through each recollection and worked again until his weariness began to mix and blur the images together and the exercise grew too agonizing to continue.

At one A.M. Thorn got up and took a shower and dressed in fresh clothes. He moved to the adjoining doors that stood open and listened to Cruz's fluttery snuffle, then he slipped out his door and walked across the parking lot toward the fast food joint. Its outside signs were dark, and inside there was only a faint glow where a young man was mopping up.

He walked beyond the hamburger place out to

the two-lane and headed back toward the ramps onto I-95. He would hitch rides, head north, catch a bus if he had to, get to Pine Haven any way he could. Take as long as he needed. Do this alone. He didn't trust Cruz. There were too many slippery places in her story. Her voice quivered and her eyes wandered. She swallowed too often as she was speaking of her daughter, Carmen. She was lying. He wasn't sure how much of what she'd said was a lie, but some of it, maybe all.

He'd do this on his own. When he arrived in Pine Haven, he'd parade up and down Main Street announcing his arrival, whatever it took to lure Flynn out of hiding, then whisk him away to safety in the Keys.

It was a crazy idea. No idea at all. But he continued to walk.

He walked beneath the underpass, a mile from the motel, then another, moving beyond the buzz and flicker of gas stations and all-night convenience stores into the darkness. Past a state park, Twelve Mile Swamp Conservation Area, and caught a cool breeze scented with ferns and pines and cypress.

Forget the interstate. He'd hitchhike the back roads. Or hell, he'd walk every step of the way to Carolina if he had to. He had nothing better to do, nothing of consequence. He could send Sugarman postcards from the road.

He was exhausted and felt old. He felt beyond

old. A paltry thing, a tattered coat upon a stick, or however the hell it went. He remembered the other phrase, the quotable one from that high school poem, the "mackerel-crowded seas," an image for the overflowing, ridiculous energy of youth, the irresistible drive and vigor, the flailing excitement, the way young people threw themselves forward, churning up the waters, high on the potency of their dreams and convictions and passionate about their ideals, a level of intensity that had also driven Thorn twenty years ago, thirty, a steadfast belief that justice must be served even if violence was necessary, and a conviction that it was also his sacred duty to assemble a moral code and live by it strictly, at least until some savage impulse tempted him to break loose from everything he'd worked so hard to build.

And that, he saw, had been his son's pattern as well, cycling between self-discipline and impulse. Flynn was a wild spirit, robust, a reckless live wire spewing sparks who'd learned to hold all that crazy energy in check, trained himself to master the tricky craft of acting, then just as his career was gaining shape and substance, he chucked all that and threw himself into the shadowy world of insurgency with equal fervor.

Along the shoulder of a road whose name he didn't know, he walked through a darkness as complete as any he could recall. Walked for another half hour until he saw ahead in the distance the golden radiance of some outpost, a town or a trailer park, or commercial gathering place. He halted in the quiet dark, listening to his pulse tick away the seconds, looking at the glow of the far-off lights.

He stared down at the earth beneath his feet, inhaled the night air of north Florida, a different scent than the sea-blown breezes he was used to. Here, well inland, the air was raw and edgy, seasoned by landlocked forests and stagnant marshes and the harsh industry of woodland creatures.

All the years, all his passions, all the loves that had come and gone had led to this empty stretch of asphalt. At that moment he could think of nothing he'd done with the heft or significance to match all that he had not done or done poorly. In all his reckless abandon, his high-minded quests, what justice had he brought to the world com-pared to the hurt and devastation he'd left in his wake? His own heedless behavior had corrupted his only son, sent Flynn off on a self-destructive path, a do-gooding quest that led inevitably to violence and injury and possibly death. Thorn's fault. All of it.

Behind him he heard a car and he turned and watched the headlights approach. When the car lights shined on him, he lifted his arm, thumb out. High beams in his eyes.

The car slowed and pulled abreast, a radio

playing loud. Two teenage boys leaning over to inspect him.

"Where you headed?" the passenger said. A thick-necked kid with spiky hair, his voice slurred by drink.

"Nowhere," Thorn said.

"Nowhere?"

"That's right."

"Hell, buddy, you don't need a ride. You're already there."

The driver laughed and gunned the engine.

"Get in," the driver said. "We'll take you far as we're going."

Thorn looked ahead at the empty road and back the way he'd come.

"No, thanks," he said. "I've changed my mind."

The boy in the passenger seat stared at Thorn for a moment, decided he'd been insulted, and reached back into the car and slung a half-empty beer can. It bounced off Thorn's chest. The wheels threw up a hail of pebbles and the car squealed up the highway. Thorn watched until its taillights disappeared.

By the time he made it to the motel parking lot, he was worn out, heavy-footed, finally ready for sleep. But heading across the parking lot he caught an odd shimmer inside the burger joint. When he steered that way for a better look, he saw the flicker and lash of flames spiraling from the kitchen.

Thorn trotted over, first on the scene.

The black kid who'd been mopping the floors was spread-eagled facedown on the floor near the front doors. He was a teenager, skinny. Dark fumes poured from the kitchen. Flames were twisting around the passageway between the galley and the serving counter, and the plastic menu signs with garish images of burgers and fries were melting, spattering molten beads of color onto the floor where more flames lashed up and over the counter, taking the napkin holders and the straw dispenser, reaching out for everything they could touch and consume.

Thorn shook the handle, locked and searing to the touch.

The kid was probably overcome by smoke. His body seemed shriveled inside the restaurant uniform. Thorn pivoted away, searched the area for a battering ram, and saw a nearby trash bin made of galvanized wire mesh.

Thorn pushed it over, knocked off its domed top, and dumped out a day's worth of food sacks and paper cups and diapers, rolled the bulky can down the sidewalk to the front window.

From the kitchen came a flash then a concussion that rattled the windows. The deep-fat fryers had exploded or some other accelerant had supplied the fire a new rush of fuel, and a ball of flame appeared at the passageway, a seething mass like some Greek serpent, an orange hydra's head with coils and loops of flame sprouting in every direction. The kid was vanishing inside the smoky haze.

Heaving the trash bin onto his shoulder, maybe thirty or forty pounds of unwieldy weight, Thorn took two steps forward and crashed the base of the container against the widest, seemingly most vulnerable sheet of glass.

A spiderweb of fractures radiated from the dent, but the windowpane didn't give way. He targeted the same spot and slammed the base against the glass. Slammed it again. The blossom of cracks spread wider and the glass flexed more at every blow.

As Thorn hammered, the glass began to sway and weaken. Behind the boy's body, the fire had burrowed under the fixed tables and chairs and was consuming them. The boy's mop was ablaze. A shallow layer of fire spread across the tile floor like smoldering surf washing up the shore toward his feet.

Thorn continued to bash the glass wall, breaking a finger-size opening, then a larger one, continuing while a mass of fire edged closer to the boy.

Thorn stepped away, moved several paces back, and took a running start, throwing the trash bin at the glass, then slammed his shoulder against the center of the web of cracks. That did it. The glass gave way, and a solid sheet of it dropped like a guillotine blade and exploded on the sidewalk at Thorn's feet.

Inside the restaurant the whooshing intake of air sent the fire rising higher, blew it into the ceiling, setting off small explosions and bursts of sparks. Thorn stepped over the ledge and grabbed the shoulder of the boy's uniform and lifted him up and over the ragged teeth of glass still clinging to the window seams.

The boy's shoes were melted to a black goo. One of them fell away, exposing the charred flesh of his foot as Thorn dragged his body beyond the swell of heat and smoke to a grassy plot beside a concrete picnic table and a flagpole. There was a siren somewhere, there were screams. They might have been there all along, people rushing toward them while Thorn lay the boy out on his back and cocked his head back at the proper angle and applied his lips to the boy's lips and tried to breathe into him.

But the boy's mouth was packed with some-thing. Thorn pried his jaws open and scooped his fingers inside the kid's mouth and flung away a gob of goo. He dug inside the mouth again, found another handful of the pinkish paste. He scraped it out as best he could and scoured his cheeks for more.

When he had the airway as clear as he could manage, he pressed his lips to the boy's again, tasting a sour reek, and the acrid tang of ash, but staying with it, counting in the steady fashion he'd been taught, finding the rhythm, pressing the boy's chest, breathing into him again and again for long, hopeless minutes until someone pulled him off the boy, a man in a blue jumpsuit, a man who hauled Thorn away from the dead child and the ruined hamburger joint, dragged him into the darkness of the parking lot.

An hour later, maybe more, when Deputy Sheriff David Randolph was finished questioning him, Madeline Cruz walked Thorn back to the motel.

"I close my eyes for a minute and you go all heroic."

"Not heroic," Thorn said. "The kid died."

"All the same."

As she unlocked the door, Thorn looked back at the smoldering remnants, crime scene tape fluttering in the wake of the departing ambulance.

"It's not the same," Thorn said. "Not even close."

Saturday at three in the morning, Sugarman arrived in Key Largo and drove to Tina's house on Oceana Drive. Her neighbors on both sides were up late, having competing parties in their backyard chickee huts, reggae cranked up on one side, Sinatra crooning on the other. Pickups and motorcycles at the reggae party, bulky American cars from the seventies filled the yard of the Sinatra house. Sugarman had met both sets of neighbors, got along well enough, though Tina had been at war with the reggae guys, who rented that house and didn't use their recycle bin and tossed empty beer cans into her yard.

Sugarman pulled in behind Tina's ancient gold Eldorado, its white Landau top peeling, a blanket of rust consuming the rear panel.

He knocked on the door, rang her bell. Waited.

"I Shot the Sheriff" coming from the east, and from the west, "It Was a Very Good Year."

He walked around to the back, went inside her small screened porch. The beat of the music was rattling her collection of beer steins on the glass shelves beside the makeshift bar Sugarman had cobbled together out of old shipping crates. One of the steins had shattered on the Mexican tiles.

Sugarman shaded his eyes and pressed his face to the sliding glass door. No lights, no sign of her return. He went around to the air-conditioning unit that sat on a concrete slab and kneeled, felt under its edge, and found the house key she hid there.

He let himself in the back door, shut it, and called out her name. Called it out again as he walked toward her bedroom. In his ten-year stint as a deputy, he'd walked into many empty houses and had acquired a feel for the unique staleness in the air that he felt at that moment. No one home, no one there in a while. But he went through the drill, going room to room.

When he was done, he went back to the living room and used her landline to call her cell and got voicemail again, Tina's cheery message. She was off on a romantic getaway. Whoopee.

Yeah, whoopee. With a duffel full of cash and a couple of high-powered shotguns. Not to mention an unsuspecting boyfriend.

Sugar left another message, told her he was back in Key Largo. Give him a call when she got this, whatever time she got in, it didn't matter, he wanted to hear from her, he was worried, and told her that whatever she'd been up to with the guns and the cash, it was okay, nothing bad had happened, but he needed to talk to her, needed to know what Thorn was getting into. He babbled for another minute then set the phone down without a good-bye.

Ten

It was Saturday morning, breakfast time in Pine Haven. Webb Dobbins and his sister, Laurie, were at the table reserved for them seven days a week. Webb on the phone, listening to Madeline Cruz's brusque voice, this hardass female speaking without a bit of civility like Webb was her hired hand. When she was done, she didn't wait for

Webb to respond, just ended the call with an arrogant click.

He stared at his phone, then looked at Laurie across the table and said, "First glance, I thought she was hot, now she's starting to piss me off."

"She's taking her sweet time."

"Had to find a way to get this guy motivated."

"How many is she bringing?"

"Four counting her," he said.

"Thought there'd be more."

"Don't need an army to root this rascal out of his hidey-hole. Just the right worm wiggling on the hook."

"The father, the kid's father."

"Guy's name is Thorn. He should get the boy's attention."

"My money says the kid's dead."

"Naw," Webb said. "He's out there. The little shit."

"You don't know one way or the other. Just because you couldn't find him in the woods, that doesn't mean diddly, Webb. It's coming up on two weeks. Either the kid's body is rotting out there or he got the hell gone."

"He wouldn't leave one of his own on the battlefield."

"You sure of that, are you?"

"These assholes are true believers, that's how they think."

"How'd you get to be an expert on these people?"

Webb looked off at the diner's empty booths. Just Millie cleaning up.

"Bottom line," he said, "till we find his corpse, we assume he's alive. A threat to all of us."

"When do they arrive?"

"Just now leaving St. Augustine, driving fast, six hours, around there."

Webb looked out the window of the Happy Biscuit Café, Main Street, Pine Haven, North Carolina. The street was bowed slightly, so from Webb's position he could see all the way down two blocks in each direction, the complete length of Pine Haven. The Country Hearth Bed and Breakfast anchored the north end and the Winston County Bar and Grill the south, and in between were two pool halls, a pawn and gun shop, five empty storefronts, and Tommy's Barbecue occupying the space where the Pine Haven Hotel had been when Webb and Laurie were growing up. You wanted Twinkies, tampons, or motor oil, or any of life's other essentials, it was forty-five minutes to the Walmart in Goldsboro, narrow country roads all the way.

Webb waved for Millie, who was cleaning the table one booth over. He scribbled in the air and she came with the check.

"Get this, will you," Webb said to his sister. "Forgot my wallet."

Born a year apart, Webb and Laurie used to be mistaken for twins when they were kids. Both were ginger redheads, tall and wide shouldered, both with a little extra jaw and brown eyes that could turn cold and harsh as arctic tundra. Over the years as their bodies filled out, the resemblance ended. Laurie turned out thin as a cedar fence post and twice as hard. Webb kept packing on meat since graduating high school, thickening in the gut and going loose in the jowls, but he hadn't noticed any of the ladies hereabouts minding much.

"Another rasher of bacon, Webb?"

"No, I'm done. Though that pig belly was mighty tasty."

Laurie set her purse in her lap, dug around, and came out with a ten and looked up at Millie.

"You ever have any trouble sleeping, honey?" Laurie said.

"Sometimes."

"I got something that'll fix you right up on those long nights."

Millie glanced over her shoulder at the kitchen and shook her head.

"Don't need a thing," Millie said. "Thanks anyway."

"If it's money stopping you, we know you're good for it," Laurie said. "No hurry either. It's not like you're running off somewhere."

Millie stared at Laurie's purse.

"No," she said. "Thanks anyway."

"Whatever you like," Laurie said. "Nobody's forcing anybody."

"Did I ever tell you, Millie, you make me happy in the pants?"

Millie produced a halfhearted smile.

"Just every single day since junior high."

"It's still true. All those years ago, and probably be true tomorrow."

"You're an amusing man, Webb."

"I'm guessing if you'd heard anything about the young gentleman we discussed, you would've spoken up."

"Haven't heard a thing, no."

"But you're keeping an eye out, from your excellent vantage point."

"You know I am, Webb."

"And Billy Joe and his helper back there?"

"Everybody's watching out."

"Because this is important."

"I know it is."

"Not just to me and Laurie, personally, but you understand it affects every citizen in Pine Haven. Our community well-being."

She drew a rag from her smock and wiped some crumbs off their table.

"We're looking out, Webb, best we can. We see anybody strange, hear anything suspicious, your cell phone jingles. We all understand what's what."

"Because it's my belief," Webb said, "there's

some people in this town, they aren't true blue, they don't understand what the fuck is what. I even heard there's a treasonous asshole or two might be giving aid and comfort."

"I wouldn't know about that."

"All the customers coming through the Happy Biscuit, sitting at these booths, you haven't heard anybody talking treason?"

She shook her head.

Laurie said, "How's your little one, Millie?"

She stiffened slowly like a woman wading into cold ocean waters.

"She's fine, just fine."

"Getting ready for Christmas, I bet. All excited about Santa."

"She is, yes."

"Something on little Emma's wish list me and Webb could help out with?"

"That's nice of you, Laurie. But no, I got it covered."

"Oh, I almost forgot," Laurie said. "Pass this on to that vegetable boy." She reached into her purse.

"Rodrigo?" Millie said.

"If that's his name. The dark-haired skinny one. He expressed an interest. Tell him if he's happy how it goes, he knows where to find me. First one is free."

Millie palmed the packet and tucked it in her uniform pocket.

Webb said, "So, Millie, you see anybody I should know about, give me a holler, you hear. The Doobies are always available. You know that."

Millie nodded again and cleared their plates.

Although Dobbins was their given name, everyone in Pine Haven knew them as the Doobie Brothers. Two jokes rolled into one.

The "brothers" part started in junior high when Laurie decided just being gay wasn't sufficient. She wanted to be flagrantly, outrageously superbutch, a style she first observed one summer at Topsail Beach where the bull dykes from Camp Lejeune paraded the sands in muscle shirts, hairy legs, and bad attitudes, and those ladies made a deep impression on the budding lesbian. For years afterward her mannish style was one of many ways she tormented her parents and martyred herself.

Although thank the sweet lord, that phase finally petered out and nowadays Laurie was all girly-girl again, smooth and feminine and lipsticked. Nevertheless that handle, "brothers," stuck for good.

"Doobie" was easy. As kids Laurie and Webb consumed way more than their share of weed. But the label stuck for good shortly after their senior year. As a graduation gift Webb's dad presented little Webb with a ten-acre parcel on the west end of the nine-hundred-acre Dobbins hog farm.

Webb Junior promptly plowed up a primo acre of his pineland and planted a hybrid ganja that was a cross between Afghan and Hindu Kush, known as Hog's Breath, a name Webb considered so appropriate, it conferred virtual legality on his enterprise. The dense buds of Hog's Breath were a beautiful dark green with bright orange hairs. The taste was cheddary and produced a tingly mind and body high. Damn good shit.

During that bountiful period, while Laurie handled distribution, catering mostly to military personnel at Camp Lejeune and Fort Bragg, Webb Junior tended the plants, harvesting, cleaning, and bagging, and in his spare time he experimented with the horticultural aspects, playing around with sativa and indica hybrids to come up with better yields, greater bag appeal, and some seriously higher THC counts.

The Doobies were way ahead of their time. Now, a dozen years later, a new wave of cannabis barons were living large in high-rise office buildings in San Francisco and Denver. They underwrote state-of-the-art hydroponic farming operations and distribution networks that supplied hundreds of dispensaries with so many varieties of weed they had to keep adding pages to their Web sites to extoll all the medicinal and recreational virtues.

But being ahead of your time in the drug game wasn't a healthy business strategy. Two years out of high school, the Doobie Brothers were keeping their profile low, their profits high, when one spring afternoon Webb's daddy, suffering from early stage dementia or some damn shit, came riding out to Webb Junior's operation unannounced with two DEA agents following in their Crown Vic. The senile fucker had turned in his son for reasons Webb Senior was forever at a loss to explain. Pure malice is what Webb always believed.

Webb was awarded an eighteen-month post-graduate scholarship at Wayne Correctional Center over in Goldsboro, a medium-security operation where he was treated to Narcotics Anonymous meetings three nights a week and a shitload of inspirational bullshit. And he met some mighty fine gentlemen in the facility, a few folks who were now his loyal customers.

Webb took the fall for Laurie, and to show her gratitude, his sister managed in the year and a half he was locked up to piss away their entire stash of dope and cash so that when Webb returned to civilian life, he had become, like his father and grandfather before him, nothing more than a simple hog farmer. Until a year ago.

When he and Laurie were getting up to leave the Happy Biscuit, Webb got another ring on his cell. He listened while they were walking out the door and said, "Be right there."

"What is it?"

"Burkhart needs me," he said. "He caught another spy."

"Well, well," she said. "Maybe we won't need Cruz after all."

"I'll find out shortly."

Webb headed west in his black F-150, passing first through the three-block section of stately Victorians where the great-grandchildren of Pine Haven's gentry were still occupying the family homes, built when cotton and flue-cured tobacco made a few local men rich. Most of the folks in the big houses were church ladies or shut-ins or renters living four poor white families crammed together. Then came four blocks of tiny brick two-bedrooms mixed in with a scattering of double-wides, the homes of Pine Haven's plumbers, handymen, and the folks who commuted to Fayetteville or Goldsboro or Cape Fear.

Shortly after that Webb bumped across a gully where the old train tracks were ripped up decades ago, the asphalt ended, and the dirt road began and he passed into the shantytown where a few hundred coloreds lived in pine shacks, most of them with busted-down front porches and taped-up windows, no bushes or grass in their yards, their communal trash pit burning constantly near the road. Since before Webb was born the area was known as Belmont Heights, though the land was as low-lying and featureless as the rest of Winston County.

As he drove Webb looked out at the brokeback houses, the ancient cars rusting in dirt driveways. At the ruined furniture in the weeds and ruptured refrigerators and stoves lying on their sides in the front yards. Disgraceful how they lived like junkyard dogs, but every time Laurie and her lady friends got it in their minds to do some community beautification and run some bulldozers through the miserable slum, all the preservationist fanatics got out their bullhorns and whipped up an army of crabbed-up arthritic ladies and put a stop to it. So nothing ever happened. The dead refrigerators continued to rust and the squalor would just keep on being squalid for another generation.

Up ahead he saw a man he'd been meaning to speak to sitting on an overturned washtub. Webb pulled over, honked twice, and Ladarius Washington lifted his head and flicked away his cigarette butt.

One more honk and Ladarius stretched himself and sauntered over to the truck, leaned in the passenger window. Webb and Ladarius had once been classmates in elementary school and on through the county high school, and they'd played on teams together, riding the team bus, banging heads and blocking each other's jump shots. They'd been friendly enough back then, but eventually the social order kicked in and now it was just a wave howdy when Webb passed by. Sometimes Ladarius nodded back.

"Something open up at the farm?"

"Not a thing, Ladarius. Not a damn thing. Got all my slots filled."

"With Mexicans."

"Your people work the slaughterhouse. There's always jobs coming open there. What's wrong, you too good for butchering hogs?"

"Too bloody for me, too much screaming," Ladarius said. "Rather work with the living."

"Well, there you go. You can't complain about not having work if there's work around and you don't have the stomach for it."

Ladarius watched a flock of ravens pass overhead.

When they'd disappeared, Ladarius motioned at the sky.

"Air's stinking again. Must be shit-spraying season."

"Got to put it somewhere."

"All the power and influence you got, Webb, you can't get the wind to blow the other direction?"

Webb smiled politely.

"Just shipped out a few thousand hogs," he said. "Another batch to the abattoir. I'm thinking I'll spray their leftovers later on this afternoon. So, fair warning, old friend, better hold your nose for a while, you hear."

"What you want with me?"

"Just say hello. Shoot the shit."

Ladarius was silent, waiting.

"Oh, and I heard a rumor some white fella might be hiding out here in one of these shacks. Might be bullet wounds in him. You hear that same rumor?"

Ladarius seemed about to say something, then shook his head.

"What is it, Ladarius? You can talk to me."

"Tell you what I told Burkhart the five, six times he been around banging on doors day and night with his bloodhounds, asking the same damn question, shouldering his way inside of people's homes without no search warrant or legal right. There ain't no white folks out here except the ones kicking up dust on this road."

"So you didn't hear a mess of gunfire in the woods back of Belmont Heights, that pine forest by the river, eight, ten days back?"

Ladarius frowned as if giving it some serious thought.

"Seems like I would've heard gunshots in them woods, living so near."

"Seems like you would, yes."

Ladarius wrinkled his brow as if trying hard to recall.

"No, sir, didn't hear no shooting."

"And never saw any of those punk-ass kids

126

coming and going from those woods. Young troublemakers."

"No kids, no shooting, no rumors like that, no, sir."

Webb eyed him for a minute but couldn't penetrate his dull-witted mask.

"If I was to give you my personal cell number, would you call me if you suddenly realize one or more of those rumors were true?"

"Would I call you?"

"Would you let me know about strangers out here, hiding out, plotting mischief against me and my business? The well-being of our fair city."

"That's a lot of responsibility," Ladarius said.

"Make it worth your while."

One of Ladarius's girls, five or six years old, wandered out onto the porch chewing on her thumb and looking out at her father.

Webb scribbled his number on a yellow notepad and tore off the page, held it out. Ladarius gave the paper an insolent look, then reached out for it.

"Day or night, you see that rumor walking around, call me. There'll be a chunk of change for you if you got it right."

"Now, that would be my lucky day, wouldn't it? Heavens opening up."

" 'Cause, Ladarius, on the flip side of my generosity is the fact that if I was to find out later on that those rumors were indeed true and some radical was hiding his sorry punk ass out here and folks like you knew about it all along and were aiding and abetting this snot-nosed criminal, well, I'd hate to think what havoc some kerosene might cause to all the kindling lying around here."

Ladarius stepped away as Webb pulled back onto the road. In the rearview mirror he watched his old high school chum walk back to his shanty, adding to the litter in his yard a wadded-up yellow ball of paper.

Eleven

Webb slowed for some potholes, then floored it through the rest of Belmont Heights and sped into the next neighborhood, the jam-packed trailer camp where the United Nations of Mexicans and Nicaraguans had their world headquarters.

A couple dozen wetbacks were lying around in the beds of their pickup trucks sipping beer and laughing, a few playing ragtag soccer in the rutted field nearby. All of them waiting to be summoned back to work by Webb's foreman.

The stink that started back at Ladarius's place grew stronger the farther west he went. "The smell of money" is what hog farmers liked to call that reek of swine manure and piss. Hydrogen sulfide, ammonia, and methane is what it actually was.

Hogs were prodigious shitters. Pound for pound they put out three times what a human did. In all, Webb's eight thousand hogs produced ten thousand gallons of soupy manure every day. No way to keep the putrid smell from drifting with the wind. The prevailing breezes swept those particles east across the migrant labor camp and into Belmont Heights, where they settled and took root in the grain of the wood houses and the weave of people's clothes and the fabric of their furniture, coated their utensils and pots and pans and dishes and glasses. A fine invisible mist of hog shit raining down on Ladarius Washington, his daughters, and the other fine people of Belmont Heights.

From time to time some of them complained about headaches, sore throats, burning eyes, ulcers, and blisters, and once in a while one of their sickly babies would cough itself to death and oh, lord, here we go again, there'd be a solemn vigil, a noisy march down Main Street or a bunch of signs posted on trees near town with pictures of the dead kid and angry messages about the hog stink they suffered from and how they weren't going to take it anymore.

But they always did. What were they going to do? Write their fucking congressman? Hey, go on, give it a whirl. That was Webb's advice. Write away, I'll lick the stamps myself. Send it to Raleigh, to Washington, D.C., express your god-given outrage like any citizen of these great United States was entitled to do. See where it got you.

Find out whose side your congressman was on. Yours or Pastureland's, the corporation that owned nine of ten hog operations from Raleigh to the coast. They'd find out quick enough who was running the world. Not Ladarius Washington, and not Webb either. It was Pastureland and their smug-ass bean counters who liked to call Webb every month and tell him how unproductive he was being, and how many more years he had before he'd paid back all the low-interest loans Pastureland generously provided him so he could expand and outfit his modern hog facility.

Back on his farm, Webb parked near containment shed number one, which he'd customized to be the nerve center of the farm. Rigged out with corrugated siding, vent stack chimneys, concrete floors, and high-tech feed monitors and blowers and misters that sprayed the hogs with a cool fog in the summertime. Hogs didn't sweat, so the fog was a necessary cost to spare the weaker animals in July and August. With all that fancy equipment, it didn't resemble any barn Webb had known growing up on his family's hog farm. But it was the way things were done these days, and the only damn way to stay in the hog game.

Webb Dobbins's farm was a seven-barn finishing operation, one of the biggest in the state. Three times a year he took delivery of eight thousand pinkish-white and cheerful piglets, spent four months fattening them from their arrival weight of about forty-five pounds to their target weight of two-fifty, then shipped them off to slaughter at the factory ten miles down the highway. Before each new drift of piglets arrived, he gave his men a two-day holiday, except for a couple whose job it was to scrub down the floors and walls and disinfect. Today was the second of those two days. The new passel would unload later on tonight.

He stood next to his truck for a moment, waiting for olfactory fatigue to set in. Weird but true, Webb had grown up on a hog farm, spent every waking hour for years within spitting distance of a herd of those even-toed ungulates, and the stink still could make him stomach-flopping gut sick.

A minute went by, then two, and his membranes dulled enough for him to walk out to lagoon number three. Filled ten feet deep with hog shit, four football fields long, it was one of seven lagoons on the farm. Holding his breath, he climbed the bank and worked up to the edge of the brown scummy pond and then set his feet, closed his eyes, and drew a long breath.

His bowels sank. He drew another breath,

pulling it down like dope smoke, holding it in until he could feel the tingle in his nostrils, the desensitizing beginning to take effect. Another minute up there, looking out across the lake of shit, and he was about as acclimated as he was going to get.

With all the water flushing through the floors of the containment sheds pumped out here, all five of the ponds were at their brims. Time to flush them out before the next eight thousand arrived.

Webb walked along the pathway around its shore until he came to the switching station. He looked out at the ten-acre pasture, a flat, empty field where his father's hogs used to graze, then reached up and pulled the lever.

It took a minute for the pumps to engage, then the giant sprinklers awoke on the tops of the steel poles and began to spray great beautiful arcs of hog shit out across the empty land. He watched them work for a while, the breeze whisking away some of the fine brown spray, then Webb made his way down from the pond edge and walked across the parking lot toward the containment shed.

Sadly for Ladarius and the rest of the folks in Belmont Heights, they got their hog shit stench in irregular pulses throughout the day and night, depending on the vagaries of the wind and the farm's spraying schedule, so their nostrils never reached the deadened state that Webb experienced by just staying put for a while at ground zero.

With his stomach settled, Webb entered the south entrance of containment shed number one. It was empty now, no squealing, no grunts, just the chug of the DeWalt high-pressure cleaner down at the far end where two of his illegals were spraying the walls and flushing the last pig turds into the louvered slats in the floor so the shit washed into the holding tanks belowground, where it would sit until he'd made room in one of the lagoons.

Burkhart, his foreman, was waiting for him down with the illegals. He saw Webb coming and slashed a hand across his throat and the Mexican running the DeWalt cut it off.

Burkhart was a sixty-year-old ex-Marine, his gray hair still in a tight crew cut, his chest chunky and his arms chiseled from a lifetime of pushups. He was Winston County's duly elected sheriff, a job Burkhart, like every sheriff before him, considered more a hobby than actual work. He'd be living in a shabby double-wide on the outskirts of Belmont Heights if it wasn't for his better-paying second job as Webb's foreman and head of security.

Both the Mexicans bowed their heads at Webb's approach.

Burkhart stepped to the side and pointed to the

culprit, then gave Webb a maître d's swoop of the arm. Have at it.

He moved close to the two workers, pushed one aside, then stepped even closer to the offender. He stooped forward, got his face near the man's, and said, "You understand English, even a little bit?"

"Little, yes, sir."

"So Jorge, you were taking pictures too, like your buddy Javier."

The man shook his head.

"No, sir. I no take pictures."

"That's not what I heard, no sir, it's in total contradiction to the information I've received. You *comprende*, boy?"

He nodded uncertainly.

"Mr. Burkhart, may I see the evidence?"

Burkhart walked over to the metal lockers against the back wall, opened one of the doors, and came back holding out a silver watch. He handed the watch to Webb and Webb spent a minute examining it. Then he pushed it into the Mexican's face.

"You recognize this timepiece, Jorge?"

"My name Jesús."

"What I'm asking you, Jorge, is about this watch, this watch Burkhart found in your locker just now, hidden in the toe of an old boot. This watch right here. You see this watch, don't you, Jorge?"

The man lowered his head and didn't answer.

The other illegal muttered something to the culprit, probably translating.

"It not my watch, Mr. Webb," the culprit said.

"So, you're denying you ever wore this watch. This watch with a little bitty video camera in the dial. Right there, you see it, Diego? The camera, that little lens right there, you see it?"

Webb pushed the watch into the man's face. He turned his head aside as if waiting for the blows to come.

"You been taking pictures in the barn and around other places on the farm, haven't you, son? And then you gave this watch to those hippies living in the woods. You were acting as their spy, consorting with the enemy. You been engaged in treasonous villainy, boy. That's how it appears. You got anything to say for yourself?"

His friend, the translator, gave him the Spanish version.

Webb looked at Burkhart and the old Marine shook his head. See the shit he had to deal with all day?

"I no spy, Mr. Webb."

"Where'd you get this watch?"

"Someone gave him the watch," the translator said. "He didn't know about the camera."

"So both of you are lying to me now. Two of my own men turning against me, playing footsie with people meaning to do harm to me and to this establishment."

"No, sir, Mr. Webb. I mean no harm."

"I put my trust in you, boy, let you wander freely about the property, and this is how you treat me in return? Because I know damn well you took some movies of the operations on the farm, and other top-secret activities, then you carried that watch to the enemy. Isn't this what happened, Juan?"

The man was out of lies, all his courage draining away, hanging his head.

"What I want to know, Jorge, and this is the point of this entire exercise, I want to know if any of those folks are still around. Those people that paid you to be a traitorous infiltrator."

There was some jabber between the two Mexicans, then the translator said, "He don't know if those people still around."

"But he's admitting he made movies for them, and got paid for spying. Is that the case?"

"They ask him to wear the watch, bring it to them every night. That's all. They gave him a hundred dollars. He didn't know it was wrong. He needed the money. Jesús knows nothing more. They were in the woods, back there behind where the black people live, now they gone."

"Except they're not," Webb said. "I believe one of those hippies is still lurking nearby. And I believe Diego here knows where the slimewad is."

"No, sir, no, sir. I don't know nothing, sir."

"Then it looks to me like we got us a classic rock and a hard place."

Webb reached out and tipped up the small man's chin so he was forced to look at Webb eyeball to eyeball.

"You know what happened to your friend Javier when I caught him with an identical watch as this one? You seen him around here lately?"

The man shook his head.

"I did nothing wrong, Mr. Webb, not a spy."

"If that's your story, boy, then here's the deal. I give you three choices."

"*Tres opciones*," the other one said.

"That's more than fair, you ask me. Number one, I pull out my phone, I dial a gentleman I know in Raleigh, man works with ICE. You know what ICE is, don't you?"

He nodded.

"So if I ask him polite, he'll drive down this afternoon as a special favor to me and he'll check to make sure your papers got all their *i*'s dotted and their *t*'s crossed, assuming you got some papers to show him."

The illegal listened to the translation and said something back to his buddy and the buddy said to Webb, "He lost his papers. They destroyed. His family papers too. No papers. Jesús is a hard worker. He never been in trouble."

"Then tell him he's got two other choices.

Number two, you tell me where this man is hiding. This man who bribed Jesús to spy on my farming operations."

When the translator had given his friend the update, Jesús said, "I don't know about anyone hiding. I wear watch, I give them watch, they give it back, and I never see them again."

"Well, then I guess that leaves us with number three."

Webb bent forward and pulled up one of his own pant legs, all the way to the knee.

"This is how my daddy handled things back in the day when he caught me in a lie. This is how we worked it out between us."

"What is that?" Burkhart said, craning forward. "He scald you?"

The slick hairless scars resembled burn marks, but they weren't.

"There's your number three, boy. So pick your poison."

The man was silent, eyes scanning slowly around the hog barn as though taking one farewell look. The two Mexicans had a short back and forth. Both of them looked like they might be ready to make a run for it. Then the culprit looked at Webb with the weary gaze of a veteran of defeat and said, "I don't know where anyone hiding, Mr. Webb. I don't know."

"Strip off your overalls, boy. I don't have all fucking day."

Jesús's face was pale and strained. But he did as he was told.

When his overalls were heaped on the concrete floor, Webb said, "Now start up the pressure cleaner, boy. Start her up."

Jorge cranked up the DeWalt's Honda engine and stepped away. His boxer shorts were white and printed with red hearts. Burkhart looked up at the ceiling of the barn and shook his head. Lordy day.

Webb picked up the spray wand and aimed it at the floor and fired a quick pulse and the wand kicked back against his hand. Forty-two hundred pounds per square inch of firepower, enough to peel the chrome off the bumper of a '57 Chevy.

"Tell me where he's hiding out, this man you been spying for."

His friend didn't bother to translate. He shut his eyes, unable to watch.

Webb turned to Burkhart and said, "When I'm done here, if this man is still alive, you put him in one of them special cells. Give him a chance to consider the errors of his ways."

Burkhart nodded and Webb aimed the sprayer at the Mex.

When the Mexican raised his hands in helpless surrender, Webb fired a blast at his ankles, the right then the left. Doing a hot-footed jig, Jorge howled. After a few seconds, the skin peeled back and blood ran onto the floor. Webb cut off the spray.

"You sure about this, Jorge? You sure this how you want it to go?"

The man was shivering, tears on his cheeks, speechless.

"I know nothing. Nothing."

"Okay, then."

Webb fired another blast, working up the man's leg to his knee, leaving a two-inch stripe, then aiming at the valentines, another blast, holding down the trigger, holding it tight until the cloth at his crotch ripped apart and darkened with blood, and the howling was almost more than a civilized man could bear.

Twelve

Thorn ordered plain waffles, thinking they might stimulate his appetite. He stared down at them for a while, then out of habit he cut them into small squares and swiped some butter across the grids and watched it melt. He tried pouring maple syrup over them but that did nothing to rouse his hunger either. He pushed the plate away and took a sip of the black coffee and sat back in the booth and looked out the window at the wreckage of the burger restaurant.

Sitting across from him, Cruz was on the phone, her second call since they'd been seated.

Speaking softly, a hand cupped over her mouth as she told someone to expect them by early afternoon.

When she finished, she set the phone beside her plate of pancakes and said, "That was our contact in Pine Haven. Name's Webb Dobbins. It's his farm Flynn's group was targeting."

Thorn watched her cut up her short stack and spear a chunk and tuck it quickly into her mouth, then repeat the process. She wasn't having any trouble with her appetite.

"What really happened to Tina?"

"Just what I told Sugarman."

"He didn't believe your story. And I'm having the same problem."

"So call her. Ask her yourself."

She dug her cell from her purse and handed it to him.

"Don't know her number," Thorn said.

Cruz recited it to him.

"I had her under surveillance for some time. I know all her numbers."

Thorn punched it in. Got her voicemail.

"Sorry. Me and my honey are on a little romantic getaway. If I'm not answering, well, you know. I'm otherwise occupied. Whoopee."

Thorn shut off the phone and set it on the table.

"She's not answering."

"She's probably sleeping it off. She smokes a lot of grass, that one."

Thorn nudged his plate of waffles farther away. "Who drove Tina back to Key Largo?"

"You still don't trust me?"

"I'm working on it. Who drove her?"

"An associate of mine."

A few minutes later, waiting at the checkout register, his gym bag in hand, Thorn looked out at the parking lot and saw Deputy Randolph speaking to a man in a blue suit. Thorn told Cruz he'd meet her outside and before she could respond he was out the door.

The man in the suit was short and heavyset with a comb-over the morning breeze had flipped up like the hinged lid on a mason jar. He was consulting an electronic tablet while Randolph was unwrapping a stick of gum.

"Thorn," he said, folding the gum into his mouth. "You're still here."

"About to leave. Unless you need me."

"And who's this?" the fat man said.

"Guy I told you about, hauled the kid's body out of the fire." The fat man looked Thorn up and down but didn't seem awestruck. "Thorn, this is Detective Dickerson."

"That fire was arson, wasn't it?"

"What makes you think that?" Dickerson took a second look at Thorn.

"Like I told Randolph last night, there was a substance in the victim's mouth. At the time I thought it might've been vomit, but now I don't

142

know. It was heavier, thicker, smelled like spoiled meat. You might be looking at foul play."

"You a forensics specialist, are you? Come to our small hamlet to share your expertise with the country boys?"

Deputy Randolph must've seen the veins rise in Thorn's throat. He took hold of Thorn's arm and steered him back toward the restaurant.

"Being an asshole," Randolph said. "It's his mission in life. Don't take it personal."

Thorn shrugged out of his hold.

Randolph said, "What you told me last night, the goop in his mouth, I passed it on to the ME and he took a look before he started the autopsy. It's all preliminary, but yeah, seems to be a big wad of ground beef in the kid's cheeks, more of it blocking his windpipe. And he wasn't wolfing down a burger. The meat wasn't cooked."

Thorn asked him what they made of that, but Randolph shook his head.

"Murder by meat is how it looks. A fire to cover it."

"You ever hear of that before?"

"No, sir, that's a new one on me. Hard to picture how a thing like that could happen, you know, the mechanics of it. Not to mention the why."

Thorn spent a few uncomfortable seconds trying to picture someone being choked to death on a handful of meat.

"One other thing came up," Randolph said.

"Early last evening apparently there was a confrontation, the kid versus some fellow in the drive-through window. Manager told us about it, thought it might be relevant. The incident was captured on the security cam. We just took custody of the disc, haven't had a look, but I don't have much hope for that."

Thorn was staring at the wreckage.

"You want to leave me a cell number, I'll let you know the outcome of the investigation, seeing you have a personal stake."

"Not personal. I was just passing by. I did what anybody would."

"Wish that were true," Randolph said. "I surely wish that were true."

"Good luck finding the guy. I'll check back if I'm free."

Across the parking lot, Cruz motioned for him to join her. She was waiting at the rear of a brown four-door sedan, an Oldsmobile Cutlass Supreme, one of those gas-swilling mastodons from twenty years back. The trunk was open, her gear and the green duffel stowed inside. Thorn tossed his gym bag beside the other bags. When he slammed the trunk and straightened, Cruz was in his face.

"Now listen. The two people you're about to meet, they're members of my team, but they can be quite volatile. So I'm asking you, please, don't antagonize them. The less you interact with them, the better. They don't need to know anything about you, and you don't *want* to know anything about them. Keep it impersonal. Clear?"

"I'm feeling a little volatile myself."

"Control yourself. Don't run this off the rails. There's a lot at stake."

The guy was sitting behind the steering wheel and in the seat behind him was a pale, emaciated young woman with gigantic sunglasses that hid half her face and a baseball cap cocked sideways. She wore a baggy black sweater and jeans ripped at the knees, and was scrolling through messages on her phone and didn't look up as Thorn and Cruz stepped close to the Olds. There was something vaguely familiar about her but Thorn couldn't say what.

Cruz knuckle-tapped the guy's window and he cranked it down.

"This is the man I told you about." She gestured with her chin at Thorn.

The guy continued to stare out the windshield at the charred ruins of the burger joint.

The young woman in the back rolled down her window.

"Hey, me and X were thinking of going retro, boys up front, girls in back. Can you dig it?"

When they were seated, Thorn riding shotgun, Cruz introduced him to the driver a second time. The man didn't say a word or look over, and he didn't offer his hand and Thorn didn't offer his.

An instant bristling standoff, the kind of hairy-chested ritual Thorn had experienced since he was old enough to make a fist. Two guys thrown into the same small cage with the clear understanding that only one of them would be coming out with his manhood fully intact. In recent years Thorn had lost interest in such bullyboy contests, but the mood he was in this morning brought it all back.

"X-88," Thorn said. "Is that with numbers or you spell it out?"

The guy looked over at Thorn. He was swarthy, in his late twenties, heavyset with overripe lips and a gleaming shaved head. Big arms swelling the sleeves of his black polo shirt. A fleshy beer keg, thick in the chest, thicker at the waist. But it didn't look like fat to Thorn.

"88," he said. "It's a number. Maybe you never counted that high."

"Good one," Pixie said.

"You use a hyphen or go without?" Thorn said.

"It's a nickname, Thorn," said Cruz. "Give it a rest."

"He's giving you a ration of shit, X," Pixie said.

Thorn glanced back at the young woman.

"What? He needs an interpreter?"

"Thorn?" X said. "Is that with a prick or without?"

"Out of the park," Pixie said, clapping her hands. "Slam dunk."

"Okay, knock it off, all of you. We're on the same side. Where we're going, what we're doing, we can't be at each other's throats. I'm warning you. Stop the smartass. His name is X-88. Numbers, hyphen. Call him X if the '88' is too much for you. And you too, X. From now on we need to depend on each other, so let's get started, no more bullshit."

They got on I-95 and rode in silence for a long while, passing through Jacksonville, taking the high bridges across the St. Johns River, then out of the city and into Georgia. Passing through the coastal lowlands, the flat watery bayous and marshes, saw grass, palmetto, live oaks with beards of moss.

After another half hour of quiet, X pulled off the interstate, turned into a service station, and got out to pee. Everyone else stayed put.

"In case you're interested," Pixie said, "me and X-88 are hardline vegans, straight-edgers. We don't do drugs, eat meat, cigarettes, coffee, anything that pollutes our bodies."

"I'm happy for you."

"X has hyperosmia," Pixie said. "A very rare condition. He smells in high definition like a dog, you know, only unlike a dog, he can actually describe what he smells, put it in words, which is an art form if you ask me. Like how a wine connoisseur talks, you know, a special vocabulary.

"He can smell your breath, tell you what you had for lunch, or you hide something, he'll walk right over and dig it out of where you put it. I didn't believe it at first until he showed me. My bra, lipstick, a toothbrush. I hid them, in like two seconds, he found them. He's freaking amazing.

"And he knew who slept on that motel mattress the night before us. Some long-haul truck driver and a black girl he'd picked up at a truck stop. He could smell the particles they left behind. And traces of the others before the trucker, layers of scent, like archaeology, how long they stayed, if they had sex or not. Most didn't, in case you were interested."

"And you believe all that?" Thorn said.

"It's genetic, from when his mother was pregnant with him, she was heavy into meth. That's what his doctors think. It corrupted his DNA. It wasn't so bad when he was a kid, but the older he gets, the more acute it is. Lately it's really been bothering him, the last month, giving him headaches, all the odors swarming the air all the time.

"He's studied the science of it to see why he's like how he is. He's seen specialists, neurologists, he's been CAT scanned to see what's going on inside his brain and what they told him, it's because his hippocampus and frontal cortex are different, a lot larger. He's got all these extra neurons in his olfactory bulb. There's nothing he can do about it, just accept it. Sometimes, all the smells in the air, it can overwhelm him, that's what he says. You don't believe in science?"

"Enough," Cruz said.

"And let me tell you, he inherited his old lady's cranked-up metabolism too, because X has stamina, I mean serious staying power. Shit, only guy I ever met could outlast me. I'm telling you, some mornings I can barely walk."

"Stop it," Cruz said. "Our private lives are private."

"You're such a prude."

"Try to act professionally, Pixie. Just this once."

"That's a shitty attitude. Boundaries, repression. Me, I'm into total transparency. Pixie, the permeable membrane. Share everything. It comes into my mind, it's out of my mouth. Just skips right over my brain. I mean, keeping secrets, shit, it gives you cancer, you never heard that?"

"You're making an ass of yourself."

"Where'd you pick up these idiots?" Thorn asked Cruz.

"Drop it, Thorn."

"I'll tell you," said Pixie. "She didn't pick me up anywhere. I popped out from between her legs. I'm Pixie Cruz, Mommy's worst nightmare."

Cruz frowned out her window and her reflection revealed the face of the woman she might become in a decade or two. Sallow skin, sunken cheeks, eyes hollowed out, whittled away to almost nothing.

Pixie said, "Mom lost the daughter she loved, the good girl, white sheep. She'd just as soon I fuck off, disappear somewhere. Isn't that right, Mom? But she puts up with me because she's crazy about X because he'll do shit she doesn't have the guts for. He's a badass, a total badass."

Cruz massaged a temple as if to ease a sudden headache.

"Thank you, Pixie," she said. "Thank you for never disappointing."

X got back in the car.

He registered the strained silence, looked back at Pixie, then at Cruz and said, "I miss anything good?"

Thorn leaned over and blew a breath in X's direction.

"What'd I have for breakfast?"

"Coffee," he said. "Black. Last night you had a bite of a fried-fish sandwich. A couple of french fries with ketchup. At the moment you've got acid indigestion."

"He get it right?" Pixie said.

"Like a speaking dog," said Thorn.

"See," Pixie said, "what'd I tell you? He could do Vegas. X-88, the Amazing Sniffer. I could see it. Me in a tight gown, showing some boob, bring people up from the audience onstage. Nobody's ever seen anything like it."

"Vegas sucks," X said. He put the car in gear. "All that phony shit, the canals of Venice, Eiffel Tower. It's Disney World on Viagra."

"Well, Branson then," said Pixie. "There's lots of venue possibilities. Soon as we finish with this deal, we'll kick around ideas. You got to cash in on your god-given gifts, share them with the world."

"And you, Pixie," Thorn said. "You have any god-given gifts?"

"Damn right, just ask X. He's experienced a few."

X's mouth remade itself into something resembling a grin, but it was a misshapen thing, as if smiling was not in his repertoire. He gunned the big car up the ramp back onto the interstate, mouth spread wide, showing a set of large teeth. X's head was tilted back a degree or two, listening to Pixie begin what became an hour-long monologue, a grand tour through her sexual history, from losing her virginity at ten to a man selling magazines door to door, to the months she turned tricks in parked cars outside her junior high, then the year she spent in juvie for some bullshit charge of dealing crack, and a few months with a South American coke dealer, living with some other girls in his penthouse on Brickell Avenue, a big-time view of Biscayne Bay, servicing his friends, men

151

and women who were partying at his condo, all the time Pixie was picking up new ways to please a man, a great education, prepping for X-88.

Cruz shut her eyes and rocked her head back against the seat with the exhausted look of one who'd long ago given up trying to regulate her daughter.

Thorn listened for a while, then turned his attention to the distances of the Georgia countryside, the blue sky broadening and deepening in color in the east as the sun pushed higher, watching the lazy, halfhearted flights of egrets and herons, rising from the waterways, elongating their bodies, catching the updrafts like spirits ascending rapturously, puncturing the blue skin of the sky, as if they were reentering the heaven from which they'd descended. And every bird he saw, every wisp of cloud, each leaf tumbling in the breeze reminded him of Flynn, the shadows cast by trees, each ripple etched in the silver marsh spreading eastward toward the sea was Flynn, his only son, lost to him out there in the vastness beyond the limits of sight and touch.

Thirteen

Herbert Shubert lived in a forest west of St. Augustine, a home with no plumbing or power, just sheets of scrap plywood nailed to some trees, formed into a box with a roof made of a blue tarp he'd stolen off a house back near the interstate after a hurricane ripped away all its tiles.

Up at dawn, Herbert was foraging near the asphalt two-lane. That's what he did with his daylight hours. Scavenging the amazing shit people threw out of their cars. Half-eaten burgers, pizza slices, beer cans with a couple of swallows left, half-smoked cigarettes, sunglasses, shirts, pants, belts, socks, even a wallet once, with cash money and love notes folded up in the pockets.

It was usually kids coming way out in the woods to park and fuck. He'd seen some filthy sex out here. Seen some porno stuff and homo stuff late at night in the glow of the interior lights. Kids trying out their bodies. Making orgasm screams.

Once or twice Herbert had been tempted to mug one. Almost worked up the nerve, but stopped when his mother spoke to him and warned him that he'd surely fuck up and his victims would escape and bring back the cops and throw him in the lockup again, with the gangbangers, spastics, and the howlers. He didn't want to go back to jail.

For an hour he worked up and down the shoulders of the road, scrounged a few butts, a half-smoked cigar, found a banged-up Zippo lighter with its insides dried out. Toward the end Herbert found a pair of black silk panties that were big enough to fit him. He sniffed them and damn if they hadn't been worn recently. What must've happened, one of the fuckers parked out in the woods probably lost them, or some wild party girl flung them out of a moving car. He stuffed them in his pocket for sometime when he might want to dress up.

On the way back to his shack he crossed the sandy path that ran near his place and saw fresh tire tracks rutted deep in the sand. He stared at them, followed them to where they stopped about a half mile from the road. He hadn't heard anybody over here last night, no pleasure screams, not a damn human sound, but then he'd been drinking the half jug of red wine somebody left at another lover's lane a mile in the other direction. So that might explain it. Drunk. Sorry he'd missed it. He liked to watch the fucking or just listen.

He poked around where the tire tracks ended. Scrounging for food scraps or beer cans or used condoms. He saved rubbers. Had a nice collection, different colors and sizes he hung around his shack for decoration.

Scrounging in the woods, he heard something. He listened some more then headed off that way into the brush. And a few feet later he heard the snort and snuffle and he knew it was the bear, an old bear that lived way back into the woods. They'd crossed paths a few times, and they got along, you could say, the bear keeping his distance and Herbert keeping his. That snorting bear heard Herbert approaching, treading on sticks and dried leaves, and the bear got up from whatever he was doing and snuffled on out of there, not in a big hurry, but going away, finished with his business.

There was buzzing as he pushed into an opening in the trees, a sandy patch covered in decaying leaves, and there was a dead body circled by flies and wasps and bees and butterflies with shiny blue wings and every other insect Herbert had ever imagined or seen. He wasn't sure which exactly he was doing now, seeing or imagining. But one of those. It didn't matter really. The butterflies were a beautiful blue.

The woman seemed real, and about as dead as a woman can get.

He kneeled down beside the stink, horseflies orbiting his head.

He touched her cheek with a fingertip and found it cold. The bear had worked on her face, torn open her mouth and cheeks, and her belly too, ripping her clothes, and it was messy there and wet and the flies were feasting all around where the bear had been.

Herbert decided he wanted to see her snatch, just a look. Nothing sick. He wasn't going to climb on top of her. He wasn't one of those creeps, though he'd met a couple in jail, at least that's what they bragged they'd done, made unholy love. But not Herbert. That wasn't sane. But just a look, maybe a feel, pluck a few hairs if there were any and take them back to the shack, put them in his stash. Just that. Nothing more.

But then, shit. There she was.

Herbert's mother said, "Herbie, what do you think you're doing? The woman's dead. It's a sacrilege what you're thinking. The woman's immortal soul would be forever damaged."

Herbert's mother was like that. Immortal souls were her main line of work. She harped on them. Not happy with Herbert living out in the woods, scrounging like he did, peeping on lovers, but tolerating it. The old woman mainly lay low and didn't bother him, but he knew she was there all the time because like now, she'd speak to him clear as pie. She'd say the words to steer him from the bad things he was about to do and direct him to the good.

But just a quick look at her snatch was all he wanted. She had blond hair on top and he'd never seen snatch that color. Just a quick look and no touching. That was okay, right?

But then his mother was back.

"You need to report the tragic death of this woman. You need to walk down to that highway, flag down a car, let someone know there's a body. She's got loved ones. People care about her just like I care about you, Herbie, and how would you like it if I just disappeared without a trace and you never knew where I was or what happened to me. Not to mention my immortal soul."

So shit.

Herbert stood up and looked around at the woods.

He knew his mother was dead and the dead didn't speak. It wasn't possible. But still, her voice was clear as pie. Clear as warm apple pie with vanilla ice cream on a Sunday afternoon on his twelfth birthday and she made it special for him, special for her only son, just the two of them having a birthday party, Herbie, her child who she watched over so carefully and cooked for and made his every wish come true, as many as she could manage.

"Flag someone down. Report it, Herbie. Do what's right."

But she wasn't real. He knew that. His mother's voice was in his head. That's what the docs told him. Not a real voice. Like a dream without the pictures. He could tune it out.

And anyway, all he wanted was a peek. Maybe harvest a few hairs.

After he left Tina's house, Sugarman went home, lay down on his bed, and tried to sleep for a couple of tormented hours, then paced around his house till he thought it was safe to call Sheffield.

At eight, Sheffield answered, clearly coffeed-up, saying sure, Sugarman was free to drop by, he'd be on the second floor of the motel painting the interior walls. It was a motel he'd inherited from his old man, a bit run-down, but it was smack on the beach, which meant it was worth a shitload more in land value than anything Sheffield could sell it for as a functioning motel even after he finished fixing it up. But, as he told Sugar, Frank wasn't interested in selling.

Sugar waited through Frank's ramble, though he'd not asked Frank about the motel. But Frank was on a tear, telling him that by now he'd sunk so much money and so many hours refurbishing the old place, restoring its mom-and-pop charm, that he wasn't going to take any amount of money for the place, not even the five mil he'd been offered last week. What the hell else was Sheffield going to do now that he was fully retired from the FBI, except run the motel, do right by the place where he'd spent the happiest hours of his life back in the day when Miami was actually a very sweet town to grow up in.

Sheffield talking without pause like he was starved for social contact. He didn't ask Sugar why he'd called, and Sugar didn't broach the subject because he wanted to see Frank face-to-face in case there was some deception at work in this mess, some interoffice ass-protecting the likes of which Sugarman had experienced often in his years of law enforcement. It could be that Madeline Cruz was working an angle that overlapped with something Frank had going on, then Frank would try to bullshit him about the whole deal, which was why Sugar was making the hour-plus drive up to Miami even though he'd just finished doing a five-hundred-mile round trip to St. Augustine and back.

It was nine-thirty when he located Sonesta Drive, hung a left off Crandon Boulevard on Key Biscayne, drove a few blocks toward the Atlantic, all the way to the end, and pulled into the empty parking lot of the Silver Sands Motel, hidden in the shimmering shadows of two thirty-story glass cylinders. The motel had an impressive hundred yards of oceanfront with a few dozen coconut palms stirring in a trickle of morning breeze.

Sugar climbed the outdoor stairway and got halfway down the hall when he saw an open door and smelled fresh paint. He rapped on the door.

"Go away, I'm working."

Sugarman came inside and Frank Sheffield

craned around a corner, held up a paintbrush, and said, "You handle one of these? Don't need to be Rembrandt."

"This won't take a minute. Just a question, I'll be out of your hair."

"How about a beer?"

"It's not even ten o'clock."

"But it's Saturday," Sheffield said. "That's got to count for something."

Frank wiped his big paws on a rag and they shook hands and Sugarman admired the paint job for a minute, said he liked that particular shade of blue, though in truth he thought it was way too purple, more like the walls of a strip joint than a family motel at the beach.

"So what's with Thorn? He start another world war yet?"

"I believe he might be working on it."

He watched Sheffield examine some recent brushstrokes that were lit by the sunlight streaming through the front window. Sugar was trying to get a fix on Frank's mood. He'd worked along-side Sheffield a few times, knew he was about as laid-back as a federal agent could be and survive in an uptight agency like the FBI, but Frank was also a canny son of a bitch who had made a career of hiding that shrewdness behind an amiable facade.

"Madeline Cruz," Sugar said. Springing it on him. Test the reaction.

160

Sheffield picked up a brush and touched up a spot on the wall. Face empty, studying the wall like Sugar hadn't spoken.

"Five seven, dark hair, pretty, carrying FBI ID. She consulted with you about the case she's working, one that involves Thorn and Flynn Moss."

Frank lowered his brush and turned to Sugar. Still giving away nothing.

"Madeline Cruz?"

Sugar said, "Yeah, that's right."

"How pretty?"

"Slim and trim," Sugar said. "But businesslike, with brown eyes. Probably Mexican descent, a little Aztec too, I'd guess."

"Never met her, never heard of her."

"Look, Frank, I understand. If you can't talk about the particulars of the case, fine. You have to keep things confidential. All I need to know is that this woman is genuine. She can be trusted."

Sheffield's mouth flattened like he was disappointed in Sugarman's approach, treating Frank like a goddamn civilian.

"Well, granted," he said, "my memory is getting spotty, but damn, I believe I'd remember a pretty woman named Cruz discussing Thorn and Flynn Moss. I'm not that far gone."

"Tell me you're kidding. You never heard of her?"

"How many ways can I say it?"

"Shit." Sugarman stared out the window at

the silver glare of early morning sunlight on the ocean. "Shit, shit, shit."

"You sure you don't want a beer?"

"She had to know I'd check, find out she was lying."

"Maybe you and I should sit in the shade, you can lay all this out. I'm intrigued by what I've heard so far."

Down at a concrete picnic table that faced the beach, Sugar told Frank the story while Sheffield guzzled his first beer quick, then opened another. Sugar explained how Flynn had been sending regular postcards, his way of keeping Thorn apprised of his journeys, then a postcard came yesterday, the Neuse River, no postmark, a call for help, and they'd set off for Carolina, and how they'd stopped at the gas station along the interstate, Cruz appeared, badged them, and Tina, coming back from the restroom, saw what was going down and made a run for it, stole a car, and fled. Guns in a duffel, a mess of cash.

How Cruz pressured them to continue up I-95, stringing them along with bits and pieces of a story, saying if they were going to find Flynn, they'd need her help because there were dangerous people up on the Neuse River, and she was running a larger federal operation, and it was Tina's job to deliver Thorn into some kind of trap, and if he and Thorn barged into Pine Haven without knowing the cast of characters, Flynn was a dead man. Then in the early evening Cruz steered them to a motel near St. Augustine, sent Sugarman for takeout dinner, ten minutes later, when he returns with the food, she's convinced Thorn to cut Sugarman loose.

Finished with the retelling, Sugar slumped forward and said, "I hear that story coming out of my mouth, and Christ, it sounds totally batshit crazy."

Sheffield took the last slug of his second beer and set it aside.

"That it does, my friend. That it does."

Sugarman stared out at the Atlantic, at the mild surf lapping the beach, at the weekend sun worshipers arriving, rolling out their towels.

"She kept dropping your name, Frank. Said you advised her Thorn might be willing to help her out. She quoted you verbatim, about Thorn being a social misfit. She was very persuasive."

"How hard would it be to know my name? Last twenty years I was a public figure, head of the regional field office of the FBI. Anybody who read the papers knows Thorn and I had a couple of encounters. And you can take one look at Thorn and tell he's a misfit. Tell me this, she say anything might be considered private information about me?"

Sugarman sighed. Shook his head.

"She sold us this twaddle, we swallowed it like a couple of schoolboys."

"A woman shows you a badge, she's a slick talker, you trust her story, not so surprising. Maybe you were a little gullible, yeah."

"Thorn was worked up. Getting that postcard, a call for help. He was emotional, off balance. Primed and ready to head off. I got swept up in his fever."

Sugarman came to his feet.

"Now where do you think you're going?"

"Fly up there. See what I can do."

"Sit down, big fellow. Being rash, that's Thorn's bailiwick. You're the levelheaded one, remember? Think this through. Say you go driving into this hayseed town, what if no one's heard of Cruz or Thorn, they're nowhere to be found? This whole Pine Haven thing, it's a fake-out, Thorn and this Cruz woman are somewhere else entirely? Hey, you've just wasted a lot of time and money and you don't know one thing more than you did already. So relax. Take twenty-four hours for Tina to check in. Maybe she's embarrassed, hiding out somewhere, licking her wounds. Meanwhile, do your research. Give me Tina's vitals, I'll call in to the office, have them put her in the system."

"I should've been tougher, more suspicious. Tina's disappeared, and Thorn's walking into some kind of setup."

"Easy does it, man. There's no need to worry about Thorn. That guy's luckier than a twodicked tomcat. And he's got twice as many lives."

"And he's used up more than his share already."

Down on the beach an elderly couple in swimsuits had begun to dance with graceful and unembarrassed intimacy. No earbuds, no boombox playing nearby, just swaying to the music of the natural surroundings. They moved together like old lovers, each step and swirl and dip synced with the roll and crash of the surf, the beat of a passing speedboat, its hull hammering the chop in rhythm with their waltz, and the sweet soaring flights of a pair of gulls that were rising and plunging in time with the dancers.

"You okay, Sugar?"

He blinked his eyes clear and smiled quietly at Frank.

"Thorn's saved my life a half dozen times."

"Yeah? And how many of those times did he put your life in danger to begin with?"

"Thorn's in trouble. Big damn trouble."

"Give me Tina's info. I'll get that part started."

"Thought you were retired."

"Still got a friend or two at the bureau. Sit tight, let me find out what I can. Give me one day."

PART TWO

Part Two

Fourteen

Passing through South Carolina on I-95, the car was quiet. Pixie had run dry of stories. Napping. From the glances Thorn took in the sun visor mirror, Cruz seemed to be reading texts or e-mails on her phone, answering some.

Thorn was looking out at the forest of pines along the interstate when a phone rang somewhere deep in the car.

Cruz craned forward over the seat.

"What the hell?"

"Sounds like a ringtone," X said.

It rang three more times, distant, muffled. Then stopped.

Cruz sat back in her seat.

"Next stop," she said to X, "find it."

The phone started to ring again. It rang five times, then ceased.

"La Marseillaise."

To arms, to arms, ye brave. March on.

Thorn stared out at the pine trees flashing past. The doubts he'd been having about Cruz and X-88 were gone. He sat quietly, unmoving, trying to breathe.

. . .

An hour later, sometime after three in the afternoon, X-88 exited I-95 onto a two-lane highway, US 13, heading north and east. Miles later at a crossroads called Spivey's Corner, X pulled into a Citgo station and the women got out to pee.

"And you, Thorn?" Cruz said through his open window.

"I'm fine," he said. "I can wait."

"Watch him," Cruz said to X.

When she and Pixie were inside the station, he got out. X-88 was watching the numbers fly by on the gas pump, holding the nozzle in place. Thorn put his palms against a supporting beam, bent forward, and pretended to stretch his back. Positioned to block X's path back to the pump.

The Olds' big tank filled slowly. A minute, another minute. Thorn continued to stretch.

Back in the station, Cruz finished in the bathroom and was standing at the checkout counter with a Coke and a bag of chips. Beside Thorn the pump's numbers whizzed by, fifteen gallons, sixteen.

He looked back at Cruz. She was talking to the clerk and Pixie was beside her, Pixie looking out the station's front window at Thorn, her big sunglasses gone, curious. He'd seen Pixie before somewhere.

The pump bell dinged.

Thorn stretched some more.

170

X-88 stepped over to him.

"Hey, asswipe," he said. "Move aside."

Thorn broke his pose, turned to X, and held out his hand. The helpful passenger—doing his part, returning the nozzle to its slot.

X gave him a leery look, then handed it to him, and Thorn moved toward the pump, then waited till X had turned back to screw on the gas cap.

He took a quick half step, raised the nozzle, and hammered the trigger guard against the back of X's head. The big man collapsed against the car, but didn't go down. Thorn thumped him again above his right ear, and when he'd crumpled to his knees, Thorn squeezed the fuel trigger and drenched his clothes with gasoline. That should slow them down.

X sputtered, flung out an arm to defend himself, and tried to roll over. Thorn kicked him in the side of the head. X groaned, breathing hard, shaking. Thorn crouched beside him and dug the car keys from his pocket, hopped over his quivering body, and hustled to the driver's side.

Cruz had spotted the action and was sprinting out of the store. She'd drawn her weapon and had it aimed his way. Twenty yards off.

Thorn was quiet inside. All the overheated fury and pain he'd felt a hundred miles ago had turned to a block of ice. He'd finished brooding and no longer cared about Cruz, about her gun, the bullets, he didn't care about any of it. He started the car, eyes locked on Cruz. She shouted at him to halt. Took a shooter's stance.

Thorn slipped the shifter into drive, hit the gas hard, smoked the tires, swung the wheel to the right, and veered toward the highway.

She didn't fire.

In the rearview mirror, he watched the three of them. Cruz lowering her weapon and trotting over to X, who was on his knees, struggling to rise. Off to the side, Pixie stood alone, arms folded across her chest, her eyes following Thorn's flight. Striking the same pose as yesterday, the girl whose car Tina Gathercole had stolen.

A half hour later Thorn pulled into the gravel parking lot of a general store with a single gas pump outside. A rusty Dr Pepper sign hung cockeyed above the screen door, and next to the metal sign was a hand-stenciled placard that said GREAT HOPE SUNDRIES.

He parked, got out, opened the backseat driver's-side door. The floor mats were clean. Pixie and Cruz had taken their handbags into the gas station restroom, but Pixie left her baseball hat behind. That's all he found. He dug his fingers between the seats, worked his way down its length and encountered grit and a couple of old coins, sticks of gum, a bobby pin, and a Metallica CD. He crouched down and peered under the front seats, knowing this was useless.

Yesterday when he'd first heard Tina's phone ring, the volume was set on high, but this last time, the sound was heavily muffled. Still, he was trying to be systematic, hoping to find the phone lodged between the seats, or under the armrests or in the door pockets, which would suggest that X had been a party to stopping Tina on the high-way after she fled the gas station in Vero Beach. That she'd ridden for a while in the backseat until she'd been deposited at some law enforcement facility. It was the reasonable, legitimate explana-tion. The other, darker alterna-tive, however, was becoming inescapable.

He repeated the search of the backseat, again found nothing.

He shut the door and went to the trunk and unlocked it. He moved the luggage aside, but didn't see her phone. He ran his hand around the outer edge of the spare tire. Nothing.

Piece by piece he removed the luggage and set it on the gravel behind the car. Cruz's backpack, a battered fake leather suitcase he assumed belonged to X-88, and a pink hard-sided roll-on that must've been Pixie's. He hauled out the heavy duffel with the automatic weapons and the bricks of cash.

He removed some old ropes and a roll of duct tape and assorted bungee cords and a leather packet of tools. When the trunk was empty, he

173

patted the carpet from one side to the other and found nothing. He did it again, working methodically, and again felt no bulges or anything out of place.

He was about to give up and dig through the luggage, when he looked back into the trunk and spotted a small lump at the far edge of the mat.

Taking hold of the corner of the carpet, Thorn peeled it back, and there, tucked in a crevice at the right edge of the trunk, was Tina Gathercole's cell phone. He drew a long breath and let it go.

He flipped open the phone, located the control button, and navigated to the recent calls menu. Several numbers on the incoming list were from Sugarman. Since late last night, Sugar had called Tina seven times. From his home, from his office. The most recent calls, the two that rang an hour ago, were from Sugar's cell. The call that Tina had answered in the car yesterday just before they pulled off at that Vero Beach gas station was from a blocked number.

Tina's outgoing list was odd. Late yesterday afternoon the last calls were a series of garbled numbers. Most were too short to qualify as phone numbers at all. A dozen or more were only five or six digits. And there was a long list of only three digits. 288, 443, 922. As if she'd been dialing in the dark or randomly butt-calling.

He stared at the phone, the list of muddled numbers. Only one thing explained it. Tina had been in the trunk of X's car, a captive, probably with her hands bound, and somehow she'd managed to work her phone free and had tried calling for help. The three-digit calls were attempts at 911, the others he could only guess.

The list of recent outgoing calls was long. At least sixty or seventy. Frantic, she must've tried again and again in the cramped airless space. A valiant, agonized attempt to save herself. It was likely when she realized the car was reaching the end of its journey, she stashed the phone in a small fissure in the trunk's floor. Leaving it behind like a note dashed off and slipped into a bottle and cast into the turbulent sea. An attempt to chronicle her predicament, to send one last cry for justice.

Thorn had never liked the woman. She was shallow and self-indulgent. She'd exploited Sugarman's generous spirit for reasons that still weren't clear. But there was more to her than Thorn had seen. A core of toughness he'd missed. The woman had been dogged and resolute at the end. And yes, the bottle with her message had washed ashore and had come rolling up to Thorn.

In the upper corner of the cell phone screen the signal strength icon was showing only a single bar, and when Thorn punched in Sugar's cell number, the call wouldn't go through. He closed the phone and looked around at the empty fields, the bare trees, the desolate expanse of a farm community clearly struggling. Prosperity had bypassed this region, their crops were no longer in demand or their land grown fallow. Great Hope, North Carolina, was dead quiet except for a steady wind that rattled the tin Dr Pepper sign and sent a paper coffee cup skittering across the gravel lot.

He considered searching the luggage, see what more he could learn about his traveling companions, then decided it wasn't a priority at the moment. He needed to move, put more distance between himself and Cruz. Thorn had slowed them down. They'd have to find fresh clothes for X-88, clean him up, and they'd have to commandeer a car, but he had no doubt Cruz would soon be back in motion.

Before he could return to the road, he needed directions. He'd taken only a quick look at Sugar's paper map yesterday, and didn't remember the road names or highway numbers that led to Pine Haven.

He put Tina's phone in his pocket, repacked the luggage in the trunk, slammed the lid and locked it, walked over to the general store, and pushed open the screen door.

Two men and a middle-aged woman were huddled around a chess board that was set up on a wooden barrel, the men dressed in overalls and denim shirts and matching sweat-stained John Deere caps, the woman wearing black jeans and a ratty white sweater that fit too tight across her ample breasts. The younger of the men, a skinny dude, looked up as the screen door slapped behind Thorn.

The other two stayed focused on their game.

"Don't have no gas," the scrawny man said. "Ain't been none for going on twenty years."

"I'm looking for the road to Pine Haven."

The woman, who'd been about to move a pawn, set it down and looked up at Thorn.

"Pine Haven, is it? That what you say, Pine Haven?"

Thorn didn't reply.

The woman rose from her chair and came around the chess board and over to Thorn, inching in close. Her brown eyes were lit with moonshine and there was moonshine on her breath.

"Now what's a healthy specimen like you be wanting to go to a god-awful town like Pine Haven? A day in that hellhole, you'll be stumbling around like a one-legged mule."

The skinny man chuckled. He was a toothy fellow with hollow cheeks and long-distance eyes.

"Never mind," Thorn said. "I'll find my way."

"You a hog man, are you?" the woman said.

Thorn stopped and turned back to her.

"That's about all there is in Pine Haven," the skinny man said. "Hogs and more hogs."

The big man, older by twenty years than the other two, was still seated at the chess board. He looked up and said, "Hogs and hog stink. Yes, sir, that about covers it for Pine Haven."

"What if I am?" Thorn said. "What if I am a hog man?"

"You don't look like any hog man I ever seen," the skinny man said. "Does he, Reb? Does he look like a hog man to you?"

"Could be one of them corporate people, Pastureland."

"Is that right?" the woman said. "You a Pastureland man?"

"Pastureland," Thorn said. "What do they do?"

"What do they do?" The woman grinned at him. "What don't they do?"

"They run the show," the skinny man said. "They run everything there is to run in these parts. If it has to do with hogs. And other things too."

"What about Webb Dobbins? They run him too?"

All three of them turned to Thorn.

"You know Webb?" the woman said.

"Doesn't everybody?"

"Just so happens, back in the day, Webb was my old flame."

Thorn didn't reply.

"You going to see him?"

"He's on my list."

"Well, you tell him howdy, you hear? Tell him Mary-June says hi."

"I'll do that."

"Webb's the number one hog farmer in all of North Carolina, that's what they say. Number one, top of the list." She smiled to herself and looked off at the empty shelves of the store. "In these parts, he's our rock star."

"That Webb, he's a healthy specimen," the skinny man said. "Ain't he, Reb? Mighty healthy specimen, Webb Junior."

The woman craned her neck out and oozed in closer to Thorn.

"Back in the glory days," she said with a dreamy tone, "Webb, he'd come in this store, I was just a wee teenage thing working at the counter, and he'd reach out with those big hands of his and he'd honk my boobs.

"Do it every damn time, honk, honk. A grab-ass boy, that Webb. Now he's all grown and owns that whole town, owns it inside and out, upside and down. If I'd played my cards smart, I'd be lying there beside that warthog today in the lap of luxury."

"You didn't have no cards to play," the skinny man said.

"Hell, I didn't. He couldn't stay off me."

The skinny man said, "These days Webb Dobbins can honk any boobs he wants. He don't need your tired-out old flour sacks."

"You a friend of Webb's? You do business with him?" the woman said.

"I might be."

"There ain't nobody in Pine Haven worth seeing but Webb Dobbins."

" 'Less you count his sister," the skinny man said. "Oh, lordy, I'd like to have me some of that tasty stew, yes I would, like to bury my face in some of that and just gargle the night away."

The man named Reb stood up and smoothed his palms across his huge belly, looked down at it, and ran his hands over it again as if surprised to find it there.

"You take highway 13 right out front here, go north about ten miles, you come to the first crossroads, you throw a left, few miles later the next right. That'll be Perkins Hollow Road. You stay on that for fifteen miles, you come directly into Pine Haven. Town's four blocks long, not much to it."

When Reb was finished, he took a step to his left, raised his hand, and backhanded the skinny man across the face—a blow that sent him staggering against an ancient Coca-Cola cooler.

"And don't be talking that way about women, boy. It's unseemly and unchristian. Makes me damn near ashamed to call you my son, hearing them words stream out of your filthy mouth."

"We were just having fun, Reb. No need to get pissy," Mary-June said.

Reb turned back to Thorn, fixing him with an uncanny look. He reached out the hand he'd used to strike his son, gripping Thorn's shoulder, digging his fingers in with the passionate resolve of a faith healer hell-bent on curing Thorn's deformity.

"I knew Webb's daddy, Big Webb. For a time, me and him ran around together. That Big Webb, he was always one mean-ass son of a bitch, kind of man should've never married, never had no family whatsoever. All that man was good at was meanness from the time he was little till he went off to the war with the gooks and when he come back he was twice as mean as when he left.

"Far as I can see, anything his boy, Little Webb, does, or his poor sinful sister, I don't condone it, not one bit, but I understand it. The apple don't fall far, is what they say, and if the tree was rotten to begin with, then the apple's gonna be rotten when it falls and it'll only get more rotten as the years go by.

"And you listen to me, mister. I wouldn't mind if you were to repeat to young Webb any of what you just heard come out of my mouth, each and every word, if you do run across him there in Pine Haven. I don't mind a bit. You tell him Reb Parker was talking about him and if he has a problem with any of that, he can drive over and sit down and we'll have us a discussion about apples and meanness."

Thorn shrugged out of Reb's hold and took a half step toward the door and the woman scooted over and pressed a soft shoulder against him.

"Go ahead," she said, pulling her shoulders back. "Honk them for old times' sake. 'Cause of Webb and all. Just a quick honk and fare-thee-well."

"This man doesn't want to squeeze your titties, Mary-June. Nobody does."

"Just once in memory of them good old days that have come and gone."

"A tempting offer," Thorn said. "But I must decline."

He looked past Mary-June, thanked Reb for the directions, and headed for the door.

Fifteen

When the phone call came from Cruz, Webb Dobbins was in the greenhouse planting a trumpet tree cutting, and was up to his elbows in pig shit. The shit was nicely aged and blended in a ratio of one to five with vermiculite, the plastic tub also holding a few scoops of crushed peanut shells, a handful of dried-out straw, a gallon of topsoil, dozens of earthworms, and a healthy dose of peat-based biofilters inoculated with bacteria to metabolize ammonia and reduce offensive odors, an idea Webb had stolen from a Dutch researcher.

"You there, Dobbins?"

"Present and accounted for."

"I can barely hear you," Cruz said.

"I'm wearing a mask. But don't worry, I can hear you fine."

Cruz was silent for several moments, probably unsure if Webb was playing games with her. He wasn't. A full-face gas mask with goggle eyes.

"Thorn got away from us. I believe he's headed to Pine Haven."

"How'd that happen?"

"Not important. We'll be there soon as we can. A few hours at most. But he'll arrive first. So get ready."

"And do what exactly?"

"Watch for him, put out the word."

"To who?"

"To whoever you put the word out to. It's your town, I believe."

"That's it? Put out the word."

"Intercept him if you get the chance, sit on him till we get there. Do whatever you need to do to restrain the man."

"What's the guy look like?"

She said he was around six feet, well built, sandy hair worn scruffy and uncombed, blue eyes, face a little beat up.

"He dangerous?"

"He got away from the three of us," Cruz said. "He's Flynn Moss's old man. You figure it out."

She clicked off and Webb brushed some crumbs of potting mix off the phone and slipped it into his pocket.

He looked out at the greenhouse. Five hundred plastic pots lined up in neat rows, each thirty-pound tub of blended potting soil watered daily and left to season for half a year before it was put to use.

That greenhouse was where Webb's momma, Hazel, grew her hibiscus and her spider lilies, golden shrimp plants, oleanders, sunshine mimosa, lantana, orange jasmine, pentas, plumbago, and porterweed. All native blooms from her homeland in South Florida, the region where Webb's father, the twisted bastard, bumped into Hazel.

Hazel was the only child of two school-teachers, a Depression-era couple, religious penny pinchers. When he met them, Webb's daddy did some fast arithmetic and realized the size of the jackpot waiting for their only daughter when these two teachers kicked off, and he proceeded to court the hell out of Hazel, and more important, he set about winning the hearts of her parents, who by that time had begun to fear Hazel was doomed to spinsterhood, too gawky, cloddish, and unappealing to ever find a suitable husband.

Big Webb, passing through Miami after his discharge from the army, took only a month to win the three of them over, and after the wedding he spirited her away from the jasmine breezes of the subtropics and the wild and gaudy hues of the flowers she cherished and brought her to the bleak landscape of the Dobbins hog farm in Pine Haven, North Carolina.

Five years into their marriage Webb erected the greenhouse, calling it a Christmas gift, when in fact it was his last-ditch bribe to keep Hazel firmly trapped in the Dobbins harness after she'd suffered repeated bouts of wordless depression, despising her husband and the isolation and the drab surroundings and yearning constantly to return to the flamboyant natural world of her youth.

All of this Webb's mother confided to him on many long afternoons working side by side, grubbing in the rich dirt of the conservatory. The story of how Webb's father had constructed the glass house himself, pane by pane, wooden beam by beam, on a plot of land within sight of the pig pens and the slaughter barns and smokehouse, so no matter what labor he was engaged in, he could keep an eye on his erratic and gloomy wife, make sure she didn't hang herself from the rafters. At least not until her parents died and the inheritance was final.

These days the greenhouse no longer contained

his mother's colorful medley of flowering beauties, for they'd been replaced by a monochromatic single plant. Its downward hanging trumpet-shaped blooms were the pale yellow of a sad winter day. Hailing from the Solanaceae or nightshade family, the trumpet flower was as beautiful and tropical and eerie as anything Webb's mother had ever grown, but it was far more than a simple ornamental. This was a plant that could gratify the senses in any number of ways and greatly profit a man willing to risk the dangers of its blooms, its pollen, its seeds, its very scent, a man willing to exploit its potency.

As he always did when working inside the greenhouse, Webb wore latex gloves and one of the army surplus gas masks he'd bought online. NATO filter and a hydration port. NBC was its nickname. Full protection against nuclear, biological, and chemical attacks. Also good for smoke, paint spray, and grinding dust and the full range of airborne microorganisms. Probably a bit of overkill, but the outfit settled Webb's nerves.

Webb's workers had to make do with paper surgical masks, and as a result a few of them, now and then, had tragically succumbed to an overdose of the trumpet flower's pollen. Losing a well-trained man was always a setback, but it was the unlucky cost of doing the kind of business he was engaged in.

The trumpet flower Webb was cultivating went by many names.

Some South Americans knew it as the Borrachera tree, or the tree of the drunken ones. Fall asleep beneath its branches and wake up plastered. Tree Datura and burundanga were other aliases. A plant used by Mexican shamans to add color and vividness to hallucinations and utilized by criminals in Medellín to stupefy gullible foreigners, then direct them to empty their own bank accounts.

Its blooms and seeds and even the invisible spores of its sugary scent contained the alkaloids scopolamine and atropine, powerful toxins that in low doses could cause dizziness, sweating, dry mouth. But at higher amounts the same chemicals could produce delirium, unconsciousness, and a wide range of hallucinatory experiences. Push the dose a bit higher, you were cold-cocked dead.

Domestic pharmaceutical companies used compounds of scopolamine and atropine in treatments for Parkinson's, or as a sedative or to prevent motion sickness, and surely some of Webb's customers had these lawful medical applications in mind when they bought a few of his bright red tablets.

But like any entrepreneur, Webb could make no guarantees about the usage his product was put to once it was in the hands of the consumer. Laurie reported that some of her customers at

Fort Bragg employed the drug for carnal adventures. Zombie rapes, as they were known. Far superior to the other date rape alternatives, which left the victim unconscious, the trumpet flower kept the prey upright in a dreamy, compliant state.

When he'd finished mixing the batch of potting soil and firmly fixed the fresh-cut stalk of the trumpet flower in its center, he washed his latex gloves in the sink, went outside in the fresh air, stripped off his protective gear, and drew out his phone again and texted Laurie.

Where R U?

A few seconds later she came back with: *Moving product, where else?*

Get your ass home. 9-1-1

Webb went upstairs, showered, toweled off, and lay naked atop the double bed where his mother and father had slept, where they fornicated, where Webb and Laurie were conceived. It was Webb's room now, but he hadn't changed their lumpy mattress, their stained sheets, their sour pillows. All his. Where he came to gather himself.

Webb stared up at the ceiling that his mother had stared at while Webb's old man had lain atop her and pounded his mass against her frail body. He traced the cracks in the ceiling plaster as his mother had. She'd seen things there, flowers and hummingbirds and butterflies. She told him about them, reported how those cracks distracted her while Webb's father grunted and labored above her. Always missionary, his mother told him. Always the same groan and unholy curse at the end.

He had a giant penis, she told him. A horse cock. When she asked young Webb, at fifteen, to present his own penis one afternoon, he'd obeyed, the two of them alone in this bedroom. Let me see it. Don't worry, there'll be no touching or any of that. When she insisted, he unzipped and pulled it out.

Though his mother only looked, Webb's penis hardened and he tried to stuff it back in his pants before it came to full life.

She said no, let me watch. Let me see it in its full glory. Those were her words. Full glory. So he did. Without touching it, without using his hands, just his mother's eyes doing the work. It rose and it rose until it was fully erect.

Yes, she said. It's his. You're his son.

No, I'm your son, yours.

You have his cock. I can do nothing for you. You're his.

And thereafter, she never again confided her private longings or memories to him, but became cool and formal, causing Webb such a deep and abiding hurt that even now all these years later the memory of it could bring him to tears if he let it.

• • •

A half hour later, Laurie drove up in her white Jaguar, came slinking up the front stairs, and sat beside Webb on a rocker. There was a halo of weed clinging to her clothes and skin and her gray eyes were fogged.

Webb said, "How stoned are you?"

"Scale of one to ten, maybe six," she said, voice hoarse. "Haven't got the giggles, but I been fantasizing about a case of MoonPies."

"You need to sober up quick, this guy Thorn is on his way."

When Webb finished recounting Cruz's phone call, Laurie said, "This woman is incompetent or nuts or both."

"I've been calling around, everybody we can trust. You do the same."

"You hear what I said? This Cruz woman is a loser. I thought she had a surefire plan."

"Make your calls," Webb said. "Put the storm flag out."

Webb looked off at the greenhouse.

Staring at him, the last shreds of dope haze in Laurie's eyes clearing.

"You been wallowing in your childhood again," she said. "I can see it in your goddamn face, Webb, how your eyes go soft and your mouth droops with that sorrowful, woe-is-me thing. You're making yourself weak and sick at heart thinking of Momma."

"What I think about is none of your concern."

"It damn well is my concern. I'm out there pushing pills eight hours a day, risking life and limb. Now's not the time for weakness. This extravaganza with Flynn Moss and Thorn and this Cruz woman, this whole deal is because you had to go into hock to Pastureland, build another barn and another one, till we were giving them every fucking penny we made and still slipping so far behind on our payments we didn't have a choice but to start our jim-dandy little sideline.

"Now we're using that smokehouse to cure blooms instead of ham, the slaughterhouse to stamp out pills by the hundred, and we've got Momma's greenhouse chock-full of enough Schedule III drugs to keep the Carolinas stoned on their ass for the next year. And why exactly are we in the fix we're in right now? I'll tell you. Because you had to outdo our daddy and run the biggest, baddest hog farm the world has ever seen. A man that's been in the grave for years."

"I'm twice the man he was, three times."

"Yes, you are, Webb, and three times as dumb. Now suck it up, get all that Mommy's boy look out of your face, and this time, let's get this done right."

Sixteen

Thorn drove with Tina's phone in his lap so he could monitor the signal strength, but for the next half hour the icon flickered between one bar and none at all. There were no mountains or valleys to obstruct cell signals, so he assumed this part of the world had not yet attracted sufficient interest from the marble halls of commerce to warrant connecting it with the rest of civilization.

He followed Reb's directions, made the proper turns, and watched as the land grew ever more flat and treeless. A patchwork of fields ran alongside the highway, but they seemed to have been left unplowed, unplanted, and untended for years and whatever crops once gave them color and value had long ago been harvested, consumed, and forgotten.

A few houses appeared, cramped brick rectangles, some double-wides with battered pickups out front. Some satellite dishes. Thorn could only imagine what was taking place inside those isolated dwellings, with folks like Reb and his family, televisions playing endlessly to ease the boredom, stoke the fantasies, and withstand the solitude of this barren countryside.

There were houses boarded up with plywood and two-by-fours, yards cluttered with abandoned farm implements, plows and tractors, old army jeeps. In every direction the land was fenceless as if the owners had long ago come to accept that there was nothing worth keeping out or keeping in.

He found the turn for Perkins Hollow Road. A mile or two later he rounded a sharp corner and discovered a river flowing alongside the highway. For a few miles the road and river meandered in unison, then Thorn saw a place along the shoulder wide enough to pull off.

He got out and stood for a moment, taking it in, then crossed a weedy patch to the river's edge. He took the postcard from his shirt pocket and held it up beside the water. The photograph had been taken midsummer with the river gleaming and flowers blooming along the banks and a profusion of leaves on the oaks and hickories. Now the trees were bare and the river itself was a dull gray as if the sediment on its bottom had been churned by recent rains.

He put the postcard away and got back in the car. A couple of miles farther down the road he saw a girl of thirteen or fourteen skimming rocks across the smooth water. Beside her was an older boy casting a fishing line out into the river. He pulled off again.

The girl turned away from the water and

watched Thorn approach. She was an African American child wearing yellow jeans and a gray hoodie. The boy stayed focused on his work. His plaid pajama bottoms were droopy and heavy boots unlaced and he had on a Marine Corps T-shirt, though he was several years too young for the service.

"Is this the Neuse River?" he asked the girl.

She stared at him for a moment as if he'd spoken a foreign tongue.

He repeated his question and after more consideration she nodded.

"My daddy's just over yonder. Don't you think of trying nothing."

"I'm looking for my son." A lie to calm the fear. "I thought I might find him fishing along here."

"Is he addled too?" the girl said, gesturing with her shoulder at the boy. "Ain't no fishes here you can eat. Though I seen lots of copperheads on the bank right along here."

The boy reeled in his line and cast again. He turned his head slightly in their direction and Thorn saw the boy had the blank stare and mechanical movements of a child with some neural disorder.

At that moment the breeze must've shifted for it was only then Thorn caught the stench of rot and noticed farther downstream dozens of small silver fish, shad, he thought, floating belly-up just below the surface. Dozens more had washed onto the riverbank, their shiny bodies blemished by red sores and missing fragments like the half-moon bite marks weevils make in perfect green leaves.

At the girl's feet, a small wave brought more dead fish onto the bank. A few were still flopping. More bloody sores.

"There's a million of 'em dead, my daddy says. More than that maybe."

"What killed them?"

She shook her head hard. She knew but wasn't saying.

"What's wrong?"

She shook her head again.

"You've been warned not to talk about it."

She picked up another stone from the riverbank and slung it sidearm low across the river. It skipped three times then went in.

"Bet I can do four," he said.

"Hell, four's nothing. I do seven all the time."

Thorn found a stone and sidearmed it with a sharp wrist flip.

It made four quick skips then arced up and skipped three times more.

"Seven," he said.

"I seen six. I didn't see no seven."

"Well, I got to be going," Thorn said. "Nice talking to you."

He was turning away when she said, "It's them hogs, their shit."

"Their shit?"

"There's lakes full of shit out on their fancy hog farms, stuff leaks in the creeks back up in there, and that shit run down here into the river and the fish come floating up with them bleeding places. Been like that since ever I can remember."

"Pollution," Thorn said. "From the hog farms."

"Naw, it ain't polluting, it's hog shit."

"Has anybody tried to do anything about it? People from out of town making a fuss?"

"Saw a man once, he came around, wrote something about the fish, then he left. Said he'd put it in the newspaper. Never saw him again after that once."

"No one else?"

The girl looked out at the river and shrugged like she'd had her say, and by god, Thorn could just get on back into his car and leave her be.

He tried rephrasing the question, but she was done with him.

Thorn was turning to leave when a man his size, a black man in his thirties wearing overalls and a striped shirt, came walking along the bank.

"This gentleman bothering you, child?"

Thorn held his ground.

"Asking about the dead fish is all."

"Did he touch you in any way?"

"No, sir. He didn't touch me."

"What you tell him?"

" 'Bout the pig shit is all. He wanted to know

about other people, strangers, if they was any of them around."

"He did, did he?"

The man moved closer to Thorn, squinting into his eyes as if to see what kind of devil he might be dealing with.

"You a lawyer?" the man said.

Thorn shook his head.

"Newspaper writer, scientist, politician? You ain't the governor by any chance?"

"Just the father of a boy protesting around here."

"Oh, yeah? Protesting the hog farms?"

"I think so, but I'm not sure. He's on the run from the law. I don't have much contact with him, a postcard now and then."

The man nodded, softening some, but still watchful.

There was an inflamed knot on the side of his throat, a sore.

"I saw the dead fish, and I was asking about them."

"Way it starts is algae blooms. You heard of those?"

"I have," Thorn said. "We got some of that where I'm from. Nitrates from fertilizer and runoffs feed the algae and it eats up the oxygen."

"And where would that be, where you from?"

"South Florida, the Keys."

"They raise hogs down there?"

"No, no hogs."

"Yeah, well, you got it right. The chemistry of it. And when that algae's been blooming a while everything in the river comes crawling up onto the shore trying to pump water through their gills. Next morning everything's dead, crab, shrimp, eels, bass, catfish."

The girl said, "That's what we call a fish jubilee. 'Cause you can just wade right in and scoop up all the free food you can eat."

"Scoop it till it begins to rot," said the father. "A day or two then it's done. River's empty. Takes months before you see a single fish again. Been doing that for years. We get people down here writing for the papers, doing studies with their test tubes, taking photos, and we got a string of politicians talking to TV cameras, they drive off, put a bill in the state house, and their bill gets crushed 'cause it's the pig farmers got the money in this state. A billion dollars always beats out test tubes and newspaper stories. Seen it happen over and again."

"My son is with an outlaw group. They're trying to attack this in a different way. Civil disobedience."

"I might've heard of 'em. The elves. That their name?"

"ELF, yeah, elves."

"Your son mixed up with those people?"

"He is. That's what I'm here to find out."

The man nodded and looked off toward the river.

"Well, good luck to you then."

"You know something."

The man shook his head, keeping his back to Thorn.

"What do you know?" Thorn said.

He came around slowly, turned his head, and spit dark juice into the grass.

"Heard there's been a skirmish. Elves against some folks didn't take kindly to them stirring things up, talking shit about their business."

"A skirmish."

"Shots fired, people hurt, maybe worse. Just people talking maybe."

"Where'd this happen?"

"Where you're headed, seems like. Up that road a bit."

"Pine Haven," Thorn said.

He hummed a noncommittal note.

"That would be Webb Dobbins's town."

The man shook his head as if Thorn had uttered a curse.

"You be careful, mister. You say the things in Pine Haven you been saying to me, it won't go so smooth. You need to keep your head down, don't make a ruckus."

Thorn smiled his thanks.

"Though I look at you, you look like a man enjoys himself a ruckus."

"Can't say I enjoy them, but I do seem to attract them."

The man half smiled, turned away, and walked over to his son and set about helping him untangle a bird nest snarl in his fishing line.

Seventeen

Back in the car, driving slowly, he gazed off at the Neuse, its gray water, its slow steady flow. A long way from a picture postcard river.

Thorn's son had come marching into this god-forsaken region to do righteous combat against another despoiler of the land, the hog shit farmers. He'd won battles elsewhere in equally deprived areas, and seemed undeterred in his commitment to protect those who lacked the means or will to protect themselves. No doubt in the year he'd been fighting this war he'd faced plenty of the hostility and backlash any do-gooding outsider would experience. So on the face of it, his Pine Haven mission was simply another version of Marsh Fork, Kentucky, and the others Thorn had read about in his postcard research.

Except it wasn't.

He followed Reb Parker's directions and in

another half hour he was cruising down the four-block main drag of Pine Haven. Two pool halls, a bar, a diner, a pawnshop, and a barbecue place, and on the east end, a decrepit hotel. Looked like an inviting place to start a ruckus. But before he got to that, he decided to take a few defensive steps.

He headed west, out of town, passing through a residential area, a couple of blocks of two-story wood homes with wraparound porches and shade trees, and within a half mile he was in the countryside again, scattered houses, big empty fields, then the road deteriorated abruptly and he came upon a cluster of wood shacks with bare yards studded with abandoned appliances.

He turned off the main road and wandered for a while through the dusty maze of streets in the shantytown. When he found an isolated stretch of road, he stopped, got out, went to the trunk, and dug through the duffel. He peeled off a layer of fifty-dollar bills from one of the stacks. Did a quick count and stuffed the seven hundred in his back pocket and continued to wander the neighborhood.

In a minute or two he came upon a two-story structure that seemed to be the hub of local social life. There was a Coke machine on the front porch, shelves of food visible through the window. The neighborhood grocery and hangout. A table and chairs were set up out in the yard and it was covered with an array of liquor bottles and vending machine food. Charlie Parker was playing his sax on a speaker inside the grocery, "The Way You Look Tonight."

Some black men were gathered around an old Chevrolet with its hood up, a gray-haired man leaning into the engine compartment with a wrench in one hand, a rag in the other. Nearby a fifty-gallon oil drum was rigged as a barbecue pit with a half dozen men standing around it watching it smoke, drinking beer, a couple of women in bright summer dresses and sweaters buttoned up against the brisk afternoon. The temperature was in the mid-fifties with a clear blue sky. In a nearby field some children were playing tag and a big hound was loping after them.

Not so different than the weekend scene in Hibiscus Park back in Key Largo, a district of the island that Thorn frequented as a kid to hang with Sugar and practice his skills at horseshoes and half-court basketball. The meat grilling on the barbecue pit in Hibiscus Park was usually fresh grouper or grunt, not the slab of pork whose savory scent was filling the air in this neighborhood, but otherwise it was the same make-do housing, the same bare-bones decorations, a flashy chrome hubcap propped up here, a pot of colorful flowers standing there, some shabby Christmas wreaths hanging on doors, the same stalwart crew of men and women gathered in a perpetual block party, same kids playing their games with an abandon that appeared unencumbered by the crush of deprivation and hardship around them.

Thorn pulled up alongside the aging Chevrolet and got out.

A couple of the men watched him draw near. But most seemed to be studiously ignoring his presence.

He stood at the front fender of the old Chevy, near the mechanic, who raised up to see who was casting a shadow over his work.

"I'm looking to buy a car," Thorn said. "Know of anything for sale?"

The men looked beyond Thorn at the Cutlass Supreme.

"Looks to me you already got a car," one of the men said. "A big one."

"Too big and too hot," Thorn said. "I'll be happy to leave it if anyone wants it. It's yours. I'm paying cash for the right car."

The men glanced at one another but were silent.

"Three hundred," Thorn said. "I'll go higher for one that runs good."

"Got this here car," the mechanic said. "Valves are knocking, and it burns a mite bit of oil, but it'll get you from here to there."

"How far is that, here to there?"

"Down the road a ways, you treat her good."

"And that's all that's wrong with it? Valves?"

"Smells like a rat died in the glove box. Other than that."

"What're you doing to it now?"

"Tuning the carb."

"Let me hear it run."

The mechanic waved at a gawky kid in jeans and an old army shirt.

"Turn her over for the gentleman."

When it started a cloud of blue smoke erupted from the tailpipe and the engine knocked for a minute then smoothed out and the clatter went away. Thorn made a shut-it-off motion to the kid at the wheel.

"Got anything else?"

"All this one needs is some forty-weight oil, it's good as new."

"That's not valves, that's a rod knocking," Thorn said. "Oil pump is working well enough because after a few seconds it circulates the oil and suppresses the knock. But that engine is about ten miles away from throwing a rod. It needs to be rebuilt. It's not worth driving to the junkyard. I'll go as high as five hundred for a decent car."

"I told you it was a rod knocking," the kid in the army shirt said.

"Shut your mouth, boy."

Thorn looked around at the rest of the men. Nobody stepping forward.

"I could even rent something short term. I'll pay the three hundred and bring the car back in a few days. The three hundred's yours."

"A minute ago you were saying five hundred," a bald man said. He stepped away from his friends. An older gentleman, two decades past Thorn.

"You got a car, sir?"

"Taurus," he said. "Runs a hell of a lot better than this piece of crap."

"Five hundred for a few days."

"How many days we talking about?"

"Can't be sure. Soon as I settle my business here in Pine Haven."

"I baby that car. Ain't got no scratches on the body, mats are clean, change the oil every five thousand miles. I want it back same way it goes out."

"I can't promise that," Thorn said.

"Why not?"

The mechanic said, " 'Cause he's looking to get into some kind of trouble, Eddie. Can't you see it? Look at this man."

The others took the opportunity to give Thorn closer scrutiny, weighing his potential for danger to Eddie's car. Thorn tried to imagine what they were seeing, a scruffy, sleep-deprived white guy, his sandy hair grown shaggy, a three-day beard. Big through the chest and long-limbed. A scar on his cheek, another that intersected an eyebrow, his nose bent a few degrees out of line, not quite a thug, but definitely a brawler, a man who'd gone into the ring more than once and hadn't always held his own. All in all, if Thorn had been estimating his own potential for damaging the man's well-kept car, he would've said no way.

"Two thousand," Eddie said.

The others chuckled at his audacity, but Thorn said, "All right, two's fair. I'll do my best to bring it back safe and sound. If I can't manage that, the two thousand should get you into a pretty good replacement vehicle."

"Let's see the money," Eddie said.

As Thorn was walking over to the Olds, a younger man came striding around the corner of the grocery. Well built, clear eyed, a tight white T-shirt and dark jeans. A cigarette tucked in the corner of his lips. The men made way for him and he could see them whispering to him, no doubt bringing him up to date on the negotiations that were taking place.

Thorn popped the trunk, kept his back to the men, concealing the duffel as he counted out more cash. When he closed the trunk, the man was standing beside him.

"Ladarius Washington," he said. "That's mine. What's yours?"

Thorn told him his name.

"That first or last?"

"Works for either."

"What's your business around here? Besides buying a car."

For the last hour of his drive he'd been playing around with various cover stories though none of them seemed to stand out as more credible than the others. So he decided to shade things as close to the truth as possible.

"I'm looking for someone."

"Are you now? Here in Pine Haven?"

"That's right."

"Who would that be?"

"Are you the mayor here, the sheriff?"

"As close to either as this broken-down neighborhood will ever get."

"The person I'm looking for is a young man. He's not from around here. He might be hiding out, might be camped in the woods, I don't know. He travels with a group of his friends. He resembles me a little bit."

"You're his father, are you?"

"I am."

"What makes you think he's hiding out around these parts?"

"I heard something along the way."

"Heard something, did you?"

"I don't know where he is. I'm simply asking whoever I meet."

"Not a smart approach."

"It's the only approach I have. Now if you'll

excuse me, Mr. Washington, I'm in the middle of a transaction."

Ladarius said, "You didn't ask me if I knew anything about this man."

"Do you?"

Ladarius held Thorn's eyes for several seconds as if taking the measure of his secret self. He must've gotten a poor reading, for he turned his head away from Thorn, giving him nothing more than permission to pass.

"Twenty dollars for a shovel," Thorn said to the gathering.

Eddie stepped forward.

"A hundred," he said. Thorn, the easy mark.

"I got an old pressure cooker works good," one large woman said to laughter. "I'd take fifty."

"Fifty for the shovel," Thorn said. "I have no need for a pressure cooker."

After Ladarius drifted away, he asked a few of the men if they'd heard anything about some kids protesting the hog farms. But no one was talking, not one of them would even meet his eyes.

Once he had the luggage transferred to the Taurus, he headed south toward the highway and when he reached it, he pulled into the side yard of the house he'd been told belonged to Ladarius Washington. It faced the highway and was no better or worse than those around it. He mounted the front porch and was about to tap on the door when a young girl appeared behind the screen.

She was holding a stuffed animal against her chest and was peering out at Thorn with a curious smile, as if she'd never seen his species up close before.

"What's its name?" Thorn nodded at the stuffed creature.

"Leo," she said.

"It's a lion?"

"A giraffe," she said. "Long neck, see."

She gripped the giraffe's head and swung it from side to side.

"Does it get dizzy when you swing it around like that?"

She tittered at the thought.

"Yes, it's dizzy. It's dizzy and can't walk. It falls over on its head."

Ladarius appeared behind the girl.

"Leo's dizzy, Papa." The girl swung the giraffe in a wide circle, bumping it against the floor. "See. He's dizzy."

"You got your car. What you want now?"

Thorn said, "I've got a cell phone. If you hear anything might be helpful in my search, maybe you could call me."

The man's eyes were stony and distant.

"Why would I do that?"

"Kindness of your heart. Or I could pay you handsomely."

"How handsomely is that?"

"Very," Thorn said.

"You throwing around money like you didn't earn it honest."

Thorn gave Ladarius the number for Tina's cell and recited it again.

"Leo's dizzy, Papa. See how dizzy."

With a gentle touch, Ladarius Washington steered his daughter aside and shut the door in Thorn's face.

On the drive back toward Pine Haven, he pulled onto a road he'd spotted earlier. An asphalt street that ran straight into a wooded area for at least two hundred yards then ended. The concrete slabs and foundations of five houses had been laid out, but the development had failed, and weeds had overgrown the slabs and broken through splits in the asphalt and were thriving.

The green-and-gold sign out front said, DOBBINS COURT.

The street halted in a cul-de-sac, where he found the largest foundation. A monster house had been planned, a palace that would preside over the lesser homes of Dobbins Court. Beside the foundation a yellow Port-O-Let had tumbled onto its side and had been sprayed with layers of graffiti.

He parked, took the shovel and duffel from the trunk. He removed a few hundred dollars of the cash for incidentals that might arise and left the rest of it along with the automatic weapons

210

inside the duffel and hauled it over to the Port-O-Let.

He pried open its door, startling a family of field mice. After taking out the three cartons of ammo packaged in a heavy Ziploc bag, Thorn zipped up the duffel and propped it upright against the edge of the toilet seat.

At the western edge of the palace's foundation slab, he picked an open area at the base of some slash pines, cleared away the layer of pine needles, and dug a hole and buried the Ziploc bag of ammo. He scuffed up the dirt then scattered the pine needles over the hole. Even if someone stumbled on the shotguns, they'd be useless without the exotic ammunition.

He was no pacifist, but until he understood exactly what danger he was facing and had a plan to combat it, he'd rather keep the big guns in reserve.

Back at the car, he hauled out the luggage. He started with X-88's fake leather case. Its contents were minimal. A man traveling light. T-shirts, underwear, a shaving kit with a single throwaway razor, a toothbrush, a motel-size tube of tooth- paste, and a travel-size deodorant stick. Nothing else. He wasn't planning a long voyage. A night or two.

He looked at Pixie's pink roll-on, thought of his rearview-mirror glimpse of her as he was fleeing the gas station. Not Cruz's nitwit black-sheep daughter blathering about her bawdy history for the last few hundred miles. But an active player in Cruz's crew.

He lay her suitcase on the ground at his feet and unsnapped it. Clothes neatly organized. Jeans, shirts, basic undies, a pair of plain leather walking shoes, no cosmetics in her toiletry bag, not even lipstick. Organized, methodical. No crotchless panties, lacy bras. Nothing to indicate the floozy she'd made herself out to be.

Cruz's backpack was a fancy model with straps to wear the usual way and an extension handle and wheels to roll through airports. He unzipped the main compartment and found a couple of changes of casual clothes, gray jeans, two identical black long-sleeved T-shirts, pajamas, underwear, a small cosmetics bag, some wires to recharge her cell phone, a pair of running shoes with socks stuffed inside. The outer zippered compartments were empty.

As he was tucking her clothes back in place, his hand bumped a bulge where the retractable handle was anchored. It might have been a part of the assembly, but something about it seemed out of place.

He emptied the bag again and ran his finger around the inner edges of the pack, tugging on the seams until he discovered a Velcro strip, an access point for servicing the retractable handle. He peeled open the slit and slid his hand under the lining, felt around till he came upon a plastic bag held in place by duct tape.

He peeled the tape loose, drew out the object, and held it up to the winter sunshine. Inside the plastic bag was a bright orange T-shirt. Thorn didn't open the bag. He didn't need to. Whoever folded it to fit inside the plastic container had left a large portion of the front exposed. There was a logo in white, a round sun halfway buried into the waterline, and printed in bold white letters: CARIBBEAN CLUB, KEY LARGO, FLA.

Thorn had given Flynn a shirt exactly like this one as a silly gift the day he and his mother had come down for a visit. The day when Flynn was cool and distant and acting disinterested in Thorn's house, his boat, his lagoon, and most of all his presence. A gift the boy took reluctantly and without comment, then set on the fish-cleaning table as he wandered aimlessly around Thorn's property.

But when he left later that afternoon, Flynn had walked over to the fish table and picked up the shirt and carried it to his mother's car. It was the same T-shirt Flynn had changed into the last night Thorn saw him a little more than a year ago as he climbed into the Ford van and drove away with Cassandra.

How had Cruz come by the shirt? Why had she taken such care to protect it and to secrete it in her luggage?

He set the backpack on the ground and stood at the open trunk trying to piece this mess together. Lies jumbled with more lies. Were they all lies or was there truth blended in? The Snitches Web site? The red *X*s across their faces, the story of Cruz's own daughter. The postcard with no postmark, Sugarman's address printed in block letters that were different from Flynn's handwriting. Tina's emergency bathroom stop, directing them to a particular Shell station and fleeing in that conveniently available car. If it was all as choreographed as it appeared, and Tina had been part of the scheme from the start, why had she been locked in the trunk?

He slowed down, then walked through it again.

For some reason Cruz had lured Thorn to Pine Haven, summoning Sugarman in order for Tina to join the party, then discarding both of them along the way. If true, it was an absurdly elaborate ploy to get Thorn engaged. Why hadn't she simply shown up at his house, laid out the scenario one-on-one? Flynn was in danger and in hiding. Then explain her plan to use Thorn as bait to convince Flynn to reveal himself. Why the convoluted scheme with so many moving parts?

Maybe it was all a magician's trick. Misdirecting his attention with shiny objects, the duffel and the shotguns and the cash, then distracting him again with Tina's flight and with the Snitches Web site, the red *X*s. All to confuse him, keep him off balance, moving forward. Because if he'd stopped to question her, stopped to do due diligence, he might've balked. Might've suspected she was hunting down Flynn to capture him and throw him in jail, and simply using Thorn to accomplish that objective.

The more he considered it, the more muddled he got. Where was the proof of a single thing she'd said? If she'd been lying about the real reason behind this journey, then perhaps she was lying about Flynn's wounds as well.

God, how he wanted to believe that.

But the sad truth was, logical reasoning had never been Thorn's strong suit. Puzzles confounded him. Riddles left him irritated and bewildered. His customary method for solving problems was simply to trust his gut, and if his instincts failed, his next reflex was to start kicking down doors, a monkey wrench in each hand.

He returned the T-shirt in its plastic bag to the slot in her backpack and retaped it in place, then he repacked her clothes as neatly as he'd found them. He set X-88's bag back in the trunk in exactly the same position. He shut the trunk and took a deep breath, then took another. He looked off at the clear blue December sky and tried to read some message there. But as usual, the sky was keeping its advice to itself.

So on his own he decided.

215

For Flynn's sake he would keep the monkey wrenches holstered for now. He would calm down. He would drive to town, present himself politely to the fine folks of Pine Haven, spread around his name and his Florida charm, and he would watch with great attention to see whose hackles began to twitch.

Eighteen

The Happy Biscuit Café was a modest white storefront with a picture window that stretched from the front door to its far wall. A smiling caricature on its sign showed a biscuit with flaky layers shaped into a pair of smiling lips surrounding a neat row of teeth. A weird and unappetizing logo.

He wasn't hungry, but decided to make it his first stop. He'd save the pool halls and bars in case things got desperate. Over the years Thorn had found that diners and luncheonettes had far more reliable local intelligence than bars and pool halls, where, in addition to an inebriated and hence less trustworthy clientele, an outsider could easily ask one question too many and find himself departing the premises headfirst.

He parked Eddie's immaculate Taurus across

the street from the diner and tried calling Sugar's cell phone. Again the call failed. Only one signal bar was flickering. Either Tina had chosen a cut-rate phone plan that didn't have coverage beyond South Florida or else Thorn had chanced upon yet another dead zone.

The only customer in the Happy Biscuit, Thorn chose what he considered the premier spot, a backless counter stool of fake red leather in the exact center of the counter. He tried it out, swiveling to his left then his right. It squeaked harshly, which drew the attention of the blond waitress who was cleaning the coffee machine. She looked up at the clock over the coffee station. Three-fifteen.

"A little early for dinner," she said, coming over with a menu.

Her tag read MILLIE, a name more suited to her grandmother's generation. She was in her mid-thirties with a tired smile. No rings on her fingers, a barrette in her hair that was hand-painted by a kid. EMMA spelled out in awkward yellow letters.

Millie was a pretty woman, maybe a decade past her innocent years, with the battle-weary look of a single mom who'd survived the worst that men could do. She'd heard all their small-town lies. Experienced every disillusionment and betrayal. Weathered the slow erosion of her reputation when one ex after another spread poisonous libels about her. At least that's how it worked for certain women Thorn knew in Key Largo.

"What's the worst thing on the menu?" Thorn said.

She wiped the counter in front of him, keeping her eyes down.

"Well, there's a line I haven't heard before."

"I like to start at the bottom, work my way up."

"And what's that accomplish?"

"If I'm expecting the worst, I'm rarely disappointed."

"Lucky you."

"I'm looking for somebody," he said.

"Now, that," she said, and met his eyes, "I've heard more than once."

Thorn smiled.

"He's a young man, a much better-looking, less battered, and far more idealistic version of me."

She gave him a closer look, and whatever she saw made her flinch and clutch her rag and take a half step back from the counter.

"The pulled pork sandwich," she said. "It's dry and tasteless."

"I thought this was hog country."

"They're dry and tasteless hogs."

"That's the worst you can do? Pulled pork sandwich."

"It's stringy and tough."

"Okay then," Thorn said. "I'll start with that."

"Fries or coleslaw?"

"His name is Flynn Moss. He probably showed up a week or two ago. He's an environmentalist. Cares more about the woods and rivers and birds and all that than he does about himself. Trying to do good for mankind."

The light had begun to twitch in her eyes, her mouth trying on and discarding various moods. Unskilled at concealing her emotions.

She ducked her eyes and said, "Coleslaw is homemade. Got raisins in it, a little on the sweet side."

"I'll go with the fries."

"Limp and greasy, cooked in oil that turned black three days ago."

"Sounds perfect," Thorn said.

She braced herself and looked directly at him again.

"Anything to drink?"

"How's the water?"

"Go with the root beer. Water's got a metal taste. Myself, I'm used to it, but people from out of town, well, they can have a hard time."

"How hard?"

"Very," she said. "A very hard time."

"Then I'll take the water," Thorn said.

"Of course you will," she said with a faint smile. "Of course."

She was right about the pulled pork. But Thorn slathered it with sauce and wolfed it down, discovering he was more hungry than he'd thought. The fries, however, were as gummy and far removed from the world of food as candle wax. The water tasted of copper and iron and something else he couldn't identify but that reminded him of the fumes released from paper mills.

Finished, he pushed the plate aside and waited for Millie to return.

Beyond the pass-through opening he could see a dark-haired heavyset man scraping the griddle with a spatula. Another man, Hispanic, was chopping vegetables, a phone wedged between his shoulder and his ear. Both had their backs to Thorn and there was no sign of Millie.

While he waited he flipped open Tina's phone. On the screen was a NO SERVICE message. He set the phone on the counter and waited some more.

The vegetable chopper stopped for a moment, cut a look at Thorn, then spoke to the man at the griddle, who also turned his head and appraised their sole customer. Thorn waggled his fingers at the men, but neither waved back.

He opened the phone and tried again but it was as useless as before. At home in the Keys, Thorn didn't have a landline and he didn't own a cell phone. He'd never been comfortable conversing electronically. Ready to hang up as soon as the connection was made. Phones were unreliable. They flattened out voices, pared away the highs and lows of emotional content. People got away with lying on phones more easily than in person, no facial clues, no telling gestures, and sometimes Thorn had spoken on phones to people who were obviously doing three other things while speaking to him, a rudeness that would rarely happen face-to-face. He'd happily toss Tina's phone in the nearest waste can except he had to speak to Sugar, needed to tell him what he'd learned about Tina, get Sugar to alert the proper authorities, start things moving.

He tucked the phone in his pocket and waited some more.

No Millie. And the fry cook and vegetable kid had also disappeared.

Thorn called out a hello.

He got down from the stool, called out Millie's name.

When he got no response, he went around the counter and pushed through the swinging doors and came into the kitchen. A knife and a half-cut celery stalk lay on a wooden cutting board. A pot of collard greens was simmering on the stove, the blue flame extinguished beneath it.

Maybe everyone was taking a smoke break. He was turning to go back to his stool when he heard a hiss from the far side of the kitchen. Thorn headed in that direction, toward the stainless-steel door of the walk-in cooler. The linoleum creaked behind him.

He swung around. But there was no one there and no one in the diner he could see, no one in the tiny kitchen. The only movement in the area was a cloud of steam rising above the pot of collard greens.

The hiss came again from behind a half-open door beside the cooler. An office, or maybe a broom closet.

Thorn flattened his back against the wall, edged forward until he arrived at the door. He reached out and nudged it open. Stepped in front of it, raising his fists.

At the sight of him Millie stepped back. She'd changed out of her waitress smock and was in her street clothes. A navy turtleneck, old jeans, with silver running shoes.

"They're coming for you. You've got to go."

"Coming for me. Who?"

"They mean you harm, I can tell you that much. It was Rodrigo, the kitchen boy, he's the one who alerted them. Don't blame him. Everyone's scared. He did what he was told, that's all. What everyone was told."

"Who's coming?"

"I've got to go," she said. "You too. Right now. They gave you something. A drug. Rodrigo crumbled up a pill and slipped it in your sandwich. I didn't know about it until a minute ago. It hasn't hit you yet, but it will soon. You need to get somewhere safe. Quick."

"What pill?"

She shook her head, not going there.

"Have you seen the young man I described?"

She sighed in resignation, and nodded yes.

"Before Thanksgiving. Just a fleeting glance. But it was him. That's how it started."

"How what started?"

"I've got to get out of here. I'm sorry. I've done all I can. I have to live in this town. You're on your own now. Get somewhere safe and stay there. It could last for hours. Go on."

"Is he injured, the boy you saw? I was told he was shot and seriously injured? You hear anything about that?"

"It may be true, I don't know. All I know is all the others disappeared."

"What others?"

"The ones he was with. Protestors, like you said, environmentalists. They were around for a couple of weeks, trying to organize people, asking questions, sticking their nose into things. They had a camp in the woods back of Belmont Heights, then they were gone. All at once, overnight. People said things, but I don't know what to believe."

"What things did people say?"

"Now look, I've got to go."

He blocked her path.

"When did this happen, the night they disappeared?"

"I don't know, before Thanksgiving, a couple of days. Something like that."

"Almost two weeks ago."

She hesitated, then stiff-armed him, pressing her hand flat against his chest, leaving it there for a moment as if feeling for a heartbeat.

"Okay, listen," she said, her hand softening. "The drug's called Devil's Breath. The dose he slipped you, it works like roofies only it won't knock you unconscious, but it steals your free will. You do whatever you're told. You're powerless, there could be hallucinations. Till it's out of your system, you need to hide somewhere quick, stay there."

She shoved past him and was across the kitchen, heading to the back door when Thorn said, "You have a daughter. Emma."

She stopped and flung him a hopeless look.

"The young man I'm looking for, Flynn. He's my son."

"I know he is," Millie said.

"You'd do anything to protect Emma, wouldn't you?"

She swallowed, held her ground but didn't reply.

"I'm the same," Thorn said. "Anything it takes, I'll do it. Anything."

"You stay here much longer," she said, "you'll not get your chance."

And she was out the door.

Thorn went back out the swinging doors and headed to the Taurus. He felt fine. Maybe he was immune to whatever they'd slipped him. But he'd decided to take Millie's advice and drive the Taurus out of town, find a side road somewhere, and park until he was sure he was okay.

He was in the middle of Main Street when the wide and cloudless sky began to wobble. He stopped and looked up just as the heavens started to rotate counterclockwise. Then the sky turned a bright flickering crimson and cracked apart in a dozen fragments like the shell of a giant egg going to pieces.

Thorn looked down quickly, focusing on the ground in front of him, and continued to plod across the street. It was wider than he remembered, seemed like half a mile of asphalt between him and the car. As he watched, the street expanded, becoming a black ocean of asphalt where sailing ships set forth long ago and were never heard from again. Where mythological creatures rose from waves of black asphalt and sucked down all voyagers foolish enough to attempt a crossing.

He stopped and looked back at the restaurant. Maybe he should go back. It was an impossibly long way to the car. It might be quicker to return to the diner, take back his squeaky swivel seat. Just wait this out. Maybe order more water, try something else on the menu.

The Happy Biscuit logo was smiling at him. The flaky lips were spread wide, and as he watched they spread wider. The Happy Biscuit thought Thorn was hilarious. He was stranded in the middle of Main Street in Pine Haven, not sure where to go, and his plight was making that biscuit even happier than usual.

Thorn turned back to the Taurus. He ducked his eyes again, focused on the asphalt as he plodded on across the endless black surface until at last he made it to the car. He steadied himself with a hand on the door handle. He was breathing hard. He could feel his heart working. He ventured another look skyward. As he watched, the giant red egg turned black, became a perfect midnight sky, then began to fill up with the brightest stars he'd ever seen.

Thorn swallowed back the gob of nausea clogging his chest. He'd been stoned plenty of times, been drunk more than that, about as drunk as it was possible to get. A few times when he was younger, he'd experimented with LSD and mescaline, so he'd seen this heavenly highlight reel before, observed a few gaudy hallucinations, brick walls melting like hot wax, the air dense with spirit orbs and auras and sparkling dragon-flies zipping at light speed.

He opened the car door and looked inside. There was a woman in the passenger seat. He didn't recognize her. She might not have been there at all. He straightened up, took another look at the sky. Which was a mistake, for now it was a sphere of stained glass, and it was gyrating, thousands and thousands of bright broken pieces of red, green, and blue glass twirling. He didn't feel euphoric. There was no rush, no exhilaration. And he didn't feel frightened or anxious or the least bit mystical. The world was erupting all around him, spinning off its dizzy orbit, but he felt quiet inside. Mildly interested in the weird events, but not particularly alarmed.

He looked back into the car. The driver's seat was empty. But he was uncertain how to enter the vehicle. The geometry and physics of getting inside seemed ridiculously complex. He was too big to fit. The space was tiny and a steering wheel blocked his way. Where was he supposed to put his feet? Which hand went where? He stood looking into the baffling car. The woman was still in the passenger seat, leaning down to watch him, and grinning like a hungry wolf. She wasn't anyone he knew, wasn't anyone he wanted to know.

He shouldn't drive. Not in his condition. Not with the sky the way it was. He decided to go sit somewhere. Find a shady patch of grass and sleep this off. He was about to slam the door and seek out a grassy plot when a powerful hand gripped his right biceps and spun him around.

He was face-to-face with a reddish-haired man

with beefy arms and a belly that hung over the waistband of his camo pants. His black T-shirt was tight across his wide chest; whatever muscles he had were buried beneath layers of flab.

"Your name Thorn?"

"It was," he said. "A while ago."

"For a lowlife he's sort of cute," came a woman's voice from behind him. "What shall we do with him?"

The meaty hand held Thorn in place.

The man considered her question, staring into Thorn's face with a mix of rage and bewilderment as if Thorn was only a stand-in for what was truly pissing him off.

This guy was a heavyweight, a gamecock by the look of him, but he'd gotten sedentary and gone to seed during his journey to middle age and he looked like a one-punch wonder who would never make the second round of any match without getting so winded and red-faced he'd trip over his own feet. Thorn was fairly sure his most threatening trait was his murderous scowl. He decided to make a fist and take a swing at the man's big face, but when he tried, he couldn't locate his hands.

The man's face turned ugly—so strangely, cartoonishly, grotesquely deformed it made Thorn titter. Like Ladarius's daughter had tittered earlier. He remembered her titter. It was sweet and innocent. Thorn couldn't recall the last time he'd tittered himself. Maybe never. It was a little sad to think he'd never tittered in his life, sad but also amusing. So amusing he tittered again.

From behind him the woman said, "Let's get started."

"She'll be here soon," the man said. "Let her handle this."

"We don't need Cruz," the woman said. "His eyes are spinning. The asshole is ours. Let's put him to work. Introduce him to Pine Haven. Start getting the word out."

The woman floated in front of Thorn. More ginger hair. This woman was very thin, very hard. A grin that made Thorn's stomach knot harder than it was already knotted.

"So, Thorn," she said. "My name is Laurie."

"Laurie," Thorn said. "Laurie."

"And this is my brother, Webb."

"Webb," said Thorn. "Laurie and Webb."

"That's right. Now I want you to go across the street, throw a rock through the window of that pool hall. Say hello to the fellows inside. They'd like to meet a man like you. Tell them your name, tell them you're looking for someone. How does that sound to you?"

"Like fun," he said. Or someone did. He felt the words rise from within, but couldn't take credit for them.

"Do you like breaking things, Thorn?" Laurie asked him.

"Breaking things, sure."

"Good, good. You're going to have a chance to break a lot of things. We're going to write your name in the sky so everyone can see you're here, everyone for miles around."

"Start a ruckus."

At that moment his head had grown top heavy and he was having trouble stabilizing it on his neck. It wanted to tip forward, chin to his chest. He had to lift the entire thing just to see the woman, lift it again, lift it. Very hard to keep the thing upright, like balancing a bowling ball on a broomstick.

He tried to remember who these people were. Were they friends of his from somewhere? They seemed to know him. That was good. In his present state he needed friends looking out for him. But he wasn't sure exactly who they were. His head was fuzzy, full of smoke, nothing much of consequence seemed to be going on inside his skull at the moment. Laurie and Webb. They must be his friends although he couldn't place them. Lately, he'd been seeing people he'd known most of his life, and their connection to him slipping just beyond reach. It didn't matter. He'd remember these people later when the sky was back to normal, when the smoke cleared.

"Thorn wants to break some things and start a ruckus," Laurie said. "Find him a rock, Webb. Find him a great big rock."

Nineteen

Thorn broke a window, a plate-glass window with the name of the pool hall painted in white letters. It wasn't the first window he'd broken in his life. He could remember at least one other from long ago, a window he'd smashed by driving a lucky golf ball into it when he was trying to save Sugarman, trying to draw the attention of a bad guy who was holed up in his condo at Ocean Reef Yacht Club, lure the bad guy out in the open. He remembered that window very clearly as he stood on the street in Pine Haven with a crowd of men pouring out of the pool hall and surrounding him.

Thorn was holding another rock in his hand. He'd been encouraged by his old friends—or were they new friends?—to hurl this rock at the next window on the block that belonged to a pawnshop and gun store. But the black men who were surrounding him blocked his way. They were pissed.

One of them had a bleeding cut on the arm.

"What you doing, asshole?"

"Who you think you are, throwing rocks through a window?"

"My name is Thorn," he said. "I'm new in town."

His friends told him to say that. Give his name to anyone he met.

"This guy's crazier than a shithouse rat."

"Somebody call Burkhart, put the asshole behind bars."

Someone tore the rock from his hand and hurled it away.

"That was my rock," Thorn said.

"Yeah, what you going to do about it?"

Thorn was experiencing something new, a form of X-ray vision. He could see through the clothes and the flesh of these men and see their skeletons and their internal organs. He could see hearts and livers and stomachs and intestines and other body parts he couldn't identify.

It was amazing. Like an excellent dream, a superman skill.

Then somebody put their hands on him and turned him from the mob of angry black men. It was Laurie, the woman with ginger hair. He looked through her clothes, at her skeleton and her organs. Laurie didn't seem to have a heart. He stared at where her heart should be and there was a black space.

"His name is Thorn," she announced. "He's looking to stir up trouble."

"He got a good start on that," one of the men said.

"His name is Thorn," she repeated, and led him away.

The sounds of her words were echoing in his head. He heard them once and then a few seconds later he heard them again and then fainter a third time. Like he was wandering inside a very deep canyon.

Behind the mob of black men, he saw a woman standing on the sidewalk. She was blond and Thorn recognized her. He had a pleasant memory of the woman from somewhere. He even knew her name. Mildred or Marlie, something like that. He waved at her, but she turned and hurried off.

Oh, yeah, he remembered, the waitress who'd given him an inedible barbecue sandwich.

"That's Millie," he said to his escort, the hard, thin woman with the fox face and the reddish hair and no heart.

"You know Millie?"

"I don't know anyone," Thorn said. "I don't know where I am."

"What's your name?" the woman said as she led him down the sidewalk.

Thorn told her his name.

"Yell it," she said. "Yell it real loud."

"My name?"

"That's right. Yell your name. Right now, yell it out."

Thorn yelled his name. As old as he was, all those years of doing crazy shit, he couldn't recall ever yelling his own name before. A first.

"Good," Laurie said. They were well away

from the group of angry men. "Now yell 'help me.' Yell it very loud."

Again Thorn obeyed. It felt good to obey. To be relieved of his own decision-making duties. It felt odd but good. He was starting to like Laurie, this woman who was giving him orders. Maybe she was a former lover or a current lover. Maybe she was his sister. Though he didn't have a sister. Yes, he did. He'd had one a long time ago but she was dead. What was her name? She'd been murdered, or maybe she got sick and died. He'd have to think about that later. Ricki, that was her name. Maybe he had two sisters. This one seemed to know him very well and she'd saved him from the pack of angry men. He hadn't had to fight any of them. He believed he was a fighter, a pretty good fighter. But he felt sluggish and slow, so fighting probably wasn't a great idea.

A man appeared beside the woman. It was Webb again. Heavyset, ginger hair. Thorn tried his X-ray vision on the man but it had stopped working. Too bad. He was enjoying that.

"Just spoke to Cruz," he said to the woman. "Told her what was going on and she said to stop and take him back to the farm."

"Why? This is working. This is getting the word out."

"She's worried we can't handle him. He'll escape, someone will snatch him from us."

"Fuck her."

"Fuck her," Thorn said. "Fuck Cruz. She's a liar. Don't trust her."

"What do you know about Cruz?"

"Fight on, fight on, ye brave," Thorn said. "I know that."

"He's useless," the woman said.

"Cruz'll be here in an hour. Let's take him back to the farm."

"But this is so much fun," Laurie said. "I'm digging this."

"Back to the farm," Webb said.

"I like farms," Thorn said. "You got any tractors? I like tractors."

Somewhere, deep inside Thorn's smoke-filled, hazy brain, a speck of light was shining. Another Thorn was waking up from a long sleep, blinking his eyes, stretching, letting go of the dream he'd been having. Deep inside, not fully awake. But that light had a voice and it was speaking to Thorn. Speaking in a whisper, saying, "You're drugged. You're fucked up and in trouble. Go with this, but look for a chance to escape. You're drugged. These people are the enemy."

"Are you the enemy?" Thorn said to the woman who was leading him across the street.

"Where'd you get that idea? We're your friends. See how friendly we're being, helping you get away from that mob."

"Yeah," Thorn said. The light down in the basement inside him was shining brighter. The voice that sounded like his own voice was whispering, "Go with it. Go with it, but look for a chance to make a break. These people are the enemy."

"I think he needs another hit," the woman said to the man.

"Can't risk an overdose."

"All I gave Rodrigo was that one tablet. This guy can handle it. He's got to be close to two hundred pounds, at least one-ninety. Two won't kill him. Just to be safe. To keep him docile."

"How much do you weigh, Thorn?" Webb asked him a question.

Thorn said he didn't know.

"You never weighed yourself? Come on, how much?"

"I've put on a few pounds. Getting older, hard to lose it."

"He's useless," Webb said.

Laurie was digging in her purse. She came out with a clear plastic envelope the size of a postage stamp. A red pill inside.

"Give it to him, Webb."

They'd walked across the street and were standing beside a car. Thorn was looking into the car. He remembered it. A Taurus, very well kept. It ran fine. This was the car he couldn't get inside. It was the complicated car. He looked inside and the upholstery was rippling the way the air above hot pavement could ripple.

"Take this," said Webb. "Open your mouth, Thorn."

Inside Thorn the pinpoint of light was expanding. Inside the light a voice told Thorn to refuse the pill.

"I refuse the pill."

"You'll do what I tell you. If I say jump, you're going to jump. If I say shit in your drawers, you'll fill 'em up. You got me, pal? We understand each other?"

"Okay."

"So open your mouth and take the fucking pill."

Thorn opened his mouth.

The man pinched the pill and moved his fingers to Thorn's open mouth.

Don't take the pill, the voice said inside him.

The man slipped the pill onto Thorn's tongue.

Thorn bit down hard on his fingers, very hard, and he spit the pill out.

"No pills," Thorn said.

The man howled, holding his finger, and he hunched over, stamping the ground. He cursed and swung around and hooked a fist at Thorn. Thorn watched it coming, watched it coming and coming through the sluggish air, and the voice inside him said, "Duck, asshole, duck."

But Thorn kept watching the fist, the knuckles taking a big arc toward his chin, the big man putting his weight behind the punch. Not much of

237

an athlete, this guy. Thorn had seen better punches. This one was molasses slow, still coming, still coming. Then against a black sky he saw an explosion of bright, electrified criss-crossing comets. Colored stars and beautiful arcs of sparks like a willow tree on fire and there was another flaming willow tree beside it, sizzling branches, red, yellow, fiery green. A forest of blazing willow trees.

You should've ducked, the voice said. *I told you to duck.*

It was dark. Thorn's teeth were aching. It was black dark.

I told you to duck. Listen to me next time, idiot.

Twenty

Thorn woke to ammonia fumes and the screams of children. No, not children. People were being tortured. Lots of them. Bellows and shrieks, war cries and groans. He squirmed and shut his eyes tighter to push the sounds away. A nightmare, it had to be.

But as he drifted to consciousness, the howls continued, a gruesome chorus close by. He tried to recall where he was, how he'd gotten here. But he was empty headed, his memory inaccessible.

He opened his eyes and shut them quickly. The wails and snorts and blubbering continued beyond his door. It wasn't children. Not human voices.

He opened his eyes again and blinked them clear, backhanded his face. Lying flat on his back, he stared up at a concrete ceiling. He reached back and traced his fingertips across the rough fabric he was lying on. It seemed to be a camp cot without a mattress.

His back was aching, his jaw too. He shut his eyes and tried to recollect the last thing he remembered. All he could dredge up was a biscuit with teeth. On a sign, a biscuit smiling.

He wasn't in Key Largo, that was clear. This place stunk like a cooped-up barnyard. That ammonia reek was burning his throat. He sat up and his stomach shuddered and clenched, but Thorn tipped his head back and drew a few cautious breaths and after several seconds his nausea backed off.

The walls were concrete. The door was a dull gray metal. A cell.

Everything was gray. Or maybe that was him, maybe the gray was springing from his own diseased mind. He was projecting his sad inner grayness on everything.

He rubbed his eyes again and groaned as he settled his feet on the floor.

No, the gray was real. The windowless walls,

the floor, a rough, unpainted concrete. A storage room converted to a cell. Just him and a cot.

No, he wasn't alone. Across the room, lashed to a chair, was a small Mexican man. He wore white boxer shorts with red valentines on them. His head was slumped forward, drowsing or unconscious.

Thorn began to remember. He remembered the Happy Biscuit Café, yeah, that was it. Pine Haven. And all of it swirled back, an unsequenced hailstorm of images. A picture postcard, an endless car drive with strangers, a burger joint on fire, a man named X-88, an uneaten waffle, a dry and tasteless barbecue sandwich, dead fish floating in a river, a cell phone hidden in a trunk, a heavy rock in his hand, the Lorelei, some kid wanting to take his photo, a woman who invited him to squeeze her breasts.

He needed to halt the chaotic slideshow and piece the images back together in some reasonable order if he was to understand his predicament, how he arrived at this cell, what it meant, what to do next.

From beyond the gray metal door came more shrieks and squeals and the clang of steel like prison bars slamming shut. Men speaking Spanish with a Mexican lilt. The grunt and shuffle of animals.

Okay. He was in a barn. On the other side of that wall, that heavy door, there were pigs, lots of them from the sound of it.

He rubbed his head and looked around at the gray.

He'd been drugged. He couldn't remember who'd done it or why. There'd been an angry mob. Thorn babbled at them and someone, a big man he didn't know, punched him in the jaw, then shoved him into a car and drove him into the countryside, and that same big man hauled him out of the vehicle and dragged Thorn through a barn where truckloads of squealing young pigs were arriving, trotting down ramps, herded by small dark-skinned men with sawed-off bats and cudgels until the pigs were crowded into storage pens.

Thorn hadn't fought back against any of it, which seemed strange. He believed he was a fighter. He didn't know why he'd complied so willingly as the big man pushed Thorn, stumbling, into a room. This room. This gray room.

His jaw hurt. His mouth and throat were parched. The drugs were still acting on him, in his system, causing the gray haze in his head. Surely it had to be the drugs, a hangover. Surely this was not how he felt all the time or how he would continue to feel. Who could live like this?

The pigs bleated and shrieked in primal outrage and banged against the metal bars of their pens, their new home. Not where they belonged, restless, frightened, and wanting out. Their misery was Thorn's misery.

The Mexican was awake and eyeing Thorn. He went over to the man and stripped the duct tape off his mouth.

The man thanked him, taking deep breaths.

"*Avúdeme*," the man said. *Help me.*

"Brother, we both need help."

He untied the man's hands and his legs, but the man was too weak to stand. There was blood on his undershorts, a stripe of dried blood running the length of his right leg. Looked like torture.

"I'm searching for my son. His name is Flynn Moss, he looks something like me, younger. Have you seen him?"

"*Es su padre?*"

"Yes, his father. You've seen him?"

He spoke in slow, simple Spanish.

"He come to my trailer, him and others. They give me watch."

"A watch? *Reloj?*"

"*Si, un reloj especial.*"

The man's head rocked back, his eyes closed. Thorn came to him and shook his shoulder.

"Have you seen him after that? Do you know where he is?"

The man shook his head. He tried to rise to his feet but was too weak and settled back in the chair.

In a quiet voice he said, "*La pelirroja.*"

"A red-haired woman?"

"*Si.*"

"There was a redhead with my son. You've seen her?"

He motioned at the wall.

"She's here? She's next door? *En el cuarto al lado?*"

"*No.*" He shook his head. "*Dos puertas más.*"

Cassandra, or some other redhead, was two doors away.

Rocky and weak, Thorn eased from one side of the room to the other, ten feet across, then retraced his steps. Circulate his blood, accelerate his heart, work the shit out of his system. He circled the room, once, twice, another time.

When the dizziness began to stabilize, he tried to jog in place, lifting his knees, bouncing on his toes, but felt heavy, and the dizziness returned with a wallop and he had to stop and steady himself with a hand against the wall. When he'd recovered, he circled the room in the opposite direction, breathing hard.

The Mexican man was watching him, blinking and mystified.

Thorn halted at the door, examined it. A slab of heavy metal, as solid as any door could be. He tried the doorknob but it was locked from the outside. The doorknob was aluminum, cheap conventional hardware. A vulnerability.

It was an odd arrangement, locked from outside, no keyhole inside. Thorn could think of no good reason for it except to use the room for confinement. A time-out space to punish lazy or disobedient workers, a chamber of horrors.

He pressed his finger against the tiny release button on the edge of the sleeve, but his fingertip was too blunt. He needed a tool, a screwdriver would be nice, a knife, even a nail of any size. He checked his pockets. Nothing but lint. He looked around the room.

Only the bare walls and the camp cot with a rough fabric sling, three crossed legs. Easily folded up, easily stored.

He flipped the cot upside down, examined the legs. Aluminum, with the joints held together with screws and washers. His heart was thumping, he was sweating. This was a workout, just moving a few feet this way, a few feet that. But the dull gray room was coming into better focus and it was brightening. The gray walls were changing to a light blue, the floor an off-white.

For no reason, he recalled an earlier scene. Some indeterminate moment when he'd been in the kitchen of a restaurant. A waitress, what was her name, he knew it but couldn't recall, she was telling Thorn he'd been drugged, the vegetable kid in the back had slipped something potent into his sandwich, and she'd even told him the name of the drug though he couldn't remember it. Millie, that was her name. A daughter named Emma. That was some time ago, but Thorn had no way to calculate how long. It felt like weeks had passed.

With the cot upside down, he worked from one leg to the next, testing the tightness of the bolts until he found one that gave a little. He twisted, got it going, unscrewed it thread by thread. Hard work. Whatever deftness his fingers normally had was blunted by the dope.

Out in the barn, the pigs were squealing again as if all of them had realized at the same instant their dire circumstance. They would grow from pigs to hogs in that big room, live there until their final day, no sun, no breezes, no smell of the soil, lying down in their own feces.

Thorn's cell was coming into sharper focus. The world returning. There were no shelves, no decorations, no attempt to dress up its bare walls. The Mexican man was still sitting but stretching his arms now, trying to revive.

Thorn got back to work on the cot's hinge, managed to unscrew the nut, then he drew out the bolt that acted as a hinge. Fatter diameter than he hoped, but it might work.

He went to the door, tried it on the release button, pressing it down, got nothing. Then he cocked it to the side so its edge made better contact. The bolt was a fraction of an inch too big. It didn't penetrate deep enough. Thorn experimented with different angles, tilting it to one side and stabbing it into the hole, stabbing it harder. That did it. The aluminum knob came loose.

Good. But there were more layers to break through, several more.

He drew off the knob, set it on the floor. He was sweating more heavily, a feverish wave was rolling through his body, and he was starting to shiver, a tremble in his hands. It was probably in the low fifties, sweater weather. Damn cold by Thorn's standards, but his shirt was soaked. Had to be the drug. His sweat smelled like the fumes of some sour industrial chemical and trickles of it were running down his forehead, burning his eyes.

Something new was happening to his vision. Now his hangover was glazing everything in the room with a slippery radiance, as if the walls and floor had been sprayed with heavy layers of lubricant. Though his mind felt calm enough, his limbs were still untrustworthy, as though the drug had frayed the link between brain and body. His stomach squirmed uneasily, and the more he focused on his work, the more it writhed.

The queasiness, the aches, and fumbling fingers, those he could cope with. It was the hollow itch in his chest that concerned him. That small hit of dope had given him a taste, a low-grade tickle of desire to regain his X-ray vision, abandon his free will and surrender himself to the sway of any suggestion, the vagaries of a casual bump or nudge.

Under its power a stray breeze might guide him left, a random shadow might steer him right. For those hours in its thrall, the drug had allowed Thorn to escape. Liberated him from his resolve and pragmatism and his almighty sense of duty and permitted the whims of others to guide him. It had been a strange and blissful pleasure to indulge in such bovine stupidity.

He blinked his eyes several times, rubbed away the blur, and forced himself back to work. He popped off the rose, a circular plate made from the same polished aluminum as the knob. Beneath it was the mounting plate, the last layer before he broke into the heart of the mechanism. The mounting plate was held in place by two screws. Tiny screws, only a few turns would release them. If he had a damn screwdriver, if he had anything with a narrow edge, a dime, a credit card, anything, it would be five seconds' work.

He tried his fingernail. Twisted the top screw. Broke the nail. He tried using the nail on his middle finger. *Screw you, screw.* Twisting carefully and breaking that nail.

So much for the top one. He tried the bottom. And found this screw wasn't as snug as the others. It budged a fraction before he broke another nail. Then tried his left thumbnail, thicker, harder, and yes, he got the little bastard moving, a quarter turn, a half turn, then finished it with a pinch and a twist. He swiveled the mounting plate aside and looked into the interior of the mechanism. Standard piece of hardware.

Using his little finger, he probed the mechanism, going deep into its gut, then twisting clockwise. The metal pins bit into his flesh. He'd done this before. He couldn't remember when. Locked inside a room somewhere, successfully breaking free. Brain still not operating at full speed, memory moth-eaten and sluggish.

He felt the latch assembly respond and rotated his finger ever so slightly in the painful slot, turning the cylinder, the tumblers reacting to his flesh. The latch drew back, then in the next instant he lost the combination of pins and was back at zero.

He'd gotten lucky, solving it so quick, but he'd lost it just as quickly. It might take hours to find that correct angle and pressure again. He didn't know if he had hours. Maybe only minutes.

He looked back at the Mexican man, who was looking at him dubiously, not impressed with Thorn's skills. And it was true. He hadn't been thinking clearly. He'd been going at this the hard way.

His eyes moved to the cot. On the underside of the heavy cotton sling was a card with printed instructions about the care and operation of the cot. He went over and fingered the card, testing its strength. It was a thin plastic sheet, the size of a business envelope. On it was printed the step-by-step process a total idiot might require to unfold and refold the cot. The card was stitched into the cot's back side.

He worked a finger under an edge and ripped one end loose, then tore the card free. Flimsy, but it might do.

In case someone chose this awkward moment to check on him, Thorn reassembled the doorknob. When he had it all snapped and screwed back in place, he got to work with the instruction card. He slid it into the door edge above the knob, working it down, forcing the plastic against the spring-loaded pressure of the latch.

As he'd thought, the card was too flimsy for the job. It bent and scrunched up at the contact point. He drew it out, studied it for a moment, then folded it in half. He planted the folded edge against the wall and pressed down hard on the crease to flatten it.

Reinserting the bent card into the door edge, he jimmied it downward, wiggling it gently, increasing the pressure little by little until he felt the latch give, then ease free of its slot. He kept the card in place as he edged the door open a notch and put his eye to the crack.

Pigs everywhere, bumping one another, squeezing their heads through narrow grates to reach the food trough, some munching at the bars of their pens. All of them young. Piglets jostling, rooting their snouts under the bellies of their pen-mates, biting at tails, playing or struggling for dominance, a sea of white flesh, pinkish ears and snouts, their rubbery, bristly hides gleaming in the sunlight that filtered through window slats high on the corrugated metal walls.

He drew the door open wider, stepped one foot forward, ready to make his move, when he saw them marching down the central walkway through the middle of the sea of pigs, a group of people headed his way.

Cruz, X-88, and Pixie. Followed by a large man and a lithe woman, both with reddish hair. It was the woman without a heart, Laurie, and the man who'd cold-cocked him out on the streets of Pine Haven. Webb Dobbins.

Cruz had changed clothes. Her new outfit was from the suitcase Thorn had searched, a dark long-sleeved T-shirt, gray slacks. They'd found Eddie's Taurus.

As the group passed by the pens, the pigs bleated and surged against the bars as if trying for a better view of passing royalty.

Thorn shut the door, slipped the plastic card in the back pocket of his jeans, and hustled back to the cot. He flipped it on its feet. There was no time to repair the hinge on the middle set of legs. If he lay on the cot, it would surely collapse.

Clearly there was no way he could take them on, ambush them, overpower so many. If he stayed on his feet, they'd know he'd sobered up and needed another dose of whatever they'd hammered him with. His irrational chemistry hungered for another hit, but his good sense told him otherwise.

"*Están viniendo*," Thorn said to the Mexican.

Thorn sank to his knees and sprawled face-down on the cold concrete floor and stretched out his arms like a shipwreck survivor clawing his way onto shore. He thought of Flynn Moss, his son, the gifted actor, and tried to summon, through some cosmic sorcery, a pinch of his son's theatrical magic.

Twenty-one

Maybe when they rolled him over and yanked him to his feet, Thorn could try a goofy falsetto, speak in a helium-laced screechy voice and convince them he was still loopy. Flip through his scrapbook of drunken clownishness and retrieve some gems. But for that to work he needed to believe it. Play it with bravura. That's what he'd seen Flynn do on the set of his TV show, and by god, his audience of grips and best boys and assorted Hollywood cynics were mesmerized.

But he didn't get a chance to test his acting skills, for no one came to his door. He lay still and listened for human voices or any indication of their passing. A minute went by, another. He heard a door shutting nearby and moments later raised voices filtered through the adjoining wall.

Because now they were occupied, quarreling about something, but it was clear Thorn wasn't going to be left alone much longer. The inquisition would be starting soon, probably another round of meds to loosen his tongue.

He got to his feet, went back to the door, used the plastic card to open the latch. He drew the door open. The pigs had quieted down, pre-occupied with their food, with acquainting themselves with their new surroundings, or napping after their long journey. A single worker was shoveling grain from a wheelbarrow at the far end of the barn. He had his back to Thorn.

"You coming?" Thorn said to the Mexican. "*Vienes*?"

The Mexican shook his head. Not going to risk it.

"*Bueno suerte*," the Mexican said.

Thorn shut the door behind him and stepped out onto what appeared to be an elevated walkway, something like an observation platform. Ahead of him were two more doors. The middle one was standing slightly ajar. He could hear their voices, the argument continuing. Nearby on the floor of the barn several pigs noticed his presence and bleated quietly as if pleading for his help.

Ahead of him, beyond the two remaining doors,

was a short stairway leading down to a corridor, possibly a back exit.

By god it better be. Trying to make a run for it out the main walkway where he'd seen Cruz and the others enter was out of the question. There was a set of glass double doors at that end of he barn, and beyond was a grassy plaza where he could see workers passing by. No way he could risk being exposed for fifty yards. He headed for the door to the redhead's cell.

When he was halfway down the ramp, coming to the final doorway, a voice spoke out behind him, deep, and belligerent. Thorn swung around in time to see the middle door come open, and Webb stepped out onto the platform. He was barking at someone inside the room, saying he didn't like this one bit. Not one fucking bit. He wasn't playing her game.

Thorn whipped open the door beside him and ducked into a darkened room and shut the door and it locked behind him. He felt around for the light switch and flipped it on.

In the center of the room Cassandra was lashed to a metal chair, mouth sealed with duct tape.

He'd never learned her last name. It was a year since he'd last seen her, on the night Flynn Moss drove away with his new comrades, the ecowarriors. She was one of their leaders. He remembered her wild red hair, her broad shoulders, her patrician manner. But in the interval since that night she'd been badly scuffed. Her hair hacked short, bruises on her face, a lump the size of a small radish disfiguring her right cheek. Her dark eyes were older, harder, but they still crackled with voltage.

In their last brief contact, Cassandra pledged to Thorn that she'd look after Flynn, protect him, that he shouldn't worry about the kid's safety, then she'd escorted his son to a van and they drove away together.

He tore off the duct tape and began to work on the knots.

In a harsh whisper she said, "What the hell are you doing here?"

"I'm getting us out of this place."

"How'd you find me?"

"Don't worry about it," he said. "Your face? They did that?"

"Fucking goons, Dobbins and Burkhart. I've got some kind of resistance to their truth serum. So they tried cruder methods. Burkhart, he's a sweetheart. I think I hurt his feelings. Tried every trick he knew, poor guy. Didn't get shit out of me."

When she was loose, Thorn helped her stand. She wobbled as she rubbed at her wrists and looked over into the far corner of the room where clumps of curly red hair were piled.

"They're next door," Thorn said. "Five of them."

"It's some kind of conference room," she said. "Donuts and coffee. Their hangout. Who is it, the five?"

"Dobbins, his sister, Laurie, and three more that brought me here."

"Who're they?"

Thorn gave her a quick run-through of X-88, Pixie, and Cruz.

"That's what she's calling herself now?" she said.

"You know her?"

"I'd recognize that voice anywhere."

Thorn waved a loose hand as if to clear the air.

"And Flynn? Is he alive?"

She shrugged and made a noncommittal groan.

"All I'm sure of, I didn't see him go down with the others. But Dobbins thinks he's alive, that's what counts."

"You're not sure?"

"There's a chance he is. He headed for the river, maybe he swam."

"Hogs? This is all about goddamn hogs?"

"Hell no. We stumbled on something else."

"What?"

"A building full of dope, not weed, some kind of trumpet flower. Potent shit, I hear."

"Yeah," Thorn said. "I heard the same."

"We got it all on video."

"What video?"

"A little spy camera video," Cassandra said.

"Their drug operation, pill-making assembly line. We had one copy, it was on a laptop Dobbins got hold of when they raided our camp, so they've seen it, know it would destroy them. They think Flynn escaped with a copy."

"Did he?"

She was slinging her arms now like a swimmer on the blocks.

"There's no copy," she said. "But I convinced them there was."

"You did what? Why?"

"To fucking stay alive. I'm their bargaining chip. Me for the video, if they can get word to Flynn, they'll offer him the swap. I convinced them it would work. Buying time, that's all, because they're never going to let me go. But now you're here, the game's changed. That's what they're arguing about in there, Cruz wants to execute me right now, Dobbins wants to wait and see how you perform. If you draw Flynn out of hiding. Either way I'm done."

She looked at the wall where the voices were heating up again.

"If Flynn's alive, why hasn't he called in the cops?"

"You're kidding, right?"

"Tell me."

"He wouldn't get the cops involved because of me. If they stormed this place, took down Dobbins, I'd be riding in the same paddy wagon.

Next day Dobbins is out on bail. No one ever hears from me again. That's what Flynn's got to be thinking. He's protecting me. If he's alive."

Thorn walked to the door.

"Did you kill Cruz's daughter? Push her off a roof?"

"She fed you that story?"

"Did you?"

"Hell no. Carmen, her daughter, I knew her in vet school, took her on a couple of incursions. She was a rah-rah go-getter. Too much so. She went overboard, people started worrying. She wanted to set everything on fire, hurt people. She was nuts, like her little sister, only more so. Finally we had to kick her out, and of course, she goes squealing to her mother. Two of my friends got ten-year sentences because we hurt the bitch's feelings."

"Who killed her?"

"Nobody killed her. She got so dark and miserable when we rejected her, she took a flying leap. Her old lady can't accept it, so she puts it on me. Mother's just as batshit as the two daughters."

Thorn absorbed that for a five count and said, "Okay, can you run, the shape you're in?"

"I can outrun your ass."

Thorn pulled the plastic card from his back pocket.

"Follow me."

"You even know where you are? The layout of this place?"

"We're about to find out."

Once he had the door unlocked, he put his eye to the crack. Down the platform toward the short stairway where he thought the back exit might be, a man stood smoking, looking out at the big floor of noisy pigs. A guy with a silver flat-top who despite his age looked very much in shape.

Thorn motioned Cassandra over and she looked out.

"Burkhart," she whispered.

"Then we use the center aisle."

"It won't work. Too visible."

"Trust me," Thorn said. "You go first."

"That asshole, Burkhart, he groped me three times a day. Stood there smirking with his fingers inside me, working me over."

Thorn lay a hand on her shoulder, felt her tense at his touch.

"When we get out of here, we find Flynn, then deal with Burkhart. Deal with all of them. Now stay in front of me. Don't look back, don't stop, move as fast as you can."

"Usually I give orders, I don't take them."

"Once won't kill you. Now go."

Thorn opened the door wide and Cassandra didn't hesitate. At a lope, she headed down the central stairs toward the floor of the barn.

Thorn held back, staying inside the room, door ajar. Burkhart spotted her and yelled for her to stop. A few seconds later he came sprinting down the platform and Thorn caught him midstride, kicked his legs from under him.

Burkhart pitched headlong, banged his face against the pebbled steel. Thorn slipped out the door, measured the distance, took a skip step, and drove his shoe into Burkhart's temple. The man groaned and rolled onto his back and Thorn was about to deliver a second kick, one for Cassandra's sake, when the door to the center room opened.

Not waiting to see who it was, he swung down the stairway, using the handrails as parallel bars, slinging himself over the six steps and hitting the concrete floor in stride.

At the first pen, he halted, searched for a latch, hearing the footsteps behind him rattling the metal stairway. He found the clasp, threw open the gate, stepped in the pen, and herded the excited pigs onto the main floor.

He skipped the next two pens to build up a lead, then flipped the latch on the next pen, waved his arms and clapped and sent another fifty pigs scrambling out to block the passageway. Two more pens, a hundred more pigs, then he was out the double doors and into the chilly sunlight, Cassandra about fifty yards ahead, running with a long graceful gait across a green field toward what appeared to be the main entrance road. Her stride as light-footed and smooth as a veteran marathoner, eating up the distance with an effortless glide.

Problem was, she should've headed for cover, the nearby woods, some outbuildings, anywhere to hide, but she was too far ahead and running too fast for Thorn to call to her. So he followed her track, sprinting to catch up.

Maybe she knew something Thorn didn't, the shortest route to safety, maybe she'd made a careful appraisal of the farm's layout when she'd been transported there. Thorn's memory of his arrival had been washed clean by the drug, so as he ran, he gave her the benefit of the doubt, hoping she had a good reason to be leading them in that direction.

He was gaining on her, nearly close enough to get her attention, when a gleaming black four-wheeler roared past him. Burkhart driving. Bouncing over the rutted gravel drive, gunning up behind Cassandra, then slowing to follow in her wake, staying just a couple of feet behind. He revved the engine as a taunt, to break her, make her surrender. But she didn't. She kept running without a hitch in her rhythm, her arms pumping evenly, legs stretching out.

After another twenty yards, Burkhart pulled alongside Cassandra. She didn't look over and didn't break stride, just kept that gliding pace, lost in the easy athletic flow of her body, as if perhaps escape was no longer foremost on her mind, but instead she simply wanted to bask in this moment of exertion, delight in the stretch and flex of muscles she'd obviously nurtured for years.

Twenty-two

Burkhart yelled at her to stop, but she didn't respond. He yelled again.

Another four-wheeler rumbled up to Thorn's right side and held its speed just beyond his side vision. He didn't look back, didn't slow, kept going for Cassandra's sake, to interfere with Burkhart any way he could.

They'd run nearly a half mile by the time Thorn closed in, choking on the whorls of dust Burkhart's four-wheeler was spinning up. Gasping, exhausted, he kicked it up another notch, gave it what he had left, pulled to Cassandra's side, and together they continued to race out the main drive with their escort of ATVs on either side.

"The woods," Thorn managed to call out. "Left, left."

The look she gave him said she disagreed, but

she veered beside him off the road and together they entered a pasture, the ground growing suddenly soft. Inches of glop were coating the earth, their feet sinking to their ankles.

"Shit," Cassandra yelled.

Yes. Pig manure, a thick layer of it, the four-wheelers still beside them in the sloppy muck. Thorn took a quick glance at the ATV dogging him. X-88 at the wheel, Cruz beside him.

"Good luck, Thorn," Cassandra called and swerved back the way they'd come, back to the hard-packed ground of the entrance road.

His lungs were aching, legs weak, but as he watched Burkhart closing in on Cassandra, raising a handgun, yelling for her to stop, Thorn found another dose of reserve.

He swung around and caught up to them at the entrance gate. There was a narrow asphalt road just beyond the entry, a public thorough-fare it seemed, but no traffic in sight in either direction, no houses across the way. Cassandra stood in front of Burkhart's four-wheeler, arms at her sides, taking deep slow breaths but not heaving the way Thorn was.

"All I ask," she said, "bury me in the same hole you buried my friends."

"Tough broad," Burkhart said. "But I would've broken you. Another day or two, you'd've been on your knees, worshipping my cock."

"In your dreams, old man."

Thorn was only a couple of yards behind Burkhart. Back in the field of pig shit, X-88 had gotten stuck, and the two of them were slogging across the pasture, Cruz yelling for Burkhart to hold on. Don't shoot. Hollering it again as they trudged.

Thorn aimed a roundhouse right at the side of Burkhart's head, at the swollen lump where he'd kicked him minutes before. But from the corner of his eye, Burkhart must've seen it coming and ducked away. Thorn's second shot clipped his chin and knocked him sideways, and before Burkhart could recover, Thorn was on him, chopping the pistol loose with his right hand, then pivoting hard and slamming his forearm flat into Burkhart's nose. The blood flooded out and Thorn hauled the man from his perch on the four-wheeler and slammed him to the ground.

He climbed into the driver's seat and yelled for Cassandra to get aboard. But she was more interested in Burkhart. On his hands and knees, he was looking up at her with blood flowing from his nose, running into his mouth, and dripping down his chin.

"Leave him, goddamn it, let's go."

Cassandra stepped close to Burkhart and spit a wad of phlegm in his face. Then spit another.

She turned and climbed onto the seat beside Thorn.

"All right," she said. "I'm good."

Thorn gunned the vehicle out the last twenty yards of gravel and was turning left onto the asphalt that he believed led back to Pine Haven, where they might find some measure of safety, when he heard the first gunshot, then another. A slug dinged the metal roll bar and sparks showered them. He ducked and Cassandra ducked beside him, her head squeezed up against the primitive dashboard, her hands gripping the hard plastic rail. Two more gunshots, then they were on the asphalt and heading east, both of them still bent low.

"Stay down!" he yelled at her.

When it came, the black Ford pickup truck appeared so suddenly beside them Thorn had no chance to evade. A deep ditch on the right, the truck on his left. Webb Dobbins behind the wheel, Cruz and X bouncing in the bed.

Thorn kept the four-wheeler throttled all the way up, but there was no way to outrun the pickup, no side roads ahead, and Dobbins was edging into his lane, bumping his running board into the steel cage of the four-wheeler, leaving behind a trail of sparks.

Thorn leaned over to Cassandra.

"I'm going to stop. Look for your chance and drive on."

"What?"

"Do it."

Thorn brought the four-wheeler to a gradual

stop, and Dobbins halted the pickup beside him. Raising his hands straight above his head, Thorn stepped out of the ATV and walked to the front of Webb Dobbins's pickup. As X and Cruz were climbing from the bed, Cassandra hit the gas and the four-wheeler roared away.

"Get her!" Cruz shouted. "Go, go, go."

But Thorn's chest was pressed against the pickup's grill, hands high. No way for Dobbins to maneuver. Maybe Thorn's calculation was right, that he was more valuable to them than Cassandra, or maybe he was about to find out otherwise.

Cruz and X trotted around the truck, Cruz shouting at Dobbins to run Thorn down if he had to, Cassandra was getting away, the roar of the ATV fading in the distance.

X rounded the passenger side of the pickup. He approached Thorn casually, his left hand upraised as if testing the air for raindrops. Two red tablets lay in the center of his palm.

"Forget it," Thorn said. "No way that's going to happen."

"Oh, but it is. It is."

With the nonchalance of someone trying not to spook a wild beast, X eased toward him. Thorn held his ground in front of the truck, listening to the rumble of Cassandra's ATV recede.

Then Dobbins gunned the engine, tapping and releasing the accelerator, pushing the revs higher and higher.

"Time for your medicine, Grandpa."

When X stepped within range, Thorn chose an angle and threw a jab at X's jaw, but he side-stepped the blow, caught Thorn's wrist, and slung him backward against the grill of the Ford pickup, then shouldered him solidly in place, leaning on Thorn with his hard belly, heavy and hot, grabbing a handful of hair in his right hand, cranking Thorn's head back at an unbearable angle.

X-88 mashed him against the hood, and though Thorn grappled for X's arm and wriggled against the suffocating weight, X was stronger, far stronger, younger by decades, heavier by fifty pounds, a rubbery power and leverage that was impossible to budge.

There'd been a time not long ago, golden years when Thorn would have squirmed loose, or found some clever maneuver to break free. But not anymore, not against this younger man who seemed to absorb pain, even relish it. The man's strength and weight were smothering him, crushing the air from his lungs.

Maybe he couldn't break X's grip, but Thorn could damn well keep his mouth shut. He pressed his lips tight, clamped his jaw.

A sly smile came to X's lips as if he'd seen this move before and knew exactly how to defeat it. Thorn felt it coming and tried to block it with his thigh, but was late by a fraction.

The big man's knee thudded into Thorn's groin, and he gasped, and damn it, X timed his move perfectly and clapped his left hand over Thorn's open lips, kept it there with what felt like a well-practiced hammer lock, and Thorn tasted the acrid burn of the tablets on his tongue, the tiny pellets melting fast, and in the next slow seconds as Thorn struggled against the rigid hold and tried to spit out the tablets, X-88's face began a leisurely dissolve, and the daylight grew gray, then a darker gray and darker still, with X's hand pressed over his mouth, and as Thorn sank again into that altered state, a dreamlike slide, not so bad, not painful, kind of pleasant actually, giving himself over to the will of others, directed, bossed, all independence gone, all accountability, and that X-ray vision, yes, strangely, unexpectedly, he'd enjoyed that part before, and he was thinking a last thought, how glad he was that Sugar hadn't come along and fallen into this same shithole, just as a strobe light began to flash as if some giant windmill was whirling in front of a pink sun, and X's round ignorant face melted like ice cream on a summer day, and right before everything blurred into unreality, Thorn made a leap of logic based on nothing more than the immense pressure of X-88's headlock, Thorn's mouth forced open and covered by X's hand. He had the answer to Deputy Randolph's question back in

St. Augustine, the mysterious mechanics the killer used to jam ground beef into the black kid's mouth and keep it there.

This was exactly how it was done.

Twenty-three

Sugarman was studying a bong Tina had covered with peace symbols and white smudges that were her attempt at peace doves. There was a row of them at eye level on a shelf in the back of Island Treasures, her shop in the Tradewinds Shopping Plaza in Key Largo. Open seven days a week, ten to six. Behind the counter was Julia Jackson, the purple-haired librarian, texting someone, her thumbs a blur.

Sugarman killed a few more minutes in the bong aisle while the overweight couple in matching I ♥ KEY LARGO T-shirts finished pawing through a bin of plaques with off-color one-liners and finally wandered out the door.

Julia didn't look up when Sugarman edged up to the counter.

"Must not be easy," he said. "Going from books to bongs."

Julia finished with her text, whooshed it away, and looked up at him.

"Sorry? You said?"

"Books to bongs," he said. "Must be a jarring adjustment."

"Not really," she said. "I get high from reading. Don't you?"

She flashed him a flirty smile.

"Tina's not here," she said. "She went off . . . oh, she went off with you."

"We got separated," he said.

"Separated?"

"Complicated story. I thought she might've checked in with you."

"Nope, haven't heard a word. Something happen?" She was keeping her eyes from him; lying wasn't one of her talents.

Sugarman looked at the shelves behind Julia, filled with cigarette papers and water pipes and glass figurines in the shapes of mushrooms and dwarfs and unicorns.

"She probably took the long way home. Nothing to worry about. The other thing is, I wanted to ask you about Thorn."

"Thorn?"

"Yeah, Thorn and his son, Flynn. The postcards you saw him looking at in the library."

She cut her eyes down to her phone.

"It's okay," he said. "Tina told me you'd mentioned the postcards."

"She did?"

She looked up, rubbed an eye with her knuckle,

smeared her mascara. For all her coquetry Julia seemed at that moment childlike and unsure, as if her coy act was a cover for deeper insecurities.

"I was curious if you ever saw Tina talking to anyone, somebody she might've been discussing Thorn with. And the postcards."

"I don't know what you mean."

"I think you do, Julia. A stranger, maybe someone who came in the store, or who Tina told you about. Thorn's name came up."

She shook her head, but her gritted teeth said otherwise.

"I know what's going on," Julia said. "Tina's gone missing, you're worried about her, trying to track her down."

Sugarman sighed.

"Am I that transparent?"

She nodded. "Pretty much."

"Well, okay. Yeah, I'm a bit concerned about her whereabouts."

"I'd say you're a lot concerned, you wouldn't be in here asking stuff."

"So help me, Julia. You remember Tina talking to anyone about Thorn?"

She looked out the window of Island Treasures at a gang of tourists in madras shorts and sun hats trooping by.

"What'll happen to Island Treasures if Tina doesn't come back?"

"Don't worry about the store."

"Tina told me to keep it to myself. The woman, I mean. Madeline, I think was her name."

Sugarman felt his heart sag. Despite all evidence to the contrary, he'd been hoping this whole episode was an elaborate case of mistaken identity, or that Sheffield was right and Tina was just hiding out somewhere, ashamed to show her face for a few days till things cooled down.

Julia straightened a tray full of key chains on the countertop. She flicked a piece of lint away. Her cell phone buzzed and she checked the screen but didn't answer.

"You met Madeline?"

"First time she came in the store was on a weekend, so yeah, I was here. It was busy, but I overheard a few things."

"When was this?"

"A week ago, around there, more or less."

"What did she look like, this Madeline?"

"Pretty, I guess, in that Latin way, sultry and cold at the same time. Long black hair, thinnish, a little thingy on her nose. A crimp or something."

"You get her last name?"

"I heard it, but I don't remember."

"Cruz?"

"Maybe. Yeah, that sounds right."

"And the stuff you overheard?"

"I shouldn't be talking about this. I don't like to gossip."

"This is to help Tina. You want to help me find her, don't you?"

She took a huge breath and held it with her cheeks puffed up as if she were about to submerge.

Julia only remembered snatches of that conversation in the store. Cruz introduced herself as a federal agent, working on an investigation that involved Thorn. Could Tina be of help? Tina stiffened, freaking out that this was a drug bust in the making. That's what Julia thought too. Weed.

But Cruz wanted to know if Tina was aware of any contact between Thorn and his fugitive son. That's when Tina glanced over at Julia, and Cruz noticed the look they were sharing and invited Julia to participate.

"So you told Cruz about the postcards?"

"A federal agent," Julia said. "I'm not going to lie. That's serious shit."

"You said earlier 'first time,' so there were other times?"

"Next couple of days at Tina's house," Julia said. "Tina told me before she left on that trip with you, not the exact details or anything, trying to shield me I guess, but Cruz wanted her to work on some kind of sting operation, go undercover, you know, top secret, hush-hush. It got thrown together very fast, a whirlwind. Cruz stayed at her place, they were huddled up together, cooking up this plan to capture Thorn's kid. I mean, he's a criminal, right? He attacks people and things, burns stuff down. Tina was just doing her civic duty."

"Yeah, her civic duty."

"That's what Tina said."

"Ever hear Tina mention automatic weapons, anything like that?"

"Whoa." Julia raised her hands to her shoulders, showed her palms. "No way. Guns, no guns. Nothing whatsoever about guns ever came up. Tina hates guns. You should know that, her boyfriend and all."

Sugarman asked her several more questions but Julia cycled through the same narrative without any variation. When two elderly ladies came in and started to cruise the store, Sugarman took the opportunity to thank Julia for her help and leave.

He stood by his car door, trying to absorb Julia's story. Cruz had been in Key Largo for several days, planning something with Tina, some kind of scheme to nab Flynn. Sugarman was wrestling with that when someone hailed him by name.

A red Chrysler convertible had rolled up behind his car, top down. The driver leaned over the door edge and called out his name again. There was an Asian woman in the passenger seat wearing a colorful scarf over her hair.

The man removed his baseball cap and sunglasses. Frank Sheffield.

He gestured at his passenger.

"This is Shirley Woo. Sugarman, meet Shirley. Shirley, Sugarman. Shirley's an artist, Sugarman's a private cop."

"What're you doing here?"

"A sunny Sunday, felt like a drive, see how you Keys characters shake, rattle, and roll."

"And you just bumped into me?"

"Hey, I may be retired but I still have skills. The FBI, this is what we do. We track people down. Now get in, let's go someplace with a view, get a fish sandwich. I got something I need to tell you. Not good news."

They went to Snappers on the Atlantic side. A busy Sunday afternoon, a live band playing Jimmy Buffett medleys. Tables outside around the basin were full, so they got seats inside by a window.

"Been here before," Frank said to Shirley. "Fish is very fresh. Get anything you like, I'm buying."

Shirley Woo took off her scarf and her glasses and appraised Sugarman with a frankness bordering on rude.

"Eat first, talk later?" Frank said. "Or vice versa?"

"What's the bad news?"

Frank scrubbed his hands together and blew out a breath.

"You and Tina Gathercole close? Engaged, going steady, like that."

"What is it, Frank?"

"Yes, well, I put Tina's data into the system, and last night late, a former colleague called me with a hit. Tina's prints were on file, a couple of drug busts back in the seventies, so the ID was quick and easy."

"Come on, Frank. I'm a grown-up."

"Very dark stuff. A vagrant found her body in the woods just outside St. Augustine. Murdered."

"Jesus Christ."

"It gets worse."

"Tina was murdered. How much worse can it be?"

"Murdered, yes. But it's the method that's rough."

When Frank described the cause of death, then described the ligature marks on her ankles and wrists, adhesive residue on her lips, Sugarman turned his eyes away and looked out the big windows. The water seemed as flat and lifeless as a chintzy oil painting, the sky a long stretch of blue desolation. All that harsh winter light began to burn his eyes.

"I'm sorry," Frank said. "It's an ugly thing."

Shirley Woo had a sip of her iced tea and continued to scrutinize Sugarman's face.

"There's something else," Sheffield said. "The way things work, maybe I would've heard about

Tina's death eventually, but it could've taken a while, a single death like that, no matter how unusual the cause, it's still a run-of-the-mill local murder, not a federal matter. But when a second victim shows up a few miles away on the same night, killed in the same unique fashion, well, now it's clear you have a predator working the area or passing through. Either way, it becomes federal, rings the phone in my old office."

"A second victim?"

"Kid in a burger joint. Choked to death on a mouthful of raw meat, then the place where he worked set on fire."

"Fast food place right off I-95? On motel row?"

Frank dug a spiral notepad out of his back pocket and flipped the pages.

"Yeah, Hampton Inn, Best Western, a Waffle House, and this burger joint. The usual franchise strip."

"That's where Thorn and Cruz were staying, where they cut me loose."

"Well, well."

"How the hell does Tina get from Vero to the woods outside of St. Augustine? How's that happen? It couldn't be coincidence. Tina didn't know where we'd be stopping for the night. Someone waylaid her and brought her three hours north and dumped her body near where we were going to stay, which has to mean that that someone is connected to Cruz, knew where she was stopping, or spoke with her on the phone."

"Back up a minute. 'Cause see, the local law up there, the St. John's County homicide guy, crime scene people, they're thinking Tina was killed at the location where the body was found. Tire tracks down a back road, two sets of footprints leading from the rear of the vehicle into the woods, the ground disturbed, signs of a scuffle. All of it consistent with her being held in the trunk of a vehicle."

Sugarman was silent, trying to picture it and trying not to.

"See, the thing is," Frank said, "to make matters more of a concern to the bureau, these two cases aren't isolated. So far they turned up two others with similar MOs. Both in the last eighteen months, all in Florida. Somebody forcibly choked to death on food."

"Two more?"

"At least two, maybe more. They're looking through case files, deaths that might have been ruled accidental or went unsolved and got filed. This could be more widespread. Or maybe it's just these four. Either way, there's one fucked-up individual at large."

"May I get started?" Shirley said.

"Yeah, yeah," said Sheffield. "I didn't tell you, Shirley's a sketch artist, best we've got. If you can describe it, she can draw it. My replacement, Gracie Rodriguez, new special agent in charge, she asked me to bring Shirley down, see if you'd consent to describing this Cruz person. They're sending a team up to St. Augustine tomorrow, wanted something to show around. Since Ms. Gathercole was apparently associated with Cruz, and Cruz was impersonating a federal officer, it's a logical starting point. You game?"

Shirley Woo dragged her purse from the floor, set it in her lap, and withdrew a small laptop.

While the computer was booting up, Sheffield rose.

"You guys have fun. Come get me when you're done. No hurry."

It took more than two hours. Sheffield wandered around on the outside deck, sat at the bar, talked to a woman for a while, made her laugh. Sugarman watched him hitting on the ladies and socializing with some old salts while Sugar described Cruz's face.

Woo worked her software and asked questions and Sugarman tried his best, not just to remember, but to label her features in a clear-eyed way.

"Her mouth," Woo said. "Lower lip, upper lip."

"Lower was thin, upper a little thicker."

"Is it a mouth you would want to kiss?"

"What kind of question is that?"

"It's my question. My way of doing things. This software, I have written it myself."

"Okay, okay. Would I want to kiss Cruz's mouth? No. Not really."

"Why?"

"It was pretty but cold. Calculating."

"Any other words of this type?"

"Imperious," Sugarman said.

"Your vocabulary is notable. You are a word-smith."

"Thank you. It's a hobby, vocabulary building. I know it's strange."

"Strange, yes." Then Woo said, "Lashes? Dense, full, sweeping, stubby?"

And on they went, Sugarman trying for the simplest descriptors, then those out-of-left-field questions throwing him off. Sugarman trying and failing to elicit an extracurricular remark from Woo. At intervals, she turned the laptop around and had him choose from sets of facial shapes, ear shapes, noses, foreheads, chins, cheeks.

"Was there sunlight radiating from her eyes? Or something else?"

"Brown eyes, okay, but with what color under-tone?"

"Which of these words describe her eyes: bedroom, bleary, bloodshot, close set, widely spaced, dazed, glassy, placid, stricken, vacant, dancing, piercing, flashing, sparkling, squinting. You can choose more than one."

"When she smiled could you see her teeth? Upper and lower?"

"Were her teeth white, yellowed, straight, crooked?"

"Cheekbones, angled, soft, none?"

"Did she have crow's-feet, deep-set eyes, drowsy, heavy-lidded, hooded?"

"On a scale of one to ten, one is icy, ten is scorching, what number was the heat in her eyes?"

Sugarman played along. Not sure if Woo was joking or trying to make him comfortable, or what the hell New Age bullshit she was slinging.

"Could this woman carry a tune or is she tone deaf?"

"Was she pierced anywhere you could not see?"

"Has this woman given birth? Has this woman aborted a child?"

Preposterous questions, which little by little erased the sharply detailed image he started with, turned it into something slippery and uncertain, then gradually awoke memories of Cruz that somehow clarified her face more vividly and with more dimensionality than he'd had at the outset. By the end of the session he was exhausted, but Woo's oddball method had dredged up elements of Cruz's character Sugarman had registered only subliminally.

"Now," Woo said. "I will show you a face, three views."

She turned her laptop around. Side, full front, head turned at an angle.

"Is this her?"

"Damn," Sugarman said. "You're good."

"Yes," Woo said. "I get that a lot."

Twenty-four

Outside in the Snappers parking lot, with Woo waiting in the car, Sheffield thanked him for his help.

"She's a bit of a wackadoodle, but she gets it done."

Sugarman nodded. Emotionally bottomed out, unable to speak.

"It pains me to admit it," Frank said. "But I royally fucked up."

"What?"

"Should've realized yesterday, that story you told me. My mind's on remodeling the motel, all the little details, I'm walking around in a daze, no more job, no office, no schedule, you know, all my adult life as an FBI agent, now the void's opening up before me. You were telling me this stuff about Thorn and you, and this Cruz woman, it should've clicked, but it didn't, not till this morning. I woke up and realized who she might be."

"Talk to me, Frank."

"That woman, the one you know as Cruz, her real name is Yolanda Obrero."

"You know her?"

Frank grunted a yes.

"She did a stint in Miami. I thought when you described her yesterday I might know her, but hey, so many good-looking Latina broads in this town, it's hard to sort out one slim dark-haired beauty from another. But the woman in Woo's drawing, that's Obrero. Maybe her maiden name was Cruz, I don't know. Women do that, lose a husband, take back their father's name."

"What do you know about her?"

"More than I'd like to. One thing, she had two daughters, both seriously fucked up. One died a year or two ago, suicide, threw herself off a building, full of dope at the time, heroin, coke. The other one, Pixie, Trixie, one of those, that little girl has a few dozen soliciting arrests. Don't remember the details."

"She was FBI, Obrero?"

"That's right, she was one of ours."

"For how long?"

"Ten years on the street, then her marriage cracks up, the guy, he worked DEA undercover, wound up drifting over to the dark side, Manny Obrero, hanging with Scarface and his friends too long, snorting the product, got converted. I don't know where he is now. Some federal facility. But right after he's taken off the street and sent away, Obrero stopped showing up for work. The girls giving her trouble, acting out and shit. She started flashing a lot of cash, new fancy car, diamonds on her hands. Clearly she's tapping into some of Manny's ill-gotten gains.

"Other than that, I can't remember how it all went, but if you think it's relevant, I'll see if I can get you her jacket. I just remember she was one of only two agents in my much-heralded history with the bureau I had to fire. Couldn't find anyone she'd worked with who trusted her anymore, nobody would stand up for her. Between her girls and her Scarface husband, man, the woman turned into a hot mess."

Sugarman said, "That's all I need to know, Frank. Don't bother digging out her file."

"No, there's more."

Sheffield grunted again as if lifting something heavy.

"Cruz, Obrero, she stopped in my office, I don't know, a week ago, ten days. I'm packing up everything from my drawers and shelves, thirty years of trinkets, trophies, plaques and shit. She said she'd heard I was retiring and brought me a bottle of rum as a present. Ron Abuelo Centuria, you ever hear of it? From Panama, smooth and rich, best damn rum I've ever tasted. So the two of us are sipping rum, she's hitting on me a little, I kind of lose my focus."

"What'd she want, Frank?"

"After a couple of drinks she got around to it. Said she was doing something private now, corporate security job, personnel investigations, and Thorn's name came up at work and did I know anything about the guy?"

"And you told her what?"

"I don't remember exactly. Like I say, there was amazing rum involved. I'm packing up my office, it's emotional, looking at my files, photos, emptying my drawers, a catharsis, I wasn't concentrating. I do recall saying at one point that Thorn was a barnacle, he's stuck to his rock down in Key Largo."

"Why'd you say that?"

" 'Cause he is."

"But why's that come up?"

"She might've asked something about his willingness to travel. Is he mobile? I don't know. It's fuzzy. But after I heard that story of yours yesterday, I started thinking about Obrero, and I think she was picking my brains about what she'd have to do to get Thorn to accompany her on some kind of trip. Like the one you were describing."

"So when Obrero was in your office my name came up too."

"Sure it did, yeah. I told her you and Thorn worked in tandem. Thorn's the loose cannon, you're the straight arrow."

"Starting to make sense," Sugarman said. "My name leads her to Tina. She gives Tina a story about capturing Flynn Moss, Tina's gullible. Cruz gets her to play along with this fake sting operation."

"But this raw meat thing," Sheffield said. "That's not Obrero. She's crazy, but not that way, not crazy violent."

"Maybe what that is, Frank, that's a distinction without a difference."

"I'm sorry, Sugar. I haven't been thinking straight lately. Too much booze, reorienting my orbit. A lot of shit has been slipping my mind lately."

"I understand, Frank. Retiring, it's a big deal."

"Look, I'd like to help you with this Pine Haven thing. I would. But I'm afraid you're on your own. I've retired for real, and I promised myself no side jaunts, no special favors. I'm strictly out of the biz."

The rumble of trucks and cars on the Overseas Highway a block away was rolling in, the sound setting up a sympathetic vibration in Sugarman's chest.

"And if I went up there with you, no way could I do it on the sly. There'd have to be other feds involved. You don't want a bunch of by-the-book agents around Thorn, the situation he's in. Minute he found Flynn, my people would be all over him, clap the kid away. Better I stay clear. But you know, just between us, from what I can tell, that kid's been doing good stuff. Illegal as hell, but nobody's gotten hurt, so I say more power to him.

"But you understand, Sugar, if I'm questioned about any of this, I'm going to have to give up

Flynn. Tell them what I know. I like the kid, what he's doing, so I'm not going to volunteer anything, but I can't withhold if they ask directly."

"I get it, Frank. Do what you have to do. I appreciate you coming down, letting me know face-to-face about Tina."

"You two were close? Real close?"

"Close enough," Sugarman said. "But that's not the point anymore."

Frank nodded.

Though it didn't need saying, Sugarman spoke the words anyway: "Nobody should have to die like that. Nobody."

Twenty-five

Thorn showed them to the Port-O-Let where he'd hidden the shotguns. Cruz was guiding him like a model airplane with a controller, a falcon and falconer, some invisible thread linking them, Cruz speaking quietly, the whisper of a hypnotist. This trip, everything was heavier, the dose different, the effect different, Thorn moving with a sleepwalker's sluggish tread, the drug's dark undertow pulling him forward.

He was obeying, but no X-ray vision this time, no exuberant visions, just this drunken lethargy as they walked around the foundations of the houses that never got built, Dobbins Court, Cruz repeating over and over, now take us to where you hid the ammo, her words coming so slow he could hear each syllable stretching and stretching like a song on a vinyl record, the turntable set at the wrong speed, where did you put the ammo, where's the ammo, each word drawn out and echoing afterward.

He tried resisting. He knew he'd buried the box of shells near the edge of the woods, but as an exercise, just to see if he could do it, like that meditation trick one of his girlfriends used to do, Monica, Lourdes, or Sarah, Alexandra, Darcy, or Rusty, he couldn't recall which, he'd learned so much from each of the women he'd loved, but this one knew a yoga thing, a Zen thing, a karate thing, whatever it was, it was simple to describe but hard as hell to do, a way to keep her mind to herself, keep all the trash and chaotic whirlwind at bay, she'd focus on her breath, the breath going in, going deep into the pit of the stomach, down below the navel to a secret place the Buddhists knew about, letting the oxygen stay down there and ignite the secret place, then letting the air loose again, feeling it leave the lungs, every inch of the way in and every inch of the way out. He tried that. Tried to keep his mind under his own control.

Thorn was a stubborn fuck. Sure, his physical

skills had declined, his speed, his agility, his strength. He'd lost his edge. He couldn't go hand to hand with bruisers like X-88 the way he once had. But he'd always been a stubborn fuck and he still had that going for him, and stubborn fucks didn't like to be bossed or controlled, yeah, okay, it felt good that first time, felt good for a brief while, a foreign sensation, yielding his will, succumbing to the power of another, a release from his own steadfast mission, but they'd given him too much dope this time, or brewed up a bad batch, or he'd developed a quick tolerance to it, or else his own stubborn-fuck brain had kicked in and was beating back the power of the pills.

"I don't remember where I buried the ammo."

"He's fighting it," X said.

Webb Dobbins was tagging behind Cruz. The other women hanging back at the car. Pixie and Laurie were lost in conversation, paying no attention to the others. Thorn watched as Laurie reached up and ran a finger down Pixie's jawline, then touched the finger to Pixie's lips.

Dobbins said, "Just keep asking, he'll do what you say. Some hardheads, it takes longer for the drug to get into their system, you got to keep working him."

"Where's the ammo? Where'd you hide it?"

Thorn didn't answer. He was having a crafty thought. His brain was fuzzy, but the stubborn fuck was sputtering to life. That breath thing working. His crafty thought was this: Give them the ammo. Make them think he was under their spell. Make them think they had him where they wanted and then later he could make a break. Later when their guard's down.

But Thorn wasn't sure if this was a genuine crafty thought or just his willpower sagging and giving him an excuse to obey their request. He wasn't sure. But he had to try it, try to fool them, fool the drug. If he was truly in control, maybe if he waited a while, looked for his moment, he could find a better chance to cut loose, escape these assholes, find Flynn, or find Millie the waitress, or Ladarius, or Eddie, or one of the others who seemed trustworthy, people who might keep him hidden until he came down from this tricky shit. Unless they were in league with Dobbins. Could a whole town be corrupt? Could every single person inside the boundaries of Pine Haven be in on this?

Was he saying all this aloud, or only thinking it? It was maddening not to know.

Cruz wore a troubled frown like she might be hearing his thoughts. She measured Thorn with her dark, enigmatic eyes.

Thorn did the breathing thing again, all the way in, all the way out, slow, focus, then cleared his throat and said, "I buried it over there, by the tree line."

"Show us."

Thorn led them to the spot. He tapped his toe on the ground.

"Dig it up," X-88 said.

"Don't have a shovel."

"Use your hands. Get down on your fucking knees, dig it up."

"Relax, X. There's a shovel in the back of the Taurus." Cruz waved at the car parked nearby.

In the next instant the shovel appeared.

"Like to help," Thorn said. "But I'm woozy."

Thorn knew his synapses were misfiring. One moment was bleeding into the next, the order of events garbled. Was he saying all this out loud?

His mouth was dry, he needed to piss.

He tried to reconstruct the events, the sequence, find his place. Cruz wanted to kill Cassandra because she believed Cassandra murdered her daughter Carmen. Cruz brought Thorn to Pine Haven to lure Flynn into the open, so they could recover a video they thought could destroy Dobbins, and when Dobbins had the video, he'd hand over Cassandra to Cruz. A simple trade, a business deal. I give you what you want for what I want. But all that was changed now because Thorn had set the pigs loose, set Cassandra loose.

This entire shitstorm was about drugs, the drug that was circulating in his bloodstream. Flynn and his friends had stumbled on the dark heart of Pine Haven, a greenhouse full of trumpet blooms, and it cost some of them their lives. Cruz had lied about everything. She'd devised an elaborate hoax. Yes, Thorn was bait, that little bit of what she'd told him was true.

Okay, okay, so he understood his situation, understood it perfectly, but, goddamn it, he wasn't sure if he was revealing all he knew to Cruz or keeping it to himself. He remembered the breathing thing and started it again, following his breath in, following it out. Trying to put things back in order, rebuild the wall between outside and inside.

X-88 was digging with the shovel and Thorn found himself taking a piss against a tree. His piss stream glowed fluorescent blue. Thorn was in trouble. Deep shit. Trying to breathe his way back to some scrap of self-control. The last trickles of piss turned flame red.

"I told you," Dobbins said. "I told you he'd go along. I haven't seen a soul yet it doesn't work on, you get the dose right. Split a tablet in half, most of them, they just fall asleep, have some juicy dreams. But two tabs like he's on, your wish is his command for the next ten hours, bark like a dog, he'll bark. Take a shit in his hand and eat it, whatever you say he'll do."

"Can it, Dobbins." Cruz flicked a hand at him as if chasing away a fly.

"What the fuck are those nose plugs?" Dobbins said, motioning at X.

"X is very sensitive," Thorn said. "He can smell

the starlight. He can smell the vacuum of space. The emptiness between atoms."

Cruz gave Thorn a skeptical look.

"Is that how people talk on this drug?" she asked, her eyes on Thorn.

"No two are alike," Dobbins said. "Trust me, he's cruising at altitude."

X-88 pulled the plastic bag of ammo from the hole and held it up.

"All right," Cruz said. "Good."

"What's that for anyway," Dobbins said. "Who you going to shoot?"

"Whoever the fuck I need to," Cruz said.

"Now what?" X said. "Go look for the redhead?"

"She won't be far away," Cruz said. "These people always have a contingency plan. If they're separated, they rendezvous at a certain prearranged location. We're operating just as we were before she fled. When we find Flynn Moss, we find Cassandra. Count on it."

"And remind me, Cruz, how's that going to happen?"

"Thorn's how. Keep showing him around long enough, one of them will make a play. They're stupid that way. They don't leave their wounded on the battlefield. Loyal to the point of self-destruction. Deluded."

Next second they were back in the car, Thorn in the backseat wedged between Dobbins and X.

Cruz driving, Pixie and Laurie up front, Laurie with an arm on the seat, touching a hand to Pixie's bare arm, whispering in her ear. It was Eddie's Taurus, the one Thorn had rented. Meticulously clean.

"Am I saying this out loud? Can you hear me?"

"Shut up," X said.

"Okay, good," said Thorn.

Back safely in his head, he worked on his breath. Hard as hell. But the stubborn-fuck voice was telling him to do it, it's the only thing that's working. *That's keeping you from stepping off the cliff. Remember how the sky split apart like an eggshell, remember how the asphalt street expanded, remember how you couldn't figure out how to get inside a car? Remember all that? So breathe, the stubborn fuck said. So breathe and breathe and rebuild the wall, and don't let the drug win, don't let these people win. Remember why you're here. Remember your son.*

"Is Flynn dead?"

"I told you to keep the fuck quiet." X-88 punched him hard in the arm.

"Don't hit him," Dobbins said. "He's your well-trained dog. You wouldn't kick your dog, now would you?"

"I hit who I want to hit and you don't have a say in it, pig man."

"Webb's right," said Laurie from the front seat. "Bad idea to punch him. I've seen it happen, strike somebody when they're tripping on this thing, it'll snap them out of it. Adrenaline kicks in or something. I don't know the chemistry, but I've seen it work that way. Better to be gentle, better to coax. Violence is counterproductive."

Thorn looked down at his hands. They hadn't cuffed him. They were counting on the drug to keep him under control. The two big men, one fat, the other who only looked fat. The guns were put away, he didn't know where. A whispery voice was telling him not to try anything stupid inside the car. Weak and whispery, it said, "Wait till they've stopped, let you out, let you wander, then make a break."

But Thorn didn't feel like waiting because when they let him out and let him prowl the streets, that's when they'd be most on guard, and he'd be on a short leash. It struck him that this was a better tactic, surprise them when they were least expecting. When the odds seemed impossibly stacked against him.

Thorn pictured it in his head, breathing slow and easy as he did it. He mapped it out, move one, move two, move three. Keep it simple. Quick and dirty. A plan even someone as stoned as he was could replay. One two three.

They were maybe half a mile from Belmont Heights, passing mobile homes. They'd be stopping in a minute or two and the window of possibility would shut.

Thorn leaned forward an inch, then two inches. Not enough to draw attention, but looking for a better angle, repositioning his feet, planting them securely.

Then he went for it. Rocked forward, bounced his forehead on the front seat, arms folded in front of his chest, and heaved backward, exploding, straightening his legs, pushing hard and throwing open his arms, hammering his elbows into their faces. Simultaneous strikes at X and Dobbins. Dobbins howled, X grunted. He didn't stop to inspect the damage but repeated the move, rocking forward, driving backward with both elbows at once.

Cruz slammed the brakes.

He reached forward and with the flat of his palms, Thorn pounded Cruz on both ears like he was banging cymbals, then a second time for good measure. X clawed for his arm, trying to pull him back into the seat, but his grip had weakened, and Thorn jerked away, gave himself enough room to deliver another elbow crack to X's face, then swiveled the other way and slammed his right elbow into Dobbins's nose.

He leaned across Dobbins, found the door handle, got it open, pushed Dobbins headlong onto the dirt road. X was clutching at the collar of Thorn's shirt, but his fingers fumbled and lost their hold. Pixie was yelling, Laurie spilling out her door, then kneeling beside her brother in the roadway.

Thorn came around to the driver's door, threw it open, hauled Cruz into the road. Her hard brown eyes were woozy from the ear claps. He grabbed her by the shirt front, dragged her close.

"You're the deluded one. You, Cruz, not them."

She was too hazy-eyed to reply.

Thorn drew back his right arm and hooked her with his forearm in the side of the head, sent her stumbling backward into the tall weeds beside the road. Snarling, X came out the rear door. Thorn pivoted and side-kicked the open door into his face. Then took hold of the handle and drove the door onto his lower legs, which still dangled outside.

He reached in, snatched the ignition keys, took them to the trunk and opened it, slung the green army duffel over his shoulder, the shotguns, the ammo, whatever cash was left. He had no plan to use them, but wanted only to deprive Cruz of the chance.

He hustled down the road toward Belmont Heights. The whispery voice in his head was nagging. Where the hell did that come from? *You're drugged, you're a creaky old guy, you're finished. Maybe this is a hallucination, maybe you're only dreaming this, imagining it, wishing it were true. Don't trip over your own drunken feet, you fool.*

Thorn stopped and looked back at the car. Cruz on her knees, fingering her damaged ears, yelling at him to stop, X-88 groaning inside the car.

He wasn't dreaming. He was a stubborn fuck, gifted with a wild and reckless streak. That second goddamn voice was the drug whispering, cajoling, undermining, trying to demoralize.

Up ahead another thirty yards he saw Ladarius Washington standing in his front yard. As Thorn broke into a trot, Ladarius started moving his way, a worried smile growing on his face. Then he waved his arm like a third-base coach bringing his batter home: *Hurry up, hurry up, move your ass.*

Twenty-six

"I known it first time I saw you," Ladarius said. "You're some kind of crazy-ass fucker."

He was leading Thorn at a jog down the dusty maze of pathways winding between the houses. Thorn catching sight of rust-stained tin roofs, windows covered with bright prints like the summer clothes of children cut up and hung to sweeten the indoor light, an old wooden boat upside down on sawhorses. A black hound, ears flapping, scooted around a corner and fell in alongside Thorn, head up, shaking himself as he ran, happy to join the procession. Clouds of insects swarmed near an outhouse where the stench of sewage was even greater than the cloud of pig shit riding the afternoon breeze.

Children stopped at their games, and men and women shushed their conversations and the humor went out of their faces as they watched Ladarius, then Thorn loping along behind, burdened by the duffel, but keeping up with the lanky man in overalls and heavy work boots.

Thorn had been doing a lot of running lately, more than since the days he used to go for dawn jogs along the bike path that ran beside the Overseas Highway in Key Largo, chased by roosters at Hibiscus Park and honked at by his fishing guide buddies on their way to the docks. When he got back to Key Largo, by god, he'd get back to running, whip himself in shape. It wasn't too late. Never too late.

Thorn hailed Ladarius to stop. He halted on the edge of the communal gathering spot, where several men were standing around the barbecue grill warming themselves in the smoky heat of charcoal, several slabs of meat broiling. There was church music coming from someplace nearby, a piano leading a choir of women's voices in "Nearer My God to Thee."

Though like the wanderer, the sun gone down,
darkness be over me, my rest a stone;
yet in my dreams I'd be nearer, my God, to thee

"Got to keep moving," Ladarius said. "They'll be here shortly."

"I need to see Eddie, he around?"

"Right here."

Eddie stepped forward from the group around the barbecue pit. Bald head gleaming in the afternoon sun, freshly pressed black trousers that shined with wear and a stiff white shirt and red sweater vest. His Sunday going-to-meeting best.

"Your keys." Thorn dug them from his pocket and handed them over. "Car's on the road. Better reclaim it now. Don't think it's been much abused, though there might be a bloodstain or two on the upholstery. A little pig shit on the mats. We got some on our shoes running through a field."

Eddie looked quizzically at Ladarius.

"They must've slipped the man some dope. That's how he's acting."

"True," Thorn said. "But I'm fighting it 'cause I'm a stubborn fuck."

"You keep on being stubborn," said Eddie. "Fight it all the way home."

"They'll be coming," Ladarius said. "We wasn't here. Neither of us."

"Course you wasn't," Eddie said. "I found these keys on the road. Get on now, get on to where you gotta go. None of us seen you passing by."

The other men nodded.

The two of them broke into a trot, going deeper into the rear fringes of the neighborhood. The duffel banging hard against his back. Thorn wasn't sure where Ladarius was leading him and he was breathing too hard to ask. They ran beyond the houses into an open field where a group of mutts were basking in the sun. The hound that was escorting them broke off and joined the pack as though he'd reached the limits of his territory, or perhaps beyond this point it was no longer safe for dogs.

The forest they entered was trackless, matted with vines, and dense with saplings and red maples, loblolly pines, sweet gum with their spiked seed balls littering the forest floor. Big white oak and sugar maples towered over the others.

"Where we going?"

Ladarius had slowed to a fast walk. A sweat stain showed through the back of his white shirt and burrs had collected on his dark blue trousers. His church clothes.

"Taking you where it happened."

Thorn's heart rolled and pitched.

"Where they were killed?"

"Just hold on, it'll speak for itself."

Thorn's elbows ached. His right arm wouldn't straighten fully, as if he'd cracked a bone when he slammed Webb Dobbins's face. His knees were sore from all the running and his forearms throbbed from repeated impacts. Thoughts in disarray, head swirling.

High above them the light piercing the canopy of evergreens and firs was diffused into a delicate twilight with a green cast that cut the temperature by ten degrees, and Thorn found himself shivering. He saw birds flitting in the uppermost branches but heard no birdsong, as if they were all waiting warily to see what these intruders in their woods had in mind.

Ladarius halted and peered from side to side through the trees, getting his bearings. Thorn heard nothing stirring, only a few stray long-dead leaves letting go of their limbs and trickling to the forest floor.

"This way," he said, and set off through an ankle-deep layer of leaves and twigs. Pushing through the dense netting of branches, ropey vines, and spiderwebs.

In fifty yards they came across a footpath, barely wide enough for a slender man. It shot straight ahead through the shadowy woods as if the deer, foxes, and Cherokees who'd carved the trail had settled on the same route to some watering hole or cave. Maybe it was the drug's lingering hallucinatory effects, but as they progressed down the narrow track, Thorn found himself conjuring the wispy spirits of the departed who'd passed this way centuries ago, leaving behind the path as a memorial to their common needs and basic fears. Those remnants of the long past, as insubstantial and shapeless as fog, seemed to be ushering Ladarius and Thorn toward some hallowed site.

A few yards later on, Ladarius halted, then stepped off the path and came to a stop beside the trunk of a large oak.

"This here was the lookout," he said. "Where your boy was crouched."

Thorn stood beside him and looked down at the ground behind the tree. The spot was bare of leaves, dirt scuffed lightly, but otherwise unremarkable.

"How do you know this?"

"His job was to alert the others, his hippie friends, if anyone came sneaking up in the dark, he blows a whistle twice. A signal to run."

Ladarius reached into his trousers pocket and handed Thorn a red-and-white plastic whistle.

"Been carrying this around, looking for the right time."

"Where is he? Where's my son?"

"We're getting to that. Didn't know could I trust you. Didn't know which side of the street you was playing. Still not a hundred percent sure on that, but the others think you're straight, so that's why we're here."

"What others?"

"We're getting to that too. You just hold all those horses you got pulling on you. We'll take this step at a time. Be sure that drug finished its business."

302

Thorn examined the whistle. Nothing special. A dime store toy. He slipped it in his pants pocket.

High above them a listless breeze rattled through the treetops and the birds up there hopped from branch to branch, playing a nervous game.

"Sure enough that night the men come sneaking up, two of them while your boy was crouched here. They was on him before he was ready, and this spot he picked, he made a mistake 'cause it was too damn close to where his friends was camped. So he blew the whistle and blew it again and the two men chased him for a while, then they split up and one of them took care of the ones by the campfire and the other kept chasing after your boy."

Thorn was silent. Prickles of cold sweat had broken out on his back.

"The campfire, it was down here."

Ladarius led him another fifty yards to a clearing. The charred remains of logs sat inside a circle of rocks. Off to the east sat a green Ford van, the same van, Thorn was certain, Cassandra was driving the last night he'd seen her, the night he'd last seen Flynn.

He walked over to it. Dozens of holes riddled its steel hide, silvery florets the size of jonquils. A large-caliber weapon, a huge clip of ammo. Thorn stopped counting at thirteen.

The tires were flat, the windshield gone, the

sliding side door was drawn open and inside were two woven hammocks slung one above the other from pegs fixed to the sides. The van was stripped of personal gear. Thorn checked the ashtrays, the glove compartment, scoured the floor beneath the seats. Not even a scrap of paper, a gum wrapper, nothing to identify it as belonging to Flynn's group. Dark spatters on the tan carpet, a dried patch of blood the size of a small dog.

While Ladarius stood a few feet away, Thorn walked around the vehicle, touching the gashes in the metal, running his fingers across the smooth finish. The license plate had been removed. The taillights smashed.

"How'd they get a van back here? There a road somewhere?"

"No road," Ladarius said. "There's a shoreline."

He waggled his hand and led Thorn down a slope of open ground, the bushes flattened or hacked away to make room for the van. The bank slanted gently down to the sluggish flow of the river, and running alongside it the hard-packed shore was barely wide enough for a single vehicle to navigate.

"Up river about a mile there's a beach near the highway where people fish and swim and hold baptisms." Ladarius motioned north. "That's where your people came in and drove down here till they found that clearing. Nice spot for camping. Nice hideout. They came and went on foot through the edge of Belmont Heights, talking to those who'd stand still and listen, mostly preaching to the folks around here about shit they already know, how bad the hog farm is for everybody, like we got to hear about that, like we haven't been living that goddamn nightmare every day of our lives, then when they were wore out talking to my people they worked their way down to the Mexican trailers."

Ladarius headed back up the bank to the woods and Thorn followed. The last of the drug's effects had faded, the tension was leaving his shoulders, a new clarity returning to his vision.

"Flynn blew his whistle then ran. Where was he shot? Do you know?"

"Don't know exactly, don't truly matter, does it?"

"You're right."

"Now I'll show you something else."

As Ladarius was leading him along a rocky crest that followed the river's path, Thorn asked him how he knew all this.

"I'm showing you this one last thing, then I'm done with you," Ladarius said without turning around. "After this you're on your own time."

"Dobbins did this," Thorn said. "All this killing to cover up his drug operation."

Ladarius pushed through the brambles and branches, taking long strides.

"Why hasn't the town done something? He's a

criminal, a murderer. He holds his employees captive, tortures them. He's polluting your water and your air, he's slaughtering people in the woods, he's dealing drugs to the citizens. Why haven't you called the state police, the FBI? Dobbins might be powerful in these few square miles, but he's not some god."

Ladarius stopped but didn't turn around. He tilted his head back as if beseeching the heavens for patience.

"Where you from, mister?"

Key Largo, Thorn told him.

"That a small place, is it? Small as Pine Haven?"

"Similar, I suppose."

Ladarius turned to face him with a sour look.

"How many different jobs can a man work at in this place you live?"

"I don't know."

"Bartenders, plumbers, people like that. How many different kinds?"

"A lot."

"In this place you from, this Key Largo, there one man who holds all the strings to all those jobs?"

"That doesn't matter," Thorn said. "He's an evil man. He's fucking up your world. He's a dictator. Dictators can be overthrown."

"So there's not one man holding all the strings? That what you telling me? You never had experience of this kind? That's what you're saying?"

Thorn was silent.

"First day you arrive, you drove a car into Pine Haven, ain't that right?"

"That's right."

"You see any thriving metropolis on your way? Any gated golf course communities, any streets paved in silver or gold? Anything like that? 'Cause I don't think so. I don't think you saw nothing but neediness and empty fields and empty highways and crumbling-down buildings.

" 'Cause see, if Webb Dobbins was to be struck down by lightning or carried off to jail as we all agree would be the rightful outcome of his criminal actions, then it wouldn't be a year before Pine Haven looked exactly like all that mess you drove through. Just as empty, just as needy and downhearted."

"Somebody else would take over, run that farm."

"Is that right? You know that for a fact, do you?"

"Why wouldn't they?"

"What you think Webb Dobbins is in the drug business for? To be a millionaire? No, sir. He's selling his poison over at the military bases so he can pay his debts to Pastureland Corporation. That drug money just gets them by. Take it away, that farm dies in a month. And those are the same debts anybody else would have if they bought that farm. It ain't going to happen.

"Then you got all the harm those hogs already done to the land and river and the air. Easier to set up shop somewhere else where nothing ain't polluted yet, where the people don't know what's coming their way, and they're all singing and happy and clapping their hands about this new business bringing jobs to town. That's what happens. Dobbins dies or goes to jail, this whole town withers up and blows away like a milk-weed bloom in August."

Ladarius stepped close to Thorn and pointed a finger at his face, then thumped that finger hard against Thorn's chest.

"So you think twice before you go screaming for the FBI or the state police. Most people in this town'd like nothing better than to slice Dobbins's throat, but they know damn well if they did, they'd be good as slicing their own and their brothers' and their sisters' and all their little children's throats too.

"Now follow me, Mr. Key Largo, and don't be talking no shit about things you don't have no damn idea about."

Twenty-seven

Ladarius led him across a gully to the riverbank, then marched down the smooth shoreline until they reached a spot where the mud was freshly chewed by tire tracks.

"Look there in the water, out about ten feet."

Thorn leaned over the river, cupped his hands against the sunlight.

The ATV Cassandra had been driving was submerged, six, seven feet down in the muddy current.

"What she did was, the redhead, she came roaring into Belmont, five, ten minutes before you showed up. We gave her directions, same directions I'm about to give you, and after she went off, we drove that machine over here and rolled the goddamn thing into the river to cover her tracks."

"I'm not following you."

"We was keeping your boy," Ladarius said. "Ministering to him best we know how. That man Eddie you met, the one you been driving his car, he was an army medic in one of those foreign places, Iraq or Iran, Kuwait, wherever the hell that war was. Eddie's as close to a doctor as we

309

got, so it was him keeping your boy alive, giving him pills and cleaning his wounds, lord almighty, he plucked enough buckshot out of his backside to sink a rowboat."

"Flynn's alive? Where is he?"

Ladarius looked over at the sunken ATV. This man was going at his own pace no matter what whirling foolishness the world threw in his path.

"Like I'm saying, Eddie, a week, ten days, he's spending every hour with that boy, keeping his breath moving in and out, keeping his heart pumping, talking to him, putting cold rags on his forehead, neglecting everybody else in his own backyard, their fevers, their coughing, their headaches, my little girl's got asthma so bad she almost died two nights ago because Eddie was doctoring the shit out of your boy.

"And every time Burkhart come around with his bloodhounds and his shotgun, kicking down doors and searching for that kid, Eddie would slide him quick onto a stretcher and a couple of the young ones would get out of bed and carry him back into these woods till Burkhart was done with his terrorizing.

"Burkhart, he had one of your boy's shirts or underpants, I don't know what it was, but he was carrying it around in a plastic bag, must've taken it from that van, and he's holding it under the dogs' noses and putting them on the scent. Couple of nights ago those tracking dogs came right up to Eddie's door. Too damn close, he barely got your boy out of there before Burkhart came busting in.

"So that's what's been going on around here. That's what we been doing, all of us in one way or the other, to keep your kid alive. Don't ask me why, 'cause there ain't no good reason for it. Boy was a fool on a fool's errand. Preaching to the choir is all he was doing. Then him or the red-head, one of those folks, they flashed money in front of the Mexicans, got a couple of them to sneak around, do some spying inside the hog farm, taking pictures or whatever the hell they did, and that got one of those Mexicans killed. Kid just trying to make a wage. Your boy and his friends coming in here, not knowing shit from apple butter, a week on after they show up people are dying because of them and me and my people, every day it gets more certain one of us is going to be shot dead by Burkhart or Webb for hiding your boy's sorry ass.

"You asking me is he alive, well, I'd tell you if I could, but I can't. All I know is, he was half-way alive when me and the others, we couldn't take it anymore, all the dogs sniffing around for him, and the danger we were putting our own people in for hiding that kid, so we brought him down here, down to the river, and we put him in a boat and we set him loose."

"Set him loose," Thorn said.

"Set him loose, exactly right."

It was a dark green aluminum canoe, one of two, Ladarius informed him, that Flynn's group brought along to use in the escape plan they never had the chance to employ. Ladarius showed Thorn where the remaining canoe was hidden inside a blackberry thicket and buried beneath a pile of leaves. Ladarius dragged it out and kept dragging it, Thorn following him down the bank to the riverside.

"Was Flynn strong enough to paddle?"

"Hell no, he wasn't strong enough. It was a miracle the boy could sit upright at all."

"So in that condition you just pushed him into the river by himself?"

"If I'd've done that, I wouldn't be much better than Webb Dobbins or Burkhart, now would I?"

"Someone went with him?"

Ladarius drew an exasperated breath and whistled it out.

"What you do, you go down this river, just paddle with the current, shouldn't tax you too much, in half an hour, forty-five minutes, you'll come to a dogleg bend to the right, and just past that you'll see a rickety little dock, all but gone, just a couple of pilings that ain't finished rotting yet, hanging on like bad teeth, and that's where you pull out. You walk up the bank a way and you don't need to do another thing, no need to shout

312

hello, 'cause they'll find you, you count on that, yes, sir. They'll know the minute you step on their land."

"You're not going to tell me what you're sending me into?"

"It ain't nothing worse than where you been already."

Thorn loaded the duffel in the bow, took a seat in the stern, and Ladarius nudged him out into the sluggish current.

"You be careful now, whatever you do next, you hear? Don't be overthrowing any dictators unless it's the only way to save your sorry ass."

The river was deceptive, the current taking Thorn's canoe more briskly than it appeared capable of. He was off and away from Ladarius before he had time to say good-bye, and when he swiveled around, the man had slipped back into the woods and was gone.

Borne into the center of the waterway by invisible tributaries within the river's flow, Thorn dug his paddle in deep and tried to gain control, but the current had commandeered the canoe and turned it broadside and was dragging him toward twin rocks spread apart no farther than the mouth of a hockey net. Before he could right himself, his stern collided hard against the outer edge of one rock, which sent the canoe into a spiral that splashed a small wave over his starboard side. He wallowed badly and it felt for a moment like he was about to swamp the boat and go for an extended swim.

It was then Thorn understood the drug had not finished with him and was at the very least slowing his reflexes if not sabotaging his entire nervous system. He back-paddled hard for several strokes, got the bow headed downstream, and finally settled into a more balanced position on the seat. At least the cold river water had toned down his delirium a bit, waking him from the drowse he'd gotten lost in.

He concentrated on piloting, holding steady mid-river, paddling with small, tentative strokes like a drunk trying to tiptoe a straight line with police lights whirling nearby. It was a lesson in control, how much Thorn truly exercised, how much was beyond him. The river had its own ideas and a capricious streak. After a while he steadied himself, steering when he could, obeying the tug of the current when he couldn't, keeping as close to the right bank as he was able.

No one lived along this stretch of water, though he saw what looked like abandoned fishing shacks through the trees, summer cabins perhaps, where city people had once come before the river grew so contaminated it lost its appeal. There were half-sunk floating docks and diving boards fixed to the edges of back-porch decks, automobile tires washed ashore, all but hidden beneath years of river mud.

A clear-cut acre appeared to his right. Stripped of timber, the land had grown scar tissue of weeds and saplings, and as he passed by the current seemed to grow faint as if the river were honoring the loss of foliage. Sunning itself in that open space, a great blue heron was flushed by Thorn's passing and with a startled cry it rose awkwardly then swooped forward in front of his canoe and raced along before him skimming the water with the tips of its wings, leaving its brief autograph.

He missed the channels of deeper water and ran through a series of small foaming rapids, the canoe scraping hard across the rocky bottom, bumping against hidden rocks, then washing over a four-foot dip, a mini-waterfall, and floundering for a moment, barely averting another pinwheel slide.

Around him the river made a low humming sound as soothing as the gentle wash of surf. In the nearby forest crickets were perfecting their tedious drone. Here and there clusters of dead fish floated in patches like shiny silver oil slicks and above him a few dragonflies who'd lingered into winter were lacing knots in the still air. He could smell the rich moldy shoreline, generations of leafy decay, the rank metallic aroma of damp clay rarely touched by the sun.

In its way the terrain was as wild and gorgeous and as jeopardized as the Florida landscape he felt so passionate about. This place needed defending too, needed people like Flynn and Cassandra who were willing to put all else aside and risk themselves to rescue what was left of it. Hog farms that fed an insatiable national hunger were clearly not the only dangers. There was a listless, undervalued quality to the land itself and to its people. They seemed more like captives than citizens. No one with the stomach for a brawl. So much already lost, there was little left to fight for.

When he came upon the dogleg bend then saw the collapsing dock, its appearance was so sudden, he had to back-paddle hard, putting on the brakes, and swing the canoe at nearly a right angle to the current, and even with a flurry of deep and urgent strokes, he missed the remains of the dock by several feet and plowed the canoe into a soft, sloppy embankment.

Thorn climbed over the duffel and hopped across to the slope, pulled the canoe forward till it was half out of water. He left the duffel behind and scrambled up the bank, punching footholes along the way as if he were scaling a snowy cliff.

At the summit of the bank there were knee-high weeds and a rickety chain-link fence that had lost its battle with rust and gravity and toppled over and was lying nearly flat before him. NO TRESPASSING signs were nailed to several trees, though they looked as ancient and unattended as the fence.

He stopped for a moment and peered into the shadowy woods, and when his eyes adjusted to the gloom, he made out the vague outline of a cabin but no sign of activity. Perhaps he'd landed too soon, and this wasn't the property Ladarius had directed him to. Then again, he'd not seen any docks farther up the river and this was the first enclave he'd seen in the last half hour with even a remote chance of being occupied.

Following the remnants of a path, he waded through the weeds, heading toward the house. He was twenty yards off when just a few feet to his right the gleam of metal surprised him.

A girl of seven or eight with blond curls that hung to her shoulders sat in an adult-size wheelchair. She was dressed in a cowgirl shirt with red and black checks and blue jeans with fancy stitching. The legs of the jeans hung loose and flapped in a river breeze. A brown paper sack with a grease stain sat in her lap.

Beside her stood an enormous yellow dog, mostly Lab but partly Saint Bernard or some other long-haired giant breed. It had been focused on the girl and the bag in her lap, but as Thorn approached it swung its massive head around, its neck hairs bristling, and began to make a low rumbling growl.

"You Thorn?"

"I am."

"I'm Emma," she said. "They're in the house.

Mom and the others. You like chocolate chip cookies?"

Thorn took a slow breath. He hadn't realized how rattled his nerves were, how trip-wired he'd become from the drugs and the violence but mostly from hearing how badly injured Flynn was.

"Sure, I love chocolate chip cookies."

She rolled forward, then tucked a hand into the bag and came out with a cookie, extending it to him. The dog followed her, still growling, and watching Thorn with an unsettling focus on his throat.

"Every Sunday Mama bakes them, a special treat if I've been good all week. Usually I'm good. Sometimes I'm not, though, sometimes I get a little peevish. Do you get peevish?"

"I do. More often than I'd like."

"It's hard to be good all the time," she said. "Don't you think it's hard?"

"The hardest thing there is." He sampled the cookie. Chewy and fresh, warm from her lap, the sun, or just out of the oven. "Your mama is Millie?"

"Everybody knows Mama. She's famous in Pine Haven, best waitress in the county."

"She's excellent."

"The boy inside, the one that's hurt, you're his dad?"

"I am. Can I see him now?"

"That's why I'm parked here. To show you where he is. This is Duke. It's short for Marmaduke, but we just call him Duke. He's friendly, you can pet him if you want, but don't touch his head, he doesn't like that, or his ears."

He passed on petting Duke but asked Emma if he could help roll her chair up to the house, and she shook her head.

"Like doing it myself. It builds my muscles. A girl needs muscles, don't you think?"

"I do," Thorn said. "Muscles come in very handy."

"Come on, Duke," she said.

The big dog followed them up the path toward the house, nosing Thorn hard in the butt twice along the way.

Twenty-eight

Sunday wasn't the best day for it, but Sunday was all Sugarman had. Mid-afternoon, blasting along I-95 at twenty miles an hour above the limit, traveling the same route as two days before, cell phone pressed to his ear, calling the Florida Highway Patrol office in Tallahassee.

After fighting through the phone cascade, then half an hour on hold and four handoffs, he finally found a state employee willing to help track down the green Nissan Tina Gathercole had hijacked from the Shell station in Vero Beach two days earlier.

Sheila Barnes had a south Georgia voice, sweetly asking him to identify himself, which Sugarman did by giving his old badge number and work history from twelve years ago when he was a deputy for Monroe County sheriff's department. Sheila sounded skeptical, then put him on hold, and Sugarman thought, shit, here we go, impersonating an officer, but she came back in a few minutes and said that, yes, in fact, two days ago a green 2003 Nissan had been found abandoned in the emergency lane three miles south of the Vero Beach exit, and it was subsequently ticketed then later towed to an impound lot servicing Indian River County. Sheila gave him the name of the trooper who'd written the violation and the phone number for the garage where the car was being stored.

Sunday must've been a big day for the impound garage because a gruff guy snatched it up on the first ring.

Yeah, they still had the car, at least for the moment. Vehicle was stolen from a Miami shopping mall three days ago, the owner was on his way up right now to collect it. No, there was no blood or sign of struggle inside the car, and nothing of note left behind. A few CDs, some cigarettes, loose change, he'd check again if Sugarman wanted, but he was pretty sure the car was clean.

Sugar asked him, if he didn't mind, to give it another look, but don't touch or disturb anything, this was a homicide investigation. The driver's body was found a few hours north of the location where the car was abandoned and Sugarman was trying to piece together exactly what happened. When the tow truck guy started hemming and hawing, Sugarman told the guy that the driver of the car was a woman and she'd been killed by being suffocated with meat.

The guy groaned, set the phone down, and came back in a few minutes. Quieter, subdued. No, he'd found nothing in the car. Clean as a new whistle.

One last thing Sugarman wanted to know. Was the tow truck guy absolutely one hundred percent positive the car was found south of Vero Beach exit 147, not north? The guy huffed, smacked the phone down again, and came back in two or three minutes, paper rattling in the background.

He had the record sheet in his hand. Yeah, yeah, it was three miles south of exit 147. South, south, south. Now you got everything you want?

"Don't go near the car again," Sugarman said. "And don't deliver it to its owner. The car's an active crime scene. FBI will be contacting you shortly."

If the car was found south of exit 147, it meant

Tina was heading home after playing her part in Cruz's bogus sting operation. Which meant somebody intercepted her, and that person was likely in league with Cruz. It was hard to imagine how the guy managed to shield what he was doing when he bound her up and tossed her in the trunk, all this going down along a busy section of the interstate. People whizzing by.

Sugarman settled on a more likely scenario. The killer hailed Tina, got her to pull over, then he strong-armed her into his vehicle, took her to a remote location to truss her up and put her in the trunk. In that case, Tina probably recognized the person in the car, which meant this encounter may have been a part of the plan from the outset. Cruz promising she'd send somebody to extract Tina from the stolen vehicle and drive her home to Key Largo, then double-crossing her big time. All of it was speculation, but Sugarman was sure it was one of those versions, or something close.

He called Sheffield. Got him as he was about to enter a Home Depot to buy a few more gallons of paint.

"You might want to call a pal at the bureau, let them know the car Tina Gathercole was kidnapped from is about to be delivered to its owner, contaminating a crime scene."

Sheffield sighed, took down the number of the impound lot.

"That it?"

"No. One more thing."

Sugarman asked if he'd be willing to throw some weight around with the St. Johns County sheriff's office, find out the name of the homicide cop assigned to Tina's case, see if he was available for a sit-down in half an hour.

"You're asking me to impersonate my former self?"

"If you're uncomfortable with that, I'll find another way."

"Will this make us even?"

"We're even now."

"I'll work on it," Frank said. "Give me ten minutes."

A little guilt, Sugarman thought, could work a lot of magic.

Fifteen miles up the interstate, Sheffield called back.

"Deputy David Randolph is waiting for you at the sheriff's office. He's not the lead investigator, but that guy, name of Dickerson, apparently he's a pompous shithead. Randolph sounds like a decent guy. I asked him to open the murder book for you, share whatever case files they've got. Told him it was part of a federal investigation. For the rest of the afternoon, you're an FBI agent. Enjoy it, because this is it, Sugar, all the assistance I can provide. I don't want them to yank my goddamn pension before I get the first check."

The St. Johns County sheriff's office was twenty minutes off the interstate on a stark stretch of roadway across from an industrial park. He found Randolph at the coffee machine refilling the reservoir with water.

Sugarman introduced himself, apologized that he was in a bit of a hurry, had an urgent appointment a few hundred miles up the road. Randolph didn't ask for any identification.

The deputy was a good six-four with a hard-looking body and a soft face. Mouth on the edge of a smile like he was easily amused or in on some cosmic joke. There'd been a time when Sugarman wore a similar smile and had a similar outlook, and maybe someday that sensation would return. But for now his own face felt like he was wearing a plaster cast set in a scowl of outrage. Behind his eyes he'd been feeling a pressure building like a gallon of hot tears dammed up back there.

Randolph led him to a conference room and laid out on a long table the documents they'd collected so far. Two murders, an eighteen-year-old African American male and Tina Gathercole.

"You want some privacy?"

"I could use that, yes."

"I gotta say, you seem pretty courteous for an FBI guy. I haven't met that many, but you're not like the others. Abrupt, abrasive. Bunch of a-holes, mainly."

"I'll take that as a compliment."

Randolph left him with the ME's two autopsy reports along with sets of photos for each, and the two crime scene accounts, photos of the scenes and investigators' notes. There was also a handful of photos that were still shots taken from the security video footage at the burger place's drive-through window and more images from another camera mounted above the rear door.

In the set of photos from the drive-through, a round-faced stocky man with big lips and a shaved head was leaning out the window of a four-door sedan.

The other security camera at the rear of the burger joint had caught the same husky guy approaching the rear door of the restaurant. The time stamp marked it at 2:23 A.M.

Sugarman didn't bother with the autopsy photos. He'd seen more than his share of those kinds of images and didn't want them skittering around in his head the rest of his life, especially the ones of Tina. He scanned the ME's report and learned the meat crammed into the mouth of the young fast food worker was uncooked, while the meat Tina had choked on was flame broiled and there were no signs of bread or condiments, mayo, ketchup, pickles, or lettuce in her airway.

The manager of the burger joint had given a detailed statement, which was translated into familiar cop euphemisms that were meant to be neutral and professional but always sounded to Sugarman like deadpan satire.

The verbal altercation with the suspect concerned three issues. First, the worker who would soon become the victim of a murder casually noted to the drive-through customer that it was unusual for anyone to order a plain burger without cheese or any toppings whatsoever. The suspect objected to what he considered the worker's haughty attitude. Further hostile interchange took place between the suspect and the victim, at which time the manager of the establishment came to her worker's side and asked if there was a problem. The suspect made further antagonistic remarks to both manager and worker indicating he found the entire fast food industry to be guilty of abhorrent behavior regarding the manner in which chickens, cows, and pigs were raised. Following his final hostile remark, the suspect drove off with the three plain hamburgers.

Sugarman found Deputy Randolph at his desk drinking coffee and reading from his computer screen. He asked if Randolph could make him a copy of a couple of the photos. They might come in handy up the road.

Randolph made the copies and escorted Sugarman outside to his car.

"You nail this guy, you'll let us know, right? Professional courtesy. I mean, this kid at the fast food place, Anthony Pope, he was a straight-A student at our county high school, track star, ran the mile, good hardworking kid with a single mom and three young sisters. Had a scholarship to go to Gainesville. Sang in the choir." Randolph's eyes were misty, his voice breaking on "choir."

"I'll let you know," Sugarman said. "You have my word."

Back on the interstate, holding it steady at ninety in the seventy zone, Sugar tugged the drive-through photo from the folder and had another look.

The guy had his hand outstretched from his car window and was about to take hold of the white paper sack from the attendant.

The man's face was fleshy with small, moody eyes, a broad forehead, and a formidable hawk nose. Thick neck, big shoulders, the kind of goon you'd expect to see working as a bouncer in a biker bar.

One side of his upper lip was curled upward in a snarl that showed a glimpse of his right incisor. The expression seemed to sit easily on that mouth as if this was a man who scowled habitually. All in all, it was a harsh, resentful face, one that would be hard to love and seemed unlikely to express either affection or tenderness. His eyes were murky and lightless, possibly a result of the poor quality of the nighttime photo, or maybe that's how the guy really looked, a pitiless and vacant stare.

Of course Sugarman knew he was projecting. He had no way of knowing if this man was ever tender or affectionate, loved or unloved. But he was pretty damn sure of one thing. Those three naked hamburger patties the man was holding in his right hand wound up choking to death a woman Sugarman had cared about a great deal.

Twenty-nine

After Thorn fled, X-88 stumbled out of the car, straightened his shoulders, probed his throbbing nose. Numb, but not flattened. He drew out the plugs to see if he could still smell and found that his nostrils were swollen but not completely clogged.

While Cruz sat in the front seat of the car and recovered, X stood beside her and made the case for returning to the farm. It was no use chasing the redhead without a fresh sample of her scent.

"Whatever it takes," she said. "We can't let her slip away."

At the farm, Laurie and Pixie stayed with the car while Dobbins, with a hankie pressed to his bloody nose, followed X's orders and went for

Ziploc bags and brought them to the room where Cassandra was imprisoned.

X was standing next to the mound of red hair piled in a corner.

"Hers?" He kicked at the pile.

"Yeah, yeah," Dobbins said. "Burkhart thought hacking it off would get her talking. It didn't work. Nothing did."

X-88 picked up a handful of hair, sniffed it, then stuffed it inside the bag and sealed it.

"You going to tell me what the hell you're doing?" Dobbins was planted in the doorway. "These fuckers are absconding and you two're playing games."

X bent over and pressed his nose to the vinyl seat where Cassandra had been bound up. He looked back at Cruz and nodded, took out his pocketknife, and sliced a square of vinyl from the seat and tucked it in the other plastic bag.

"Colored town," X said. "We'll start there. Where Thorn was headed."

X was getting in the car, Dobbins and Cruz already in their seats, when Pixie tapped him on the shoulder and motioned for him to follow.

When they'd moved a few yards away, she said, "I know what you're thinking, X. You want to burn this place down, destroy it. It's horrible, all these pigs in the cages, your worst nightmare, hell on earth. But I'm pleading with you, don't do it, X. Please, as a favor to me."

"Favor?"

"I know this is sudden, and I'm sorry, but I'm staying here."

"Staying where?"

"I mean staying for good. She invited me and I said yes."

Pixie cut a look toward Laurie, who was leaning against a tree nearby, smoking what looked like a joint.

"You and her? Hell, you just met the woman a few hours ago."

"There was a day when I'd just met you, X. You were an impulse and that worked out pretty good."

"I haven't seen you say two words to her. I haven't seen you and her even look at each other. Who the hell is she anyway?"

"You haven't paid much attention to me lately."

"You don't even know that girl, Pixie."

"You sound like my mother. Can you hear yourself?"

Yeah, he did. He sounded like fucking Cruz.

"I wouldn't even consider it except when you tried to push me off on Varla in St. Augustine, then what you said about the train coming to the station, you meant that, didn't you?"

"I meant it."

"Soon?"

"Can't say. But yeah, feels like it should be arriving shortly."

"I'm sorry, X. I'm really sorry. You're hurting, aren't you? The headaches?"

X waved off her question.

"Your old lady isn't going to like this."

"Are you kidding? She doesn't care. She's never cared. She'll be glad to get rid of me. I'm the sick and twisted daughter, an embarrassment."

From the car Dobbins yelled at them to hurry the fuck up.

"Pixie living on a hog farm." He said it, adjusting to the idea.

"So now you can't burn this place down, X. I see it in your face, that's what you were planning, some way or another blow it up, but you can't. I'm staying here, and listen, I know it sounds crazy, but I was thinking maybe you could stay too.

"I had this idea, the three of us, we get rid of Dobbins. Laurie hates him, wants to be rid of him. It could be just the three of us, we could fix this place, make it right, put the pigs out to pasture or whatever, go natural, you don't need to burn down everything just because it's wrong the way it is."

"So that's what this is about? She's angling for me to kill her brother?"

"No, it's about fixing this place, making it right. What you believe in."

"Let the pigs loose? Let them run free in the fields? Let them get old and die a natural death?

You can't make a living like that. It's a fantasy, Pixie. That's some silly-girl dream."

"Stay, X. Don't destroy it. Stay with me and Laurie. You're always saying you want to fix things. Well, this is your chance. Fix this place, don't tear it down."

"It's a fantasy."

"We could make it happen," Pixie said. "I know we could, the three of us could make it work. We'd throw in together, become a weird, fucked-up little family, find a way."

"Okay, look," he said. "For you, Pixie, just because it's you, and because the promise I made to your dad, I won't burn it down. But you got to know I can't stay. This is everything I hate. This is the worst fucking place in the known universe. But hey, you're welcome to it."

He reached out and ruffled her white-blond hair, scratched his fingernails into her scalp the way she liked. She closed her eyes and went a little slack. After a few seconds more, X stopped and Pixie's eyes came open.

Cruz shouted at them to hurry up.

"Goddamn it, I'll miss you, X. You're fucking unique. I'll miss you."

"Yeah," he said. "You probably will."

X-88 left her standing there, got behind the wheel, and drove them the ten minutes through the Mexican slum and parked on the road on the outskirts of Belmont Heights. He felt bad.

Maybe it was about losing Pixie, or maybe it was just his goddamn nose, swollen and sore from Thorn's punches. If it hadn't been for the plugs in his nostrils, his nose might've been smashed flat and pouring blood like Dobbins's was.

They got out and he took a few quick sniffs of the air.

"We're close," X said, and led Cruz and Dobbins into Belmont Heights.

They wound in and out between houses. Children peeked from windows, and a pack of mongrels tagged along barking till X halted and glared their way and they scattered.

There was no sign of men anywhere.

He was carrying the three plastic Ziploc bags. The red hair, the vinyl swatch, and in the third was an orange T-shirt from a bar in Key Largo. Cruz picked it up on her first trip to Pine Haven, loot she'd found in the tree huggers' van, the shirt was Flynn's. A while ago X took a single snort of the T-shirt. Its scent was a blend of wet wood, caramel, vanilla tea, and toasted bread, sharp and distinctive though not nearly as zesty as Cassandra's aroma.

Her mass of red hair was dense with odor.

Though it was a challenge to smell anything at all beneath the haze of pig shit blanketing the area, in that tangle of red hair he'd detected the nuttiness of marzipan, damp stones, a grassy pasture with a tinge of mint, and a background of cat piss and yeasty warm biscuit. All of which told him she'd been living outdoors, sleeping on pine needles, bathing in river water, using no deodorant or toothpaste for months, and she'd been engaged in unsanitary practices, employing neither soap nor toilet paper. Her hair was sour and greasy, flecked with fecal matter.

A unique flavor, but still hard to track because molecules of those same odors were floating everywhere in this neighborhood. If he'd had to rely solely on this bag of hair, X might easily blunder around for a week without finding her, drawn to an empty field where moist rocks lay hidden in a bed of pennyroyal, or attracted to a house filled with cats where someone was cooking cornbread. He could bat from smell to smell and never locate that particular blend of fragrances in one place.

However, once he was in close proximity to Cassandra, he knew her scent would guide him the last few steps, but at such a distance, the collection of aromas in her hair didn't point anywhere in particular.

Fortunately he didn't have to rely on her hair alone. There was another scent available, her aromatic signature, a pungent strand of her bodily odor that was as distinct as a ten-carat diamond in a box of river rocks.

"Can you do it?" Cruz said. "Or do we call for the bloodhounds?"

"Fuck the dogs," X said. "She's been through here in the last hour."

"You're shitting me," Dobbins said. "He's pretending he can smell her trail?"

Cruz said, "X-88 is a fragrance savant. Better than any dog."

"Give me a fucking break. This freak?"

X spun on Dobbins, gripped a handful of his hair, and yanked his head backward, locked him in place with an arm around his throat. He spoke quietly into his right ear.

"I'm going to give you a free science lesson, redneck, so pay attention, I'll go slow. My olfactory receptor neurons are as sensitive as a beagle's. You, if you're lucky, you got five million receptors, where I'm at something north of two hundred million. Which means, even on a bad day, I can tell whether or not there's a single drop of human piss in an Olympic swimming pool.

"But that's just the start. Because those neurons send messages to my olfactory bulb and it ships those signals to three places at once, the frontal cortex where odors are perceived, the hypothalamus amygdala where the emotional shit is stored, and to the hippocampus that handles odor memory.

"Normal-size hypothalamus, it's an almond. Mine's a lemon. Regular hippocampus is shaped like a sea horse. Supposed to be about an inch long. Mine's triple that. I've been lab tested, X-rayed, and CAT scanned half a dozen times. Reason I had all those tests, it's because my lemon and my sea horse, they started out big, but this last year, they started growing. They're double the size they used to be, and they're still growing. If they don't stop, in a month or two, maybe less, my skull's going to crack wide open. So yeah, damn right I'm a freak of nature, but I'm the exact freak you people need at this moment.

"There it is, hotshot. You don't believe it, think I'm a joke, a fake, whatever, fine, stand back and watch, then decide if I'm for real. But I'm not taking any more of your bullshit. You got it?"

Dobbins made a throaty noise that sounded like agreement. X released him, pushed him away, and kept walking through the warren of houses.

It took a few more minutes before the scent trail led him to a two-story shack. The shack was neater and larger than those around it, with flower boxes, a gleaming tin roof, a fresh coat of white paint.

X-88 tilted his head back, shut his mouth, and inhaled deeply, and inhaled again. He smiled at Cruz.

"You got something?"

"Blood's a bitch," he said. "Nails you every time."

"What's that mean? Cassandra's wounded? She's bleeding?"

X-88 held up the Ziploc bag with the vinyl inside.

"Having her period," X said. "Squirming on that chair, her blood and sweat soaked in pretty good. Normally vaginas are acidic, and that keeps germs at bay, but blood changes the pH and kick-starts bacteria. At the moment our girl's got some very nutritious organisms thriving in her crotch."

"Where is she?"

"She was here a while ago, maybe an hour, I don't know, maybe less."

"Which way?"

"Slow down," he said. "I need another whiff of the T-shirt."

"They're together? Cassandra and Flynn?"

"A hit of this, I'll know for sure."

He peeled open the plastic bag, drew in a deep breath, then closed it up again. Turned in a half circle, breathing evenly.

"In there." He gestured at the two-story house. "Both of them."

"Eddie's place." Dobbins sounded chastened, pitching in to help. "They call him Doc. Old-timer, him and his wife, they handle all the colored births."

"You're sure?" Cruz asked X.

"In there," he said again.

"Dobbins." Cruz waved at the near corner of the house. "Around back. Nobody gets out of here. Nobody."

When Dobbins was set, X shouldered open the front door. The living room was shadowy and was crowded with black men in dress shirts and dark trousers, at least a dozen, shoulder to shoulder, some with hammers in hand, others holding knives, a couple with long-handled axes, all of them bristling with anger.

From her waistband Cruz drew her Glock.

"You break into my house, wave a gun, I'm within my rights to defend myself any way I see fit." The man was bald with a fringe of white hair.

"Are you Doc Eddie?"

The man gave a curt nod.

"We're on the trail of a terrorist," she said. "We have reason to believe he's hiding in this dwelling."

"What reason you have to believe that?"

"Because I can smell him," X said, pointing. "He's back there."

"You can smell him?" one of the men said, and a few others chuckled.

Cruz stepped forward, prodded the weapon at the crowd to clear a path.

Eddie said, "It's okay, boys, let 'em look. They won't find no terrorist in this house."

Grumbling, the group parted, opening a narrow lane to the kitchen. X-88 said nothing, kept his head tipped back to scoop up the scent and passed through the kitchen, following the trail into a cramped room where a dryer was stacked atop a washing machine.

"So your terrorist, he's hiding in the washer?" one man said.

X-88 pulled open the door of the washing machine and reached inside and dragged out a white bedsheet soiled with bloodstains.

X wadded up the cotton sheet and pressed his face against it and closed his eyes. After a few seconds he dropped the sheet on the floor.

"Been staying here the whole time," X said to Cruz. "Lying on those sheets, bleeding, sweating, feverish, infected, couldn't control his bowels. He didn't leave more than an hour ago."

Cruz turned to face the men, who'd crowded into the kitchen and were watching her with hair-trigger hostility.

"I'm not going to ask you where Flynn Moss went, because you people have proven yourselves to be deceitful. But mark my words, gentlemen, you'll be paying dearly for this treachery. I'll leave it up to Sheriff Burkhart and Mr. Dobbins to decide how best to execute the punishment. But you will pay."

They exited through the rear door, gathered Dobbins, then went a few yards east of Eddie's house before X-88 picked up the scent again.

"This'll be easier now," X said. "Those sheets, there was more than blood on them."

In the lead, X-88 was striding past an open field where dogs lay sunning.

"What else?" Dobbins moved alongside Cruz and X.

"Mortuary workers call it tissue gas."

Cruz stopped. They'd reached the edge of a stand of trees.

"Explain," she said.

"A bacteria you've smelled before, everybody has. Spoiled meat, decaying vegetation, marine sediment, the stink of low tide at the beach."

"I don't get it," Dobbins said.

"Don't know the full Latin name," X said, looking off at the woods. "But the genus is *Clostridium*. It was stinking up the sheets. Even a yokel like you, Dobbins, once you've smelled it, you never forget."

"Spoiled meat?"

"You could call it that," said X. "Yeah, spoiled meat."

Thirty

Thorn followed Emma up a long, steep plywood ramp fixed to the front steps. The cabin wasn't grand but it had a gracious, stately feel with a stone chimney, shake roof, chinks filled with cement, big windows across the front, a wide wraparound porch.

The great room's cathedral ceiling swam upward into shadows, the furniture covers done in deep greens and russets and rich golds. The glossy varnish on the knotty pine walls had yellowed with age. Big bass and rainbow trout and a good-size sailfish were mounted on the walls of the large room. Racks of vintage fishing rods with heavy reels filled the wall space between built-in bookshelves that were crammed with old leatherbound books and paperbacks.

Comfortable couches, ancient leather chairs, oak and mahogany side tables, a far wall covered with photos of family gatherings. THE JOHANSSON TRIBE was inscribed on a plaque above the wall of photographs. Emma and Millie were members of a blond dynasty, Nordic pioneers, tough and serious. Generations of them were on the wall. Dressed in antique garb, sitting atop buggies, leaning against jalopies, saddled on fine-looking horses. Men in vests and hats holding up strings of fish, women in wide-brimmed hats with babies in their arms, tow-headed children wearing white Sunday clothes standing stiffly on the stone stairs that led into this lodge.

Emma rolled deeper into the house, aiming down a hallway where the honeyed late-day sun was slanting in from rooms on the west side,

Emma continuing to the end of the hallway where voices were speaking low.

"He's here," she announced and rolled into the room. "It's Thorn."

Thorn's eyes landed on Millie first, in blue jeans and a white T-shirt, standing stiffly in a corner of the room, the harsh late day's sun making her squint as she told him hello, her voice quiet, tense.

Cassandra, seated in a straight-backed chair by the head of the bed, was holding Flynn's hand. The sheets were pulled halfway up his naked chest. Flynn's face had dwindled since he'd seen him last. His cheeks sunken and his flesh so pale it had the translucent luster of ice. His damp hair was plastered against his skull. The blue of his eyes was a hazy facsimile of the color they'd been, his eyes red rimmed and swollen as if he'd been distance swimming in an overchlorinated pool. From the little Thorn could see of his body, Flynn appeared to be thirty pounds lighter than a year ago. A fit young man before, emaciated now.

Only his smile seemed as lively as ever.

Before Thorn could speak, Flynn said, "Isn't it a great house? Reminds me of your place, Thorn. Not as spartan as yours, but the same genre, rustic, authentic, tough."

"It's fine."

"See all those trophies, those antique rods and reels? What a collection, all still functional,

Millie says. Emma's granddad was a fishing guide. He took anglers deep-sea fishing out of Wilmington, and he fly-fished the streams around here. He sounds like a great guy. Somebody you'd respect."

"He does."

His delivery was breathless and rushed, the words mushy in his mouth.

"I'm doing fine," Flynn said. "Don't look so worried. I'm fine, really I am. We're all together, that's good. But the others, Jellyroll, Billy Jack, Caitlin, my friends, goddamn it, they were gunned down. All my doing. I set up the lookout post too close to the camp. You wouldn't have done that, Thorn. You would've picked the right spot. Those bastards caught me napping. Burkhart and Dobbins, that's who it was. I saw them, then I ran, blowing the whistle too damn late. They got me in the legs, the back. Eddie dug most of the lead out of me. He's good, Eddie's a good man."

"Calm down, Flynn. Relax."

"I knew you'd come. I didn't know how it would happen, but I knew it. I told Eddie and Earlene, his wife, about you. I told them you'd come, then yesterday Eddie walked in and told me you were here, that you'd arrived. He'd given you his car to use. What a wonderful coincidence, huh? He was amazed, but I knew it was going to happen all along. It's just like you to figure things out."

"Are we safe here?" Thorn asked Millie.

"I don't know. Probably for a while."

With a long sigh, the dog lay down in the hallway just beyond the door. His gaze focused on Emma.

"I'm going," Cassandra said. "Now you're here, Thorn, I can leave."

"You *should* go," Flynn said. "You should go while there's time."

"Best case," she said, "Cruz and her people will chase after me, leave the rest of you alone."

"Cruz is only one piece of this," Thorn said.

"You need to go, Cassandra," Flynn said. "There's other fights that need you. Go on, spread the word, we'll be fine."

She squeezed his hand in both of hers, leaned forward, and pressed her forehead against his chest. After a moment, she raised up, her eyes wet.

"I fucked up," she said. "I told Dobbins you had a copy of the video."

"There's no copy," said Flynn.

"But I told him there was and you had it. I only did it to stay alive, to make myself a bargaining chip he could trade for you. I put him on your trail, Flynn. I made everything worse."

"Come on, let's cut the guilt," Flynn said, smiling. "It was already worse. As worse as it gets." He started to chuckle but it turned into a cough and his body shook, the loose pieces in his chest rattled, and he fought for breath.

Thorn came to his side, pressed a solid hand against Flynn's shoulder, feeling helpless but keeping his hand there until Flynn finished riding out the cough. There was a smell hanging around his son. A bad smell. The more he breathed it the worse it got.

Flynn gave Thorn an exhausted look and smiled again.

"I'm fine," he said. "Really."

He patted Thorn's hand, then he closed his eyes and sank away. In a sudden panic Thorn searched for a pulse, finding a slow bump in his wasted neck.

"He's been doing that," Millie said. "Swooning in and out."

"He's not fine," Emma said. "He says he is, but he's not."

Cassandra came to her feet and drew aside the sheet covering his legs. Eyes still closed, Flynn didn't stir.

On the toes of both feet the blisters were green, the flesh split open from the swelling, and both grotesquely puffed ankles were shiny black as if he'd been wading to his shins through hot tar. Scattered from his calves to his thighs were a half dozen bloody lesions the size of silver dollars.

"It's called gangrene," Emma said.

"Eddie did the best he could," said Millie. "But this place, the hog manure, it's everywhere. Soil-borne, airborne staph bacteria resistant to antibiotics. They pump so many drugs in those pigs superbugs develop, new kinds of pneumonia, MRSA, and other things. We fight it every day around here. Even a small infection can get out of control fast. Flynn, jumping into the river after he was first wounded, that's probably how it started."

"We need to get him to a hospital," Thorn said. "Right now."

"No hospital," Flynn said, opening his eyes halfway. "No way."

"You've got a car, Millie?"

"I do."

"Stop it," Flynn said. "I'm not going to any damn hospital. They'll patch me up and send me straight to prison. I'll spend the next twenty years wishing I were dead. Living like those pigs crowded in their death chambers. I'd rather die here, in this nice house, with those fishing rods and those old reels. This is an excellent place to leave from."

"He was fussing like this the whole time he was at Eddie's," said Millie. "Eddie wanted to take him to Goldsboro, the regional medical center, but Flynn said the same thing he said just now. He wouldn't hear of it."

Thorn said, "Have you killed anyone, Flynn?"

Flynn's face seized up and he looked stricken. "Hell no."

"Well, good. You can plea-bargain, hand

Dobbins over to the law, his drug operation, that should reduce your sentence. The crimes you've done, that thing in Marsh Fork and the others, those are property crimes, they won't add up to more than a year or two. If that. We'll get you the best defense people there are. You haven't hurt anyone, that's what matters."

"It should be what matters," Flynn said. "But it isn't. Tell him, Cass."

"Twenty years is the going rate," she said. "We've got friends serving longer for doing less than we've done. It's a fucked-up system, stacked against us. We're lumped with Islamic terrorists because we attack corporate big shots. Twenty to thirty years. That's how it is, Thorn. By the time he got out, Flynn would be almost as old as you."

"Yeah," Flynn said. "A damn geriatric."

He began to chuckle again but caught himself, face glossy with sweat.

Cassandra leaned down and kissed Flynn on the forehead. She cradled his cheek in her hand and stared into his eyes for several seconds, then drew her hand away and moved to the doorway. She patted Emma's shoulder.

"Thorn, your son is a stubborn shit," she said. "Once he makes up his mind, forget about changing it. I should be going. I need to be a long way down that river before it gets too dark to paddle."

"Go," Flynn said. "But stay in touch, okay?"

Cassandra worked her mouth into a reassuring smile, gave Flynn a wink and a thumbs-up. Glanced at Thorn, desolation in her eyes, and left the room.

"Come on, Emma," Millie said. "They need their privacy."

"He'll get better, right? Gangrene, it's not cancer or anything. Right?"

"We'll talk about it. Now come on, tomorrow's a school day."

Before she closed the door, Thorn said, "There's a duffel in the canoe. Could you get it out, bring it up here? It's a little heavy."

"Oh, I can handle heavy."

"Yes," Thorn said. "I see that."

When the door was closed, Flynn said, "So many good people, risking themselves to hide me, help me. So many good people, here, everywhere we've been this last year."

"The hospital, Flynn, we need to do it. You're in bad shape."

"You're telling me? Eddie was giving me pills for the pain, morphine or Oxy or something, I don't know. But I made him stop. I want to feel this. I don't want to be cloudy. I want to be right here, experience this as close to natural as I can."

"None of this is natural," Thorn said.

"Let's not argue, okay? Can you just follow my wishes?"

Thorn came around the bed and took Cassandra's chair. Flynn held out his hand and Thorn gripped it in his own. Feeble, bony, trembling.

"We never really got to know each other, did we?"

Thorn couldn't find an answer.

"It's okay, I know you don't do schmaltzy. That's fine. But we do need to discuss a couple of things."

"Anything you want."

"We have to find Jellyroll and the others, where they're buried. The law will need their bodies for evidence, but we need to give them a proper funeral. Let their families know."

"I'll make sure of that, yes."

"Then there's the question of what to do with my ashes."

Flynn smiled at Thorn's awkward silence.

"I'm serious," he said. "It's about the only decision I have left."

Before Thorn could respond, Flynn winced and closed his eyes, bit down hard on his pain, and in a minute or two he drifted away again.

Thorn watched the tick of his son's heartbeat in his throat, slow but steady, and felt his own heart downshifting to match it. While Flynn was out, Thorn drank in the young man's face, his elegant cheekbones, his solid chin, his mother's sensitive mouth, her lashes, Thorn's eyebrows arching over the young man's deep-set eyes.

The room darkened but he didn't rise to turn on the lights because it would mean releasing Flynn's hand. So he sat in the expanding shadows and listened to a wood thrush give its final call of the day and a while later in the full darkness a barn owl began to practice its strangulated screech in the nearby woods. Each of them searching for a mate or defending its territory. Doing what was necessary to keep the species alive.

X-88 tracked the dual scent trails through Belmont Heights then through the thick stand of woods behind the shacks and to the river's edge near where the hippies had been camping. He wandered up and down the shore for twenty minutes, stopping now and then to crouch and bring his nose near the ground.

"Who lives downriver?" Cruz asked Dobbins.

Webb was bone tired and sick of these people, sorry as hell he'd ever given Cruz the time of day. His nose was stuffed up with blood and swollen tissue and his entire face ached. He was certain the nose was broken. Last time that happened, Ladarius Washington was the culprit, basketball practice, Dobbins jigging left when he should have jogged right.

"Depends on how far downriver you go," Webb said.

Cruz stepped close to Dobbins, peered up into his eyes.

She slapped him across the left cheek, then drew back fast and slapped him again. Neither strike was hard but they stung his flesh and Webb could feel a bulge of anger rising up the column of his spine.

"Wake up, you fool," Cruz said in a harsh whisper. "Wake up and focus. They're getting away, both of them. From the very first you've screwed this up and you're goddamn lucky I came along to save your ass, but I'm out of patience. Do you understand? Now who lives downriver that might be sympathetic to their cause and take them in?"

Dobbins fingered his burning cheek.

"You want names?"

"Let's start with how many there are. A dozen?"

"About ten miles down there's a state park, the river runs past it without any private homes for a long way. Most of the cabins this side of the park, they've been abandoned since the river went bad. Out-of-towners, they found somewhere else to vacation."

"Nobody local?"

"There's one down there, a woman and her kid. I know her pretty well."

"And she's loyal?"

"I always believed she was."

"Her name?"

"Millie, waitress at the diner in town. Kid's

name is Emma. Pretty little girl, lost her legs in a car accident. Coming back from the beach, her daddy was drunk, ran their vehicle head-on into a tree."

"Nobody else lives down there?"

"Hey, you didn't need to hit me. I'm not a god-damn punching bag. I've got my entire liveli-hood riding on the outcome of this hoo-hah. So give me some room, lady."

"Anybody else down there beside this waitress and her legless kid?"

Webb stared at this cold bitch for a moment, considered striking her back, how good it would feel.

"No," he said. "Nobody this side of that park but Millie Johansson and a bunch of abandoned houses, then it's twenty miles of state land. After that it gets populated again."

Cruz watched X-88 coming back up the shore.

She said to Dobbins, "Can you locate a boat for the three of us?"

"It'll be dark in another half hour. There's rocks downriver, boulders. It's shallow in places."

"Then we'll just have to get some goddamn flashlights, won't we?"

X-88 sidled up beside them, dusted his hands off on his pants leg.

"They went downstream, both of them, traveling together."

"Will you be able to catch the scent from the middle of the river?"

"Hey, this kid smells so nasty even Dobbins could handle that."

Thirty-one

"Someone's coming."

Thorn heard the woman's voice filtering down the deep shaft where he'd fallen. He opened his eyes, but it took a moment to locate his place in the story. Pine Haven, drugs, pigs, his son badly wounded. Then snapping awake.

He'd fallen forward, head sagged against Flynn's mattress. Someone was stroking his hair. He raised his head and found Flynn's hand brushing the back of his head, the boy comforting his old man.

Millie stood in the doorway in pale blue pajamas.

"Someone's out on the river in a boat with a spotlight. Emma saw them from her upstairs room. They'll be by here in a minute or two."

"The duffel?" he said.

"In the living room. I'll get Emma and we'll stay in here with Flynn."

"Bolt the door."

Flynn groaned and winced, his head pressing

into his pillow, his grimace stretching his lips like a grin gone terribly wrong.

"You have anything for pain?"

"Aspirin is all," she said.

"I'm fine," said Flynn, struggling to form the words. "Go save the world, Thorn, save us one and all."

His mouth made a noble attempt at a smile.

"Go, go."

Thorn found the duffel laid out on one of the corduroy couches. He hauled out one of the Atchisson shotguns, and from his memory dredged up the instructions Cruz had given him back in St. Augustine in the motel room eons ago. He loaded the twenty-round drum with FRAG-12 cartridges, grenade rounds that looked exactly like twelve-gauge shells, but enclosed within them was a small projectile that erupted from the casing and flew like a small stabilized warhead arming itself as it left the muzzle and detonating on impact. A miniature grenade launcher. At least that was Cruz's sales pitch.

He locked the drum in place, and with the heel of his hand he bumped it hard to make sure.

The black, stainless-steel shotgun was sleek and futuristic, a gorgeous piece of hardware whose grim purpose was concealed by its artful design. It was lighter than his own Remington twelve gauge and felt twice as solid and a hundred times more lethal.

He dragged the couch away from the wall, slid the duffel behind it, and scooted the couch back into place. Hiding it there as a safeguard, considering the vulnerability of his son lying in the other room, considering Emma and Millie and this house full of other people's memories.

The boat hovered offshore, the beam of the flashlight searching the bank for a place to put in. Thorn snuck down the stairs, angled toward darker shadows south of the lodge, listening for voices, watching for any glimpse of faces or clothes, a flicker of recognition. He didn't need much evidence to end this now, distant from any courtroom or legal babble.

Pine Haven existed in some extrajudicial time zone, abiding by its own corrupt due process. A battlefield without even a rudimentary code of honor. Take what you can. Kill what threatens you. Brutalize the weak, hold hostage any who endanger your throne. Add Cruz on her mission of revenge and X, who was driven by forces beyond Thorn's reckoning. They'd disposed of Tina, killed three idealistic kids, cut them down in the woods and buried their bodies. They tortured Cassandra and a Mexican worker, shot down Thorn's son and left him dying. Any retaliation he took was legit.

He pressed his back against an oak but kept the shotgun lowered. Two men were speaking quietly, one deep voice, one even deeper, though they were too faint to identify. He leaned forward, pressed the weapon to his shoulder, kept it aimed to the ground. As the boat turned in a circle, the putter of the small outboard shielded their conversation.

They weren't trying to hide, weren't shy about this landing. Which made him second-guess. Could this be Cruz, the crude way she would stage an assault? Or were they simply so certain of their superior firepower and numbers, they didn't bother with stealth?

If he took his shot while they were in this tight cluster, his chances were better, much better before they came onshore and scattered. He didn't know the tightness of the trigger pull, the accuracy of the sights, so he had to account for missing at least the first few rounds. Still, the shotgun was full-auto, Cruz had informed him, holding the trigger down would empty the drum in less than thirty seconds.

After it was empty he had no backup plan. He didn't know the terrain, where to retreat if one of them was left standing, he didn't have a flash-light, hadn't thought to ask Millie for any of that. If the three of them made it to land and fanned out quickly, he could be outflanked in no time.

The spotlight raked through the trees around him and Thorn pressed his back against the trunk. He crouched, settled his left elbow against his bent knee, sighted on the man in the bow who was directing the flashlight, trying to see past the glare, make out the face. All he needed was one face of that trio.

They chose their docking spot, and the one at the throttle nudged the dinghy hard against the embankment, and the man with the light jumped across from the bow onto the muddy slope. He scrambled up the hill, the beam shining in front of him, briefly passing across Thorn, blinding him, then the boat reversed, dislodged the prow, and swung into the river, heading back upstream.

Thorn's finger was tight against the trigger, lifting the barrel until he settled the sights on the man with the flashlight. Maybe the others had jumped to shore when he was dazzled by the light and had moved out of his line of sight and were just now skirting the open grassy area and heading through the bordering trees. Maybe the man in the boat was going to make a second landing nearby and he and the others would blitz from a different angle.

Thorn eased the sight to the left and right of flashlight man, spotting shadows moving across the grassy yard, the shadows of men or oak branches in the moonlight, or the shadows of nothing at all. Training his sight again on flashlight man, Thorn tightened his finger on the smooth steel of the trigger, letting the man come closer, while the shadows to his left and right appeared and disappeared in a flutter of moonlight.

He gave the man a few more feet, allowed him to enter an oblong of moonlight. Thorn increased the trigger pressure, a sudden swell of doubt holding him in check, not sure if the drug was playing a role in this, some chemical trickery impairing his judgment, holding him back when he should be letting go. No way to know.

The man stopped. He swung his beam of light to the left, then brought it around to the right as if signaling his team to converge. Thorn scanned the area to each side of flashlight man but saw nothing, only the erratic shadows of limbs swaying.

Flashlight man inched forward as if he sensed Thorn's presence, and he targeted his light on the front steps of the house only three or four yards to the left of Thorn's position and kept moving forward, the beam so bright and held waist high, there was no way to see anything but flashlight man's legs.

Thorn's trigger hand was slippery. He wiped the sweat on his jeans, reset his grip on the weapon, pressed his cheek to the stock, focused on the man's midsection. He decided to shout a one-word warning, to be a hundred percent certain and maybe flush the others out of hiding, if there *were* others.

He let the man come a few more steps toward the house. And was about to call out when the recognition came with such a rush of gratitude and relief Thorn could feel a lump of heat rise into his throat. He lowered the shotgun, gripped it by the barrel, and stepped out from behind the tree. He recognized flashlight man's gait. The unmistakable limber-legged stride of Sugarman.

"Up ahead," Dobbins said. "Just beyond that next bend."

X-88 was in the bow, holding his weapon at port arms, his body wobbling as the boat threaded through narrow passages between boulders and jagged rocks, some that were hidden below the surface. Dobbins was at the throttle while Cruz managed the flashlight.

X felt like shit. He didn't like boats, didn't care for water of any kind, rivers, ocean, lakes. He hated swimming pools. He couldn't even dog-paddle, sank like an anchor, didn't have whatever flotation tissues other human beings possessed. He was beginning to feel queasy from the boat ride, riding all those dips and swells, trying to keep his balance as the boat bobbed and slid sideways then bobbed again.

And dead center in his chest something was throbbing. Maybe from the tension of the moment, then again, it struck him this feeling might be about Pixie; he might be experiencing heartache. Over the years he'd heard songs about it, lots of sappy songs, but he'd not felt the sensation himself as far as he knew.

He'd gotten along better with Pixie than with any female before. She had a slinky way about her that X found hot. He liked the way she talked, so wild, so giddy. But he'd never felt heartache before, so he wasn't sure this hard pinging in his chest was it. More likely it was just a touch of seasickness.

Dobbins kept the speed slow, the motor burbling quiet. The plan was to cut the engine a distance before the dock and drift with the current to the pilings, lasso them with one of the lines, use the boat hook to pull themselves in. Dobbins claimed he was an experienced seaman. They'd find out shortly.

Doing his part, X-88 was still fetching for Cassandra's scent. It came in pulses, not the reliable spoor it was on land, but clear enough.

Back at the farm Dobbins had provided X with an AR-15 with a thirty-round staggered column magazine. Not X's weapon of choice, but it would do. Dobbins carried a Remington twelve gauge, telling them that he and Burkhart used the same weapons to waste the hippies who were trying to destroy his business.

"And you didn't dispose of them after," Cruz said, acid in her voice.

"This was my daddy's gun," Dobbins said. "It's a family heirloom with strong sentimental value."

"Tonight when we're done," she said, "they go into the river. The AR and the heirloom."

"We'll see about that," Dobbins said.

X-88 felt the power shifting from Cruz. She was losing her hold on them. She'd also lost Pixie, and she'd lost X long ago with her fanatical focus on the redhead and her lack of attention to loose ends. And Dobbins seemed ready to mutiny, bonding with X-88, choosing him as the natural pack leader. Which he was.

He'd never been in any group where that wasn't the case. He was usually stronger, more vicious, willing to do the crazy shit no one else had the stomach for.

After so many years of falling in with groups of brutal thugs and cold-eyed hoodlums and every time rising to the dominant position, X believed he'd gathered a force field around him. People deferred. They didn't have to be told or shown. He never had to demonstrate it, he simply walked into a room, didn't say a word or act tough, and the seas parted.

Even lately as his brain ballooned and the pressure inside his skull grew, even as the migraine pain doubled and tripled, he didn't reveal how much it cost him, didn't complain, didn't even admit it to himself. He was the big dog. That's what the big dog did.

Yeah, Thorn had faked him out, pretending to be drugged, and he'd sucker-punched X, knocked him semiconscious, and earlier he'd pulled that stunt with the gasoline hose, hammered him from behind, left a painful knot on his skull, but those were the early rounds, and no way that was happening again, next time the guy was going down, all the way down, and staying there.

"Cut the light," Dobbins hissed at Cruz.

The light went off, the engine shut down, and they drifted through the darkness. A minute of silence, another minute, the boat gliding near shore.

"Still got her scent?" Cruz asked.

X nodded.

"Getting stronger?"

He nodded again.

When the collapsed dock appeared, Dobbins handled the boat hook, reaching out, snagging a piling smoothly. He drew the small boat up to it and looped a line around the piling and tied it off, then the boat swung around, facing into the current, and Dobbins used the hook to pull the rear end up close to the shore.

"Good work," X said quietly. "Handled like a pro."

Dobbins grunted his thanks, and even through the darkness X could make out the cold look on Cruz's face. Not liking what she was witnessing, these two men forging a connection, getting along fine without her.

One by one they jumped to shore, Dobbins pointing the way toward the house. At the crest of the slope, they stepped across a fallen chain-link fence and entered a weedy field. X stopped them with a hiss.

Cruz asked him what was wrong.

"I believe the woman may have crisscrossed her own trail."

"What?"

"There's two trails. One cold, the other fresh."

"Where's the fresh one lead?"

"From up there to down here," X said. "She came along this path, went to the house, stayed a while, then left recently, no more than half an hour ago."

"Left?"

X-88 motioned at the river.

"I'd say she probably left the way she came, in a boat."

"Then we get back in the boat, go after her."

"Fuck if we are," Dobbins said. "I'm getting that video. The kid's up there, right? That spoiled meat smell."

"Yes," X said. "He's up there. You can't hide that."

"We're going after Cassandra." Cruz had drawn her Glock, holding her arm slack at her side, the gun pointing down.

"Take the fucking boat yourself," Dobbins said. "My gift to you. Go on, chase after her. I'm getting that damn video."

"Fine, Dobbins. Do what you need to. But X, you come with me."

"Why's that? Why am I coming with you?"

"I need you," she said. "I need your skills."

"I like that. You need me. First time I've heard those words out of your tight little mouth. It's always been the other way around, hasn't it? Me needing you, me needing the cash you're handing out. Me staying true to your husband, Manny, my oath to him, to guard your ass, make sure the money was still there when he got out. But the truth is, you need me more than I need you. That's how it's turning out, isn't it?"

"Don't do this, X."

"Here's how it is, Cruz. We're here right now. Shouldn't take long, we grab the video, then we sit down, discuss what's next. Do it democratic."

"There's nothing to discuss. She's getting away. We'll lose her."

"I'm not bargaining," X said. "I'm telling you how it's going to work. First, the video, take care of the asshole Thorn, then we see how we feel, if we got any energy left to chase after the redhead. It's been a long day, that drive alone has me tired out."

"What is this about? What're you doing, X?"

"Doing what I should've done weeks ago. Now let's get that video."

Thirty-two

Dobbins said he knew the layout of the house.

"Millie's folks had parties, everybody in town invited. Black, white, even the Latinos. Music, lots of cold beer and booze, dancing on that lawn, skinny-dipping in the river. Real party people, the Johanssons, big-time drinkers."

X could see Cruz chafing to be on her way down the river, pissed Dobbins was wasting time reminiscing. The guy had to see it too, how angry Cruz was, how frustrated. Every delay getting deeper under her skin.

"That Millie used to be a looker." Dobbins winked at X, enjoying his chance to stick it to Cruz. "Always had a sweet spot for that gal. Can't believe she'd betray me like this, hiding that son of a bitch when she damn well knows the future of Pine Haven depends on handing him over to the lawful authority."

"Burkhart," X said. "Real lawful guy."

"He's got the badge, that's all that's required."

"You guys want to do this?" Cruz waved her Glock at the cabin. "Or you planning on staying out here, chitchatting like a couple of teenage girls?"

"Okay, okay."

Dobbins laid out the floor plan of the house, one bedroom downstairs, the master at the top of the stairs, two other bedrooms beyond that. Kitchen in the back, big living room in front. A back door leading into the kitchen, front door opening into the living room. Just those two entrances.

X-88 figured the kid to be in the downstairs bedroom. Sick as he was, they wouldn't haul him upstairs. So they agreed to attack from the rear. Storm the kitchen, go into the hallway, bedroom was first door on the left.

X and Dobbins would take the kitchen route, Dobbins in the lead since he knew the way and had the room-clearing shotgun, X would follow as mop-up. Cruz, with the least firepower, just the fifteen rounds in the Glock 19's magazine, she'd take out whoever tried to exit the front.

"Side windows?" X asked. "One of them jumps, that could be an issue."

"House has a ten-foot elevation," Dobbins said. "Flood protection. Another few feet for the window height, that's a hard landing. Could be done, but if they're in a hurry, first choice, they'll go for the doors."

"And what if Cassandra took the video?" Cruz said. "We're losing her."

"Decision's made," said X. "We're going in. Once that's done, we'll deal with your obsession."

Even in the gloom X could feel the heat of her glare. An odor radiating from her, something new from Cruz he hadn't smelled before. Flop sweat of a special kind. Vinegary with an undertone of curdled milk. She'd worn through her baby powder deodorant and this, he believed, was the woman's natural scent. Rancid, brackish, like the stagnant water in a vase where flowers were left too long. Her adrenal gland was working overtime. The woman's sweat was ripe with hate.

"We're taking down everybody?" Dobbins said.

"Only way to go," said X. "Anyone in that house is fair game."

Cruz was silent, looking downriver.

"Even little Emma? I don't think I can shoot an eight-year-old."

"Kid that age can tie a noose around your neck tight as anyone. If you're squeamish, I'll do her. But Thorn is mine."

"Main job is the video," Dobbins said. "Don't kill everybody right off, they could've hid it, we'll have to tear the damn house apart, might never find the damn thing."

"Sure, sure." X was going along with him, making nice. Even feeling a soft spot for the redneck. But when the time came, none of that would matter. Dobbins was a fucking pig farmer. Lord of the concentration camp, emperor of abominations.

Cruz dropped back while Dobbins and X-88

slipped around the north side of the house. Lights on in the living room and in the back, and upstairs a couple of rooms were lit. Voices coming from an interior room on the ground floor. An argument of some kind.

X ducked around the corner of the house, brought his rifle up, covering Dobbins as he slid from the corner to the back porch. A single yellow bulb was burning on the small screened-in entryway, attracting bugs that battled at the mesh. He could smell a vapor trail of the kid's rotting flesh like candied sewer gas, stronger than out front, so harsh and cloying it was a wonder the jackals and hyenas hadn't started to swarm. A feast for vultures.

The chatter inside the house continued, slow-talking man versus high-pitched woman, a debate. Dobbins mounted the steps up to the screen door.

He had his finger inside the trigger guard, holding the weapon one-handed, bad gun safety, could shoot off his own foot that way, but it was too late to teach him anything. X hustled over to the steps and took them two at a time and settled in behind Dobbins. He could hear the man swallowing back his fear.

He whispered over his shoulder to X, "They could be expecting us."

"Don't be a pussy."

"Do we yell and try to scare them, or sneak up?"

"Sneak," X said.

"I can smell that stink now. Like a zombie's halitosis."

X punched him lightly in the middle of the back. No time for jokes.

"Tell me when to go."

"Count to three, that should do it."

Dobbins bobbed his head once, twice, then threw open the screen door, ducked into the small porch, X on his heels.

The sewer gas was switching around, some ahead of him, some behind. Could be a random breeze tearing apart the trail. But it concerned him. Inside the voices were still hashing out some problem. Preoccupied and gathered in one place. All good.

Dobbins tried the knob to the back door. It turned and he glanced over his shoulder at X and gave X a *you ready?* shrug.

"Go," X said. "Get it done."

Dobbins pushed through the door and stepped inside the lighted kitchen. Ancient wood-burning stove, knotty pine cabinets, black and white floor tiles, white walls peeling here and there, bright overhead lights, calendar on the wall, a little girl's drawings fixed to the fridge. Beyond the kitchen entryway the hallway was clear. The voices sounding close by.

X signaled Dobbins toward the closed door on the left. The single downstairs bedroom where the voices were coming from.

Planting himself on the hinge side of the door, X motioned Dobbins to go ahead, throw it open.

The redneck swallowed, put his hand on the knob, looked at X hard as if trying to absorb some of his courage. The voices inside the room reached a peak, a woman yelling out, "I'm sick and tired of you being sick and tired." And there was laughter, an entire TV studio audience laughing in unison.

"Shit," X said.

He felt something shift inside his skull, a stab of pinkish-green migraine lightning that made him cringe.

He blinked hard and pushed it away, threw Dobbins aside, kicked open the door, and sprayed the empty bedroom with a dozen rounds.

Afterward, going room to room, door by door, it took him and Dobbins another jittery ten minutes to be sure the house was vacant.

"Where'd Cruz go?"

By then X and Dobbins were standing on the front porch looking out toward the dark river.

"Where else *would* she go?" X said. "That woman's got only one destination."

"She stole my goddamn boat?"

"You got a cell phone," X said. "Call Burkhart, have him pick us up."

"We're fucked. We had them cornered, now they're gone. That bitch took my goddamn boat.

370

That video is going to crucify me. I'm finished, man, I'm fucking finished."

"Call Burkhart to come get us," X repeated.

Another thunderbolt fired inside his head. This one shut his eyes.

"We can track them," Dobbins said. "At least we got that. They couldn't have gone far. We can track them. Your nose, man. I didn't believe it was true. That's one fucking amazing skill you got, pardner."

Dobbins wandered down the porch searching for a good phone signal. X-88 looked out at the river and inhaled the night air.

Nothing.

Not even the aroma of the muddy riverbank, the nearby evergreens, the ever-present pig shit hovering in the air. Something inside his head had finally grown too large, maybe the hippocampus swelling an extra millimeter against the inside of his skull, extinguishing its glow like a cigarette crushed against stone. Maybe it was the blow Thorn gave him to the back of his head. He couldn't smell a goddamn thing. He could barely breathe without setting off another zap of current behind his eyes.

"Burkhart's bringing my truck," Dobbins said.

Dobbins followed X down the front stairs.

"We go out the driveway, meet him on the road. Shouldn't take him more than ten minutes. Hey, you feeling okay? You look like ever-loving shit."

Thirty-three

After hurried introductions, Sugarman shaking hands with Emma and Millie, everyone piled into Millie's station wagon. With the tailgate down, Duke jumped into the back, lay down, and released a long sigh that seemed to capture the mood of the moment.

Emma was strapped into a high-backed booster seat behind her mother, with Flynn stretched out beside her, his head on a bed pillow propped against the door behind Thorn, his lower legs wrapped tightly in sheets. Sugar was squeezed in the middle of the front seat. All the windows were open because of the smell.

They were silent till they reached the end of Millie's long drive. A dark night with a dreary drizzle just beginning, a hard north wind blowing the sprinkle into the car. Alongside her driveway the naked limbs of runty trees clattered like loose bones in a tin can.

The Carhartt jacket Millie had dug out of a closet full of her husband's old clothes was already damp from the rain, and even with the collar turned up, the chilly breeze whispered across Thorn's neck.

Millie stopped at the asphalt roadway beside a

row of mailboxes and a wooden sign pointing the way to the Johanssons' residence.

"Where to?"

"Dobbins Farm," Thorn said.

"You're not serious."

"It's time to turn the tables."

"No," she said. "I can't do it, not with Emma. It's too dangerous."

"It's just a farm, Mama. It's not dangerous."

"Drop Sugar and me out front." Thorn bent her way and lowered his voice and said, "Then take Flynn to that medical center."

"No hospital," Flynn said. "No way."

Thorn turned around and confronted Flynn's steady gaze.

"It's not about you, Flynn, not anymore. You've got to do this for Millie's sake and Emma's, and Ladarius and Eddie too. The longer you float around Pine Haven in your condition, the longer you're putting everyone around you in danger. You don't want that, do you? Risk innocent lives because you refuse help."

Flynn was silent.

It was Thorn's last hope. Play the guilt card, appeal to Flynn's principled instincts. The car was quiet for several moments, then Emma said, "I don't want you to die. Won't you go to the hospital, please?"

And in the long silence that followed, it was settled.

Several miles down the road, Thorn leaned forward and spoke to Millie.

"We appreciate your help. I know this is going to be a problem for you later."

"No," she said. "I've been quiet too long. Got lazy, lost my gumption."

"Well, you've got good allies. Eddie, Ladarius, I've met a few. There's probably lots more. They just need a nudge."

"That Ladarius," Sugar said. "He's a solid man."

"More than I knew," Millie said. "It took some serious guts bringing you down the river, risking everything like that."

"Always count on a brother," Sugar said. "Little town like this, when I drove in, I said, now how do I go about locating my buddy Thorn? First thing I did, I looked for a beauty salon, because I know they're the nerve center, got all the breaking news, but the only one I saw was closed, then I stumbled on Belmont Heights, and it was the smell in the air that did it."

"What smell?" Emma said.

"You ever want to know what's going on in a place, Emma, sniff out the best barbecue pit, stand around for five minutes, chat with the folks, I guarantee you'll get a helping of high-grade gossip along with your ribs."

"You're a detective, aren't you?" Emma said.

Sugarman hesitated, then swiveled his head to look at her.

"I used to be," he said. "I used to be a darn good detective."

"Did you quit?"

"I'm seriously considering it."

"I'd love to be a detective," she said. "That would be so awesome. Mama, you think I could do that when I grow up? A private eye."

"I think you have no limits, Emma. Anything you put your mind to."

Emma made a noise in her throat Thorn hadn't heard in years. A shiver of eagerness, the deep churn of a child's imagination fixing on a thrilling future.

As they drove, Sugar switched on the map light, fished inside his jacket, and handed Thorn two black-and-white photos.

"Tina's grim reaper." A euphemism for Emma's benefit.

"You sure?"

"As close to positive as I can be. Details later. These are from St. Augustine, the burger place where I got our supper the other night. Worker there was done in the same manner as Tina."

Thorn groaned, told Sugar he was sorry.

"You seen this man along the way?"

The first photo showed X-88 leaning out his car window at the burger joint. The second was later that night with X's head ducked, trying without success to shield his face with his hand as he approached the rear exit of the burger joint.

"I have."

"Thought it was likely, the circles you've been traveling in."

"Cruz takes her daughter Pixie everywhere. This guy is Pixie's boyfriend. Calls himself X-88."

"What is that, a gang name? X-88."

Thorn said he didn't know. But he and Pixie called themselves hardline vegans or straight-edgers, maybe that was a gang, though not one he'd ever heard of.

"Straight-edgers," Sugar said.

"Heard of them?"

"Indeed I have."

"You get around."

"Met one in the flesh a year or so back, called himself that, a straight-edger. Freaky guy named Wally, that time I was working the runaway case in Key West. Guy was an ex-con, it was something he'd picked up at Raiford. Bad as the Taliban. Guy thought he was holier than the pope. He could do no wrong, the world could do no right. Mean man, full of spite. Teetotaler to the tenth power."

Emma tapped on Sugar's back and asked what a teetotaler was and he explained the idea to her as they rolled through the night.

"Mama, are you one of those, a teetotaler?"

Millie glanced back at her.

"I am," she said. "Have been for a long time. Don't miss it a bit."

"But you're not full of spite, are you?"

Millie looked over at Thorn and they shared a smile.

"I try not to be. I try real hard."

The drizzle had become a downpour, the wipers slapping double time to little effect. Everyone rolled up their windows and the smell of Flynn's decaying flesh quickly became palpable.

"Cold front," Millie said. "Dropping to the forties tonight."

"Perfect weather for what I have in mind," Thorn said.

"I'm not even going to ask," said Sugar.

Millie said, "You sure you know what you're doing, Thorn? These people are ruthless, they'll do anything to keep the show running."

"I heard about a certain trumpet flower," he said. "Know anything about that?"

Millie frowned out the windshield and was silent.

"What I heard," Thorn said, "this flower is the linchpin for Dobbins. Without that plant the farm wouldn't survive. Did I get that right?"

"I believe you did."

"So Pine Haven has no choice but to look the other way on Dobbins's sideline business because without that part everything else collapses. His farm, eventually the town."

"Sounds like we got two detectives riding with us, Emma."

"What trumpet flower is he talking about, Mama?"

"I'll explain later," she said.

"You always say that."

At the entrance to the Dobbins farm, Millie pulled onto the shoulder, the wipers slapping at the rain, ahead of them in the headlights the road was a foggy smear. Millie switched on the overhead lights and Thorn turned around in his seat to face Flynn.

"They'll fix you up. You'll be healthy in no time. I know you will."

"Go on, I'm fine," Flynn said. "Don't worry about me. And don't forget what I asked you to do."

"I won't forget."

"This isn't good-bye," Flynn said. "So no big scenes, okay?"

Flynn extended his hand and Thorn clasped it in both of his. Flynn's grip was firm and dry, squeezing hard, and in those few seconds his son managed to transmit a message as rich as any human hand Thorn had ever held.

"No worries, Dad. I'm getting my second wind. Just chill out. We'll go to the hospital, I'll beat this infection, then I'll take on whatever's next."

He released his son's hand. Blinking back the burn in his eyes, Thorn kept his face stiffly composed, a stoic habit from the schoolyard and fields of play, the athlete's maxim: never rub an injury, admit to suffering. But it wasn't easy. His eyes were blurred and the bottled-up sob obstructing his throat made breathing a sudden chore.

After he and Sugarman climbed out and Thorn retrieved the duffel, there were no more goodbyes. They stood in the drenching rain beside the car. Flynn saluted, Emma waved, and Millie gave them a simple raised fist, then switched off the interior light and drove off into the rising wind.

Thirty-four

"No apologies required."

"I was an idiot, persuading you to go," Thorn said. "She tricked me and I fell for it big time."

They were plunging ahead through the lashing rain.

"She tricked both of us. And Tina too. She's good at it."

The outdoor lights near the main barn lit their way down the gravel drive. Thorn was soaked. His jeans had doubled in weight, the coat was shedding water, but was a size too small and the driving rain leaked in and plastered his shirt to his skin. Shivering against the biting wind, he hugged the coat to himself while the two shotguns in the duffel thumped against his back.

"I talked to Sheffield a couple of times, yesterday, earlier today. Cruz came to see him two weeks ago, wanted to pick his brains about you, Thorn. Her real name is Obrero, by the way, husband was DEA, she was FBI for a while till her older daughter's suicide. Girl was jacked up on heroin and coke, jumped off a building and after that Obrero fell apart, totally lost it."

"So she's tricking herself too. Putting her girl's suicide on Cassandra."

"The woman's completely stripped her gears."

As they trekked through the darkness and the pounding rain, Sugar filled him in about Cruz's meeting with Sheffield, her questions about Thorn, clearly trying to find a way to manipulate him. And about Cruz enlisting Julia's and Tina's help by convincing them this was an antiterrorist operation.

Remembering that he was still carrying it, Thorn halted Sugarman with a hand on his arm and dug Tina's cell phone from his pocket and handed it over.

"Where'd you find this?"

"Trunk of X-88's car. Hidden near the wheel well. At the end she was trying to call you, Sugar. You and nine-one-one."

Sugarman examined the phone, checked the recent calls, stood blankly for a moment, then snapped it shut and stared up at the pelting rain and the black heavens, his mouth yawning open as if he were unleashing a silent howl.

When he recovered, he wiped the rain from his face and tucked the phone in his pants pocket. Thorn clamped a consoling hand on his shoulder and Sugarman reached up and patted his hand. All forgiven, back on track.

They tramped on through the sludge, the rain bearing down harder.

"So is there a plan? You're going to try to take out all these folks on your own? Dobbins, X-88, his girlfriend, Cruz?"

"No," Thorn said. "Not that way."

"I'm angry enough to disembowel a few people," Sugar said. "What they did to Flynn and his friends and the thing with Tina. But you know I can't do that. It's not who I am. I'm not like you, Thorn."

"Then why are you still here?"

"I want the guy who killed Tina. I'm taking him in, and making sure he goes away forever. I sure as hell don't want him to die on the field of battle."

"We have the same intention then."

"Okay, then why aren't we calling in the feds, the state police?"

"Dobbins is holding the whole damn town hostage. I don't want to injure a lot of innocent folks by pulling Dobbins's plug without a backup plan."

"Spell it out for me."

"We're going to do what Flynn would do."

"Yeah?"

"What they did in Marsh Fork and the other places. Creative approach. Nonviolent. Strategy was always the same. They changed the shape of the playing field, and that changed the way the game was played."

"You mean blowing up that retention pond, the toxic sludge destroys the school. Government has to build a new one in a less dangerous place."

"Yeah, maybe that's an approach you and I can agree on. Try our best to see nobody gets hurt, make sure the bad guys lose, give the good guys a chance at a fresh start."

"You got all this figured out, do you?"

"Are you kidding? When have I ever figured out anything? I'm just trusting the seat of my pants."

There were a couple of drowsy Mexicans in blue jumpsuits working the midnight shift in the main barn. It appeared their job was some kind of sentry duty, marching up and down the main corridor watching the piglets sleep, watching other pigs, the insomniacs, pace back and forth inside their stalls, and a few others who were chewing listlessly on the cage bars.

Thorn and Sugarman stood dripping just inside the double doors and watched the two men parade up and down the aisle with the kind of stiff attention that suggested they'd been caught slacking on the job before and the punishment had been harsh and memorable.

"What now?"

"I need to show you how to work this thing."

Thorn hauled the unloaded Atchisson out of the duffel. He inserted the twenty cartridges into the drum and smacked the drum into its slot and held the weapon out to Sugar.

"You said nonviolent."

"Nobody gets shot, nobody dies," Thorn said. "That's our goal."

"Are you playing with words?"

"No, I mean it. Nonviolent."

"And by the way," Sugarman said, "those bricks of cash Cruz used as a stage prop to incriminate Tina, that's part of the drug stash her husband, Manny, left behind."

The Mexican workers had spotted the two of them and were frozen in place. Those black, sleek shotguns had that kind of spellbinding power.

"*No te preocupes*," Thorn called out to them. "*Está seguro.*"

They shouldn't worry. They were safe.

But the men weren't convinced by this strange Anglo and his African American partner. They raised their hands high and backed down the main corridor, and when they were close to the rear exit, they broke into a sprint.

Thorn led Sugar up the metal stairs and across

the observation platform to the small concrete room where he'd been held captive.

As Thorn had guessed, the Mexican who Thorn had untied was back in his chair, still wearing that pair of white boxer shorts with red hearts printed on them. His mouth was again covered with duct tape, hands bound with rope, and now his face was swollen and there were gashes around both eyes.

Dobbins had made him pay dearly for his few moments of freedom.

He recognized Thorn and stiffened. Thorn peeled away the duct tape.

"*Quieres ser libre o es demasiado peligroso?*"

It seemed only fair to ask him if he wanted to be free or if that posed too great a risk.

The man considered the question, eyeing the ominous weapons. After another moment he nodded his head.

"*Si, señor. Quiero ser libre.*"

Thorn asked him his name and the man replied that it was Jesús.

"*Te pido solo una cosa, Jesús. Si quiere.*" Thorn was asking for one thing, but only if the man was willing.

The man asked what that one thing was.

"*Por favor llevemos al invernadero.*"

Sugar said, "I got everything but that last one."

"I've asked him if he'd be willing to show us the way to the greenhouse."

• • •

"You're sick? You can't smell anymore?"

"Sick, yeah," X said. "Call it that. Swelling in the brain. It's been coming for a while."

"Then what're we supposed to do about that goddamn video?"

Burkhart said, "The man tells you he's dying, you're worried about a video?"

"Dying? He didn't say anything about dying."

The cab of Dobbins's truck was steamed up by the three men tightly packed. The wipers slinging away the rain as they sped back toward Belmont Heights.

"You want to know the truth," X said, "it's a relief."

"What? Dying?"

"Not smelling anymore. And yeah, sure, dying too, getting on with the next thing."

Dobbins had nothing to say to that. Dying wasn't high on his bucket list. They were headed back to colored town because Webb decided he needed to have a sit-down with Ladarius and Eddie and whoever else wanted to attend. One by one, he was going to turn Burkhart loose on them, let the old soldier use his military tricks to get the truth.

One of them would know where the Moss kid and Thorn had run off to.

As Webb had suspected, Ladarius and Eddie and their people were working with the hippies all along. As soon as this rain passed and things dried out for a day or two, he was going to stock up on kerosene and Belmont Heights was going to feel Webb Dobbins's wrath. Time for a community bonfire, get started on that beautification project Laurie had been campaigning for for so long.

But first they'd do a little enhanced interrogation. Begin with Ladarius, that insolent son of a bitch.

"That one," Webb said, pointing at the shack where Ladarius lived.

Burkhart swung the truck off the road and bounced into the front yard with the headlights shining bright against the door. As they were getting out, a curtain twitched in the front room.

"Need anything special, Burkhart? Tools of the trade that could speed this up? I could run to the farm, pick up whatever sharp objects you'd like."

"I don't think that'll be required," Burkhart said. "Common household utensils should be sufficient. You did say the man had a couple of daughters."

"Three little girls," Dobbins said.

Burkhart smiled.

"Even better."

Thirty-five

Jesús stopped in a cloakroom near the exit and pulled on a blue jumpsuit, the same uniform the sentries were wearing, and in a row of lockers he found a pair of work boots that fit him. When he was dressed, he led them outside the barn and guided them along a meandering path that circled around one after another giant pond of pig manure then past three other barns where Thorn heard the indignant squeals and grunts and mutterings of pigs, a mixture of protest, outrage, and yearning.

The deluge had died away to a drizzling mist, more fog than rain. The temperature was dropping fast and Thorn had to shift the shotgun from hand to hand to prevent them from going icy numb.

Sugarman was silent, bringing up their rear flank, glancing to each side into the dark hollows of the night.

They hiked across a large gravel parking area, then another just like it, and came to a county highway, crossed it, then slogged through a ditch on the other side, and clumped ahead through a muddy field and went another mile down a private paved road.

Thorn moved alongside Jesús.

"*Cuánto más lejos?*"

Not much farther, Jesús replied. One more mile.

When they finally rounded an old wood barn that smelled of damp hay, Thorn realized they'd hiked far enough from the farm that they'd left behind the stink of the manure lagoons and the pig barns.

Jesús halted and pointed to the lights of a two-story farmhouse skirted by porches. Rockers and hanging swings and potted plants decorated the verandas. Several outbuildings were clustered so close to the house that they fell inside the halo of illumination from its many windows. A silo, a granary, a smokehouse, a tobacco barn, and what looked like the original settlers' log cabin, as if the Dobbinses had preserved these structures as family shrines in memory of their hardy ancestors.

About fifty feet to the left of the house was the glassed-in conservatory.

On the other side of the house, parked in the driveway, was a white Jaguar.

"*Quien es este coche?*" Thorn asked him.

The car, he replied, belonged to the sister, Laurie.

"Wait here," Thorn said.

"What're you doing? You said no one gets hurt."

"And I meant it. We're playing by Flynn's rules."

Thorn entered the house, shut the door quietly

behind him. A stairway with ornate bannisters stood directly in front of him. He took a quick look into the parlor, whose furniture and decorations were at least a half century out of date. A stage set that looked unlived in. No magazines strewn about, no signs of human occupation or any contemporary touch, as if the room had been decorated just so, then left to collect dust. A museum display of roughly the same vintage as Millie's living room, but this was a stifling formal room where no entertaining had ever taken place.

Back in the foyer, he heard music playing upstairs. Smoky New Orleans jazz, heavy on the sax. He followed the music up one flight, then another, past a collection of metal-framed photos that showed the gradual evolution of the Dobbins clan and the farm they operated, from the small circle of log buildings Thorn had just seen outside to the massive aluminum structures that now housed thousands of pigs.

And many photos of a frail woman with a despondent air holding a young boy on her lap, and more photos of the same woman grown even frailer, this time cradling a baby in her arms, the boy growing into a burly lad, standing apart looking bewildered and bereft, and in her later incarnation the mother became so delicate she seemed to be hardly there at all, standing stiffly beside that adolescent boy and the smug young daughter in their crisp matching Easter outfits and later their high school graduation robes.

Mingled in were photographs of a bulky, robust man with a flamboyant mustache whose resemblance to Webb Dobbins was unmistakable. In every image the man seemed to loom over the other family members, an impression produced more from his severe and contemptuous countenance than his height.

At the top of the stairs Thorn heard voices, the low murmurs, croonings, and giggles of what sounded like erotic play. Both voices he recognized as he moved to the door. Pixie's bright and chirpy inflection and the low throaty growl of Laurie.

He turned the doorknob and nudged open the door with the barrel of the shotgun. They'd kicked the bedsheets to the floor and were intertwined in a naked knot of damp flesh. Pixie was pressing a pillow to her face as if to muffle her cries of pleasure.

Laurie looked up, her face glistening with the jelly of Pixie's release.

"Well, look who came to the party." Laurie scrubbed her palm across her mouth and licked a finger clean.

She climbed off Pixie and got out of the bed and stood facing Thorn, as if daring him to gawk at her nakedness, while she lit up a roach, took a drag, then handed it to Pixie.

"Three things," Thorn said.

"Oh, good, a man who likes to dominate. My favorite kind."

"Can you run this farm without Webb's help? Without drug money?"

"What're you talking about?"

"Can you? A smaller version maybe, like the farm you grew up on. Can you do that? Do you know how to manage that?"

"If I wanted to I could. Sure."

"Well, you do, you want to," he said. "You want to because you don't want Pine Haven to die. You want to because this is your home, these are your roots. Even though you act like you despise everything around you, you haven't left, so there's still some kind of bond to this place. But most of all you want to because you don't want to go to jail with your brother. Agreed?"

"You're a presumptuous asshole."

"Because when this is done, I'll be coming back from time to time to make sure you've fulfilled your side of the bargain. If you let the farm go down, then I'll do everything I can to make sure you serve the same sentence as your brother."

Laurie's mocking smile was tightening into a frown.

"Okay, the second thing is this. When I leave the room I want you to call Webb, tell him I'm here. He needs to get home quick so he can watch everything he's worked so hard for go up in flames."

"Are you insane?" Laurie said, taking back the joint from Pixie.

"You're going to call him as soon as I leave the room."

"You bet your ass I am."

"And third, you're going to tell me where the bodies are buried. When you tell me exactly where they are, we'll hang those murders on Webb and Burkhart and you get a pass. You get to stay and run this farm, have your fun. But if you lie or stonewall me, you're going down with your brother. Make up your mind and do it quick. Where are they buried?"

"What're you, an attorney?"

"No," Thorn said. "I'm the guy offering you a second chance."

"Que vas a hacer?"

Jesús wanted to know what they were going to do.

Thorn told him they were about to destroy the greenhouse and everything inside it. He held up his shotgun.

With a faint smile the man nodded his assent, as if he'd been hoping for that answer.

"Vamos a necesitar protección contra el humo si ese edificio le incendia, no?"

Thorn suspected they'd need protection against the fumes from the fire.

"Un incendio? Si, si, absolutamente. Entonces sigueme."

"He wants us to follow him," he told Sugar.

"Lourdes teach you all that Spanish?"

"Oh, yeah. That and a lot more. A memorable month at sea."

"Why?" Sugar asked as Jesús led them to a cabin beside the greenhouse.

"Why what?"

"Why attack that building?"

"It's the cornerstone," Thorn said. "It's the lake where the billion gallons of coal slurry are stored."

At the door of a small cabin beside the greenhouse, Jesús told them to wait a moment. He went inside and returned with two gas masks that looked like army surplus Second World War gear, full-face with goggle eyes and a filter canister mounted to the side.

Jesús fit one on his face, demonstrated how to tighten the straps, then took it off and held it out to Sugarman.

Sugarman took the mask and edged closer to Thorn.

"This part of your master plan, is it?"

"How about if we write up the master plan once we're done?"

"That's a history, not a plan."

Sugarman pressed the gas mask to his face, wiggled it around, looking for a comfortable fit.

"Get it airtight," Thorn said. "You don't want to

be inhaling these fumes, believe me. You don't want that."

When Sugar's mask was in place, Jesús told Thorn he would leave now. He would stand far off in a field and watch the greenhouse burn with great pleasure. And if anyone came close to the fire, breathed those fumes, then whoever was stupid enough to do that thing would be stoned. Dead on their feet, hammered.

"*Ahogado*," he said. "*Flipado*."

"*Gracias, Jesús. Bueno suerte.*"

When Jesús had disappeared into the night, Thorn fit his gas mask on and asked Sugarman if he was ready.

"Ready as I'm going to be."

Thorn raised the Atchisson shotgun to his shoulder.

"Okay," he called through the mask. "Let's take these babies for a spin."

The fire took a while to catch on. Each of them unloaded five rounds, exploding great sections of the glass walls and rattling the earth beneath their feet, but they didn't ignite the flammable portions. After ten rounds they were starting to get the hang of it, spreading apart, aiming into the lower areas of the structure where the heavy timber beams and posts and braces intersected.

The greenhouse shook and shifted and when finally the first tentative flames took hold and the fire began to swell, glass panes in the roof popped and shattered and fell in bright spiral chips like waterlogged fireworks, no exhilarating rockets bursting high in the air, but a dismally subdued inferno whose intense heat and thickening smoke drove Thorn and Sugar back a few yards, where they fired more rounds and more after hat.

He could barely see through the smoke as the trumpet plants ignited, their stalks melting; the blooms blackened and withered and released a bluish gas that coiled into the black smoke from the burning wood. He saw a tube of fire burrow under the wooden floor, then reemerge a few feet later, uncoiling atop the old planks like a bright orange snake slithering forward, then dividing into three more orange snakes, each of which began to explore a different aisle between the potted flowers.

Cruz had chosen her artillery well. The shotgun had almost no recoil and its destructive capabilities were beyond any weapon Thorn had ever encountered. Each round was a mini–hand grenade, detonating with a deep concussive force that shattered several of the upper-story windows in the farmhouse and knocked an old rope-pulled dinner bell off its stand.

They were down to a handful of rounds, maybe three or four each, when Burkhart and X-88 and Dobbins arrived. The pickup truck slewing into the driveway, barely under control, ramming the rear fender of the Jaguar and coming to a stop. The men piled out and Thorn caught glimpses of a shotgun, an automatic rifle, and the glint of a handgun in X-88's hand.

He motioned Sugarman to follow him as he waded deeper into the smoke, to conceal themselves, trusting that their wet clothes could withstand the heat and that the gas masks were up to the task.

That was Thorn's grand idea. Draw the men close, lure them into the acrid haze. Drug them on their own product.

Through the crash of glass and heavy timbers and clamor of the blaze, he heard Dobbins's horror-struck scream, heard Burkhart yell Thorn's name then a curse and another curse.

An automatic weapon sprayed a half dozen rounds a few feet to their right. Thorn and Sugar ducked and hustled to their left. A shotgun roared and more glass shattered at the entrance to the greenhouse, which broke loose the door and sent it tumbling facedown onto a stone walkway. Thorn signaled Sugar to stay put, no shooting, stay hidden in the smoke. Hold on a little longer, let the burning trumpet blooms do their work. Sugarman shook his head as if to say he was doing as instructed but this was a mighty risky ploy.

More gunfire raked the glass just above their heads and moved farther down the remaining wall. Dobbins whooped. A sound somewhere between a howl of anguish and a call to war. More rounds splintered the flaming posts behind them, shooting drizzles of sparks onto their clothes. Thorn slapped the arm of Sugar's coat to extinguish a small eddy of flames and Sugar dusted a glowing bit of coal out of Thorn's hair. A stray round ripped the sleeve of Sugar's jacket, drew blood. He tore open the material to have a look, then waved off Thorn's concern.

Close behind them the last of the supporting posts gave way and in a cascade of sparks and an overheated rush of inky smoke the rest of the greenhouse came down with such a thunderous jolt it knocked Thorn forward, sent him stumbling out of the safety of the black smoke onto open ground only a few feet from where Dobbins stood with his shotgun raised.

"Put the weapon down," Thorn said. "Do it now."

He aimed the Atchisson squarely at the big man, then slid it to the right to include Burkhart. X-88 was nowhere in sight.

"I said put it down, on the ground at your feet. Do it now."

Dobbins blinked and seemed befuddled to find himself at this place, at this moment, in this condition.

"Put the fucking weapon down. Do you hear me?"

"Okay, if that's what you want, sure, no problem, happy to do it."

Something like a giddy yip escaped him as he

bent forward and laid the weapon on the grass with the care of a well-oiled drunkard who must expend extreme effort simply to stay upright.

"You too, Burkhart. On the ground beside the shotgun."

"Yes, sir. Right away, sir."

The older man's eyes were watery and his movements were as automated and silly as one of those Saturday morning cartoon robots from Thorn's youth. Burkhart had clearly drilled for so many years and was so ingrained with the ironclad rules of command and obedience that this submissive behavior was his default state. After he raised up, his shoulders drew back, his chin pulled in. Standing at firm attention and ready to salute any ranking officer in the area.

"Now tell me," Thorn said, "where I can find some ropes to tie you two fuckers up."

"Right over there," Dobbins said, waving at a small shed nearby.

"Get on your knees, both of you, and walk over to the shed, do it now."

They both kneeled and together they began to waddle toward the shed.

Thorn looked around. He didn't know where Sugarman had gone, didn't know where X-88 was lurking. And more important, he had no idea how stoned these two men were and how long this compliant state would last.

Thirty-six

Sugarman followed Tina's killer through the smoke and shower of sparks across the yard and out the drive. After he was beyond the haze, he tore off the gas mask and tossed it aside. Glancing back once, he saw with relief that Thorn was in control of the two men, their weapons lying in the grass at their feet. Both men kneeling before Thorn, hands laced behind their heads.

For once he was doing things by the book. Though Sugarman had tried over the years to get Thorn to see the virtues of reason and order and the rule of law, this new, more disciplined Thorn was nothing Sugarman could take credit for, because this change was all Flynn's doing.

Sugarman had seen what happened in Millie's car, in fact he'd felt it physically, his shoulder pressed hard against Thorn's as he held his son's hand. He'd sensed the surge of energy flowing through him at that moment, every fiber in Sugar registering that tearing apart of the two of them, that thunderclap of pain as father and son said farewell without saying anything at all.

X-88 was ambling out toward the county road,

in no particular hurry. He'd turned his head once to see that Sugarman was following him and then again a little later to see that he was still there. Leading him somewhere. Sugarman was in no hurry either. At the current pace, he was gaining on X-88 little by little and that was enough. He needed some extra time to calm himself, to flush away the image of what this man had done to Tina Gathercole. To regain his composure, his equanimity.

Words only. But they were the words that guided him, that he returned to when he wobbled toward one extreme or another. Touchstones that brought him back to center, those words. He wasn't sure why.

Woo had noticed it. The quirky sketch artist calling him a wordsmith. He wasn't sure why they held such power for him. No one else he'd ever met seemed to care so much about finding the precise formulation of terms. For most people, words were simply units of communication, bills in a wallet to be doled out for acts of seduction, persuasion, deal making, or simply the ordinary transactions of getting along.

No one he'd ever met, not even Thorn, thought words had the power to actually shape a person's thoughts or control the heart. To them, words were slaves. But for Sugarman it was just the reverse. He was enthralled by them, defined by them, made whole, compelled by them, and sometimes overcome by their power. He was the slave, words the master. If he could not find the exact words for something, it did not fully exist. And if he could say it well enough, almost anything was possible.

X-88 seemed to be slowing. Sugarman was less than fifty yards behind him. The shotgun had grown weighty in his hands. But he wasn't going to rush this. He still needed a moment more to recapture the poise that was his natural state. His outrage and horror were almost quelled.

A few more steps, drawing closer.

X-88 climbed a fence alongside the road and entered a muddy field. The lights from a double-wide trailer lit his way. He walked out into the center of the field and stopped, then turned around and faced Sugarman. Waiting there.

He'd picked his spot, his feng shui, his harmonious center. The exact location where he meant to do battle.

Sugarman climbed the fence and jumped down into the sloppy mud.

No, "quelled" was wrong. There was no use trying to suppress his outrage. That never worked, at least not for long. What he had to do was simpler. He had to let it go. Release it, allow it to drift off like the poisonous smoke from the ruined greenhouse, let it disperse until it had no more potency.

He aimed the shotgun at the man who'd gagged

Tina with meat. And in those next few steps, because he had named it properly, because he had found the right words, his rage and his revulsion fell away. Whatever happened now would not be fouled by those dark emotions. He felt lighter, freer.

Oh, but every bit as lethal as before, maybe even more so, for now he could strike, if the need arose, without the weight of doubt, regret, or the unbalancing force of hate.

Sugarman halted twenty feet away from the man.

"That's a big gun," X said. "I've just got this little bitty thing. That seem fair to you?"

X lifted his pistol into the narrow band of illumination thrown out by the trailer's security light.

"What do you propose?"

"The usual," X said. "Put them both down, hash this out the old-fashioned way."

"How's that? You want to talk?"

The man laughed.

"I don't think we can discuss our way past this situation. It's too mountainous for that."

"Mountainous," Sugarman said. "Yes, that's good."

"So we put them down? Count of three? That work for you?"

Sugarman felt the scowl soften on his lips.

"Go ahead. Do the honors."

402

X-88 spoke the numbers in a slow cadence as he bent forward, his pistol hand extended to the ground. Sugarman mirrored his move.

On "three" they both straightened, both unarmed.

"So far so good," X-88 said. "We're halfway there."

"And what's the other half?"

"Are you a talker too? Like Tina?"

Sugarman felt the sharp tightening in his throat. Her name on his lips.

"She wanted me to tell you something if I were to see you. You're Sugarman, right, the boy-friend?"

"I'm Sugarman."

"Maybe it'd be better if we stepped away from our armaments, what do you think?"

Sugarman followed his lead and stepped two paces closer to the man, leaving the shotgun sinking in the mud.

"I know it's bound to make you angry, hearing me talk about the woman you cared about. The one I killed. I know that. I'm not unfeeling. I'm not that kind of monster."

"What did she want you to tell me?"

"She got involved with Cruz and all this mess just for money. I don't know why she thought that was important for me to tell you. That's pretty much what makes the globe keep spin-ning, isn't it? Money?"

"That's all she said?"

"She loved you. She said that, for whatever it's worth."

Sugarman nodded. He wasn't sure what it was worth. He'd save that consideration for later. Now was the time to stay focused. Even-tempered.

"Your girl Tina was a tough one. A negotiator. She ran some kind of shop, right? Sold shit, maybe that's where that bargaining thing comes from. She thought she could haggle her way out of dying, but no, she was good, but she wasn't that good."

"Why meat?"

He asked for no other reason than because he wanted to know. To understand the sick logic of this man. Not that such knowledge would benefit him in any way in the future, and not so he might even have a tingle of empathy. That wasn't possible. No childhood trauma, no failure of nurturing or nature could justify this man's acts.

"Meat was available," X-88 said. "It didn't have to be meat. Sure, meat's got a symbolism to it, I guess you could say. Me being who I am, having the feelings I do about the mistreatment of animals, it's meaningful to me, though I don't expect anybody else to grasp that. A man I met in prison showed me the importance of those values. How throwing people into a concrete cell isn't any different than doing the same thing to an animal. One can't be right if the other isn't. And neither is. It's an abomination, locking men into cells, squeezing pigs and chickens and cows into tight little boxes.

"I'm saying that using meat to kill a person, it's not meant as one of those codes some serial killer scrawls on the wall next to a murder scene, a taunt or whatever for the cops to decipher, nothing Hollywood like that. I just prefer using meat if it's available. And that night it was.

"So hearing my explanation, does any of that make you feel better?"

"No. Not a bit."

"Did you realize it's Ahab and the whale, not Ahab and a shark?"

Sugarman didn't answer. He had no idea what the man was saying.

"She corrected me. I had my movies confused, mixed up *Moby Dick* with that shark movie, with *Jaws*, you know. Tina told me I had it wrong. We had a nice conversation, we were relating, getting along about as well as two people can in that kind of circumstance. I was listening her out, letting her talk. Trying to be patient."

"So what you're saying, you're actually a good man?"

"No, no. I'm not good. See, I don't go in for any of that good/bad shit. I'm who I am, you're who you are. Isn't anybody giving us grades, coming down from heaven saying Sugarman, you get an A, X-88, you failed, man. The big F. It doesn't work that way, far as I can see. People do what they do then they're gone. They get replaced by others who do whatever the hell they can get away with and then they're gone. No grades. Just one big mosh pit writhing with everybody squeezed together. That's all I can see."

He was compressing the distance between them, doing it in such small increments, Sugarman wasn't certain it was happening till he saw the strip of light was no longer shining anywhere near him. X-88 was drifting forward.

"You're not getting out of this," Sugarman said. "If we fight, you might get the better of me, you might not. But either way, you're done."

"Oh, I'm done, all right. I know that. It's no secret. I'm terminal. Brain's swelling, everything's shutting down. At the moment, the only reason I'll fight you is because I don't want to be passing my last hours in another goddamn concrete box. I like it out here, free in the air. I'll fight you, I'll kill you if I need to, if only to have a few more hours of this."

Sugarman was doing his own slow waltz in X's direction. The mud sucking at his shoes.

"I notice you got real short hair, Sugarman. Keep it trimmed close."

"Yeah."

"Makes it hard to yank, I bet. Tina ever try to tug your hair? You know, pull it backward so she could plant a big kiss? She ever do that?

"Reason I ask, I usually rely on longish hair. It's part of my technique. But since I got my training in the martial arts in lockup, and inside there, most guys are shaved clean, I practiced other ways to accomplish my ends."

Sugarman didn't actually decide to charge. He simply did it. Not in anger, not off balance, but because the man seemed to be distracted by his pathetic monologue and Sugar sensed an opening.

Fists up, he feinted with a left jab then threw a straight right to X's nose. Hands loose at his sides, using a Muhammad Ali shuffle, the man backpedaled, drew his chin back just far enough so Sugar's knuckles skimmed past his cheekbone.

"Fast hands," X said. "For an old coot."

The mud made Sugar's footwork sluggish, and the karate kick he sent toward X's groin missed badly and threw him into a sideways stumble.

X-88 was on him. Turning him and wrapping an arm around his throat, locking it hard. Then X let his body drop backward to the muddy ground, flopping, taking Sugarman down on top of him. One arm fastened across Sugarman's throat, cutting off his air, X's other arm behind his head, levering Sugarman's head forward. Both men on their backs wallowing in the slop.

X-88 was outmuscling Sugar with ease, his burly arms, his thick chest, his heavy legs all coordinated. He'd managed to pin Sugarman even though Sugar lay atop him.

Sugarman got a breath, twisted hard to the left then to the left again, screwing both legs to the right to get traction in the slippery glop. But he couldn't break the hold.

"You asked about the meat," X said quietly in his ear. "Let me show you."

Somehow X had managed to scoop up a handful of mud and was holding it out for Sugarman to see.

His legs were scissored tight around Sugarman's legs, ankles locked together. Sugarman writhed, and tried to elbow his way free, taking shots, but the man hid his face behind Sugarman's head and seemed perfectly content to let Sugarman thrash around as much as he desired.

After less than a minute he was out of breath.

"I only got a little left in the tank," X whispered. "Don't make me waste it flailing in the mud."

"What do you want?"

"Let me show you how it works, is all. How it goes down. You happen to know the word 'gavage'?"

Sugarman knew the word, oh yes, he knew it.

He grappled for X's face, clawed, swiped. Got nowhere. He gripped the man's forearm that was cutting off his air, used both hands trying to pry it loose. But the arm was as rigid and unyielding as an iron pipe cemented into place. Brute strength that far outmatched Sugar's.

The hand cupped with mud was moving toward Sugar's face.

He slapped at the hand, knocked it away, the mud went flying.

X-88 reached out and scooped up another lump.

He ratcheted his arm tighter against Sugar's throat, then ratcheted it another notch. Something crucial popped deep in Sugarman's neck, and he saw a blast of light in the back rooms of his brain. Cells dying, a candle flame sputtering.

"Here we go. Nice and easy."

X's body lurched, tightening the hold of his legs and wrenching his forearm harder against Sugarman's throat.

Sugar gasped, and in the same instant the mud was filling his mouth.

Sugarman tried to spit it out but X's hand was clamped hard over his lips. He sucked air through his nose, threw his body to the left, tried to spin, but was cinched tight by X's legs.

The mud was leaking down his throat. Sugar gagged, heaved, but the mud had nowhere to go.

"You're a tough nut," X said. "It'll just be another little bit, hold on."

He tried to bite X's hand, but his strength had faded so badly the act was feeble and meaningless.

The sky swam with stars, a convoy of clouds flew past, two words flashed bright against the heavens as if projected by a celestial laser.

Let go.

Let go.

All right. Sure, that was fine. Made perfect sense. Sugarman let go.

His body relaxed in the man's hold, that death cradle. His finish line coming up fast.

Sugarman was sorry he'd missed what happened next. Sorry to have drifted off into that zone he'd heard about but never experienced, no longer in his body, but not yet crossing the threshold. Hovering in limbo land, beyond the inexorable pull of gravity, beyond the tangible world, hovering, hovering.

He was sorry he wasn't around for Thorn's arrival. Sorry to have to rely on Thorn's taciturn recounting of the moment. He wished he'd seen it, wished he'd been there to enjoy the whole unfolding. Thorn hauling X-88 out of his crablike hold on Sugarman. Yanking him upright. Thorn pushing X-88 backward into the mud and hammering him in the skull with the butt of his shotgun, doing it one more time to crush the man's nose.

Then Thorn dragged Sugarman out of the blast zone and went back to stand a few feet from X-88 and unloaded three explosive rounds into the man's chest. Turning his body into some cut of meat, ground sirloin or chuck roast or pork tenderloin or however Thorn put it in his tight-lipped poetry.

Thirty-seven

Thorn was once again in the Key Largo library confounded by the balky search engine the library used. He had to call over a stout and handsome older lady named Betty to help him navigate the process. The picture postcard had arrived yesterday, the twenty-third of December. On its front side was a glossy image of the governor's mansion in Tallahassee, a brick dwelling with six white columns. Greek Revival style with a central portico meant to echo Andrew Jackson's Hermitage.

With Betty's help Thorn found a series of recent newspaper articles featuring the mansion. Once he had them in sight, Betty excused herself and left him alone. Like everyone in Key Largo, it seemed, she knew what Thorn was dealing with.

Sometime late on a Sunday night a week ago, a group had managed to assemble a ten-foot-tall replica of an oil derrick on the front lawn of the governor's mansion. Then they'd poured some combination of oil and tar over the grass and slung more of it onto the white columns and the porch and the windows and the walls, then set it on fire. The fire was extinguished quickly, but not before so much smoke and water damage was done to the mansion the governor would have to find new quarters for at least the next few months.

How they'd come and gone without the governor's security team discovering their presence was a mystery. They were protesting the governor's plan to open Florida's waters in the Gulf of Mexico to offshore drilling. In the press release they sent to the papers, ELF promised more oil would be spilled and more fires would be set at other government offices in the coming weeks. This was war. All-out war. No attempt to find compromise.

Adding to the mystery was the presence of a woman's body on the governor's lawn, lying just beside the oil derrick. She'd been killed by a single gunshot to the heart and her naked corpse was covered in the oily mix. The body had been identified as one Yolanda Madeline Obrero, a former agent for the Federal Bureau of Investigation. The Miami field office was withholding comment on Obrero's death pending further investigation.

But Thorn knew what had happened. If anybody had called him from the FBI or the press, he would gladly explain it in detail. Yolanda Madeline Obrero had finally tracked Cassandra down. And Cassandra, no known last name, had been waiting for Ms. Obrero, and she'd defended herself with lethal force as all citizens of Florida were legally entitled to do.

Thorn invited Flynn's mother, April Moss, to come along today, but she told him no, she'd done enough weeping at Flynn's funeral. This was something Thorn should take care of alone since it was Flynn's request made specifically to his father.

He supposed those excuses were partially true. But he suspected April turned down the boat ride because she simply could no longer tolerate the sight of Thorn, whose own lawless behavior and devotion to the natural world had inspired Flynn to set off on the self-destructive path that caused his death.

So be it.

This was a trip best taken alone. Sugarman knew when and where Thorn was heading, but he'd known better than even to hint he wanted to accompany him. He'd cancelled his job interview with the county sheriff's department and had begun working on a new case. He'd been writing letters to Emma Johansson, describing in some detail the nature of his investigation. Emma was thrilled.

Thorn had honored Flynn's other request already. Standing naked beside her bed, Laurie Dobbins had revealed to Thorn where her brother and Burkhart disposed of Flynn's comrades. The bodies of Caitlin Evans, Billy Jack Foster, and a young man known only as Jellyroll had been weighted by slabs of concrete and sunk in Manure Lagoon Number Four on Dobbins Farm. Found nearby in the same lagoon was the mutilated body of one Javier Ortiz, his wounds so extensive that it was clear to the medical examiner that he'd been tortured for several days. The ballistics evidence acquired from the bodies matched a Remington twelve-gauge shotgun and an AR-15 automatic weapon found in the defendants' possession. With that and the detailed testimony of Laurie Dobbins, the case against Webb and Burkhart was overwhelming. Their trials in Raleigh each lasted less than five business days.

Thorn took the skiff out to the Atlantic, skimming across the white sandy flats, spooking stingrays and a school of bonefish, running out farther and farther until the deep blue seam of water appeared. He had not prepared any kind of speech. He had nothing left to say and no desire to say it. Fifteen miles offshore, the water was as smooth and sleek as icing. The sun was gathering itself behind a bank of dawn clouds that seemed rooted to the horizon.

He didn't know what Flynn's favorite time of day was, but this was his. All the promise still to come. All the hours to create something new. So much ahead. So much still to be discovered, sampled, and embraced.

He'd sprinkled ashes before and knew how it was done. Knew there was no grand finale, no resolution or anything magical that flashed into view when the gray dust was released. The ocean stretched in every blue direction, no interruption, no end.

He opened the paper carton, climbed up on the bow, and looked out at the morning sun working its way beyond the hold of the clouds. He shook out Flynn's dust where his son had wanted it to end. Not the finish the young man was hoping for, not the grand sigh of triumph, but just this. A southerly breeze scattering his body across the flat calm sea.

Center Point Large Print
600 Brooks Road / PO Box 1
Thorndike, ME 04986-0001 USA

(207) 568-3717

US & Canada:
1 800 929-9108
www.centerpointlargeprint.com